Morton's Fork

Enjoy!

Morton's Fork

Windy City Publishers
2118 Plum Grove Rd., #349
Rolling Meadows, IL 60008
www.windycitypublishers.com

Published in the United States of America

First Edition: 2012

ISBN: 978-1-935766-19-3

Library of Congress Control Number: 2012930805

Cover Design by Andy Carpenter
Author Photo by Buschauer Photography

MORTON'S FORK

Dale Coy, M.D.

Chi-Towne Fiction
An Imprint of

FRIDAY

CHAPTER ONE

Dr. Roger Hartley bent over the hospital bed and gently laid his hands on the old woman's upper abdomen. His fingers curled softly around her protruding ribs and then pressed deeper into her body. His eyes focused sharply on her skin, as if he could see inside the hidden cavity with his sensitive touch.

"Tell me if I'm hurting you," he said, noticing her fear.

Supporting his lower back with his hand, Hartley straightened to think. His paraspinal muscles felt tight. At forty-six, he found that leaning over a patient to perform an extended exam was much harder than it had been when he started his practice as an internist twenty years earlier, and he mentally scolded himself for not taking the time to raise the bed. He pressed the button on the side of the bed rail and waited for the bed to rise to a comfortable height. The motor droned, accentuating the idle moment. He felt the scrutinizing stares of his patient's relatives on his back, pressuring him to work faster and give them an answer. His mind worked quickly. He hoped his gut feeling about his patient's condition was wrong. Something was robbing his patient of nutrition. Her temples were hollow, and the crests of her iliac bones made sharp points under the sheet. The whites of her eyes were the yellow-orange color of a duck's foot.

Hope of a diagnosis of cirrhosis was fading. The putrid odor of *fetor hepaticus* was not on her breath. The nodular edge of a hard liver didn't slide past his fingers when she took a deep breath. A smooth, round tip of a giant spleen didn't bump on his fingers. For an instant he wondered if the blind tips of his fingers could be trusted; spleens were not easy to feel.

Carefully, preserving the patient's modesty, Hartley lifted the bed sheet from her upper chest to examine for *spider angiomata*, the tiny, cherry-red spots of snarled, dilated capillaries on the skin that occur as a sign of shunted blood around a scarred liver. He put one hand under the woman's crooked elbow, the other under the base of her neck, and gingerly helped her sit up. Her shoulder blades and the knobs of her spine protruded into his palm. He placed his stethoscope at the base of her lungs and listened as if he were eavesdropping on a private conversation inside her body. She eased back onto the pillow. Hartley placed his hand once again over the edge of her liver. The surface was smooth— it wasn't cirrhotic. He had hoped to find something different. Cirrhosis would be a gentler diagnosis than the pancreatic cancer that he now suspected, but he was careful not to let disappointment register too soon on his face.

The jaundiced woman's family remained respectfully silent while he examined her, but nonetheless he felt their hidden distrust as they leaned casually against the white walls. Their eyes scrutinized his every movement. The patient's son stepped forward aggressively. The tattoos on his biceps swelled when he folded his arms across his chest. "What do you think?" he asked in an imperative tone. "The ER doc said she has cirrhosis and grilled us about alcohol use like she was a drunk."

Hartley paused, letting his impressions crystallize before he spoke. "Are you a relative?" he asked cautiously, well versed in HIPAA laws.

The son's eyes screwed into a glare. "I'm her son. And she's no alcoholic!"

Hartley winced as he saw another relative scowling from the other side of the double room. She was stretched across the empty patient bed, propped up on an elbow as if she felt right at home. The small, white sign that requested visitors to stay off the freshly made bed was pushed aside. Hartley smiled kindly, weighing whether to tell them all at once, or draw them slowly toward the truth by waiting for test results. He hoped to avoid stripping away any of their unfounded optimism too soon. He looked at each visitor in turn and mustered a smile. It appeared they had no idea that their mom had cancer, or that she would soon go through harsh testing and therapy.

"Can I ask those who aren't relatives to please step out into the hall?" said Hartley, feeling his neck muscles tightening.

Stiffly, the son stood his ground. "We can all hear."

The sick woman lay silent, her bony hands holding the white sheet tightly to her neck. Her yellow eyes shone fearfully from deep sockets.

"I don't believe this is cirrhosis," said Hartley, directing a cajoling smile to the son. "Right now, I'm guessing the yellow color that you see in her eyes is being caused by something else."

The son's eyes widened as he unfolded his arms. "She's been here since last night and you're still guessing?"

Focusing his gaze on the son, Hartley calculated how to explain all the possible causes of jaundice in easily understandable terms. He knew his white coat and advanced education drew the man's suspicion, and he was accustomed to walking a fine line between kind optimism and frank reality when discussing serious illness. But people like this were guided by a new code of ethics, believing that a demonstration of anger would elicit better and immediate service. His unforgiving attitude was meant to show that he was not afraid of a doctor. Hartley knew from experience that the next words from the man's mouth would be a threat.

"Give it straight, or I'm calling a lawyer," said the son.

"A lot of things can cause jaundice, so I'm not—" said Hartley, trying to speak with sincerity.

The woman on the opposite bed sat up abruptly and interrupted. "It's six o'clock, Doctor. She's been here since last night."

Hartley glanced up apologetically with a disarming smile. He knew that uncertainty was stressful for patients and families. "I'm sorry," he explained soothingly. "I couldn't get away any sooner. The hospital is terribly busy."

The son crossed his arms and widened his stance as though gripping the floor with both feet. "You're too busy?"

"I'll order a CT scan for tonight," said Hartley, attempting to win back the family's trust. "By tomorrow morning, we'll know something definite. She needed a day of fluids before we could do that. She was dehydrated, and her kidneys wouldn't have done well with the contrast."

"We want an MRI," demanded the younger woman. "I read on the Internet that's better."

"A CT will provide the information we need," replied Hartley, knowing that the insurance company tracked his use of expensive MRI scans.

"If it's the money, we don't care about that," said the young woman indignantly. She slipped off the rumpled bed and stood by her brother.

Hartley glanced at the deep wrinkles left on the freshly made bed. He scratched the cowlick on the back of his head. Avoiding expensive tests and extra costs was becoming a bigger part of his job, and his efficiency was tracked and ranked against his peers. His reimbursements were tied to these rankings. He had to be frank. His face filled with solemn compassion. "I'm afraid that your mother's bile ducts are blocked by a cancer. It's usually the pancreas, but it could be the bile ducts. A CT scan will confirm it."

The young woman's mouth dropped open with shock, and she stared indignantly.

"Cancer?" asked the son. Fear tinged his expression. "My mom has cancer?"

Hartley wanted to be reassuring, but he couldn't. The word *cancer* was charged with despair and doom. He hated to utter it prematurely in case he was wrong. As whispers flew around the room, he sensed the quick change of mood and allowed the family members to feel their emotions. "Your mom's got a lot to go through," he said sadly.

"We want a specialist," demanded the son.

This caught Hartley off guard. "Let's first see if anything's there. We can arrange a specialist consult and biopsy for Monday. Biopsies aren't performed on the weekend unless the situation is an emergency."

The son arched his back in surprise. His eyes riveted on the doctor, his pupils shrinking to pinholes. His face flushed red. "What kind of hospital is this? Does it just shut down on the weekends?"

Hartley could have corrected him but didn't. "I know this is all very upsetting."

"Christ! Look at her. She's going to a university hospital—tonight!"

Hartley scratched his cowlick again and gazed quizzically at the son. The forthright approach had caused the situation to slip out of control. Hartley exhaled slowly. "I understand—but we don't need to transfer her now."

"You're not listening!" exploded the son, overcome by mistrust. He flexed his folded arms.

The old woman's eyes misted, as if she felt forgotten. Instinctively, Hartley reached for the tissue box and held it steady so the woman could pull out a sheet. She dabbed the tissue deep into her sockets and then smiled faintly. "I'll make sure the CT scan is done right away," promised Hartley. And for an instant it seemed as if the two of them were alone.

Hartley turned, contempt beginning to cloud his face. "I would listen to your mother," he said calmly to the son.

"But I have a right to ask questions," blurted the son.

Hartley's stomach growled, and he tasted rising bile. He stepped back defensively, but the son's voice grew louder. Hartley's voice lowered to a whisper. "We've got to find you a miracle," he said to the sick woman—and only to her.

The old woman cleared her throat with a gurgling cough. She dropped the bed sheet and reached out to take Hartley's hand. Her smooth and featureless palm felt cold in his grasp, but when she smiled, her teeth appeared glowingly white in contrast to her yellow skin. "I don't want to be transferred," she said. "I like the care I get here."

"Thank you," said Hartley simply. "I will be back in the morning."

Hartley washed his hands in the basin, dried them with a paper towel, and dabbed at the sticky, yellow dollop of phlegm the woman had coughed onto his sleeve. He studied the glob for pus or blood, and then dropped the crumpled wad into the trash. He looked directly at each family member around the room, sympathy showing in his face. "Can I answer any last questions?" He put out his hand, hoping the son would take hold. Their eyes locked. But the son shook his head without speaking. "If you think of questions, write them down."

Hartley circled the nurses' station in search of an empty chair. He sulked over the woman's chart, trying to summon the better part of his nature. He understood himself well enough to know that bursts of self-doubt flared up when he was overly tired or when his care fell short of his own expectations. But he kept his negative thoughts to himself. He knew it was better that way. Thoughts became words and words became actions. His professional discontent with "health care reform" was now coupled with diminishing rewards. He gripped his pen tightly and began detailing the facts of the jaundiced woman's illness in concise sentences. He relived in his mind his fingers' exploration of the jaundiced woman's liver and spleen. He debated whether his touch had been accurate. His pen pressed down firmly on the page.

"Obstructive jaundice. Suspect pancreatic or biliary cancer."

Hartley smiled lopsidedly over the well-constructed record. His body relaxed as he signed the bottom of the page with a mark that resembled a hairpin. The signature was short and quick out of necessity, although he always added the date, time, and his pager number more carefully. But realizing that in his fatigue he had transposed the last two digits, he scratched out the mistake in disgust. It frightened him that his long-dormant dyslexia could be resurfacing with age.

"You giving the poor nurse a whole page of orders, Hartley?"

Hartley's head jerked up with surprise at the voice over his shoulder. Standing behind him was a young hospitalist named Fogg. His slicked-back brown hair and stylish clothes under his pressed, white lab coat made him seem like a businessman, even though a stethoscope bowed from his side pocket. Fogg was a HMO-salaried doctor hired to manage patients with an eye to the insurance conglomerate's bottom line. He focused on getting sick people treated and discharged from the hospital more quickly and less expensively.

To Hartley, Fogg represented change. Hartley's friends were regular office doctors who still visited their patients inside the hospital doors. Medicine was becoming more of a business, and in Hartley's opinion, the profession was weakening by drifting away from the doctor-patient relationship. "No, I just wrote a few orders," he answered callously, resenting that a specialist's consult or MRI could lower his physician ranking. "I'm done, and with luck I'll catch a meal with my family."

Fogg smiled casually. "Why do you always look so tired?"

Hartley straightened. Fogg's remark touched a nerve. The young doctor was half his age and seemed to be working only to supplement his trust fund. Hartley glanced down to hide his pain and for an instant studied his worn brown bucks, tarnished with stains collected over many years at the bedside. Maybe Celeste, his wife, had been right—well-respected doctors wore suits and well-polished shoes—but in practice he found that the soles of Italian loafers wore thin even before they had stopped feeling new and that a prescription pad would quickly rub holes in the back pocket of tailored pants. He found that simple ties and more durable, machine-washable clothes allowed him to treat the sick without worrying about some misguided body fluid soiling dry-clean-only attire. "Is it that obvious?" snapped Hartley, without hiding a hard edge in his voice. "Haven't you had a long day?"

Fogg laughed. "You've just had a bad day, that's all. I heard a little part of your conversation down the hall. Tough family. People spread misery like MRSA. Why do you stand for it? It puts you on the defensive if you care. When people treat *me* that way, I let them know I don't approve."

Hartley looked up at this disclosure. "You get angry at sick patients?"

Fogg laughed again. "When I need to," he answered. "But mostly I let things roll off my back. If it gets really bad, I keep a tally of the number of people who get angry."

"I hope you don't find the number embarrassing," said Hartley sharply.

"Some days I find it amusingly gloomy," answered Fogg. "Like how many steps I take in a day when I wear a pedometer. It's sick. You don't realize you've taken that many."

Hartley regarded Fogg curiously. "You done for the day?"

"Shift's over at seven," smiled Fogg as he peeked immodestly at the logo on his breast pocket. "Best day of my life was the day I sold my practice to the HMO. Limited hours. No business headaches. I don't even pay my malpractice insurance."

"You probably couldn't afford it," answered Hartley. "What happens with phone calls? What happens when patients don't fit into your schedule?"

"It doesn't always have to be me. Anyone can read lab reports and x-rays. And I have my social life back."

"This hospital has been my social life for twenty years," answered Hartley. He was staring testily at the logo on Fogg's pocket when a page issued from the intercom speakers and flooded the hallway.

"Doctor Hartley—four-four-four-four."

Fogg shook his head slightly as the color drained from Hartley's face. "The old residency adage is still true: 'The longer you stay, the longer you stay.' The ER is calling."

Hartley glanced at his wristwatch as his stomach growled. "I need to get that," he mumbled. "It's the way I was trained."

"That's right. It's the way *you* were trained," answered Fogg. "In my training we worked together."

Hours later, Hartley's soft-soled bucks fell soundlessly on the asphalt as he strode toward his old, red Suburban parked in the spot nearest the hospital. He had arrived early that morning, and warm stale air escaped past his face as the car door creaked open. It was a muggy July night, and sweat was gathering under his collar. He turned the key and aimed the air-conditioner vents at his face, a hollow feeling expanding inside him. "Get mad at a patient?" he repeated.

Hartley recalled the only time he had allowed himself to express anger at one of his patients. About two months ago, Maxwell Moll, was a longstanding patient in renal failure because he wasn't taking his medicine. It was late in the evening, and the ER had kept Hartley uncomfortably busy. Moll was not waking up to cooperate with his physical exam, and his dismissive behavior had made Hartley uneasy. Lupus had absorbed Moll's better self, and Hartley sensed that Moll no longer wanted to get well. His disease had become his identity as well as his scourge, and he felt bitterly entitled to all compensation that a generous society might bestow.

"Have you been taking your meds?" asked Hartley.

"No," answered Moll resentfully, without making eye contact.

"Maxwell, I gave you free samples so you would take them. You're in renal failure because you don't do what I say."

Moll glanced up indifferently. "I ran out."

Hartley grinned, remembering Moll with so much medicine he had to carry it home in a box. "I emptied my shelves," he entreated. "You got all I have."

"You promised they'd make me better," answered Moll. His eyes flashed with anger.

Hartley paused with astonishment. Moll's earlier gratitude and appreciation were gone. Moll had been as sick as a patient could get without being dead when Hartley had first picked him up as an uninsured patient on ER call. He didn't have a regular doctor. Everyone else had abandoned him because he blamed everyone but himself for his illness. But Hartley had enjoyed Moll's obstinate grumpiness and never scolded him for missing appointments or neglecting to take his medicine. He understood that lupus had robbed Moll of a promising life and had made him lonely and hopeless.

"Maxwell, you have a chronic illness," pleaded Hartley. "I hope to make your life better."

"You haven't."

"You should have come to my office if you weren't feeling well. I might have kept you out of the ER. But when I don't know…"

"I can't get to your office when I'm sick."

Hartley paused, mystified by the reasoning. "You know I'll take care of you over the phone."

Moll's eyes shifted around the familiar ER bay before he turned away from Hartley. "Your office staff is terrible," he said to the wall.

Hartley gazed at Moll's back. "Maxwell, I can't take care of you if you act like this. I want you to start taking your meds."

"The meds make me sick—bloated."

"But they work. I told you that without prednisone you'd go into kidney failure. That's where you are now. Don't you remember the crippling arthritis you had when I first met you? Wasn't it right here in this same bed?" Hartley laughed proudly at his accomplishments over the years.

Moll thought of the many doctors who had previously treated him. Heart specialists. Rheumatologists. Nephrologists. Internists. Hartley had replaced them all. "Laugh now," Moll said, with disgust.

"Maxwell, you have no insurance. I helped you fill out the assistance papers and even put a stamp on the envelope. But you never mailed the application." Hartley grinned at the irony. As bad as public-aid reimbursement was, at least it was something. Moll had never paid him a cent. That had never mattered when there was gratitude. "You've got to take prednisone."

His soft tone rankled Moll. In his eyes, doctors had privileged lives, sending their children to private schools and driving Lexus sedans. "You never told me that drug had side effects."

Hartley's eyes widened. "What? We discussed that on multiple occasions. I don't like steroids, but you don't have a choice. Prednisone is all you can afford."

Moll turned his back and regarded Hartley hotly. "I do have a choice. I want a new doctor," he growled. He craned his neck to peer across the nurses' station at the callboard. "How about Fogg?"

Hartley's jaw dropped with shock. "Just like that, after ten years?" he said. Picturing Fogg caring for one of his longstanding patients particularly hurt. He showed his disgust. "You do whatever you feel you have to do, Moll. I don't have to agree with it. The hospitalist on call will see you, but the care won't be the same. It will be just what you asked for. I'll note this conversation, and you'll get a registered letter from me next week. Good luck to ya."

Hartley pushed into traffic and sped away from the hospital. The simmering heat magnified his fatigue, and he felt a festering guilt. A senior doctor had reminded him once during his residency that it is the patient, not the doctor, who suffers the illness. But sometimes in practice this was hard to remember.

Hartley had blossomed in medical school. The first two years in the classroom, he devoured the textbooks and spent long afternoons dissecting human cadavers. The first year focused on the normal, healthy body and then moved on to diseased states. The ways a body could go wrong often seemed infinite, and this made it seem like a miracle when things went right. The volume of information was incredible. He learned to scribble lightning-fast notes during lectures and rely on their accuracy when studying for exams. But Hartley liked medical school's third and fourth years best. He began to treat disease in the living, and to him, the human body made perfect sense. He could see, feel, and sometimes smell the difference between health and disease. Instead of working for grades or praise, he was motivated by knowing the answers when they were needed. And when he had completed medical school and stood on the platform to receive his degree and pledge the Oath of Hippocrates, Hartley smiled, completely confident in his knowledge and skills.

Chapter Two

The law firm of Hendricks, Kennedy, and Johnson occupied the entire forty-second floor of the prestigious John Hancock Building that anchored the skyline of Chicago's Magnificent Mile. The spacious honeycomb of offices was lavishly appointed with a blend of glass and mahogany that symbolized the firm's harmonious merging of progressive and traditional values. The oversized foyer was adorned with two five-foot-high abstract oil paintings splashed with broad bands of thick crimson paint smeared over a background of deeply textured white. The canvasses appeared similar, but a minute difference became apparent with careful inspection. In one painting, thin yellow streaks were barely visible over the red, and once noticed, the painting seemed vastly dissimilar.

Anita Johnson rushed through the glass entry doors and glanced at the law firm's marquee stretched above the receptionist's counter. The partners' names were spelled out in gold block letters, and it secretly irked her that hers would never be first. For the past five years she had been the firm's primary rainmaker, and she took full credit for expanding the business to forty-five lawyers. She took pride that she had been invited to become a senior partner before many others with greater seniority. The unusually swift promotion had raised eyebrows, but in her eyes all reproach was acceptable. She had broken up the old-boy network and smugly flaunted her role as the first female partner.

Anita was born for the practice of law. Her handshake was firm like a man's, and she confidently took risks when necessary. She dressed as she pleased with a New York designer-influenced personal style that pushed to the front edge of fashion. Her cosmopolitan flair often caught people off guard, especially in conservative Chicago, and led mistaken adversaries to underestimate her skills as a lawyer. Their resultant casual arrogance fed into her strengths: a perfected sharp wit and icy condescension that put opponents on the defensive. But anger was Anita's most poisonous weapon.

Rushing down the long hall to her office, Anita held her briefcase and purse close to her body so the straps wouldn't cut into her shoulder. She dropped into the high-backed, rose-colored leather desk chair and slid soundlessly on the casters. As a matter of habit she glanced in the large gilded mirror on the wall beside her desk. The teardrops of jade that hung from her ears danced as she moved her head. Their color matched the dark green of her eyes, which was exactly the color of money. Squaring her shoulders she flipped open a file and read through its contents. Her first appointment for the day was an initial consultation for medical malpractice. Seeing a slam-dunk, she smiled, hoping to get this one to settle.

The receptionist escorted in her new client. Mr. Moll worked his way across the office with deliberate slowness, an audible moan with each step. His edematous feet splayed the tops of his tattered house slippers as he shuffled across the carpet. Anita rose to her feet and extended her hand, deftly concealing a mild sense of distaste and annoyance. The man looked vaguely infectious and her arm recoiled quickly after they'd touched. He wavered as he neared the desk and then dropped into an empty armchair across from Anita.

"Mole..." she began. "Is that an English name?"

"It's pronounced 'Mall.' You pronounce the o like an a—as in all."

Moll's bright eyes suggested that he was much younger than he appeared, but they were edgy, and he stared at Anita by twisting his neck to look obliquely from the side. The curious gaze accentuated a tortuous, hunching curve in his back. His bloated, moon-shaped face was covered by shiny, red skin, and shallow wounds from incessant scratching dotted his forehead and cheeks. Wispy, colorless hair covered his head in patches.

"Can I get you coffee or water?"

Moll shook his head slightly, saying nothing. A large window behind Anita framed her in scattered light, and Moll squinted to distinguish her features. His stare slid down her body before shifting nervously to the heavy volumes of law books filling the bookshelves.

Anita opened the legal-sized folder that contained the details of the wretched man's case. "So—what can I do for you today, Mr. Moll?"

Moll's face conveyed profound bitterness. "I have lupus! But the doctor did *this* to me with his treatments." Perched precariously in the chair, he stretched his arms out like a scarecrow for her inspection. His frayed garments hung loosely from his emaciated body.

Anita hid her ignorance behind a veneer of polite concern "I'm so sorry. Fill me in on the details of your condition. Tell me about lupus—I'm not a doctor."

Moll's face twisted into a curious sneer as he began a narrative that rapidly veered off into a morass of vague, unimportant details. Anita bristled with impatience. "Please speak up—I need to hear which details are important if I'm to make you a case."

After moistening dry, cracked lips with a shaky tongue, Moll cleared the residual white film from the corners of his mouth with a finger and nervously wiped it off on his pants. He leered horribly as he attempted to smile, showing teeth that were broken or missing. "Lupus is a terrible illness, but Hartley's steroids are what left me broken like this. I have osteoporosis so bad that my bones fracture and my spine collapses if I so much as sneeze. I can't sit straight. I can't even breathe without pain. My skin rips like tissue paper—look at these sores." Aroused by disgust, he sat up straighter to display his wounds.

Anita recognized the importance of these grotesque deformities in developing a jury's empathy in a malpractice case. Nonchalantly she placed a hand over her breastbone and sat back in her chair, unmoved to real compassion. Her mind worked with a template to identify someone to blame. She pictured a faceless doctor in front of a jury.

Anita's first target of choice was always a doctor. It was simple to steer a jury to find a doctor at fault. Scared of making mistakes on the stand, doctors were nervous and fidgety and made bad witnesses in their own defense. Doctors easily became defensive when second-guessing choices they had made years before coming to trial, and juries interpreted resentment and egotism as a mask for wrongdoing.

"This doctor of yours—Hartley. Do you think he would settle or take this case to trial?"

"I—I don't know him that well. I know he'll be mad."

Anita smiled curtly and leaned forward to get a better read of her potential client's deformities. In her opinion Moll's case wasn't that strong. Moll avoided her eyes and glanced uneasily at the bookcases lining the sidewalls from floor to ceiling. He looked confused by the complexity of the laws he would be testing and the rigor of the courtroom, and he shivered. He cupped his hands tightly together and pressed them between his knees to keep still. He envisioned the pointed lines of questioning that he would be required to answer, and his growing uncertainty doubled under the weight of his burden. "My doctor treated me for years with his poisons, and look where I am! It's cost me hundreds of thousands of dollars in lost wages."

Anita smiled slightly, zeroing in on a figure. "I agree with you—none of this is your fault. Someone should be held responsible. Just let me think for another moment." Anita could look for medical negligence anywhere in malpractice cases. Every organ had a specialist, and she suspected that many were involved in the treatment of lupus. Somewhere someone could always be represented as careless. There weren't standards or templates for appropriate treatment in the practice of medicine, and ultimately the hospital itself could be named. She contemplated a shotgun approach, naming multiple defendants—and then her eyes suddenly widened.

"Informed consent!" she blurted. "Mr. Moll, think back carefully. Do you remember if your doctor ever informed you that steroids could leach your bones of calcium?"

Moll searched Anita's face for a glimmer of hope. Her eyes had brightened as the idea caught hold. "Do you think I have a case?" he asked impatiently.

A smile now took hold on Anita's face. Doctors couldn't afford the precious time that a trial monopolized, and ninety-five percent of her cases settled without going to jury. "I'll make a case for you," she said, laughing heartily and breaking the tension. She closed the legal file on her desk. "Even if you did discuss side effects, I'm sure the doctor didn't write it down in your chart." She swiveled in her chair to peer out of her office window at the Lake Michigan shoreline. People on the concrete bike path far below looked like ants on the march. Colorful sailboats dotted the water. But she had no envy or interest in joining the recreational outdoor activities. Trials were her fun. She turned to face Moll with an air of finality. "So there you have it—we have a case. But we may not have a verdict for years, so hang on to your health."

Remembering his last contact with Hartley and picturing the registered letter that dismissed him from Hartley's practice, Moll's moon face brightened with thoughts of retribution and greed. "How much do you think we can we get?"

"Did you have a job before you became ill?"

A glimmer of forgotten pride momentarily shined on Moll's face. He had been a young man before his chronic condition, and the treatments that lupus required prematurely aged him. "I was studying to be an engineer—a civil engineer—before I got sick. But that was twenty years ago. I've never really been able to work."

Anita smiled shrewdly. She mentally calculated the annual earning potential of a promising young engineer and multiplied it by the years of lost income to the age of sixty-five. She added a rough guess of the incurred cost of past and future medical expenses, and factored in a generous percentage for pain and suffering. "We'll ask for five million," she declared abruptly.

"Five million dollars," Moll whispered. To him the figure seemed like more money than he could make in multiple lifetimes. His hollow eyes stared into the inscrutable future.

"Whoa, Mr. Moll," said Anita. "Don't think about five million. It's strategy. We pitch a ridiculously high dollar amount that surpasses the doctor's malpractice coverage by a huge margin. It makes taking cases to trial frighteningly risky. A jury of laypeople is so unpredictable. They can't possibly understand which injuries are from the steroids and which are related to lupus. That's the crucial card in our hand. Hartley will be well aware that if he takes a case to trial and loses, the amount that exceeds his malpractice coverage comes straight from his personal assets. That's money straight from his pocket. Doctors simply can't take a chance, no matter how strongly they believe in their innocence. We drop hints that we'll settle for the limit of their malpractice insurance. That's at least two or three million for us. That keeps his nest egg safe. And believe me, doctors settle just to dispose of the nuisance."

"But haven't they put a limit on malpractice awards?" asked Moll nervously.

A condescending laugh escaped from Anita's lips. "Tort reform laws will never stay on the books. If caps on malpractice awards ever hold up in court, the time invested on contingency won't be worth it. Clients like you wouldn't have representation." She wanted to boast that the strong hand of lawyers controlled the world, but professionalism made her refrain. Again she turned toward the window. The waves had kicked up, and the lake had turned a dark navy blue. Hundreds of yachts were moored in the harbor, and she wondered if many of them were ever used. "You've got to love our politicians," she said under her breath.

Moll was intoxicated with avarice. He pushed himself out of the chair. "I heard your radio spot," he said, almost giggling. "I must say that I was a little hesitant, because you're a woman." Anita's reaction made Moll's bruised hand swing up to cover his grin. "That was a mistake," he corrected.

Stifling her seething disgust, Anita stood and offered her hand. "Plan to start working on this on Monday. It will be a lot of hard work with at least twenty hours of prep time, coaching with clerks before your deposition. You'll learn everything we tell you and repeat it verbatim." She stared at Moll to ensure his comprehension. "Every word will be carefully chosen. You'll practice your testimony to make sure it's consistent. And by the end, it will all become the truth. You want this case to come out in your favor, right?"

Moll cleared his throat and nodded his head.

As if time suddenly mattered, Anita glanced at her watch. "I'm sorry that you won't see much of me during this prep time. My junior staff will help you with most of your preparation, and they will keep me informed. And if there aren't any more questions, my receptionist will help you sign a contract. Ask her to explain whatever you wish. You'll get sixty percent of the settlement, minus expenses. It was so very nice to meet you." Gesturing elegantly, Anita was gone.

Moll blinked a couple of times with confusion as he arranged his disheveled clothing. His mind raced to comprehend all that he'd heard. He was not sure where he was going or what he was supposed to do, but he trudged out of the office and stopped at the receptionist's desk. On his way out, after signing the papers, he paused between the two oil paintings in the foyer. He stared at the canvases apprehensively. Both had broad slashes of crimson splashed across white. They appeared so much alike. He stretched his arm to touch a thick streak of paint to see if it was still wet.

CHAPTER THREE

Hartley's commute home in the rapidly advancing dusk seemed longer than usual. Early in his career he would have focused on the day's healing successes, but now fulfillment was fleeting and negativity was growing. It didn't matter that most of his patients got better. Remembering Moll and stewing over the jaundiced woman's son made it hard to recall the good parts of his day. He rounded the corner and slowed the Suburban at the top of his street. For many years his detached two-car garage had functioned solely as an oversized toy box, and he was accustomed to hunting for a parking spot along the parkway. His eyes lit on a rare space near his house, and he maneuvered the vehicle in with one try.

Just after his residency, Hartley had married Celeste and moved to Logan Square, ten miles northwest of downtown Chicago. It wasn't quite the swank Lincoln Park neighborhood of which he had always dreamed. Ragged hedges hid the crumbling foundations of houses built by early-century artisans,. The yards were small and fenced off. But the houses in this area had been in line with a young internist's salary. And even so, Hartley had had to work extra nights in a two-bed ER in the heart of one of Chicago's most dangerous neighborhoods to acquire the down payment for this first house. Moonlighting was baptism by fire. With only one year of residency under his belt, he was often the lone doctor staffing the small hospital. It felt good to be a young physician, unsupervised and out on his own. Idealistic and eager, and armed with fresh knowledge, Hartley found that the benefits were more than financial. During his thirteen-hour shift, patients presented with traumas and illnesses that he had never seen, and the raw challenges assured him that he would be prepared for anything in the future.

Hartley entered his yard through the chain-link fence gate and turned to make sure it had latched. He strode up the dark sidewalk, eyes fixed on the front windows, hoping to catch a glimpse of his family. At that time of night, the white spindled railings on the front porch and the two brightly lit upstairs windows made the house look like a spirited face. The old wooden door burst open with a squeak. From the small foyer, he peered up the stairway, analyzing the blur of familiar sounds for the voices of his four children. He grasped the newel post and gazed up the stairs toward the second floor. "Hello!" he said, to no answer.

Hartley's family consisted of two boys and two girls born exactly two years apart. He missed the days when the children were smaller, and all four would cascade down the stairs and battle for his attention. He headed for the kitchen without stirring a peep of attention and retrieved his dinner plate from the warmer. He sat down at the empty table to eat. Asparagus-scented steam escaped as he lifted the foil. Evan's voice drifted in from an unseen spot in the family room. "Dad, why does your pee smell so nasty after eating asparagus?" Hartley looked up with slight annoyance. His ten-year-old son had been sitting in the family room all this time without saying hello.

"Why are you asking me a meaningless trivia question?" asked Hartley.

"We were wondering. Mom didn't know."

Evan leaned lazily against the doorjamb. He was the student, needing little guidance in starting and finishing things on his own. Hartley noticed how much the boy had matured physically, as if overnight. The contrast between Hartley's coarsening middle age and Evan's unblemished youth was emphasized by their resemblance when they stood together. Hartley stuffed a forkful of asparagus into his mouth, picturing his family around the table with an empty chair at the head. He knew the answer to their trivia question—some people didn't have the enzyme that broke down asparagine, so the kidneys disposed of the amino acid in the urine—but now, the moment had passed, and the knowledge seemed useless. He pushed the remaining food around the plate with his fork.

"Where's Mom?" asked Hartley, swallowing hard.

"Drew got new Legos and everyone's building the Trojan horse."

Hartley set his half-eaten dinner in the sink, aware of how his muscles had stiffened in the time he had spent sitting.

"You didn't answer my question," said Evan.

After providing the answer, Hartley followed the sounds that drifted down the stairs. As he reached the last step the telephone rang intrusively. Knowing it was the hospital, he turned away from the bright lights of Drew's room. "The CT scan shows a mass in the pancreas and a dilated bile duct," said the nurse. "You were right."

The result wasn't what Hartley wanted to hear, and he stifled the smile that he knew would be wrong. "I was afraid of that."

"The husband is crying so hard it's hard to watch."

"You told them?"

"I didn't have to. Everyone could tell from the look on my face."

Hartley strained to think. "Don't tell them anything tonight."

The nurse's voice became panicked and hushed. "The son's right behind me at the nurses' station. He's demanding to talk to you now."

Hartley's jaw became taut as laughter streamed out of Drew's room. Work or family—he had to choose. But telling someone that his mother had pancreatic cancer wasn't something he could do over the phone. "Tell him I need to review the films before I can talk."

Guilt welled up immediately as Hartley hung up the phone. He entered Drew's room and sat quietly in the corner, watching the Lego Trojan horse nearing completion. He wanted to join in the delight, but his patient's diagnosis competed for his emotions. He feared how his patient would react in the morning and lamented that he wouldn't be able to heal her.

"Did you find your dinner in the warmer?" asked Celeste.

"It was delicious, thank you," he said, hiding his melancholy. He lifted Drew onto his knee. Of the four children, Drew's personality was the closest to Hartley's. He was quiet, and his feelings were difficult to discern until he reached a breaking point. "Nice horse," said Hartley. "What's inside the trapdoor?"

"Trojan soldiers," Drew answered, beaming over the completed project.

"It looks great. Did you do any reading today?"

Drew's body stiffened. His frustration with reading suggested he too suffered from dyslexia, which reawakened the awkwardness Hartley had felt himself as a child. "Dad, can I have a pocketknife?"

"Drew, you're six. Your brother's ten and he doesn't have one."

"But we're different. I want one."

"They're dangerous. I don't have time to teach you how to use it. Besides, you just got Legos."

Drew twisted out of his dad's encircling arms and proudly picked up the Lego box. "It says this is for ages ten to twelve. Even though I'm six, I finished in an hour."

"Drew, no pocketknife," said Hartley, and moved by his son's disappointment, he slipped away to the quiet of his bedroom and plopped down on the seat between the two bathroom vanities. He peeled off his bucks and let them fall to the floor with a thud. His socks were damp from long confinement. His arches were tender, and he squeezed out the soreness by cupping his toes and bending them back.

Celeste entered the bathroom with a laundry basket and set it on the edge of the sink. She dropped a kiss on the top of Hartley's head. "Tough day, honey?"

Hartley rose nonchalantly and leaned toward the mirror to scrutinize the deep creases etched in his forehead. "Good," he said, hiding his emotions. A heavy silence filled the bathroom. Celeste lifted a stack of towels out of the overstuffed basket and put them away in the cabinet. "Tomorrow morning the ladies are walking," she restarted with a hopeful tone in her voice. "I'm taking the kids to the Lincoln Park Zoo after that. Come with us? The kids would love to spend a day with their dad."

Brushing his teeth with a mouthful of paste, Hartley couldn't answer. He spit into the sink and strung out a long line of floss. "You know I have to work," he answered, popping the string between his teeth.

"Tomorrow's Saturday!" Celeste stopped what she was doing and looked at him directly. Her husband did not respond, so she tried a more honest tack. "Look, I need you to come. It's hard for me to manage four kids at the zoo. Please come."

"Don't make me look forward to something that I know I won't be able to do. I can't just turn people away when they're sick." Absently, Hartley gazed back into the mirror. "I've been extra good to everyone. If good karma really exists, then maybe God will keep people well tomorrow so I can go."

"Oh, Rosey! That's not how it works," exclaimed Celeste as she walked into the closet to change. In recent years, Celeste had begun to dislike the name "Roger," preferring to call her husband by a pet name instead. "Roger" reminded her of his tendency to always say "yes" to patients no matter the personal cost.

"Don't call me that," he fumed.

Celeste emerged from the walk-in closet wearing her favorite baggy pink pajamas. She stood in front of the mirror, brushing her hair with long steady strokes. "I want you to be happy—that's all."

"I am happy," mumbled Hartley.

Celeste stopped brushing her hair and let her arm fall to her side. She didn't mind managing the household without much support, but the kids were like four spinning tops, and sometimes it seemed like too much. "Rosey, I'll be honest. I need you to be around more."

Hartley kicked his bucks out of his way and plopped down onto the seat. "I know, and I'm sorry."

Celeste stared at her sulking husband. "Stop leaving the house before the children are up, and stop coming home when they're just ready for bed. Start working less. Be part of this family again!" Celeste looked back into the mirror and pulled the brush through the same spot in her hair again and again.

"Now is not a good time to remind me." Hartley stood abruptly and picked a fistful of clean socks out of the basket. "Look at these—they're all black and blue. It's the middle of summer, and there's not one pair of white." He snapped the socks into the basket and fell back onto the seat. His face twisted into a scowl.

Celeste stood with both hands firmly on her hips and stared at him earnestly. "Listen, Roger! Your pouting is making me angry. What is imperceptible to you at this moment is all too obvious to me. You're living in your own little world, completely preoccupied with your work. You take no time for your family. You've withdrawn from everyone who cares about you, even me."

"My own little world?" he seethed.

"I'll call it anything I want. Rosey, don't expect to heal every sick patient. You've got to know your limits."

"I said don't call me that!"

Hartley felt like shouting, but didn't. He swiped his worn bucks off the floor and marched into the closet, leaving a wake of resentment. Enjoying late-afternoon Cubs games from the bleachers with the sun on his face were remote memories. Weekend days relaxing on Oak Street Beach in the shadows of the John Hancock and other majestic skyscrapers of Chicago's spectacular skyline were now lived only through old photographs. Those types of excursions had balanced his life.

Celeste stared into the open closet doorway waiting for an apology that never came. "Be honest," she said. "You're not taking time. Pay more attention and listen. The girls especially!"

"I listen to people all day," he snapped defensively. "That's why God gave me two ears and one mouth, so I can listen twice as much as I speak."

"He also gave you two eyes."

"I'm a doctor, for Christ's sake! That's who I am! That's what I do!" Hartley shouted over the racket of shifting clutter.

"Rosey, you're like a caged lion in there. What on earth are you looking for?" asked Celeste.

Hartley reappeared with his forgotten Italian loafers pinched between his fingers. He raised them to eye level and studied the worn soles in the light. His jaw worked as he thought of Fogg. Smiling impishly, he stepped across the bathroom and let the shoes fall into the trash can with a loud thud. "Have you seen my sneakers?" he asked. "The comfortable ones—the old ones?"

Celeste gawked silently at her husband as if she no longer knew him. "Rosey..." she said finally, in a cautious tone. "What makes you complete?"

Hartley's face tightened. "What do you mean? I am complete."

"Then maybe I should say content. When have you been truly satisfied with your life?"

Hartley's eyes narrowed. His mind jumped back to his residency, when self-sacrifice was his means to a dream and convictions were drummed into him like he was a marine. His life at the time required few choices. His dedication was nothing more than the product of interest and willingness. Smiling lopsidedly, he thought of his children and scrutinized the price he paid for his idealism. His eyes misted slightly. "When I understand why a patient is ill and make him well," he answered with frustration. "I never planned on being just an average dad."

Chapter Four

Applause from the lawyers and patient advocacy activists roared as the keynote speaker stepped down from the podium. Using both arms, the congressman glad-handed his way back to his seat. Anita gaped at the response of the large gathering. She was impressed that there were so many followers willing to pay five hundred dollars a plate for this event. But Congressman Robert commanded a presence. His upright stature and broad shoulders gave him a formidable presence behind any podium. The spotlights highlighted the salt-and-pepper hair at his temples. His honest smile beamed across the room. Anita waited patiently for the room to partially clear. Her wineglass was full and untouched. Her napkin was still folded in the crook of her waist. Their eyes met from a distance. The congressman smiled warmly and made his way to her table. Anita laid the napkin on the table, smoothed her dress, and sat up straighter. The evening's topic had generated tension, and her uneasiness increased as Robert came closer.

"I liked your comments about tort reform," she said, taking his hand while still in her seat. "We do think alike." She wondered if Robert noticed the cool dampness in her grip while she felt only his warmth.

"I've known that for years," he answered, his face carrying a slight hint of desire. He sat in the chair by her side. "I hear from these trial attorneys that they'll be forced to turn away low-income clients if caps on damages ever take hold. What do you think?"

"Losing that business will certainly hurt," Anita answered truthfully. "Some of my colleagues insist they'll leave the malpractice field entirely if damage awards don't generate enough income. And I wouldn't advise seeking medical care in any state that's gutted the rights of injured patients. In those states, malpractice lawsuits can no longer be counted on to police the profession." She set her jaw nervously and glanced around the room, as if assessing the strength of their forces. "I hope this topic never becomes a part of Obama's national health care package."

Robert laughed calmly. "The whole issue of tort reform is pretty much DOA now. If it couldn't be passed in the last eight years, it's certainly not going to happen with this administration. Tort reform died in 2006 when the Republicans lost control of Congress. All those foolish physicians who supported the Republicans in the name of tort reform took the bait. As smart as doctors may be, they are political idiots."

Anita grasped her wineglass and took a small sip. The cheap wine's bitterness mixed with her emotions as she carefully set the glass back in its place. "The next thing physicians will ask for is to allow countersuits, potentially naming both us and the patient as defendants. The compensations could be sizeable if all physician hardships from a lawsuit are taken into account. Lost revenue. Increases in malpractice premiums. Legal fees. Even libel damages could be claimed."

As if he were in control, Robert touched her arm and smirked. "Don't expect countersuits to become legal anytime soon. This is a zero-sum game, and you'll discover that the players involved make choices in their self-interest." He glanced around and leaned forward to speak into her ear. "The vast majority of our lawmakers are attorneys, and they have no interest in fairness for a small group. I wouldn't lose any sleep over the issue."

Robert's hand lingered on her arm, and his expression grew sincere. This wasn't a new flirtation, and for Anita, it was hard to separate admiration from love. She felt that their bond was advancing over the past months, but were they thinking the same way? She was good at judging people in the courtroom, and she had spent a lot of time thinking about Robert. She wondered about his home life. Anita had met Robert's wife, and the couple struck her as a mismatch. Perhaps they had married before his career had taken off.

Robert sat back with a satisfied smile and glanced around the room. "Someday I'd love to talk with you more," he said. "You have hard opinions, I'm sure."

Anita's eyes fell on the glass of wine, but she resisted taking hold. "I have a softer side," she replied.

"You make me curious. Perhaps you would join me and discuss this with a view of the skyline? I have access to a yacht on the lake."

Anita froze with clashing emotions. This was new to her, and it would be embarrassing if she guessed wrong. She looked at him with suspicion. Why would two smart, highly ambitious people risk everything on uncertain love?

"Perhaps," she answered. "I'll let you decide."

SATURDAY

CHAPTER FIVE

Hartley couldn't recall what his horrifying nightmare was about. Most mornings he could remember his dreams. They were realistic and vivid, and in their midst, he was always overwhelmed with frustration and helplessness. Sometimes he was a soldier shooting blanks at an advancing enemy, and in others, he was a boxer punching with leaden arms. Strangely he was never injured or killed, or even in pain. Nonetheless his dreams were still nightmares, and he often woke up trembling and in a cold sweat.

A mug of hot coffee was sitting on the nightstand as usual, quietly placed there by Celeste. She did this every morning to help him get going. She never awakened him to receive the appreciation that he so ardently felt, but nearly always he mentioned it later. He rose onto one elbow and clasped the warm mug. The aroma was soothing. He took a small test sip and then slurped a big gulp before slumping back onto the pillow. Celeste strode into the room and rolled up the blinds. The ashen clouds outside the window looked as if they were deciding whether to float away or build to a thunderstorm. Hartley smiled slightly after accepting a good-morning kiss.

"Sleep well?" she asked.

"I slept okay."

"It sure looks like you didn't. Your cowlicks are twisted into a bed head."

"That phone just never stopped ringing."

Celeste laughed with fresh amusement. "I know. And I hear only your side of the conversations. 'How many times did you vomit? Was it bloody? Is the diarrhea black? Does it smell horrible? If that doesn't work call me back.' And then there are the calls to the pharmacy when you have to turn on the light to read people's birth dates and phone numbers."

"People think I'm working a night shift. They don't know any better." Hartley had grown tolerant of the overnight calls, but he felt sorry for Celeste after the first two or three. "It was a bad night for us both," he said.

"It's okay. I'm just glad you didn't have to go in."

"I might as well have. At one point I lay wide awake, thinking about what the ER doctor might have missed."

Most of the calls had been fairly important. Hartley had quelled intractable hiccups, soothed insufferable pain, and helped an asthmatic to breathe. But a call at 2:00 a.m. for a sleeping pill seemed abusive.

"Shouldn't people say 'thank you' for a free phone call?" asked Hartley.

"People feel entitled. They pay a lot for insurance and think you're paid well enough."

Hartley laughed pathetically and splashed hot coffee onto his chest. "Ouch!" he cried, sitting up in a panic and lifting his pajama shirt off his skin to ease the burn. "When people have no insurance, appreciation is all I get. And if that goes… Sometimes I feel people are more easily finding the bottom of my well of tolerance."

Hartley slid back between the covers to savor the bed's heat until a sense of commitment robbed him of the enjoyment. He dressed quickly and gingerly pulled the frayed shoelaces of his bucks. When one snapped off in his hand, he stared dejectedly at it, as if it held some meaning, and then flicked the lace into the trash can. He drew out the discarded Italian loafers and squeezed in his feet. The shoes pinched in the heel, and he wondered if the pain would be with him all day.

The doorbell cut through the early-morning silence, its suddenness giving Hartley a start. The children raced the length of the hall to be the first at the door. "Are you expecting someone?" asked Celeste.

"It must be your friends. Aren't you off for a walk and then the zoo?"

"They wouldn't ring at this hour—it's Saturday."

Hartley's voice sounded bitter. "You're right! It is Saturday."

"I do hope you'll join us," she answered.

The doorbell rang loudly again, and Hartley rushed down the hallway. The front door creaked open amidst the sounds of giddy children. But the hullabaloo died down in a heartbeat. "Is your dad at home?" said a deep, sobering voice. The children shrank back. Sunlight streamed in, and a sheriff's broad silhouette filled the doorjamb. His hat brushed the lintel. Only Sophie was smiling. She filled every stressful moment with laughter, often flashing a tiny version of her dad's infectious grin.

"It's a policeman, Daddy," she said with youthful innocence.

The sheriff smiled briefly at the children then turned a piercing gaze to Hartley. "Dr. Roger Hartley?" he asked in an official tone.

Reflexively, Hartley counted his children to see if any were missing. He felt a strong wave of nausea. "Yes, is something the matter?" he asked, masking his displeasure.

The sheriff reached out with a clipboard. "I have a summons. Sign at the X."

Hartley scanned the numbered lines of the routing sheet half-filled with signatures and found his name at the bottom. He wrote out a very neat signature. The scrawl was clumsy and awkward, and he accepted a large, yellow envelope with trepidation. His mind whirled. He slid the sheriff's pen into his own breast pocket without thinking, streaking a long line of black ink down his shirt. His hand found the doorjamb for balance.

"Thank you," said Hartley, his face flushing red at the incongruity of the courtesy.

The sheriff's pork-chop-shaped hand extended. "I'll take my pen. Don't let this spoil your day."

The sheriff's leather gun belt squeaked as he turned on his heels. He descended the three porch stairs to the sidewalk with two purposeful strides. From the doorway, Hartley watched the man as he went down the path and out through the chain-link fence gate. The squad car was double-parked on the parkway, its red and blue lights slicing the daylight. As the car pulled away, a small group of neighborhood women shied back to the edge of the Hartleys' yard. They peered at Hartley standing at the front door guiltily clutching the yellow envelope, then hurried away like an impromptu jury without a word. Hartley's face flushed hot. His stomach churned with nausea. Mortified, he whisked the envelope behind his back and slunk back into the house. His fingers dug hastily under the envelope's seal. He pulled out the summons with pained disbelief and scanned the contents. His arm went limp. "This can't be happening," he said aloud, closing the door and turning to face his frightened huddle of children. Celeste cautiously stepped down one step, gripping the banister.

"Is that man going to put you in jail, Daddy?" asked Sophie.

Hartley fought a wave of dizziness. "Someone must be upset," he mumbled anxiously. "That's all."

Celeste frowned imperceptibly. There was nothing she could say to put a positive spin on the moment. As Hartley's mind began to refocus, he scanned the apparent lawsuit for a plaintiff. This was the first summons he had ever seen, and his eyes were drawn to the capital letters.

YOU ARE SUMMONED AND REQUIRED TO FILE AN ANSWER IN THIS CASE IN THE OFFICE OF THE CLERK OF COURT WITHIN THIRTY DAYS. IF YOU FAIL TO DO SO, A JUDGMENT BY DEFAULT MAY BE TAKEN AGAINST YOU FOR THE RELIEF DEMANDS REQUESTED IN THE COMPLAINT.

Hartley's questioning eyes darted across the page. Besieged with the first stirrings of panic, he spotted his own name, grouped in bold with multiple defendants, many of whom he knew. His eyes kept searching, but still it was hard to locate the plaintiff's name. He finally found it in the upper left corner of the page in small italic letters. Saying the name out loud forced Hartley to believe that one of his patients had turned against him.

"Maxwell Moll," he said with a discharge of emotion. "This is a crock!"

The children huddled closer together and stared at their father, waiting for a sign to restore their faith. Celeste descended the stairs. "What is it, Rosey?"

His face was drawn. "I'm being sued. I never even sensed it was coming."

"What patient? What for?"

Hartley's forehead furrowed. and his lips drew taut as he struggled to control conflicting emotions of compassion and hate. "He fired me as his doctor about two months ago. I thought we got along well." Recalling that final meeting, what compassion he had left dissolved in a flood of resentment. He flipped through the pages of the legal document. The language was confusing, full of run-on sentences strung together by compound prepositions. "He's asking for five million bucks!" yelled Hartley. "Failed to appreciate! Failed to monitor! Failed to advise! Careless and negligent behavior? Compensatory and punitive damages? This guy did his best to make my life miserable. And I never got paid a nickel," he fumed.

Storming into the family room, Hartley flopped on the overstuffed couch, his eyes still riveted to the summons. His mouth gaped when he read that Moll was claiming injuries sustained as a result of treatment with prednisone, when Hartley knew they resulted from his chronic illness, compounded by his self-neglect. "That piece of shit," he seethed, regretfully glancing at the children, who stared at him like four baby owls.

Timidly, Evan came forward and laid a hand on his father's knee. "It's okay, Dad," he said, with compassion. The others stepped forward as well, gathering in a consoling group around their father. When the girls crawled into his lap, Hartley failed to draw them close as he measured the treatments that he had prescribed against the ideals that he had sworn to uphold. He had promised to never do harm to a patient. "I didn't do anything wrong!"

"Everyone gets sued, Rosey," said Celeste with a comforting expression. "That summons doesn't mean you're a bad doctor. The best doctors see the most difficult cases. And they maybe get sued more often."

Hartley brushed the kids off his lap and tossed the summons onto the coffee table as though it were contaminated with some fatal virus. He couldn't believe that a medical expert agreed that Moll's treatments with steroids were the proximate cause of the man's suffering. It made Hartley furious that the expert's qualifications were unstated. The only credentialing in the deposition was a statement that the doctor had practiced medicine within the previous six years. It didn't say where. "This expert can't be much of a doctor if he has to do this for a living." Tramping to the window, Hartley stared out at his dilapidated garage and bare backyard. If he had felt that he had committed an error, the situation would have been easier to bear, and he might have been glad to see Moll compensated for his mistake. He believed the purpose of malpractice insurance was to compensate a patient when something went wrong. Although nothing could turn back time, an award would bring a patient as close as possible to his uninjured state. Malpractice lawsuits in this situation weren't for punishment or for personal gain.

Celeste went to his side and took up his hand. "You're a great doctor, Rosey," she whispered, gently turning him so she could look him in the eye. "Half the doctors on the medical staff come to you when they're sick. You do everything you can to help people, and everyone knows it."

Hartley wrenched out of her grasp and glared at her with unfamiliar, coldhearted eyes. "It will be on my record. With that yellow envelope, the damage is done." He stalked back to the coffee table and glared at the summons, incensed that anyone could sue a doctor for anything. "And if I get past this one. there will be others." He violently swiped the summons off the table onto the floor. He couldn't practice medicine more carefully or do anything better to help him avoid repeating this nightmare. Pushing past the children, he trudged up the stairs. Celeste looked up at the ceiling and followed the creaks in the floorboards. She braced for the bedroom door to slam, but it closed quietly, and there was silence.

Flat on the bed, Hartley's back ached as if someone were pressing a sharp thumb into his sacrum. He stared up blankly. There were no tears, although that might have been better. Feeling as if the summons proved he had committed a crime, he tried to take hold of his feelings, but they pressed onward from denial to anger and then to self-doubt. Overlaying it all was a sense of profound vulnerability. He listened with heavy indifference to the children playing in the tiny backyard. His world seemed irreparably damaged. Quitting medicine right then and there crossed his mind as the only response. As a cynical smile crossed his face, a child's shriek of pain pierced the silence. Hartley jerked upright with panic and jumped off the bed. He ran down the hall and took the stairs three at a time. Celeste was already holding Christine in her arms at the breakfast table. The child's mouth was wide open, but no sound was escaping. Tears streamed down her red face. As soon as her breath returned, she held one hand cradled in the other and howled again. Her little body convulsed in shuddering spasms.

"Christine's been stung by a bee," said Celeste, with more maternal concern than alarm.

Christine had inherited the best of Celeste's features. Her face was perfectly oval, and her long, blond hair fell to her shoulders. With thin, athletic arms and legs, she was always first to smother Hartley with hugs and kisses when he arrived home. Gently, Hartley opened his daughter's hand and raised her middle finger to the light to study the white wheal of allergic reaction. The stinger was gone. Remembering how it felt to be stung by a bee, he tenderly kissed her on the forehead and smoothed back her hair. "I'm so sorry, honey. This is the first time you've been stung, isn't it? The first is always the worst. Let's make it numb with some ice. Being numb makes it feel better."

As Christine pressed the ice into her finger, Hartley quickly groped for his vibrating beeper. Seeing that the page was from the nurses' station on the same floor as his jaundiced patient, he let his arm fall to his side.

Celeste read his reaction. "Rosey, please..." she begged. "Don't go to work today. I'm worried. At least have some breakfast."

"I'm late already," he answered, looking crestfallen. "If I go now, I will miss a patient's family who I won't be happy to see. I can't take them right now."

Celeste ran to the cupboard. "At least take a vitamin." She pressed a vitamin C and a stress tab into his hand. Hartley stared at the vitamins in his open palm. They seemed small and impotent. "What time will we see you?" Celeste asked.

Hartley closed his fist and looked up sadly. "I don't know," he answered. "This day isn't starting off very well, is it?"

Chapter Six

Hartley eased the Suburban away from the curb, feeling his wife's concerned gaze following him down the street. He gripped the wheel tightly and glimpsed at his house in the rearview mirror. "I went through hell to pay for that house," he said out loud, as though to his wife. Scattered debris of phone messages, fast-food wrappers, and newspapers littered the passenger's side floor of the car. His life seemed pathetic, and he felt he could do nothing about it. He twisted the mirror to study the lines on his face. Graying hair. The life he had worked so hard to build now seemed remote, like a fading dream.

Karma, he thought. *What crap! The good you do doesn't come back one hundred times.*

Logan Square was in the midst of a recession. Rusted wire screens covered dirty store windows. Tumbling litter and weeds filled vacant lots. A gun shop and liquor store now shared the same block that once housed a family grocery and a shoe repair shop. At the back of the uneven gravel parking lot between the stores loomed a large billboard. Hartley's eyes narrowed as he read the advertisement's bold print. "Medical negligence. Call now." His hands squeezed the steering wheel so hard that they pulsed. *Those bastards,* he thought. *Parasites!* He squirmed restlessly. *Liquor stores. Gun shops. Perfect places for ambulance chasers to advertise. They go after the drinkers. The angry. The uneducated.* Hartley had never fired a gun. In fact, guns scared him to death. But a thick and ugly feeling of revenge welled up in him from a place he didn't recognize just as his beeper again agitated his belt. The page read, "Where are you? Patients waiting."

It was just before nine when Hartley finally arrived at the hospital. For the first half hour he slumped in the sagging corner chair in the back of the medical library. Over and over he questioned his decision to prescribe prednisone for severe lupus. Waves of nausea upset his stomach, and his skin went clammy as doubts about his medical competence rose to taunt him. He thought of the jaundiced woman waiting to see him. He wondered if the son might arrive. He stood up and sat down repeatedly, unable to step forward. And each time his shoes pinched his Achilles' heel. *How can I be correct one hundred percent of the time?* he asked himself.

"Seems like you live here, Hartley!" said a sharp, intrusive voice, shattering the silence. Fogg was dressed in a golf shirt that accentuated his tan. As he pulled a bottle of water from the doctor's lounge refrigerator, the interior light illuminated his wrinkle-free face. Hartley slumped deeper into the armchair and studied Fogg furtively. It was difficult to discern how old he might be, as his smile made him look youthful. He watched him casually unscrew the cap of his water and drink a third of its contents, wiping his mouth with the back of his hand.

"I don't! And what are you doing here? You don't work Saturdays."

"It is Saturday, and it's gorgeous, and I wouldn't call what I'm doing work. I'm signing charts."

"Check the weather," mumbled Hartley, staring sourly into the blackness of his coffee cup.

"Your dog die or something, Roger? That face should be on a horse."

Hartley rose swiftly at the sound of his first name and regarded Fogg angrily. "Have you ever been sued, Fogg?" he asked bluntly, as if this would be a measure of Fogg's character.

After taking another big gulp of water, Fogg pitched the empty bottle in the trash and regarded Hartley more carefully. "A few times," answered Fogg freely. "But the HMO keeps me out of court. And they pay my malpractice premiums." He shrugged his shoulders. "So why should I care? Settling makes it easy for me."

Hartley asked himself why he would broach the topic with someone for whom he had such little respect. "The sheriff paid me a visit today and dropped off a little gift. I think you might know the patient who's suing me. He's your patient, too."

"Who's that?"

"Maxwell Moll. I transferred his care to you a while back in the ER."

"I remember. Oh, he left before I could see him—against medical advice." Hartley gave a swift, disapproving glare. "Was that the next morning?"

"Doesn't matter. He's had plenty of doctors." Fogg laughed.

"You mean he had no insurance."

"That too." Fogg shoved his hands deep into his pockets and shrugged his shoulders. "Look at you, all depressed. This is your first lawsuit—I can tell."

"Don't look happy, Fogg; it's immodest."

"I can't very well thank you for a referral. I hope your assets are in your wife's name?"

Hartley raised his eyes sadly, picturing his house.

"It hurts," replied Fogg. "We've all been there."

Hartley plopped back into the deep-cushioned chair. "What would you do? They're asking for five million, and I... I could beat it! It wasn't my fault."

"You have two million in malpractice coverage, right? Settle! Be done with it."

Hartley shook his head in consternation. "My premiums will double."

"So you'd rather risk a decision by a jury of laypeople? Listen to me. If you lose, you'll pay the extra three million out of your personal assets, or worse, have it garnished from your future income. Forget about it! Even a nuisance case isn't worth it." The thought of Moll holding a windfall check for two million dollars was revolting to Hartley. It was more than he ever hoped to save for colleges, weddings, and his retirement combined. "The lawyers know you won't fight," added Fogg. "That's why they ask for five million. It's the game! You're a 'rich doctor' and..."

"I hate that 'rich doctor' crap! Granted, I don't work for just a buck, but I don't work for negative dollars, either."

"It's not that bad. You'll be all right."

Hartley was taken aback by Fogg's detachment. But he had noticed that unlike Hartley's generation, the younger doctors didn't resent the changes in medicine, but prepared to meet them instead. After his pager reactivated, Hartley pushed himself out of the chair and parted with a retiring salute. "I'll be all right." He grabbed a nearby phone to answer his page and leaned against the wall with the receiver pinned to his ear by his shoulder. "Ludwig's angina?"

he said. "Yeah, I know what that is." Ludwig's angina was an illness that few internists encountered outside of a textbook. Hartley remembered the severe infection. A tongue depressor in a patient's mouth might cause the throat to swell and close off the airway. "Take that patient off my census," he said, loath to take the risk. "That's an ENT surgeon's case, not mine." After he had hung up the phone, Hartley paused momentarily with his hand on the receiver. A rare disease should have excited him, and he was frightened that it didn't.

Hartley pulled himself together as he neared the jaundiced woman's room and knocked as lightly as possible on the door. It swung silently inward. The room was quiet. He glanced around nervously, relaxing when he did not see the son. "Good morning, Edna," he said, choosing the familiarity of her first name. She sat up in bed, looking much stronger. Her hand felt warm when he touched it. The IV of dextrose and saline was steadily dripping. An appropriate volume of tea-colored urine filled the catheter bag that hung from the side of the bed. Gently he pinched the skin over her bicep and watched it spring back elastically. He pulled his stethoscope from his front pants pocket and listened at the base of her lungs. There were no faint crackles to suggest that fluid had accumulated in her lungs overnight.

The patient's husband observed the exam while standing respectfully at the end of the bed, rocking his body and working his hands around the brim of a fedora. His pleading eyes were full of trust. He spoke after an inviting smile from Hartley. "Sorry our son was a little overexcited yesterday," he said anxiously. "He doesn't come to visit very often, and he's making up for it now."

"Please, don't apologize," said Hartley, easing the patient back against the pillows. "Any son would do the same thing. He must love you very much." The words seemed to comfort. Hartley attempted a warm smile, but the conflicting lines of worry that crisscrossed his face foretold what he had to say. Being honest while preserving optimism and instilling hope was going to be difficult. "The CT scan shows a spot in your pancreas," said Hartley directly, "and it's most likely a cancer. But the spot is small, and it doesn't look like it's spread. I think you'll be lucky."

Despite an obvious effort to maintain composure, the husband's lip quivered. Edna pulled up the sheet to cover the exposed parts of her body and eyed Hartley like a frightened, delicate bird. Without waiting, Hartley knew the questions the couple should ask, and he did his best to provide the answers. "A Whipple operation is a highly specialized surgery. The surgeon removes a block of tissue around the tumor and puts you back together with slightly new plumbing. It's a big surgery and we don't do a lot of them here. I think you'd do better if we transferred you to a university hospital." Picturing a university surgeon with a team of eager residents zealously immersed in her case, Hartley gazed regretfully at the floor. "I think your son was right."

But the husband's eyes widened fretfully. He clutched the brim of his fedora so tightly that it formed into a curl. "We have HMO insurance. Will they pay for the surgery?"

Edna surprised Hartley by taking hold of his arm, her yellow eyes blazing through a brim of tears. "Please! I'm an old woman."

"We have some savings," added the husband anxiously.

"Don't make him do that," said Edna, reaching out to Hartley with her withered hand.

Hartley regretted not checking his patient's insurance coverage before deciding on a care plan. If the HMO wouldn't allow a transfer, he was painted into a corner. The husband's fedora circled rapidly. Tenderly, Hartley rested his hand on the patient's frail shoulder, but inside his heart was tearing in two that his loyalty was to the insurance company and not his patient. "I'll do my best," he said, forcing a smile. "Please, have your son call me when he comes in. I'm sure he'll have questions."

"Oh, thank you. Thank you!" said the husband emphatically.

Hartley felt uncomfortable hearing those words.

It was well after ten when Hartley finally arrived at his office. He scurried, head down, through the waiting room, avoiding the glares from patients who had been waiting to see him since nine. He made straight for his desk to dial the HMO number.

"Lakeside HMO," said a woman's voice. "Please hold."

With his free hand, Hartley quelled a nervous twitch of his knee. Long holds trying to get insurance company authorization were always frustrating, especially when he was running behind, and each time, he questioned whether the whole process was designed to discourage doctors and save the company money. Flipping the call onto speakerphone, he browsed through the pile of lab and X-ray reports that cluttered his desk.

"I'm sorry," came the voice over the speakerphone. "How may I help you?"

Hartley fumbled to pick up the receiver. "Medical approval for care out of network."

"Transferring…"

Without another word the phone clicked on hold. Hartley fumed that he was infantilized into asking for permission to treat his own patients. "Will I beg a nurse this time, or a physician?" he asked himself as he tapped his pen impatiently on a pile of charts. His nurse stood outside the office door, miming for him to hurry; patients were getting upset.

The medical director who picked up Hartley's call sounded as if he were an out-of-practice physician. Hartley condensed his sales pitch for Edna's surgery into a tight synopsis, pumped up with both necessity and urgency. "But a Whipple can be performed at your hospital," said the medical director. "I can't authorize a transfer for that."

"I… I…" Hartley stammered. "A Whipple surgery performed at a community hospital? How can I recommend that for my patient with a clear conscience? It's a difficult surgery. Our surgeons do one a year—if that."

"Then this year they'll do two."

"But…"

"It was your patient's choice."

"What?" screeched Hartley. "She chose how?"

"Your patient purchased our cheapest health care insurance. Her choice was to save money. She's managed care, so she forfeited her right to choose. We tell her what treatments she's able to have and where. That's the agreement. Your hospital has a contract with us to provide the same care for less. And that's where she'll stay."

An emphatic hand gesture caused Hartley's pen to fly into the air. After it bounced under the desk, he stooped to his knees and groped to retrieve it. The phone cord, stretched to its limit, pulled a stack of charts to the floor. A few crashed on his head. "Maybe you've heard of the *Oath of Hippocrates*?" he yelled with compounded irritation. "I took that oath upon graduation from medical school. I promised to provide the best possible care for my patients."

The annoyance in the medical director's tone made it clear that he wasn't enjoying his job. "Somebody's got to be the watchdog for health care. When physicians and patients are allowed to determine what care is provided, the system spirals out of control. You guys just want to cover your butts."

Hartley gripped the receiver and spun in his chair. From somewhere in the building a jackhammer echoed through the concrete foundation. "I want my patient to get the best care. 'No' is your final answer?"

"I said *we* wouldn't pay for care out of network. It's her choice."

It wasn't unusual for Hartley to argue vigorously in support of his patients, but this morning he especially needed to win. "People make choices when they're healthy, under a veil of ignorance," he said forcefully. "They have no idea what level of care they'll need in the future. And you hold them accountable when they are under duress? This woman with pancreatic cancer has a chance for a cure! Doesn't that mean anything to you?"

"When patients gamble and lose, should they escape the consequences?"

"You get what you pay for? Is that what you're saying? Patients will love to hear that. Can I please have your name so I can quote you directly."

"Quote me all you want. I'm the gatekeeper. That's what I get paid to do."

The medical director clearly thought his view was a product of reason. Hartley pulled the receiver away from his ear as if it burned him. The thought of informing the defiant son why his mother couldn't be transferred made Hartley nervous. He would take the blame for the unfairness. People expected high-quality medicine—and they deserved it. Hartley rose to his feet and started to pace, but the phone cord tethered him like a leash. He couldn't stratify care in this litigation-happy, entitled society. If expensive tests and medications were refused to a patient, he felt insurance companies should take the blame—but he knew that blame would fall on him. "How can you do this job with a clear conscience?" he asked tersely.

"Physicians have multiple loyalties."

Hartley didn't give a damn about the insurance company's profits. "I'm the one in position to decide what's best for my patients," he argued. "Try putting a stethoscope in your ears and give me a listen."

"Wake up, Doctor! Soon we'll have guidelines and protocols for every possible illness. Physician assistants will replace the likes of you."

"And the dislikes," yelled Hartley.

"We're going to need a lot fewer doctors."

"People aren't ready for cookbook medicine," scoffed Hartley.

"Ha! People won't have a choice. Business is business. Get used to it. Physicians have become a generic commodity. Bought as cheaply as possible. Packaged together. Sold on the open market like a widget."

Hartley's jaw fell agape. After so many years of extra school and training, he had been reduced to a widget. "I've had enough," he said emphatically.

"As have I. Doctors like you drive medical directors like me out of our jobs."

"A conscience should drive people like you out of your jobs. If you're an MD, you swore an oath to take care of the sick. And if you want to be addressed by that title, you should uphold that oath." Hartley jammed the receiver back onto the cradle. He shoved the piles of charts in front of him to the back of his desk and rested his elbows on the edge. He bowed his head and pressed his fists into his temples.

The nurse slipped in noiselessly. "Doctor?" she said. "The ER is wondering why you haven't called back. Nursing homes have been calling with problems. The ICU needs a call—your pneumonia patient is gasping for breath. You were supposed to see her first thing this morning." Hartley looked up with an expression that carried a dozen emotions. "I'm sorry," she said, seeing his haggard appearance. "But our patients in the waiting room are livid. One guy rapped on the receptionist's window and accused us of booking so many patients just to make money. You've got to get going."

Slowly Hartley rose to his feet, his stethoscope around his neck like a yoke. The jackhammer pounded away from some unseen location. "For God's sake— it's Saturday and I'm here."

Hartley spent extra time with each patient to compensate for being late that morning. No one noticed that he was in the midst of an unusually bad day, because working harder took his mind off his problems. The late hour surprised him when he finished, and he made his way to the small office kitchen. As he scanned the leftover cold and congealed food in the refrigerator, the smell made his stomach churn. He rubbed his belly gently to soothe the pang. Over the years he had taught himself to go without eating. There were the long nights of his residency when a rolled-down metal gate locked the cafeteria and his only meals came from cast-off patient food trays left in the metal carts at the end of the halls. A glistening yellow peach-half in syrup would take the dryness out of his mouth, and a large sugar cookie provided a quick burst of energy. Sometimes cold beef stroganoff aided him in getting to sleep. The rules were simple—the tray had to be untouched with nothing out of place, the napkin had to be clean, and the silverware had to be banded together. But most importantly, the forager had to be desperate and famished. *Times haven't changed*, he thought.

Mari, the office manager, peeked in from the doorway. "You've got to start taking better care of yourself," she said cautiously.

"Everyone's been telling me that."

"Then you should start listening."

Hartley's face hardened, but he said nothing.

"Can't you muster a smile?" teased Mari. "You're almost done."

Hartley gazed out the window at a day that he knew he would never get to enjoy. The clouds were darkening, and he worried that his family would be at the zoo without raincoats. "Sorry, no," he said, swallowing hard. He stepped out of the kitchen into his office.

Mari followed him in. She slid into a chair by the side of his desk, fidgeting at the sight of the piles of charts. "I know that's a lot of callbacks."

"People are sick. I should be happy."

Hartley's hand massaged his stomach, but his pang wouldn't ease. "Is it me?" he asked. "Or do people these days show less respect for their doctors?"

"Certainly they want immediate gratification," answered Mari, knowing that illness provoked anxiety. "It's a service-oriented profession. They trust you'll make them feel better."

Hartley glanced at his diploma framed on the wall. The brittle, yellowing paper looked like it would fall to pieces if it were taken out from under the glass. "Times have changed—we're widgets," he mumbled. He gazed up with concern. "I'm afraid I'm beginning to dislike my patients."

Mari pressed her clenched hands between her knees. She had never seen the underside of Hartley's emotions. "You don't see people at their best. Why don't you make a few of those calls today, and let the rest wait until Monday?"

Suddenly Hartley's face twisted into a sneering smile. "I got it! I'll call the well-insured patients today, and let the HMO patients wait until Monday. That seems fair to me—or at least that's what I've been told."

"Maybe you need to stop taking on new patients and reduce your hours."

"I've been taught to buck up."

Mari frowned pensively. "Have you ever heard of the Peter Principle?" she asked.

"Yeah, I know it," he answered sourly. "People get promoted in business until they reach their level of incompetence."

Mari's eyes were full of sympathy. She knew Hartley's professional pride was getting the better of him. "Why should the practice of medicine be any different? Well-educated, compassionate, caring physicians get busier and busier until they can't keep up. Look at you. Sometimes you're going hair-on-fire and still not living up to your own standards. I'm telling you—do something about it. You'll self-destruct."

"Or get sued," Hartley fumed. "By the way," he added abruptly, "I got served my first summons this morning."

All expression drained from Mari's face. "I am so sorry!" she said with surprise. "Why didn't you tell me? I could have cancelled the office."

"No," said Hartley. "It was better to work. I got back on the horse."

Mari could see his heavily shadowed reflection in the glass of his diploma. "Please, tell me if you're having trouble," she said timidly.

"I'm just scared—that's all." His eyes misted over as a slideshow of sickening images passed through his mind. The disease-ravaged Moll. The large, yellow envelope. His children's terrified faces.

"You know what a great doctor you are. Don't you?"

Hartley plucked the top chart off the first stack of messages. "I have my doubts," he said dolefully.

Mari mustered a bittersweet smile. "Oh, I almost forgot," she said. "I put that first message on top. Her colitis is flaring, and she needs an infusion of Remicade. Apparently it costs six thousand dollars per dose, and her HMO won't approve it. They said she could be treated with steroids."

Hartley's head snapped back, and a wild glower overtook his face. "Don't give her prednisone," he answered sharply. "A surgeon should remove her colon."

CHAPTER SEVEN

The front doorman sprang out of his seat and stepped ahead of Anita with fawning agility. Tufts of curly, gray hair sprouted untidily from under his hatband. "Evening, Ms. Johnson," he said, a white-gloved hand touching the brim of his cap. She smiled wanly as she strode past. A long-term employee of her condominium, the doorman knew the residents far too well for Anita's taste. She ignored his sociability and deflected his toadying praise, guarding her contempt that stemmed from a long-held grudge. Years ago, he had keyed in to the elevator that lifted straight up to her penthouse, supposedly not knowing that it opened directly into her living room. She was in the kitchen at the time, pouring a glass of pinot noir after a particularly frustrating day in the courtroom. She heard the doors open and peered cautiously around the corner from behind the jamb. The doorman was standing in the elevator car with his jaw hanging agape, eyes scanning the riches that adorned the room. Anita believed that he had eavesdropped on the residents' gossip and hoped to see firsthand how a New York designer had spared no expense in filling her rooms with museum-quality pieces. There were plush, luxurious chairs, gleaming ebony tables, rich brocade drapes, and an original Degas washed in soft light over the sofa. He had frozen when their eyes met and quickly proclaimed it had been an innocent mistake. But as if he were a defendant in a criminal trial, Anita had seen through his account. Her anger was brutal and cold, and the mistake would have cost the doorman his job if other residents hadn't intervened on his behalf.

"Get me a cab," she now ordered, fixing her eyes well beyond him. She was wearing her favorite gown—a backless, very expensive Armani of black silk that was perfectly flattering. She liked the way it accentuated her black hair and svelte figure and deemphasized the small breasts that she secretly hated.

The doorman scurried to open the condominium's heavy brass and glass doors. "Where to, Ms. Johnson? Looks like you going somewhere special."

Noticing him eyeing her dress, Anita glared with haughty disdain. "Never mind," she answered. "I'll get my own cab." This evening, her condescension masked a doubt that had been preying on her mind since midday. She remembered how Robert had captured her interest at the fund-raiser and how she felt when she heard his cautious invitation, which she could have deflected with a flippant remark. She didn't know why she had accepted, aware that a night like this couldn't take her anywhere good.

The doorman beat her to the curb and bowed slightly after extending a gloved hand toward Michigan Avenue. "That's all right, Ms. Johnson. I'll help you get to anywhere you want to go." He felt the weight of her resentment and grew desperate. "Hot out tonight. Sometimes people get outta hand on nights like this. You gots to be careful."

A yellow cab pulled up at the curb. The doorman held open the door without eye contact, instead focusing on the street's gutter. The oily surface of a stagnant puddle reflected the streetlights that were just turning on. Anita's expensive Prada shoes passed under his gaze as she settled herself on the back seat. The doorman shut the door gently, patting the roof with his hand. "Ain't no chink in that armor," he said. "Nobody getting in there."

Chapter Eight

Except the patient with pneumococcal pneumonia who would expire within hours, Hartley's emergency room admissions had been typical—a patient with a blood clot that had embolized to the lungs, a nursing-home patient with infected urine, and a young girl suffering from abdominal pain and diarrhea. Each illness was familiar, but Hartley focused on the rare causes of each common ailment that he could possibly have overlooked. The embolism might indicate a rare coagulation disorder. The urinary tract infection could be due to an obstructing bladder cancer, a difficult-to-diagnose infection like tuberculosis, or even a foreign body inserted by a corrupt nursing-home orderly. The young girl's abdominal pain was a vague symptom that could be caused by anything between the covers of a thick gastroenterology textbook. The words *failure to diagnose* kept popping into his head, and he began to order specialized tests for each patient. Whether they had any worrisome warning symptoms or not, a fear-driven hypervigilance replaced his keen intuition and common sense. The extended work carried him deeper into the early part of the evening. Patients complained that his fuss and excessiveness were unnecessary—they were sick and tired, and wanted to get better as simply as possible. But Hartley suppressed his anxiety over the small impositions. He jettisoned his desire to protect patients from excessive testing and exorbitant bills. In one way, he was more caring, but in another way, he was less.

Knowing that he wasn't bringing good news, Hartley delayed his return to Edna's room until the end of his rounds. As timidly as a first-year resident, he rounded the corner and scanned the corridor for signs of the defiant son. His hard-soled loafers clip-clopped on the floor, accentuating his nervousness and slowing his pace even further. Both of his heels stung from the blisters. He knocked and swung open the door.

"So my mom has a pancreatic cancer?" said the dreaded son as soon as their eyes met. "How come she's still here?"

Hartley stared for a moment at the man's heart-pierced-by-a-dagger bicep tattoo, then looked him in the eyes. "I tried," he said with sincerity.

"You tried?"

Hartley's eyes fell on Edna. "Yes, I tried." Experience told Hartley that an argument would do more harm than good. He turned and spoke more dispassionately to the son. "The HMO director simply wouldn't approve her transfer. I encourage you to take the matter up with him. I have his name and number."

Hartley stepped quickly out of Edna's room and took a deep cleansing breath that was arrested immediately by the foul odor of putrefied flesh. His nose wrinkled. Three doors down was an uninsured patient, assigned like Moll to his care through an ER rotation. She had a gangrenous leg tumor that resembled a beehive, but she was not legally competent to consent to the surgery to have it removed. She was a schizophrenic with no family or guardian, and the lawyers were waiting to make her a ward of the state. Until then, Hartley continued to give her proper care. He took a deep breath before entering her room. "How is your leg today, Francine?" he asked.

Francine smiled brightly. "I seen you before," she crowed gaily. "You're that nice doctor who always carries a coffee cup."

Despite his dark mood, Hartley grinned widely at her incongruous good spirit. He tested the air with a sniff and the odor seemed bearable, so he moved closer. "At least you're not angry with me," he said.

"Why would I be angry? You helping me," said Francine with obvious gratitude. Her mouth worked like a cow chewing on its cud. "Leg feels better. Whatever you're doing is working. Beehive's getting smaller. Ain't seen no bees in days."

Knowing full well her leg would be amputated, Hartley nodded. There had never been any chance that she would be cured. He glanced at the uneaten food tray that sat on her nightstand. The napkin was untouched. In a small dish in the corner was an uneaten, glistening peach half. He glanced at his watch, realizing that he hadn't eaten all day. "Are you getting enough to eat, Francine?" he asked kindly.

Francine beamed with radiant grace. Her straight, white teeth gleamed when she smiled. "I'd be dead without you," she said. "From now on I see no other doctors but you. Thank you! Thank you so much!"

Hartley grinned self-consciously. Her statement was a beautiful delusion but at the same time a comforting satisfaction.

Now that Hartley had a moment alone to think, the unpleasant parts of his day came to life. He glanced at his stethoscope on the passenger seat, clearly hearing the coarse, wet gasps of his pneumococcal pneumonia patient's last breaths. He thought of his patient losing her colon, and the life she would suffer with a colostomy. The black-and-white X-ray images of Edna's cancer came to life in the shadows, and he pictured her eyes looming in the yellow headlights of every oncoming vehicle. Once in Logan Square, he slowed the Suburban and drew near the curb by the liquor store.

"Being numb makes it feel better," he said under his breath.

Hartley wasn't much of a drinker, and he seemed lost once inside the store. He gazed uncertainly at the bottles of whiskey, scotch, and vodka before deciding on a twelve-pack of beer. He looked around guiltily as he paid the cashier and quickly shoved the change into his pants pocket. He tossed the beer into his car, and it fell heavily on top of his stethoscope. The rubber tubes stretched and then snapped back into his hand when he pulled the instrument free. Sourly he studied one of the thin metal arms that had bent under the impact. The earpiece broke off in his hand as he tried to straighten it.

"Damn it," he yelled.

When Hartley walked into the kitchen, Celeste eyed the brown bag but said nothing as he nonchalantly opened the refrigerator and stuffed it onto the shelf beside the milk. He pulled out a can and moved to the table, plunking down hard on a straight-backed chair. "What's for dinner?" he asked. "I haven't eaten all day."

Celeste sensed his residual anger but chose to ignore it. "I thought we'd go out for dinner," she said, gathering patience. "Throw on a t-shirt. Everyone will feel better if we get out of the house."

Holding the beer tightly in his hand, Hartley slouched down in the chair.

"It's already late. Besides, it's not like you haven't been out. You already went to the zoo."

"We didn't go," she answered. "Nobody was in the mood without you."

Hartley stared in disbelief. "You stayed home?"

"We hoped that you'd call. Now, come on. It's Saturday and we're going out as a family."

"That's right—it is Saturday," he said testily. "And I've been swimming in pneumococcus, *E. coli*, HIV, hepatitis C, and God knows what other vile contagions all day. Let me sit quietly and let the contagions take hold."

Celeste stood by the kitchen island and stared. "I hope you're not planning to just sit there and drink that whole twelve-pack. Alcohol isn't an antiseptic to sterilize emotions."

"You're right—it's an anesthetic, and maybe that's what I need."

"Save it, Roger," she said petulantly. "Let's not have a pity party."

As though a breath of oxygen would make him burst into flames, Hartley refused to step out of his vacuum. "That Moll was trouble," he said, shaking his head and tramping back to the refrigerator. He pried his finger under the tab of a fresh can of beer. The white foam hissed and ran over the top onto his hand. He cleared the suds with a loud sip, then quickly guzzled an inch. "Why should I care for unappreciative, disrespectful, litigious people who never pay me a dime? Why should I take the risk? If I could pick and choose my patients..."

Celeste turned and faced him, arms akimbo. "*Roger!*"

"People have changed," he said bitterly. "For every mischance in life, there has to be some doctor to blame."

"Roger, it's you that has changed. What's happened to you?"

"People cash in on infirmities, like it's a handout. Five million?" Hartley washed the figure down with more beer.

"Roger! You've been doing this for twenty years. Why did you do it before?"

"I don't know anymore," he answered in a harsh tone. "But I now know that the cliché 'No good deed goes unpunished' is true."

"You're not the first good doctor who ever got sued. Get over yourself. You'll survive this."

"I just can't practice this way," he said, crushing the empty can with his hand. "It's that simple."

"Roger!" pleaded Celeste. "It isn't that simple. You have a family."

Moving slowly, Hartley withdrew to the bedroom and shut the door behind him. He collapsed onto the bed and let his eyes fix on the white ceiling. Shadows danced on the featureless surface in the dim light. His breathing slowed. The noise and disorder of the house grew less chaotic. His thoughts became less oppressive as the soft, distant clatter of silverware and dinner plates drifted in and out of his consciousness. In his mind, he saw his empty chair at the head of the table. He imagined a dinner plate under a blanket of foil in the warming drawer. He dozed until awakened by the familiar bedtime routine.

A worried child's voice carried under the crack of the door. "Where's Daddy?" asked Sophie.

"Daddy's not feeling well," Celeste said softly. "We'll go into your room. It's time for our prayers."

"But—what about Daddy?"

"Let's pray for Daddy."

Hartley's muscles relaxed as he listened to the muffled sound of their prayers. Usually the whole family prayed together, but tonight he felt unworthy to join them. Celeste closed up the house and slipped into the bathroom without a word. After her nightly rituals, she silently crawled into bed, pulled the edge of the blanket tight to her neck, and nested her head deeply in the center of her pillow. Hartley slid over.

"Go away," she said. "You're disturbing my chi."

His hand touched her thigh under the covers. "I need to feel something."

Immediately, Celeste flipped onto her side to face him. "The day has been rough on me, too," she fumed. "I gave all I had. And as I said, I don't remember a 'thank you.'"

With that, Hartley threw off the covers and twisted himself out of bed. His eyes were wide open, but he couldn't see in the dark. "Poor thing," he said, unable to contain his frustration. "Born without a libido."

"Are you kidding me? On your worst day you have never stepped on me like that."

"It was a joke," said Hartley feebly, hiding his scowling face in the dark.

"Listen, Rosey! Stop transferring your anger to me! Tired and angry sex isn't love. Besides, who would want to make love to *you* behaving as you are? As a matter of fact, you've been in this resentful mood for quite a while now. Why don't you try a little tenderness? Ask me how *my* day was and show that you care. It might take one minute or thirty, but that's the foreplay that I need. What's happened to you?" With an armful of covers, she rolled away.

Hartley winced as though he'd been slapped. In the depths of his confusion, all he could do was strike back. "Maybe you need to go back to work," he said tersely.

Celeste twisted onto one elbow, her expression aghast. "What do you think I do all day?" she asked defensively. "Parenting is a two-person job, and I've been doing it alone. Where have you been? I need understanding. I need you to give *me* credit, and say 'thanks' when it's due."

Gasping for breath, Celeste could barely hold back her tears. "At this moment you have two choices—you can shut up, or sleep somewhere else." Just then, the loud ring of the telephone cut through the air like a bell at a boxing match. Hartley's mouth snapped shut before he could compound the damage that he had done. But his self-pity grew stronger when he saw the ER number on the caller ID. "What have I done to deserve this?" He jerked the handset from the cradle and stabbed at the button.

Chapter Nine

The bull-necked cab driver sped down North Lake Shore Drive, catching a string of green lights. "It's gonna be a hot one tonight," he ventured, easing his foot off the gas when the sailing was clear. He tilted his head to peek at his new fare in the mirror. Anita saw a reflection of a heavy, formless jowl that pulled his lower lip into a droop. "Where to?" he asked with a South Side accent. Anita looked away from his thick, hairy neck and offered a brief description of where she was going. Speeding up, the cab rattled loudly. She welcomed the noise as an excuse to not engage in conversation. The cab driver's bland Chicago accent made her miss the sharp, colorful tone of New York City cab drivers.

Anita stared out the window, fighting off her memory of the fund-raiser and any visions she had of that casual meeting progressing to ardor. She was on her way to a clandestine affair, and suddenly everyone seemed to want to know where she was going. Robert was increasing his lead in the polls. He had become the frontrunner. His coffers were full. Outside the cab, the summer night was in swing. A chain of brake lights strung along Michigan Avenue. Pedestrians crowded the restaurants and bars, filling the sidewalks on both sides of the street. Horns blared at drivers caught in the intersections, and people on foot moved twice as fast as the gridlocked cars. The cab driver worked the steering wheel casually, rolling one hand over the other. As he made their way toward Monroe Harbor, Anita searched ahead, picturing the bobbing yacht.

"Fourteen hours on the road today," boasted the driver. Her thoughts interrupted, Anita looked at her watch with a quick twist of her wrist and said nothing. "Miss, you want me to stop at the tender?" the driver asked. He craned his bull neck and looked at Anita directly.

Anita turned away from his judgmental stare. "Let me out here."

"What's your hurry?" he asked. "I'll get you closer." But a twenty-dollar bill fluttered into his lap by the time he heard the back door opening. Anita had both feet on the street, not looking back for the change. She strode briskly toward where she had been directed to go, wrapping her arms tightly around her purse and pinning it to her body. With growing hesitancy, she fixed her eyes on the dark harbor. *Why couldn't he meet here?* she wondered. *We could have gone out together.*

A tug-shaped water taxi was waiting at the dock. "A gentleman paid your fare," the boat tender shouted over the noise of the engine. "He said you'd be coming. Ms. Johnson, right? I'm supposed to take you to slip 280."

The boatman's loud call made Anita shudder, and she stepped in unsteadily. The boat rocked away from the shore as the powerful engine surged. She stumbled sideways and fell onto the open bench that rimmed the periphery. She steadied herself with both hands flat on the seat at her sides. All her adult life she had kept a secret. She had never learned to swim. In the full moon, her embarrassment showed on her face. She blushed, and then smiled in spite of herself, picturing a solitary candlelit evening aboard a safe yacht. No phones. No distractions. Only Robert. She felt a shiver of excitement. Never before had they been all alone. This night had been coming for months. The unknown was there. It didn't have to be spoken.

Chapter Ten

Hartley left his bedroom without a look, a kiss, or even a good-bye. In his heart he sensed that the phone call had been a blessing, preventing him from saying things that he might deeply regret. As the hospital came into view, his thoughts roiled. Every window was brilliant with light, like a factory that never halted its production. He parked the red Suburban deep in corner of the parking lot. The lonely night-shift cars sparkled with dew. The rusted door hinge creaked loudly in the night, breaking the stillness. All was quiet except the click of Hartley's loafers. The sound echoed with loneliness off the stone façade of the building as if he walked with a ghostly double. Usually he felt a rush of adrenaline that he might find an interesting patient with an illness or injury that he'd never seen or treated before, but tonight trepidation replaced enthusiasm. He trod across the rubber ER doormat. The door's motor whirred loudly, and he winced at the onslaught of bright light and commotion. People bustled in a state of subdued pandemonium. Beeping monitors mingled with groans and brusquely shouted commands. Hartley's senses quickly adjusted to the familiar soundtrack as he focused on his work.

"I know who got you out of bed," said the head nurse behind the front desk.

Hartley plunged his hands deep into his pant pockets, feeling his stethoscope dig into his wrist. "Doesn't this hospital ever close?" he asked. The nurse looked up from her computer, noting that Hartley appeared nothing like his usual, grinning, good-natured self.

"Welcome to Bedlam," she answered, without an apology. "And I'm sorry if I don't stop to chat. Full moon brings out the crazies." The nurse pushed back from her desk and dropped her guard. "This job is nothing more than a paycheck," she said. The harsh fluorescent light of the ER highlighted the tension in her face. The nurse had been at the hospital since before Hartley had started, and he had never before heard her complain. "I would do something else if I could. But one more hour on this shift, and that's another one closer to retirement."

"You'd rather spend your nights at home?" Hartley frowned sadly. "Where's Mr. Friendly?"

"Same place as always, bay number seven."

"He must not like his wife or something," answered Hartley, feeling a pang of regret.

"He's in here all the time, like we're some kind of hotel."

Hartley glanced at the chart. "How's his chest pain?"

"He has no heart, so it's reflux."

"You're sure?"

"A GI cocktail made him feel better in minutes. But he keeps popping off his mouth that he's a lawyer."

"Now you know why I'm here," said Hartley bitterly. "Defensive medicine."

The nurse looked up and smiled. "I know why you're here."

"Yes, because he's old and fat, and treats himself to all the wrong foods. The first night I fail to get out of bed is the night he'll have the big one. And sleeping with the thought of wide complex spikes dancing across his monitor is impossible."

"At least you might get the satisfaction of laying the defibrillator paddles on his chest and dialing up the juice," she responded without hesitation. She laughed. "He'd flop like a fish. Why can't you just refuse to treat patients like that?"

"I'm wondering that, too," replied Hartley sadly. He glanced around the busy ER. "People should realize we treat everyone exactly the same. Teeth or no teeth. Money or no money. We give one hundred percent all the time."

Hartley made his way to look at the man's X-rays. As he popped the films on the view-box, it lit automatically. The ER doctor, Dr. Mates, stood next to him, studying an X-ray of somebody's ribs with a magnifying glass. "Hope you're not planning on admitting that patient," he said without turning away from the light. "Hospital's full. The ones you see will be mine for the night."

"The patients parked in the hallway aren't looking so happy already."

"Half of their problems could have waited till morning. But they don't have a good family physician who will care for them over the phone." Unsmiling, Mates straightened and glanced around the room as if he had the power to sweep out all the sore throats and coughs, leaving only the true emergencies.

"You're open 24/7," said Hartley.

Mates's mouth set in a firm line. He knew that uninsured and underinsured people found it hard to find primary-care doctors who would take them on as patients. They waited until their problems were serious. "Here, it's no appointment necessary," he said, frustrated that every patient had to be fully evaluated for even minor complaints. "That's why they all wait." He ripped down the X-rays and shoved his magnifying glass into his side pocket of his white coat. "And I have to be careful. The retro-spectroscope is a lawyer's favorite instrument because it's always twenty-twenty."

"They prefer a proctoscope," said Hartley dourly. "I just got served."

Mates's eyes widened with surprise. "You?

Hartley responded with downcast eyes.

"I've been named fourteen times," blurted Mates. "I walked around in shock for a day after the first. I almost bagged my career after the second. I didn't know what to do with myself, so I climbed Mount Kilimanjaro. I was vomiting from altitude sickness at nineteen thousand feet and shivering with cold. I decided being an ER doctor wasn't that bad."

"That's what I can look forward to," said Hartley dolefully.

"It certainly takes the fun out of the job. Look at my new doctor over there. Just out of residency, poor kid. Nobody around here is better trained, but he gets paralyzed. Can't make decisions. He's afraid he may be wrong, or that he'll miss something. Six months and he's already thinking of quitting. Imagine that, after all those years of training." Mates shook his head sadly. "I'm afraid for him."

Hartley stared silently. He had calculated the damage his own lawsuit would do to his insurance premiums. Several doctors he knew on staff had already left their practices when the numbers tipped over two hundred thousand. His stomach churned as though he was going to be sick.

"Yeah, you see him," said Mates pathetically. "I decided to fight for people like that. It's their future. Malpractice insurance premiums aren't skyrocketing solely because of colossal payouts. Those huge awards have simply driven malpractice carriers out of the marketplace, and the few giant publicly traded companies now enjoy a monopoly. There's no competition. And since we physicians are obligated to carry malpractice insurance, they can charge whatever they want. And why wouldn't they gouge us? They're under stockholder pressure to increase their profits. They're recouping their losses from a depressed economy. Their bad investments make them extort money from us. They know antitrust laws prevent us from banding together. We can't collectively bargain to negotiate rates. Business principles should apply to medicine—but they don't? It's not a level playing field. We're the commodities in short supply. Look at these patients waiting. Somebody has got to do something."

Hartley studied Mates more carefully. He looked like Danny DeVito with the same jovial smile. "Didn't you go to the tort reform protest in Springfield last week?" asked Hartley.

Mates laughed pathetically and shook his head in wonderment. "Yeah, some grand statement we made! The rally was so poorly attended that it was useless. About twenty docs standing around drinking coffee. You'd think more of us would be willing to speak out."

"We aren't the demonstrating type," said Hartley. "It's a curse of our social conscience. We lack aggression."

"Not me," answered Mates hotly, hearing the three shrill tones of the code-trauma alarm. "My dream is to help do something about it, or I'll have to say no if my kids want to be doctors." As Mates strode away, the commotion doubled. The wide sliding doors of the ambulance bay slid open. "Oh, before I forget," he yelled back. "There's a patient in bay six. I think you're his doc. Sorry, I think he's been waiting in triage for quite a while."

CHAPTER ELEVEN

The massive yacht was moored to a buoy in the far side of the harbor. Anita could see Robert on deck, then slipping below and reappearing as if attending to last-minute details. She straightened an earring, her hand lingering over her temple to quell a slight frisson of emotion. She couldn't remember ever feeling this nervous when meeting someone before. Her knees pressed together, and her eyes swept the skyline for a visual anchor. In the distance, the John Hancock Building glinted with its lighted windows, and she strained to focus on the forty-second floor to see who was working late hours on Saturday. A door opened at the waterline on the near side of the boat as the water taxi pulled alongside. Robert stood framed in the opening.

"Venus rises once more from the sea," he said, with exaggerated gallantry.

Anita enjoyed hearing his warm, resonant voice that so belied his campaign. When the water taxi heaved on a wave, she put out her hand, and his grip tightened around her small wrist. Their fingers entwined, and she felt herself lifted aboard the vessel.

"You look delightful, my dear," he said pleasantly, waving the tender away.

His eyes swept over her head-to-toe in a way she didn't find offensive, and she retaliated by doing the same. He was dressed casually, much like any other boatman at the marina, yet his dignified, broad shoulders gave him an alluring presence. "I've never seen you like this," she said.

Robert hid the glint in his eyes and replied with firm self-possession. "Maybe I prefer casual," he answered, grasping her hand once again to gently lead her through the passageways, past several sleeping cabins, and up a small flight of stairs to the poop deck.

"Does anyone know that we're out here?"

"Only the owner."

A fresh breeze put the hem of Anita's dress in motion and raised goose bumps on her thighs. "Who owns it?" she teased. "Honest politicians don't do *this* well."

"A trial lawyer," replied Robert. "You know him, but I won't tell you his name."

"Then my competition must be getting a competitive edge? And *nobody* else knows we're out here?"

"It's my hometown—I can come and go as I please." He smiled and popped open a bottle of Krug 1990 vintage Brut. Nesting the cork in the palm of his hand, he deftly poured the champagne into two tall crystal glasses. "He makes it available to me anytime for the asking—I'm not exactly sure why. Please, sit; you're making me nervous."

"You're making me nervous! You come and go unseen like the wind? Impossible. You're a huge public figure!" Anita eased into a deep, cushioned seat, slipped off a shoe, and curled her leg under her. A table off to the side was laden with food. "You did all this yourself?" she asked, struggling to control the smile that played about her lips.

Robert handed her a platter of fresh ahi tuna set on small cubes of white rice. "I tried to make it special. But one problem—no music."

A candle flickered under a hurricane lamp. Anita glanced at Robert's shiny, manicured nails as he sipped his champagne. "No music? You expect me to use my imagination?"

"You're a trial lawyer," he quipped. "Pretend you're setting the scene."

"You were a trial lawyer, too, before you went into politics. So your imagination is active, as well."

"I like my current job better," answered Robert, remembering how it took a few years to find the right platform, but he had it right now. "Your support is appreciated, as always."

Anita nodded demurely and reached for another piece of tuna. She popped it whole into her mouth, and it melted without the need for much chewing. The two sat for a minute in silence with their thoughts. The candle flickered, and each time it went out, Robert carefully relit it. Finally he gave up with a laugh and threw the matchbook onto the table. "I hope artificial lighting's okay."

Seeing Robert fall short so gracefully helped Anita settle down. "This is nice."

"I was trying for something a little more real."

The last word was pronounced with an emphasis that Anita hoped she understood. The evening was a threshold of some kind, and she wasn't quite sure what lay on the other side. Their flirtation had been increasing for many months, inching closer through mutual compliments and casual innocent touches to prolonged glances that trailed off into smiles. She, too, had felt a growing attraction and, in secret moments, yearned to find out more about Robert in private.

"So, Congressman," she began, gently tapping the side of her glass to make the bubbles rise to the top, "you brought me out here because you were looking for votes?" She studied his face in the ambient light of the city, trying to discern the subtleties of his reaction.

With a steady hand, the politician raised his glass to his lips and took a delicate sip. His manicured hands appeared smooth and soft. "I wanted to talk," he said with clear sincerity. "I only see you at parties and fund-raisers, and I can't say or ask what I want—mostly because I don't trust myself."

"Not trust yourself? You expect to win an election with that kind of reticent attitude? I'm not sure I can give you my endorsement if you can't state what you believe," she teased, not yet ready for conversational intimacy. She laughed her way past seeing his wedding ring glistening in the light, but her heart wished he had removed it. Robert pried off his shoes and relaxed back into his seat. Anita took his cue, wiggling her toes until her remaining shoe slid off onto the carpeted deck. Without hesitation, Robert's warm foot covered hers and caressed it playfully.

"That's right. I can freely say what I believe. But I can't trust myself to avoid saying what I feel. I don't want to be obvious. I just wanted this chance to maybe get to know you a little better, that's all."

Anita's face eased into neutrality. "Then let's do it this way. Why don't you tell me everything you think you know about me already? And then I'll do the same for you." Smiling enigmatically, she pulled back her foot and nestled farther into the chair. "You have to start."

Robert felt mildly discomfited by her challenge. "All right," he agreed. "I'll play—but no blame if I get you wrong. After all, I hardly know you, and I bet you're complex." Now with license to stare, he tilted a meaningful eyebrow and refilled their glasses. "Okay, here goes, but I hope neither of us will be offended. Promise?"

Anita nodded. "Promise. And hope to die."

Robert inched forward to the edge of his seat. "You wrote a book, *The Bible of Malpractice Law,* and you love when it's quoted. You like to be interviewed, and sometimes seen on TV."

"That's easy! It's not even a guess," she said, focusing on Robert's boyish, whiskerless face and sincere, dark eyes. "My commercials are all over the networks. But I'll give you credit for doing your homework and remembering the book, even if you haven't read it." She smiled aloofly, focusing again at her office windows glowing far off in the distance, glad she didn't have to work those hours anymore. She had built a reputation that carried her practice forward with a life of its own. She was known for setting new standards in personal injury law and for being ruthless to get the most for her clients. She pulled her knees close to her chest and encircled her legs with her arms. She fixed her eyes back on Robert. "When it's my turn, I can say the same about you in the public eye, but I won't."

"But you do like the attention," he added playfully.

"And what's wrong with that?" she retorted immediately, smiling inscrutably into her champagne. "You'd better try harder—or this won't be fun." Her legs extended and returned the warm, playful caresses of his feet. "Now it's my turn," she said. Looking him straight in the eyes to see what they revealed, she took a blind sip of champagne. "You were a lawyer once—a great one, I've heard—but the practice of law wasn't a big enough stage to satisfy your ego, so you remade yourself into a congressman. But law is your bloodline. Your father was past president of the bar association, which means you hold a strong stance against tort reform and are heavily funded by the special-interest pals of your father."

"I'm against tort reform because I believe it's unconstitutional," he said, a bit testy. "My dad has nothing to do with it. And leave it to a trial lawyer to pick that out of all my policy positions."

Hiding her admiration, Anita wrapped her long fingers around the thin stem of her glass and sipped daintily from the rim. As the champagne bubbles tickled her tongue, she squirmed with a vague, nameless sorrow. Momentarily she had pictured herself as a young girl, eating breakfast with her father sitting across the table. Every day he would read the sports page in silence, and often she wondered what he found so engrossing in the endless columns of figures. She longed for him to look up from the scores to ask her what she was thinking and what she had planned for the day. Carefully Anita replaced her glass on the table and forced a bright smile on her face. "Okay. That was an excellent first round," she said smartly. "But don't expect to get off so easily the next. Try to look deeper."

Robert laughed a bit self-consciously. "I don't want this to be painful."

"Oh, keep going," she said with amusement. "It's your turn."

As Robert sat straighter, his legs retracted under his chair. He cleared his throat apprehensively, giving himself a brief chance to think. The chilling wind lapped over Anita's newly exposed feet, and she shivered in the raw, uncomfortable silence. His eyes narrowed. He focused hard on her face. "My turn?" he asked. He started with a quick smirk. "You work long hours for prestige, not money, though you like the power of both."

"You're getting warmer. I like both. So much the better."

"You're beautiful and smart—a rare combination—but intuition's your gift."

Anita flushed. "Oh, no, no, no! Now you've gone cold. Intuition would have told me *not* to meet you out here."

"Okay then. I'm glad intuition's not your strong suit."

Rarely opening his mouth without a well-planned-out thought, Robert pinched the stem of his glass. After a moment, his eyes lit up and he smiled. "Now I am guessing. You're an only child—used to getting things your own way. You don't like your mother, but your grandmother was your best friend. You were sad when she died, even lonely. Maybe even lost. And your father..." Robert paused when Anita fidgeted slightly. "No—you tell me," he said.

Suddenly realizing that she had less control over the situation than she believed, Anita felt a wave of uncertainty. "Baseball," she said, her past laid open. The solitary word punched out starkly from her childhood. Her father had constantly preached the paradigms of his passion. A game of skill and strategy that was played like a chess match. Every move was deliberate. Brute force was useless. The ebb and flow of the game were really cause and effect. If you played hard, you'd win. When you didn't attend to small details, you lost. Like life, you kept playing the game until it was decided. She took a larger sip of champagne, the harsh bubbles burning down her throat and causing pressure in her chest. "I... I... Perhaps I wasn't the apple of my father's eye," she said with her emotions finally in check. "But in an indirect way, his love for baseball made me a great lawyer."

"Makes sense. You became a trial lawyer because the courtroom proceedings are games of skill and strategy. Your father found a connection, right?"

"Trials *are* games, and I play them well," she said sternly. "But his silly ardor for a kids' game wasn't the reason that I went into law. I hated him. I was an only child, and I felt my father had wanted a son. I believed he loved baseball more than me."

"How can you say that?" protested Robert. "No father..."

Her father had never said it in so many words. He didn't have to. His free time was spent coaching the neighborhood boys and bragging about their laurels as if they were his own. He went to their ballgames even on her dance recital days, offering excuses. "You don't need me to be there—you know you're a star." Hundreds of these comments quietly hurt, and their echoes reverberated in her head on the day she had bought the expensive Degas that she displayed in her living room. The graceful, self-made ballerinas reflected her hidden side that had never been adequately admired. Anita bit her lip gently. "It's okay," she said, with a tone of resentment. "My father had nothing to teach me. He needed a protégé to pass on his secrets of a powerful swing. I can still hear him say what hurt me the most. 'The fans value hitting. Everyone wants to see the ball knocked out of the park. They want the big bang. The long ball. The home run!' And I knew that I could not hit one."

Robert thought like a lawyer, tracing her development. "You wanted big settlements—home runs—that's why you're a personal injury lawyer."

"I reinvented myself," she said neatly. But reliving her formative years was uncomfortable. Just after middle school, she had ditched her middle-class, Long Island childhood friends, hating their commonness and lack of ambition. She had learned early and on her own how to dress for success and act like she deserved it. "I tended to the small details. I made the adjustments. And here I am now, hitting it out of the park. Too bad he's not around to see."

Robert studied her carefully. With that kind of success sometimes came solitude. "Unbridled self-confidence," he said. "That's what makes you a good lawyer. But exploiting the weakness of your opponents sometimes makes you unpopular," he added with a chuckle.

"I pretend not to notice." She downed the last sip of champagne and held out the tall glass for a refill. "Politicians aren't always so popular, either," she said with good humor.

A full smile conveyed Robert's enjoyment, but as he rose and refilled the two glasses, he mulled something over. He plunged the empty bottle upside-down into the ice bucket and returned quiet and preoccupied to his seat across from Anita. "It's the issues that aren't always so popular," he said, as if he'd been bothered for more than the moment. "Look what happened to us in last November's elections. People blew like the wind from one party to another, and many of my friends are out of their jobs. Even me. I'm in a Democratic state, and I barely squeaked by."

"I think this year will be better. I watch the polls. You're far out ahead."

Robert's expression became almost worried. Anita watched him keenly but gave the impression that she held no concerns. Her eyes strayed over the boats that bobbed in the harbor. Sailboat riggings clanked metallically against the masts. Small waves lapped against the sides of the boat. "Is your father still living?" Robert asked gently.

"No," she answered. "He's been gone a long time."

"I'm sorry. Too bad he can't see how his daughter turned out. If the legal profession were like baseball, your picture would be on a trading card with your average yearly settlements on the back. You'd be an all-star!"

"I got what I wanted." She looked up, leaving her thoughts. "Now—isn't it my turn?"

Robert nodded sheepishly, afraid of his own hidden shortcomings. "I'm sure you'll zero right in. But remember, you promised to be gentle. It's a long swim back to the dock."

Anita shivered. "I sink," she said with a titter. "You missed that fault. Okay, here goes. I'll start with an easy one. Your stature makes people think you're an athlete, but you're no good in sports."

"Ouch!" he said with a confident smirk. "That hits a man below the belt. But you're perceptive. I never was very coordinated. I pretend to like sports when they mix with politics."

Instead of gloating, Anita pursed her lips. "You like to win. But merely winning isn't enough. As a politician, you want every vote."

"All politicians dream of getting every vote. I'd have gone on practicing law if I didn't believe in my policies."

"How forthright," she said, sarcastically. Her face flushed, but at the same time her approval led to a surge of desire. She glanced away before her eyes could broadcast her feelings. Under the glow of champagne, the skyline lights blurred into a backdrop. Robert was the first person she had ever met who was more than her equal. She pictured a future filled with sparkle and glamour. Contrary to common belief, she wondered if two people so similar could form a bond stronger than opposites could. Growing tired of the game, she had only one more question that now mattered. The answer wouldn't involve law, sports, or politics. She worked to control her breathing and dove to the heart of the affair.

"Let me broaden the game a little. Your wife is your opposite."

Robert's eyes drilled into Anita's. "Home run," he replied, with rueful enthusiasm. "The woman hates public life. But sometimes I do, too. When I have to escape to a borrowed yacht in the middle of a harbor to find a private moment with you, my life is not in my control."

Robert edged forward. "I really looked forward to coming out here tonight."

Anita rolled her champagne glass slowly over her lips. Their toes mingled together. There was no hiding their feelings now. "I hope there won't be any unpleasant consequences to lifting our public masks," she said.

Robert sighed. "I thought I knew what I had wanted," he said sorrowfully. "I was too young. Things changed." He looked up with an apologetic expression and drank in her beauty. There was no way to resist her.

Chapter Twelve

The conversation with Mates left heavy emotions with Hartley. Doctors were leaving their practices. Someone had to do something. But the weight of the lawsuit blinded him to the future. It wouldn't matter if medical economics and health care reform drove him out of his practice. He was headed in that direction already. *The longer you stay, the longer you stay*, he thought, feeling only the present. He spun the chart carousel at the nurses' station with dulled enthusiasm and pulled the chart for bay six. He trudged to the room without checking the name and slid the curtain open with one finger. There lay Moll. Hartley's mouth fell open and anxiety gripped his stomach like a fist. "What are you doing here?" he asked with unchecked hostility.

Moll appeared just as surprised to see Hartley and looked away instantly. "I'm doing the same thing as everyone else in this ER—waiting for doctors."

"Fogg is your doctor now," said Hartley. "And if he hasn't seen you, too bad."

"Who?" asked Moll coldly, turning his head just enough to see Hartley's face. "And why are *you* here?"

Hartley resisted throwing Moll's chart against the wall. "The ER doctor told me I would find one of my patients in here. Sadly he was mistaken."

Moll's face became defiant. "I got the registered letter. You abandoned me like all the rest."

Hartley froze. "So you sued me?" seethed Hartley.

"Why not? It didn't cost me a penny. And there's more."

"More?" yelled Hartley. "Five million bucks is enough!" He glared at Moll in disbelief.

Moll smiled as if he enjoyed the moment. "Oh yes, there's more. At first—since there was no other way to get even—I wrote negative comments about you on all the Internet sites." Moll's piercing eyes turned up to enjoy the pain he was inflicting. "I love those sites," he said, his mouth curling into a sneer. "I can say anything I want, and you have no recourse. I think I got every one—but that wasn't enough. I only felt good for a moment."

The shock on Hartley's face didn't pass quickly. He pictured Moll typing away, his swollen fingers stabbing at the small keys. "The stuff on those sites doesn't represent what I do or how I do it," replied Hartley defensively, crying inside that thousands of satisfied patients he had in his practice would be happy to write flattering posts. "No one pays any attention to the two or three posts on each site."

"But they do!" answered Moll with cold cruelty. "And a bad post rings true, no matter how many others there are. Doesn't that bother you?"

Hartley studied the flaming butterfly rash on Moll's face. He needed care, but Hartley's heart hardened further. "Look at you, Moll. You're pathetic. At death's door with your illness, and you're still doing the devil's work. I would shove a thousand prednisone pills down your throat if I could. That would fix your illness for the rest of your life."

"Now you're threatening me?" said Moll. "Certainly that plays into my hand."

Seeing his mistake, Hartley stiffened with rage. But he could say nothing. The front desk nurse had appeared at the curtain. "Is there a problem, Dr. Hartley?" she asked.

"Yes, there's a problem!" he said stiffly. "This isn't my patient." He stuffed Moll's chart in her hands and stepped away, ripping the curtain closed as he exited.

CHAPTER THIRTEEN

As the breeze over Lake Michigan swept the humidity from the harbor, the night air grew fresh and enticing. Robert gazed into Anita's eyes with unmistakable interest, impulsively twisting his wedding ring from his finger. He dropped it casually into the empty champagne glass next to him on the table. The gold band clinked crisply on the thin crystal. Anita glanced shyly away. Her right hand cupped self-consciously over the left to hide the naked spot on her ring finger, where she imagined a diamond catching the sparkling lights of the city. Money equaled success. Success equaled prestige. But success and prestige couldn't compete with what she was feeling right now.

"This is a very comfortable boat," she said softly.

"As boats go," replied Robert, his eyes not leaving her face.

Anita smiled demurely, and her eyes beamed invitingly. She leaned forward, sliding her drink across the tabletop while watching his eyes follow her movements in the dim light. A moist heat gathered behind her ears, spreading over her face and down the back of her neck. Their warm bare feet intertwined, and she pictured Robert stepping around the table to whisper romantic words in her ear. She longed to hear meaningful words—words that she had never heard before—and the thought made her yearn for him to show her exactly what those words could mean. She glanced with a tinge of guilt at his wedding ring, its outline distorted through the delicately incised flute of the glass, and a delightful tingle arose under her skin. She blushed, struggling against letting go.

"What's happening in there?" Robert asked, gently probing the source of her restlessness.

Knowing better than to look into his eyes too soon, Anita let her hair fall coquettishly over her face. "Not a thing," she replied without thinking, still not quite sure of herself. She peered dreamily across the water at the city, once more finding the Hancock Building and noticing that the lights had gone out on the floor where she worked. The corners of her mouth turned up slyly. "It's sad that your wife is so different," she stated deliberately. "Does she know what she's missing?"

"I hope she doesn't know," he said as he watched her intently.

As Robert inched further to the edge of his chair, the rhythmic striking of the sailboat's metal rigging against the aluminum masts seemed to intensify. Anita reached for her delicate Chanel purse. She was alone with a powerful congressman on a luxury yacht in the middle of a harbor illuminated only by city light. Her lawyer's mind ran the evening ahead in fast-forward, playing out all the possible scenarios. She brushed aside the unfamiliar, conflicting tensions that niggled at her. There was no longer a need to be subtle and feign innocent compliments or hint at hidden desires with innuendos. He had to lead with frankness and trust that she craved. She let her purse fall unnoticed onto the floor.

When Robert reached out his hand, Anita studied his face for any trace of an egotistical smirk. It was easy to picture him winning the next election. His quiet, stoic manner appeared genuine. She was in no hurry to dance, but her heart beat strongly, and her chest grew tighter with each passing moment, her breaths quickening. Casually, she arched her back and sat straighter, raising her arms to pull her silky, black hair into a tail. Then she reached out to meet Robert's hand, and their first touch brought a shivering pleasure. As he pulled her toward him, Anita slid into his warm lap.

"This is a stupid thing to do," she said, releasing a sensuous, giddy laugh. "Usually I know where I'm going before I take a first step."

"It's hard for me, too," Robert said, softly caressing her back.

Giving in was easier than Anita expected. Robert's hand slid soothingly up the nape of her neck and plunged into her hair. Shyly, Anita fingered the gold chain that hung around his neck, wondering if a special charm was concealed at the end. "You're making me do something I normally wouldn't do," she whispered, slowly unbuttoning his shirt and finding a small gold cross. "I'm not sure I like that."

Robert rubbed down the goose bumps that bristled along Anita's arms and casually swept his fingers across her stiffening nipples. "I could use a little extra up there," she said defensively, with unguarded self-doubt. She lowered her head to his shoulder. The champagne had anesthetized any lingering feeling of guilt. The yacht bobbed among the waves. Anita felt as if she were rocking in the quiet of a cozy bedroom. All sense of time disappeared. She nibbled seductively at the crook of his neck, continuing more fervently as he tilted back his head to enjoy the sensation. The wind blew her hair into her face. Robert's mouth drew close to her ear.

"This means a lot to me," he breathed.

A chill stiffened her body. The words seemed empty, devoid of the meaning that she'd hoped to hear. "For me, too," she answered, retreating slightly by tucking her chin and pressing her ear to his chest. Robert's heart pounded with a quick rhythm. He put a hand to her cheek and softly lifted her face.

"I think I'm starting to love you," he whispered.

Anita's head drew back, her eyes widening so she could see his whole face. She searched for a moment and then smiled. "This is becoming a wonderful idea," she said, starting a slow, sensuous kiss. His fingers slipped under the hem of her dress, sliding smoothly up her thighs until he found the thin layer of cloth between them. He whispered something close to her ear.

"I love you," he said.

Anita's inhibitions melted away. The chill night air no longer seemed cold. She hastily glanced around the harbor before loosening his belt and freeing him from his clothing. Hurriedly, she lifted the front of her silk Armani dress and knelt over his waist. Robert's head tilted back as he waited, eyes closed, hands tightly gripping her hips. Her pelvis tilted and lowered.

CHAPTER FOURTEEN

Doctors and nurses streamed out of the trauma bay doors. Crash carts were lined up open and ready in the hallway. On his way out of the ER, Hartley turned to get a glimpse of what was happening inside the room. A young Asian doctor was on top of a gurney, kneeling over a middle-aged man, compressing his chest at quick, rhythmic intervals. A nurse squeezed a manual resuscitator bag, forcing air through a clear plastic tube into the patient's lungs. Bags of crimson blood dripped into three separate IVs. Calmly, Mates directed the flow of activity, his voice rising above the din without ever rising to a shout. Hartley craned his neck to get a better view of the man lying unconscious at the center of all the attention. He looked like a white-collar professional, but his features weren't visible from where Hartley was standing. By now the man was naked from the waist up, and a nurse used a large pair of scissors to cut off his pants. His body looked blue and lifeless, apparently crushed in a horrific freak accident. No external wounds were apparent, but it appeared he was bleeding to death internally. *A random event*, thought Hartley. The man had been mortally wounded through no fault of his own.

Abruptly the fervor intensified as the young Asian doctor jumped down from the gurney. Nurses swiftly wheeled a defibrillator machine closer and pressed the paddles against the patient's chest. As everyone stepped away, the patient's arms and legs flailed briefly with each shock. When the crowd had parted around the gurney, Hartley glimpsed a nurse pulling off the man's shoes—much like his own well-worn bucks. She tossed them through the air into a far corner like discarded props.

Breaking into a cold sweat and fighting the harsh wave of nausea that flooded up from his churning stomach, Hartley staggered a few steps back and steadied himself against the nearest wall. The ER was spinning, his vision grew blurry, and distorted noises swam in his head. After a moment, he lurched out the door. The door's motor whined as his foot hit the mat, and the cool night air rushed in to envelop him. He loosened the red tie cinched tight around his neck and took several deep gasps of fresh air. Barely able to keep from falling headlong onto the sidewalk, he walked unsteadily toward the parking lot, knowing that it was going to be hard to get home.

SUNDAY

CHAPTER FIFTEEN

The rings of the phone sounded three times louder in the dead of the night. Hartley jerked awake and blindly grabbed for the receiver. "Hello," he said quietly. Turning away from his sleeping wife, he glanced at the clock. He kept his eyes closed, hoping the call would be brief and he would be back to sleep without fully arousing his senses.

"Dr. Hartley, this is the call center. I have Susan Lynch on the line. She says her father is dying."

The woman's voice sounded monotonous and detached, like a droning machine, but when Hartley heard the word *dying* his eyes opened wide, and he searched his memory for an image of the patient's face. "Put her through," he said. There was a click and then he heard nothing, but in the silence he could feel someone waiting on the other end of the line. "Hello?" he said.

"Dr. Hartley?" said a small voice, thin and breathy with panic.

"Yes."

"My father can't breathe, and I can't wake him up."

A rush of adrenaline roused Hartley fully. Immediately his mind generated a list of possible scenarios, and none of them sounded good. He rose from the bed and slipped into the bathroom as quietly as possible, closing the door behind him. The room was dark, and the tile floor felt cold under his bare feet.

"Tell me your father's name."

"Tom Lynch," the woman answered wildly. "You're taking care of his liver cancer."

Cancer, thought Hartley, now remembering his patient well. He sank down on the bathroom seat between the vanities and relaxed his grip on the phone. He liked Mr. Lynch, an alcoholic with cirrhosis who had abandoned his self-destructive ways too late and now had an untreatable cancer. It had been agonizing to watch the man's already-ravaged body deteriorate further, knowing there was nothing he could do to halt the relentless progression of the disease. The cancerous mass had eaten its way through the surface of Lynch's liver and now bled freely into his abdomen. In the office they had discussed his prognosis and the limitations of endless blood transfusions. Lynch had decided on the comfort of hospice care. He understood the grave implications and chose to die in the calm of his own home. With a resigned sigh, Lynch had said simply, "I'm tired—I just want to rest."

"Yes, I know him well," Hartley said evenly. "Is he in pain?"

"No! But he's barely breathing!"

"Are his breaths fast or slow?"

The woman's words were choked with terror. "Slow—really slow! And every so often he gasps with a gurgling sound, as if his lungs are full of water."

Hartley knew the sounds of the "death rattle" that usually marked the last stage of a terminal illness. "Susan, you know that your father wished to die comfortably at home—we worked through this together. He's in a coma, and he doesn't feel any pain. Just stay by his side, and he'll know you're there."

"But he can't breathe!"

"A coma's like a deep sleep. He isn't suffering, I promise."

Hartley listened for an indication that the woman had understood and accepted what he had told her. She was losing her father, and he understood. "Susan?"

"Yes." Her voice had grown firmer.

"If you can't handle this by yourself, call 911. They can bring him into the hospital, and I will see him in the morning."

"Can I call you?" she asked, with an edge of fear.

"Call if you need to," he answered.

After an awkward silence there was a *click*, and then nothing. Silently, Hartley replaced the phone in its cradle and gently slid into bed, finding that the warmth under the covers on his side was gone. He wrapped his arms around his spare pillow, curled up on his side, and fell into a light sleep, his jaw and tongue working vigorously through a dream. This one was simpler than the others—a piece of sticky chewing gum tenaciously adhering to his teeth.

When the phone rang again, Hartley's body twisted with an involuntary spasm. The darkness was disorienting. He flailed blindly for the receiver, sweeping it off the nightstand onto the floor with a thud. As he leaned far over the edge of the bed, the blaring rings continued. He swiped his hand violently across the carpet, inadvertently pushing the handset farther out of reach. He slid out from under the warm covers onto his knees and managed to grab hold and silence the blaring racket. He pressed the phone against his head as he rose to his feet. "Hello," he said as if wide awake. The clock showed that he'd been back asleep for two hours, but he felt more drained than before.

"We're losing him! We're losing him!" a hysterical voice shrieked, without introduction. Hartley wondered if he was in the midst of another frustrating dream. "Huh?" he said, trying to gather his thoughts. His eyes focused in the early dawn light, and he realized who was calling and why. "Susan?"

"I've called the ambulance," she said wildly. "You need to see him tonight!"

"I can't do that," he declared, with helpless simplicity.

"Then you go straight to hell, you son of a bitch. You stupid fucker! You fucker! You fucker!" The phone slammed in Hartley's ear.

Hartley flopped heavily into bed and lay on his back, trying to comprehend the short conversation. He tossed restlessly from side to side, his pajama shirt twisting around his body and cutting into his neck. When there was no point in trying to fall back to sleep, he sat on the edge of the bed, massaging his face hard with both hands. A single light lit the upstairs hallway. He tiptoed past his children's rooms and made his way down the stairs, the floorboards squeaking along the way. He opened the front door a crack and quick-stepped his way to fetch the Sunday paper that lay just inside the enclosed yard. The stiffness in his back and hips made each step painful. He shook the paper out of its blue plastic bag onto the kitchen table, the headline jumping out with bold letters: "Fifty Million Without Health Care." He dug for the sports page. The news there seemed typical, too. "Cubs Lose in the Ninth" captioned a picture of two outfielders and a second basemen sprawled out on the grass, a baseball lying between them. He crossed to the kitchen window to glower at the crimson sky in the east. Lynch had probably died. He understood that there was nothing more he could have done, but a gnawing, irrational inadequacy ate deeper into his soul.

Soon invisible feet began to patter above, the quickening tempo contrasting sharply with the slow, rhythmic tick of the clock. Hartley spread his fingers over his temples, propping his head and bracing for the onslaught of commotion. Celeste shuffled by her husband, not noticing his awkward position. "Will you start the bacon?" she asked, covering her yawn with a hand.

"Shit on a shingle would be more appropriate," grumbled Hartley, robotically obeying. He stood at the stove, eyes out of focus, turning the strips of hot bacon. They popped in the grease, curling and shrinking away from the hot surface. Hartley poked them with a fork, his mind rummaging through his worries. His hand jerked back from a splatter. He dropped a bacon strip onto a paper towel to cool. His stomach rumbled. He had no interest in eating a morsel.

"I can't go to church today," said Hartley curtly.

"What do you mean, you can't go?" Celeste tilted her head inquisitively.

"I need time for myself."

"Church is something you do for yourself."

"I just can't," he replied simply, feeling that nothing would make him feel any better. He stabbed absently at the bacon in the bubbling fat and the sizzling intensified.

"We're all going to church," Celeste insisted.

"Except for me. I need to work through a few things," he explained vaguely. His arms dropped to his sides, and he dragged himself to the chair in the corner. He sat silently stewing over the twenty years of his life that had been defined by being a doctor. All of a sudden, he didn't want to do it anymore.

Celeste studied her gloomy husband. "You'll figure this out, Rosey. But it will be harder if you try to get past it on your own. When things get out of focus, it's better to seek more structure, not less. Come on—we'll all go to church. You'll feel better, I promise."

Hartley stared in amazement at his wife's face, which was glowing with an inner calm that contrasted with his own. He shook his head resentfully. He had been raised a Protestant, attending church only on Christmas and Easter. It was hard for him to pretend his way through the unfamiliar Catholic rituals that he robotically followed. His mind seized the pragmatic thoughts of a scientist. Without concrete evidence that God existed, he wasn't sure a higher power could break him out of his emptiness. His problems had always worked out in the past. But the contrast between his former attitudes and current needs was painfully clear. At the moment, self-reliance wasn't his strength.

Snatching the sports page off the table, Hartley gawked at the photograph of the botched, easy pop-out. "I'm not going to church, and that's final," he said with disgust. "Religion makes me feel like a fraud, and I already have that in spades. Yesterday I had this epiphany called a summons. And apparently, I'm not the omnipotent healer that I once thought." Thinking of Lynch, he pushed away from the table. "I just don't know what to believe anymore."

At that moment, Evan entered the kitchen dressed in a button-down shirt and red clip-on tie, looking like a youthful version of his father. He gazed at his dad with surprise. "How come you're not dressed for church?"

Without saying a word, Hartley plodded to the bottom of the stairs, gazing up with grim resignation. He smiled weakly. Faith might give him the best chance to be whole.

Chapter Sixteen

The wind had stiffened since daybreak, and the giant yacht rocked in the small swells that cut across the harbor. Standing at the side of the waterline hatch, Anita clutched the handrail and watched the water taxi chug toward her, shuttling passengers to and from the boats at anchor. She hoped the small vessel would be empty by the time it pulled up to collect her. She hadn't planned the previous night to turn out as it had, and she was embarrassed to be still clothed in her black evening attire. But it seemed so easy—so right—to have spent the night with Robert out on the yacht, away from everyone and everything. At thirty-eight, she was still single, and she was beginning to question whether she would ever find any man equal to her beauty and intelligence who could win her heart. At first her interest in Robert had been only professional. But now she had crossed over the line, and she found herself wondering if love and desire would surmount everything else and allow the relationship to become something more.

Robert stood next to her, watching the tender nearing, and she wondered if he was as nervous as she was. "What if someone finds out?" she asked, feeling his strong body solid against hers.

"This still bothers you?" asked Robert.

Anita looked silently away from the approaching water taxi. The thick, gray clouds had lowered, creating a colorless ceiling over the city. She stared at the skyline, her mind sequencing any possible event that could make the pillars of her life topple like dominos in a row.

When Anita looked back, Robert was grinning. "I meant what I told you last night," he said, in an offhand way.

"And what *was* that you told me again?" she asked, resisting lightheartedness.

The change in Robert's face mirrored her serious mood. "I think you know—but if I have to tell you again..."

Anita scrutinized his expression and gripped his hand tightly, hoping that she could trust him. The water taxi was nearing. "Do we really need to leave separately?" she asked hesitantly, knowing they must.

"I just need to stay and clean up, that's all," answered Robert. "This boat's a loaner, remember?" The small boat pulled alongside, bobbing inches away from the yacht. Feeling Anita's hesitancy, he leaned into her ear and spoke to her privately over the water taxi's idling engine. "I love you, and no one is going to find out."

Anita eyed the widening and narrowing chasm between the two boats with sudden fear. The deep water looked cold and foreboding, and she paused before jumping across the gap. "I don't think I can do it," she said, groping blindly for his hand as it slipped away. Robert took hold once more and helped her forward with a slight push in the small of her back. "I've got you," he said softly. "Easy does it."

Anita landed unsteadily on the white fiberglass deck, regained her balance, and moved to a seat in the bow. The engines revved, and the water taxi heaved before it began to swing away.

"Don't forget!" yelled Robert, twiddling his fingers at his waist in an inconspicuous wave. He mouthed the words silently, "I love you."

Anita traced the Chicago skyline to find the forty-second floor of the John Hancock Building. In the daylight, things looked different from the way they had in the glowing light of the moon. She shifted in her seat, smoothed down her dress, and clutched her purse. *He loves me*, she thought. But when she looked back into the hatch of the yacht, Robert was already gone. She took a deep breath, hopeful that she could go home to rest with a clear conscience.

CHAPTER SEVENTEEN

Approaching the end of the street where Hartley had left the Suburban, Celeste asked, "You want me to drive?" Hartley loosened his grip on the keys without resisting and opened the door for the children. Celeste happily stepped into the car on the driver's side. Hartley climbed into the passenger seat, moved the seat back, and sank deep into the leather. "Rosey, you need to let go," said Celeste, turning the key in the ignition. "Just sit back and enjoy the ride."

Riding in silence, Hartley tensely stewed that his life might have been better if he hadn't become a doctor. Celeste swung the car into the parking lot across the street from the church. "Look at that," she said, glancing at her glowering husband. "There's a parking spot right in front." Hartley shoved the door open with his shoulder. The cumulous clouds overhead had coalesced overnight into dense, billowing masses, their dark centers blocking out the sun. He reached for Sophie's small hand and led his children across the street. Once inside, they slid down the varnished oak pew until the six of them fit comfortably. The priest's lips moved with the opening rituals, and the congregation gave its prescribed responses. Each time, Hartley was assailed by a pang of guilt. But something else bothered him even more. Looking around casually at the faces of his friends, they seemed focused on their hymnbooks with exaggerated concentration. He sensed furtive glances of pity. As paranoia clouded his brain, he became light headed and started to sweat. *Celeste's walking group*, he thought, as though a scarlet "S" were blazed on his chest. He cast his eyes downward. "Sued," he moaned painfully.

Immersed in his emptiness, Hartley's paranoia festered and grew. When the worshipers rose for the Eucharist, he hesitated. *I can't take the host*, he thought. *I'm not Catholic. The priest will know this time. It's the way my life is going lately.* But his family slid down the pew and propelled him toward the altar. The priest robotically extended his arm. "Body of Christ." Hartley tried to step backward, but the person behind him kept him from bolting. He was face-to-face with the priest. The wafer dropped into his cupped hands. "Amen," said Hartley, as he placed the host onto his tongue. It stuck like a postage stamp, dissolving quickly to nothing. He folded his hands in the mechanics of prayer.

Hartley pulled his family toward the exit ahead of everyone else when the mass ended. The muggy heat of the day gripped him immediately, and his collar seemed to tighten around his neck like a rope. As they neared the car, he held out his hand to Celeste for the keys. Anxiously, she searched through her purse and rapidly patted her pockets. A panicked expression overcame her face. "I guess I must have locked the keys in the car," she said mournfully.

Hartley peered through the car window. Celeste's keys dangled from the steering wheel column. On the keychain ring was a tiny Virgin Mary figurine, teasingly just out of reach. "How could you be so forgetful?" he yelled.

Celeste stared stupidly, her eyes begging forgiveness.

The children had frozen in mute confusion. "Give her a break, Dad," said Evan. "We all make mistakes."

"I can't make a mistake!" shouted Hartley. "Maybe that Virgin Mary will open the door for us. No—those doors are locked, and they'll stay locked."

"It's okay," said Evan without delay. "We'll walk home. It will be fun."

Hartley studied his son's solemn face as if it were his own younger reflection. Compassion wasn't learned, it was innately felt, and his son was born with his genes. As he unclenched his fists, Christine lovingly took hold of his fingers. "Come on, Daddy," she said. "I'll lead the way."

After the car was retrieved and Hartley was back at home, he brooded in a living room chair. Ever since he was young, he had believed that he was born to be a doctor, and his gifts had steered him toward that profession as though it were destiny. "Could I have been wrong?" he asked as Evan and Drew burst into the room. Since church, they had been exploding with energy. "Can we have friends over to play?" they asked excitedly.

Reluctantly Hartley agreed and withdrew to his room. With a laptop computer, he accessed the Internet from his bed, keying in to the web sites that rated him as a physician. His eyes skimmed over the positive comments, as he was focused on hunting for Moll's. His mind cried for him to not care, but his insurmountable angst made it clear that he did. His expression fell sadly. "This doctor is awful," he read. The worst comments were signed by the name Golden Gofer. He pictured Moll. "I'm supposed to learn from these sites and improve?" he stewed. "But what is there to learn? Internet sites are not fact-checked. They hurt my reputation, and there is no recourse."

Setting the computer aside, Hartley sat behind his desk to pay bills. He wasn't saddled with a huge mortgage, private school tuitions, or car payments, but the numbers in the checkbook kept shrinking, and reality dictated how he had to live. *Just a smidgen of luxury would be nice*, he thought, as his mind wandered incessantly. When he was a medical student, Hartley had never thought of making money by practicing medicine. He had just wanted to make people feel better. But doctors were being asked to achieve more for less. He felt he had taken his eye off the ball for just a moment, and when he looked up, the familiar solo practitioners were disappearing and going the way of the dinosaur.

Faced with lower reimbursements, physicians were opting out of the traditional models for payment. Some continued to go it alone, practicing "concierge medicine" or taking payment only in credit or cash. Their only other option was to become hospital employees. Sixty percent of the once-independent doctors in Hartley's area were now owned by the hospitals. Most sold their practices for $100,000 or less, and some were so deep in overhead expenses that they agreed to simply hand over the reins and join hospital-backed practices for flat annual salaries.

In some ways, he thought it would be nice, not having to care about day-to-day office decisions or worrying about the economics of running a practice. But the MBAs and accountants had no interest in sharing a bit of their power, and they used physicians to generate maximum profits. They enjoyed lording over the doctors and had a revolving door for those who complained. In Hartley's mind this was a Morton's Fork dilemma, a choice between two equally unpleasant alternatives. Low pay and long work hours led to an unsustainable income, and there was always the fear of losing your job when monthly production numbers weren't met. But the worst problems weren't financial. The psychological stress of having to deal with bureaucrats hiring lousy staff and doctors who held no interest in ensuring quality meant risk. A lawsuit was bound to happen to him again.

A strong odor of garlic made Hartley increasingly queasy. He wandered the room taking intermittent deep breaths, but it finally drove him downstairs to hunt down the source. In the kitchen, Celeste stirred a vat of spaghetti sauce that bubbled on the front stove burner. He gazed over her shoulder at the steaming red sauce, his stomach churning with nausea. On the back burner, a deep pot contained a tangled whorl of thin noodles that, to him, resembled a pale, submerged brain. He imagined it splattered with the fiery sauce. "You know spaghetti gives me heartburn," he said with a shudder.

Celeste cocked her head to one side but didn't look up. "Not again," she said harshly. "I'm tired of your angst. Go outside and work in your garden. The fresh air might divert your mind from your troubles."

"The garden is dead and gone to weeds." He opened the refrigerator and stared at the beer sitting next to a large green apple. He poured a cup of hot coffee and sat down at the table, sliding the empty sugar bowl closer. He scraped the crusted corners with a spoon and dumped the scant loose grains into his cup. "I'm going to die hitched to the plow. The rich physician," he scoffed.

"What if I was offered a great job and you didn't have to work? How would that make you feel?"

Hartley was taken aback. He rose to his feet and emptied the bittersweet coffee into the sink. He pulled the beer from the refrigerator and took two quick gulps in succession before retreating back to his chair. The chill from the liquid spread through his body. He drained the whole can of beer with a quick chug, and crushed the can in one hand. "All I want is to live decently and provide for my family. Maybe four kids were too many."

Celeste's jaw dropped with surprise. "Rosey, you don't mean that! Neither one of us set out to be rich," she said. "Our family is more about values. Look at your children—aren't you proud of them? What has gotten into you? You're not the same person that I fell in love with. And right now, you're not the kind of person that I can continue to love."

Hartley slowly lifted the tab on a new can of beer, enjoying the prolonged hiss. "People don't realize that doctors' fees are being cut to the bone by the same massive health care conglomerates that are booming on Wall Street. And what do we do when the Medicare dollar gets tighter? Refusing care to older people will be shameful." After downing the rest of his beer, Hartley pushed himself heavily out of the chair and took a staggering step toward the refrigerator.

Celeste blocked his way. "Listen, Rosey," she said. "Doctors let this happen. Their heads have been in the sand. They should have banded together. That would give them some teeth. People wouldn't like being sick."

"Laws make it illegal to strike. We can't unionize. When we do band together to set fees, they call it collective bargaining. The government wants to keep us standing alone, with no say whatsoever. It fits in with their agenda." Hartley lowered his head. "I didn't tell you this, but I got an unsigned letter from a patient the other day. It read, 'When your doctor becomes a businessman, where do you go for your health care?' Don't know who it was, but it upset me."

Against her better judgment, Celeste opened another beer and set it in front of her husband. "Frustration can be inspiring, but merely complaining won't help. Somebody has got to do something."

"Did you say, 'Somebody has got to do something'?" he asked.

Celeste smiled broadly, with enigmatic surprise. "Yes—somebody. Events don't alter character, Rosey. Events reveal what is basic and unchanging in our personalities. Doctors are passionate about their profession."

"I'm not so sure about that anymore," returned Hartley, still unwilling to smile. He teetered on the edge of his chair and slowly rose to his feet to set the full beer in the sink.

"Where are you going?" she asked, pushing the saucepan away from the heat.

Hartley stepped toward the front door with a slightly sprightlier step. "I think I'll go pull some weeds."

"Don't go through the foyer," called Celeste, running to catch him.

"What are those?" asked Hartley, pointing to a couple of boxes in the front hall.

"Oh," answered Celeste with a tinge of fear. Watching him bend over to read the return address, her hands covered her mouth. "They arrived by special carrier yesterday afternoon while you were at work."

As Hartley peered at the two large boxes, his stomach turned over, driving a sickening mixture of beer, acid, and bile into his throat.

HENDRICKS, KENNEDY, AND JOHNSON
ATTORNEYS AT LAW

He got down on one knee and clawed at the packaging tape before ripping open one box from the corner. Hartley grabbed a handful of pages and saw Moll's name on each one. He glared at the second unopened box, his mind racing through ten years of unpleasantness. His jaw was clenched tight, and his mind raged with protest while he cursed himself for not documenting Moll's difficulties more thoroughly. In the months ahead, he would have to relive it all. Standing hastily, Hartley drew back his foot and kicked the side of the box hard. The heavy carton budged less than an inch, but tipped just enough to spill over. Steadying himself with a hand on the wall, Hartley hopped on one leg and rubbed out the pain from his great toe.

Just then the children's playmate strode past, undressed from the waist up. His shirt was clutched in his hand. "What's going on, Alex?" asked Hartley, struggling to regain his footing.

"Everyone's shirts are off downstairs," said the boy. "I'm going home."

Forgetting his sore toe, Hartley leapt over the scattered records and bounded down the stairs to the basement. "What are you doing?" he asked his children, his face full of thunder and lightning. "Evan!" he shouted, redirecting his anger toward the oldest. "What's going on here?"

"We were... We were just playing doctor," said the boy feebly, alarmed by the look in his father's eyes.

Hartley glared at the children, their youthful innocence filling him with bitter resentment. He stormed to the back of the basement. Ragged blankets were spread on the floor, a toy doctor bag open nearby. A plastic stethoscope, thermometer, and reflex hammer lay scattered, dropped in the midst of the game. He recalled his own career ideas and when they had first begun to germinate. "Go to your rooms!" he yelled with unbridled rage, not wanting them to be a part of that world. Too frightened to cry, the children flew up the stairs through the kitchen. Hartley followed two steps behind, slamming the basement door with enough force to knock a family picture from the wall. It tumbled down the steps and smashed at the bottom.

Celeste stood immobile in the kitchen as the children ran by. With a head of lettuce in one hand and a knife in the other, she shouted, "Get out of here, Roger, you miserable beast! First you bully me, and now you're scaring the kids. Get a grip on yourself, and don't come back until you do!"

Hartley went outside and crouched on the bottom tread of the porch steps, curled into a tight ball. He started to weep. "I can't do this anymore," he moaned. "In the end, a physician must lose every battle." And feeling his life's sudden change of direction, he banged his head against the railing until there were no other feelings but pain.

When darkness fell and no one had come out to find him, Hartley began to stir. Tumbling over and over in his mind, the sharp edges of his thoughts had worn smooth and settled like black pebbles in the bed of a rushing river. Having nowhere else to go, he tiptoed back into the dark house, moving with care to preserve the deathly stillness. He inched up the creaking stairs to the bedroom and sat gingerly on the edge of the bed. Celeste's breathing was easy. Hartley couldn't tell if she was pretending to sleep or if she had truly given in to fatigue. He hoped his own sleep would come soon but was afraid that his nightmares would return. Lying in bed, he kept his eyes open, staring at the red numbers of the alarm clock and waiting for them to advance. But soon the diversion no longer worked and Hartley's anger began to contaminate the comforts of apathy. He wandered the house from room to room, trying to take joy in the threads of his life woven invisibly through the meager surroundings. There was no pride in the hard path he had taken to this point in his life, and he questioned how he would make his way in the future. When he looked ahead, vast unknowns drove his thoughts back to the present. For a while, he lingered in the bedroom doorways of each of his children, watching them sleep. Tenderly, he bent to kiss each sleeping face, but the kisses felt empty. *I can't even feel love when I try*, thought Hartley.

MONDAY

CHAPTER EIGHTEEN

Startled by thunder, Hartley awakened from a state of half-sleep. The alarm clock glowed brighter than usual. Dense storm clouds blocked out any hint of the rising sun. He still trembled, and he tried to keep his eyes open to prevent the nightmare from creeping back into reality like an elusive, malevolent spirit. In his dream Hartley had been outside on the grounds of the hospital, rounding on patients lying on gurneys that were aligned in two rows. A hot summer sun beat down on his head. Windless, muggy air trapped an antiseptic scent that hung like a sickening fog. There were dozens of bodies, some motionless with their skin discolored purple by rigor mortis, the blotchy pigment of death, while others were barely breathing and comatose. Flies buzzed in halos over the heads of the corpses as if by sinister design.

Hartley moved quickly between the rows, running from one patient to another. He propped the heads of the living on pillows. He covered the dead in sterile white sheets. At the end of one row, a white-haired man lay moaning, blood gushing from his nose and ears. He vomited blood. Foul-smelling, tarry-black liquid stool welled up between his legs. A urine bag bulged with a thick, clotting juice. The man pleaded for help. Hartley ran to a closed ER door and repeatedly stepped hard on the mat, but the door failed to activate. Frantically, he pushed buttons on the house phone next to the door. But it wouldn't connect. A voice repeated from the treetops, "Code blue! Code blue!" But Hartley had no crash cart with which to respond. He tried another phone and then another in a seemingly endless row along the wall. But none of them worked. He peered through the window at nurses seated around a table. He knocked, and tapped, banged, and yelled. But no one took any notice. Doctors in white HMO coats worked behind desks piled with enormous stacks of medical charts. Their necks were drawn forward, weighted by heavy stethoscopes that looked like cast-iron cowbells, seemingly ignorant that a crisis was unfolding nearby. Hartley ran madly in all directions until suddenly he stopped dead in his tracks. At the moment he had awakened, he was staring into a puddle of blood under his feet, seeing his body's reflection—without a face.

Hartley dangled his feet over the side of the bed for a moment. He rubbed his eyes, straightened his crooked back, and took a deep, sighing breath. His chin slumped to his chest. Behind him, Celeste's slow, easy breathing paused. She rolled, sleeping, toward his side of the bed, attracted to the warm, empty space. Hartley's mind raced through half-formulated and fragmented thoughts. When the ringing phone shattered the silence, Hartley's muscles froze in fear. There was no way he could go back to work.

"Get the phone," mumbled Celeste. She awakened only enough to speak before rolling away. Hartley obeyed mechanically.

"Your patient expired," a Filipino night nurse informed him.

"Who?" asked Hartley, with confused panic.

There were shades of resentment in her sharp voice. "The old woman with pancreatic cancer. We coded her for almost an hour. Her ribs snapped with the first few compressions. Her chest felt like a wet sponge when we called it—poor woman. She was so brittle. Someone should have written DNR orders before we put her through this."

Hartley's jaw hung slack with surprise, and he was unable to utter a word. He pictured the long "Do Not Resuscitate" discussion that he should have had with the son. She should have been allowed to die in peace, but at least now she was at rest. With interest close to envy, he wondered what that was like.

"Have you called the son?" he asked gloomily.

"No, but I will."

After Hartley hung up the phone, it rang again almost immediately. Apprehensively he raised the receiver. "Doctor, you need to come in. The death certificate needs to be signed right away, and the son is coming in, too." Hartley faltered in responding, and it produced an uncomfortable silence. "Just to warn you, he wants to see you. He's upset that he wasn't here when it happened. Says you never told him that she was so sick." There were still no words from Hartley. "He wants her out of our hospital. The funeral home's coming to pick up the body at eight."

Hartley staggered down to the kitchen. He looked through the windowpanes and studied the dark towering clouds, heavy with rain. He yelled as if to someone outside. "It's going to storm! I can't go out!"

He started the coffeemaker with shaky hands and sat down at the table listening to the drip and struggling to extricate himself from the nightmare that was weaving itself seamlessly into his waking world. The coffee machine hissed, shooting out bursts of steam. He stared blankly, his mind not engaging. But it was Monday and the children would soon be awake and coming down to breakfast. He dreaded that they would see him overwhelmed with emotion. He rose with forced vigor and strode up the stairs, taking two at a time, hoping he could get out of the house before anyone saw him. He slipped quietly into the bathroom and stood in front of the mirror. His face was ragged and thin. Splotchy, graying whiskers peppered his hollow cheeks. His tired, red eyes protruded. Suddenly the sound of retching from down the hall stirred him out of his reverie. Celeste still lay quietly sleeping. He followed the sounds to Drew's room and peered in through the door.

Drew was sitting upright in bed with vomit covering the sheets in front of him. He was crying in little whimpers.

"What's wrong, Drew?" he asked, dumbfounded. It seemed as if this was part of his dream.

"I want Mommy," he moaned.

In the next moment, Celeste stepped quickly around him. "Roger, get some towels," she ordered.

Hartley obeyed without thought and brought towels from the bathroom, dropping them on the bed. Numb to his child's sickness, he moved helplessly to the window. It had started to rain, and the panes looked as if they were melting. "I'm leaving," he said without much emotion. But tears welled in his eyes.

Celeste looked up in astonishment. "What about Drew? Do something."

Someone needs to do something. The words resonated in his mind. "You take care of it," Hartley said. "He asked for you. And frankly, I can't help him."

Celeste stared at her husband incredulously. Drew quit his sniffling. The other three children had gathered fretfully in the hallway. In the awful silence rain beat on the roof. "You don't look well, Roger. You need to stay home."

"You deal with it—I'm checking out."

With hardened resolve, Hartley dashed out of Drew's bedroom and ducked back into his own. He ripped open his dresser drawer and dug under his socks, grasping a small wad of bills. He stuffed his hand in his pocket and turned with the money held in his fist. Grim determination was etched on his face as he pushed past the little crowd that clogged the hallway. He rushed down the stairs. "Roger, come back," cried Celeste, her voice cracking with fear. She handed a wet towel to Drew, then rushed to the top of the stairs. "Where are you going?" she yelled.

A slam of the door echoed through the house. Celeste galloped down the steps two at a time. The heavy front door squeaked open, but Hartley was already in the red Suburban, speeding away. She chased him for a few futile steps, oblivious to the torrential rain that soaked her thin nightgown. She stopped at the fence gate.

"Come back," she whispered. "What are you going to do?"

CHAPTER NINETEEN

The wet, morning rush hour was bumper to bumper, and cars crawled through the main streets of Logan Square. Hartley squeezed the steering wheel, his knuckles a bloodless white, and glared intently into the brake lights ahead. His chest was tight with the frantic pulsing of his heart. His breathing was shallow and rapid. His foot pumped the brake, eager to slide to the gas pedal and race around the traffic. The rain was coming down harder, and the wipers beat back sheets of water with rhythmic thuds. He lowered the window to gulp the air hungrily, without caring that rain spilled in to mingle with his sweat-saturated clothes. The side-view mirror reflected his raw appearance. "The risks I've taken, exposing myself to contagious infections. I've probably got TB or AIDS," he said out loud, as if to God. "Some destiny!" he snarled, with a determined laugh. "Well, I'll change that in an instant."

The gun shop was one block away, but it seemed to take half a lifetime to get there. When horns blared, his mind screamed back. *I'm worth more to my family dead*, he thought. The big red Suburban heaved like a breeching whale as Hartley swung it recklessly into the parking lot. He slammed on the brakes, skidding to a stop over the popping gravel. Only the torrential rain beating on the metal roof of the car broke the sudden quiet. Hartley was relieved that the gun shop was open. He stepped hurriedly out of the car and squinted up through the rain. A billboard loomed over his head in the back of the parking lot. His eyes scanned the photo of a hard-shelled female attorney. She looked attractive, but her expression was self-serving and cruel. The words tasted bitter in his mouth as he read them aloud.

MEDICAL NEGLIGENCE?
Get the money you deserve.
Call now!

The heavily barred door swung open more easily than Hartley expected, and he found himself inside at once. His breath quickened, and he took a few halting steps. Rainwater trickled off his soaked hair and ran uncomfortably down his neck. He gazed deliriously around the room, his eyes adjusting slowly to the darkness cut by the harsh, bright light streaming from rows of rectangular showcases. Mounted animal carcasses crowded the walls.

"May I help you?" said a thin-faced man, coming forward from a dark recess behind the counter. His inviting smile seemed incongruous with his piercing eyes and pointed goatee. As if Hartley's thoughts and plans were somehow visible, he shrank under the man's gaze. "May I help you, mister?" the salesman repeated.

"I-I need a g-gun," stammered Hartley, pushing away revulsion and fear. He was barely aware of what he would need.

The salesman moved down the display case with his hand gliding seductively over the edge. Hundreds of handguns, perfectly lined up, flashed brightly. "What do you need it for? Target practice? Self-defense? I've got everything." The man folded his arms and relaxed back against the wall, his piercing gaze never leaving Hartley's ashen face.

"Self-defense," said Hartley robotically. He peered into the case, his hands clasping and unclasping behind him. The guns appeared large and heavy, and he studied them with a mixture of awe and disgust.

"You want small or large caliber? Semiautomatic or revolver? Large or concealable? You got to give me some help here, pal."

Hartley thought his eyes betrayed his guilt, but he ceded to his will. "That one," he said, decisively tapping his finger on the glass. "I need something simple, and under five hundred. That's what I have in cash." His hand touched the roll in his pocket.

The salesman slid the cabinet door open and lifted the pistol as carefully as he would a china teacup. "You have a good eye," he said approvingly. "Black Glock nine millimeter. Semiautomatic. It's our most popular model." The salesman released his grip on the handle. The pistol spun, dangling invitingly from his pointed index finger. Hartley hesitated. "See how it feels," the salesman said coaxingly, waving his finger slightly to put the gun in motion.

Setting his jaw, Hartley reached out to accept the gun, but halfway his hand retracted. He extracted his vibrating beeper and cradled the device in his palm like a poker hand. His disappointed eyes projected his conflicts within. "Funeral home waiting," the text read. He thought of Edna.

"Do you want the gun or not?" pressured the salesman.

Torn between unpleasant options, he looked up uncomfortably, his confusion turning to painful embarrassment. He reached out decisively and seized the handgun, gripping it comfortably in his palm.

"Sight down the barrel," the salesman prompted eagerly.

Hartley's finger easily found the gently curved trigger. He peered through the sights, finding that the gun almost aimed itself. He turned the barrel toward his face and gazed inside the cylinder. The darkness seemed infinite. "I'll take it," he said abruptly, handing the weapon back to the salesman. He wanted the sale to be completed as quickly as possible so he could get away from that place. But where he was going? He hadn't decided. Events were unfolding without a plan.

"Here—fill this out," said the salesman, placing a clipboard on the showcase between Hartley's hands. His rueful mouth curled into a crooked smile.

"What's this?" asked Hartley.

"The Brady Act," the salesman grumbled, shaking his head with an ironic cant. "Mandatory background checks. There are two hundred and fifty million firearms loose in America. You've got five days to wait before there'll be one more."

Hartley's face went slack with dismay. "I need it today," he almost pleaded.

"Believe me, I wish I didn't have to ask, but it's required by law."

Hartley stared in helpless consternation, feeling his resolve deflate.

"You're still going to buy it, aren't you?" the salesman asked with narrowing eyes. "You'll have it the rest of your life."

Despondently Hartley turned away without answering.

"Hang on," said the salesman. "A few days aren't going to—"

The salesman's voice broke off as the gun shop door snapped closed behind Hartley. He stood in the prickling rain, watching the traffic drag by, his momentum gone. Behind him the door opened again, as if someone had followed him out of the store, and a hushed, conspiratorial voice mingled with the wind that swirled past his ears.

"Hey, pal, you need a gun?"

Hartley's squint transformed into a wide-open stare of surprise. He shielded his brow to see the speaker's face. A short man stood calmly beside him with hands tucked loosely into the pockets of a lightweight, camouflage jacket. He chewed on an unlit cigar with ruminant ease, letting Hartley scrutinize him thoroughly.

"Couldn't help hearing your discussion in there," the man said, deftly shifting the unlit cigar to the other side of his mouth. "That Brady Law is against your constitutional rights, you know. The right to 'keep and bear arms.' The Second Amendment. 1791. And in this day and age, everyone needs self-defense." The man plucked the cigar out of his mouth and motioned toward his rusted pickup truck. "Right there in that vehicle, I've got a clean firearm you could have for three hundred." He spat on the ground and wiped his chin with the back of his hand.

Acid and bile surged in Hartley's throat. He could almost taste the bitter, nauseating tobacco. Feeling faint, he glanced up at the billboard behind the battered vehicle. The rain pricked his eyes. The personal injury lawyer looked down at him with gleeful indictment. Hartley clenched his teeth. "Let me see it," he said with loathing.

The truck's door creaked on its hinges. Hartley bowed his head to climb in, kicking off to the side the clanking beer cans that littered the floor. Rain pounded on the roof like a steady snare-drum roll. The man opened a suitcase and stared admiringly down at a silver-plated revolver. Hartley's heart pounded as it passed into his hand. The revolver was heavy and crude, resting in his palm like a stone. It reflected the light and glinted just like the new ones in the shop. After a moment, Hartley gazed up with final, forlorn resolve. "I have the money," he said, not able to look the man in the eye. "I'll need a bullet, too."

Chapter Twenty

Hartley pulled slowly out of the parking lot and headed in the opposite direction from the hospital. Buying a gun was as far as he'd gotten in his desperate plan, and he had nowhere to go. The Saturday night special rested on the passenger's seat, gleaming more dully than before. The Brady Act had almost worked, he thought with grim irony as he covered the gun with a coat. Now he had reason to feel like a criminal. His eyes darted aimlessly. *Where should I go? Some quiet, isolated place, like the lakefront, or someplace that might make a statement?* He let the Suburban move forward in a long snake of traffic, its wipers beating out a monotonous rhythm. A radio talk show droned. When his pager vibrated, he grasped it in his fist without looking to see who needed him. He pictured Edna's emaciated, yellow body lying under the white canvass top of the morgue gurney. He smashed his finger on the button to roll down the window, raised his arm high, and slammed the pager onto the pavement. He watched in the side-view mirror as the exploded plastic casing and electronic guts slid along the asphalt as if chasing him. Rain slapped his face. He rolled up the window and sat back to preserve his new sense of freedom.

The stop-and-go traffic crept along slowly. The moment of freedom might have lasted seconds, or minutes, but it crumbled suddenly as he became aware of a woman's voice calling forth in a teasing, seductive tone from the radio's speakers.

Have you, or someone you love, been victimized by medical negligence?
A failure to diagnose?
A failure to treat?
A wrongful death?
Perhaps a nursing-home accident resulted in injury, or death?

As Hartley began to discern the words, he was jolted out of his trance. A man's voice took over the monologue in a more commanding, urgent tone.

Attorney Johnson has over ten years' experience fighting for the rights of the injured, with total settlements exceeding hundreds of millions of dollars. Let Counselor Johnson get YOU the money that you deserve. Don't wait! Act now! No fees will be charged, unless you're successful. Call now for a free consultation. 1-888-783-8436. That's 1-888-SUE-THEM.

As the announcer repeated the number, Hartley broke free of his hopeless torpor, and his stinging anger surged back in a flood. He glared at the radio, fists tightening on the steering wheel, wondering where he had heard that name before. He envisioned the billboard over the gun shop parking lot. He pictured the summons. "That's Moll's lawyer!" he realized. "That's her!"

"Get the money you deserve?" he seethed out loud, swerving at the last second to avoid a collision. He returned another driver's rude gesture and added his own vicious curse. He dug into his pocket and groped for his cell phone. The ringer was off, and he had missed several calls from the ER, office, and hospital. He ignored the text messages from Celeste. He dialed the mnemonic that was fresh in his mind. It wasn't hard for him to remember.

"Hendricks, Kennedy, and Johnson. You mean business."

"I want to see Counselor Johnson," demanded Hartley, struggling to conceal his burgeoning rage.

The receptionist's voice had a warm, personal quality. "Have you been injured?"

"Yes," spouted Hartley. "And others, too."

"Was there a wrongful death?" the receptionist asked, as if knowing that protracted suffering was always better for business.

"Maybe by the end of the day," spat Hartley.

"Counselor Johnson can see you next week. Would you like to make an appointment?"

"Next week's too late. I need to see her today."

"I sense that you're angry, sir, but I'm sorry. Counselor Johnson can't see you without an appointment."

"Then make an appointment for me today," he insisted, forcing himself to conceal his anger under a thin veneer of calm. "I'd like to see her now, while my injury's fresh. I'm halfway to your office."

"Please hold on," the receptionist said impatiently. "Tell me your name."

Hartley's jaw worked impatiently in the pause, and he spewed out the first name that popped into his head. "Jack," he said, with a hard edge to the single syllable.

"Jack what?"

Hartley sneered. "Turner," he answered, on the verge of saying more.

"Let me check, Mr. Turner," she said peevishly.

Hartley listened intently for signs of suspicion in her tone as he glanced toward the revolver within reach under his wrinkled rain jacket. He had pulled together his fragmented thoughts, and he was absurdly aware of the nervous system physiology behind his rage. He pictured his brain's temporal lobe and amygdala glowing red-hot with firing neurons. The chemical signals released from the myriad of synapses shot impulses down his brainstem. His glands pumped out adrenaline. *Fight or flight? Which impulse will be stronger?* he asked himself curiously.

"Can you get here at ten?" interrupted the receptionist.

Hartley pressed the cell phone tighter to his ear. "Where do I go?"

"The Hancock Building, forty-second floor."

"Thank you so much. Please tell her I'm coming," he said calmly and closed the phone with a satisfying snap.

A sense of purpose supplanted despair as Hartley calculated the time it would take to cover ten city miles. He circled the red Suburban in a U-turn and found the traffic lights were timed for the southbound commuters. He sped down the street toward the Hancock, his muscles tightening when a police car passed harmlessly in the oncoming lane. His foot eased off the gas, and he slid the silver revolver under the passenger seat. He turned down Addison Street and passed Wrigley Field. His neck craned to glimpse the flagpole soaring over the bleacher scoreboard. The Cubbie-blue "W" flag was not flying. He swung onto Lake Shore Drive and stepped hard on the gas. Raindrops were exploding on the windshield. Lake Michigan tossed up into chaotic waves, the water reflecting the dark gray of the sky. He veered onto Michigan Avenue with relief that he was nearing his purpose.

The Hancock Building overshadowed the Magnificent Mile. Hartley turned onto a side street, illegally parking across from the building. He reached under the seat for the gun, wrapped it in his coat, and stepped into the street. He scanned up the face of the blue-black steel building to locate the forty-second floor by sheer intuition. His mind's eye pictured the unfeeling lawyer sitting in a sumptuous office behind a vast desk. He glanced at Northwestern Hospital three blocks away. The flagpole atop the medical center flew three flags over the city. Hartley remembered seeing them many times during his residency, and he forced back a wave of guilt as if he were a child caught in an act of wrongdoing. He peered into the windows of the Hancock. A barricade and security checkpoint protected the building, but he saw no airport-style metal detector. He pushed through the revolving door and passed the guards with confident self-possession as he made his way to the elevator lobby. He pressed the button, suppressing his intense nervous excitement. He stepped forward as the elevator doors slid open, colliding with the exiting passengers. The impact drove the gun painfully into his thigh. In a moment of panic, his hands quickly folded over the bulge. Facing forward in the back of the elevator, he breathed a sigh of relief at the lift of the elevator. The elevator doors opened, and he forced a measured gait into the opulent foyer of Hendricks, Kennedy, and Johnson. The extravagance seemed unreal and foreign compared to the workplace in which he practiced.

"You're ten minutes late," scolded the receptionist when Hartley announced his impromptu alias. She looked him over with slight contempt, her eyes searching for some sickly deformity or injury. "Can I get you a coffee or water?"

Hartley shook his head without speaking.

"Can I hang up your coat?

Hartley clutched his coat like a football, shaking his head more emphatically. "No," he blurted, more pressured than he would have liked. Relieved that the coat hadn't attracted suspicion, he watched the receptionist disappear down the long carpeted hallway with short, high-heeled steps. His hand adjusted the butt of the pistol, itching to take a potshot at the gold-lettered sign on the wall.

For an instant Hartley wondered if he was in the midst of another terrible nightmare. His trembling finger worked in the cowlick on the back of his head. His feet couldn't keep still. His stomach cramped. He shivered and plucked his damp shirt away from his body. Formulating his options, his eyes bounced nervously back and forth between the vast twin oil paintings on either side of the foyer. The abstract smears of crimson called up imagery of blood. "She'll see you now," said the receptionist.

The door to Anita Johnson's book-lined office shut behind him, and the room was utterly still. Hartley hesitated, staring at the lawyer in silence, clutching his coat to his chest. She wasn't the sharp-featured, cold witch that he had imagined, but instead an attractive, intelligent-looking woman, with a hard air of self-confidence. There were no sinister lines marring her beautifully made-up face. She remained seated behind her desk and extended her hand with a warm introduction.

Hartley recoiled, remaining just out of reach. "Do you know who I am?"

"You're Mr. Turner, I'm told. My ten o'clock malpractice case." She waved her hand toward a chair. "So tell me, what's so urgent that you needed to see me on such short notice?"

Hartley spread his feet and wiped his mouth with the back of his hand. The hard gun under his crossed forearms dug into his chest. "I am your ten o'clock malpractice," he said, controlling his words carefully, "and I'd like to settle this right here and now."

Noting the fierce cant of his rigid demeanor, Anita's eyes narrowed. "Don't play games with me, Mr. Turner. You seem angry. Please sit down, and tell me what this case is all about."

"This case is about egregious wrongdoing," he sneered. "That's the term you people use—isn't it? But it might also be called greed."

When Anita rose quickly to her feet and reached for the phone to call security, Hartley took a quick step forward and swept the phone onto the floor. He plunged his right hand into his twisted coat, grasping the butt of the revolver. He rose the weapon and glared down the barrel at the object of his hatred. The heavy Saturday night special seemed weightless. He cradled it in both palms, drawing an unfaltering bead between her eyes. Anita froze, gawking at the long, shining nickel barrel, her hands clutched into fists. Hartley stepped forward menacingly, imitating a ready-to-fire stance that he had seen dozens of times in the movies. Unable to scream, Anita retreated, crowding the leather chair against the windows. In that moment, it was hard for Hartley to imagine how such a slight person could have caused such enormous pain and razor-sharp suffering in his life. He lowered the barrel to aim at her heart, getting a better view of her face.

"My name is Hartley," he said with all the dignity that his wounded soul could muster. "You sent me a summons from a patient named Moll. That lawsuit might bring millions of dollars to you—but to me…" Hartley churned with rage and his hands started to tremble. "But to me, that document embodies an attack on my character, my self esteem, and my work ethic. You stole my life with that paper and took things that you have no right to." He spat on the carpeted floor. "And Moll… You have no clue as to who he really is. Do you even care? That poor wretch will get only half of what is *rightfully* his, and you'll keep the rest for yourself, won't you?" He pushed the gun pushed forward six inches. "I have no sympathy for your contingency-fee system inciting greed," he added with disgust. The gun wavered as Hartley laughed bitterly. "You make things right for people, *do you*? A watchdog for the people? Ha! It's greed! And you expect me to just hand the money over out of my own pocket?"

Anita scowled, her arms bending stiffly at the elbows, hands clenched. Her eyes flicked around the room as if choosing an escape route. In her peripheral vision, she saw volumes of law books lining the walls that would absorb a bullet. The door was closed and her receptionist had been instructed never to disturb her when she had a client. Her chest was so tight she couldn't speak. Helplessness was foreign to her. She shuffled slowly toward the edge of her desk to circumnavigate her attacker. She glared into his eyes more to find weakness than to seek understanding.

"Until now," Hartley continued, pulling back the hammer of the revolver. A series of clicks sounded as the cylinder spun, freezing Anita in her tracks. "Until now—I was a nameless, faceless doctor. But now, *Counselor*, you can put a face with the name. It's time to make you think. And feel."

As Hartley watched the trapped and defenseless Anita, his anger gave way to bewilderment. "What do you know about medicine, anyway? Every doctor will make a mistake eventually at some point in his career. Have you no sympathy?" Hartley closed both eyes for a brief moment as if to recollect his situation more clearly. Tears welled. "How do you think it feels to make an error?" he asked with gloom, grasping the memory of his remorse that Saturday morning when the yellow envelope had been placed in his hand. He opened his eyes and aimed the revolver just to the left of her sternum, wondering if a bullet in the heart felt the same as the shock of being sued. His finger was tight on the trigger. His anger told him to squeeze. "And I wasn't even to blame!" he said disgustedly.

His arm began to get heavy. His breathing quieted. With budding remorse, he played with the thought of turning the gun on himself. "Convince me that you should live," he said anxiously, feeling the turn of uncertainty. His eyes left the gun sight and refocused on her face.

"You can't do it," she hissed coldly.

Conflicting emotions echoed from the depth of Hartley's spirit. *Someone has got to do something*, he thought.

"You won't do it. You took an oath."

His anger instantly dissipating, Hartley looked around as if just awakening from a nightmare. All those years he tried to do good. His dreams. His future. He looked into the thick-framed mirror by the side of Anita's desk. His hair was disheveled. His hollow cheeks were unshaven. A savage light glowed in his eyes. His image was unrecognizable. Hartley's heart filled with sympathy, and the rage that he had focused on Anita melted away. His arm dropped limply. His hand released its tight grip on the weapon. The gun spilled from his fingers, hitting the floor with a thud and a deafening bang. Glass shattered to his side, and Anita dropped to the floor.

In the two or three seconds of eerie silence that followed, Hartley stared numbly at the last triangle of broken mirror that remained in the thick frame. The shard teased him with a fragmented reflection. He saw a wild eye. A twisted mouth. And then he saw nothing as the last piece of the mirror dislodged and crashed to the floor.

Chapter Twenty-One

In the moments that followed the gunshot, Hartley saw dizzying, pulsing images punctuated by stark, blank moments. Anita's office door flew open, and he was tackled from behind. His forehead bashed against the corner of the gleaming desktop. A surge of bright light flashed through his brain. Sounds slurred together. "Somebody's shooting! Get down! Get out!" As Hartley spun onto the carpet, a knee fell heavily onto his back, compressing his chest and making it difficult for him to breathe. His face was pushed hard into the carpet, the coarse fibers abrading his skin. Blood flowed from a gash over his right eye. There were frantic, echoing shouts. Screams filtered in from the outer offices. Secretaries dove under desks. Lawyers crouched behind chairs. Some hesitated, debating whether to stay or flee. Those who scrambled for exits tripped over one another and collided violently. Clothes tore. Curses flew. People spilled down the exit stairs.

"Freeze! Drop your weapon!" Hartley heard from somewhere above him.

A security guard had taken cover behind the doorjamb and was aiming his gun with deadly menace at Hartley's head. Hartley eyed the guard's blue silhouette, fearful that he would die. A foot swept by his face, kicking the Saturday night special off to the side. It slid over some loose papers and hit the wall. "Don't touch that gun," he heard someone yell.

The knee riding on top of Hartley's back released its pressure, and his unseen captor stepped away. Slowly, Hartley rolled into a sitting position, crossed his legs, and stared catatonically at the bloodstained threads of the carpet a few feet in front of him. He thought of his wife and his children and the many patients who would have depended on him that day.

When Anita emerged from beneath her desk, she swept her tousled hair from her face and flung her arms until her twisted dress hung free. She resisted the guard trying to pull her toward the door and spun to face Hartley. "You two-bit sham," she fumed through clenched teeth. "If you think you had problems before, you have no idea what you're up against now." When Hartley didn't react, she whirled herself completely free from the security guard and slapped Hartley hard across the mouth. She glared at the security guard who jerked her back and turned with graceful defiance, cutting through the onlookers to stride out of the room.

With the rapidly breaking news of violence in the workplace, the area around the Hancock Building was quickly transformed into a war zone. Within minutes barricade teams had blocked off the Magnificent Mile. SWAT police carrying military-style rifles had surrounded the building. German shepherds on short leashes scented people as they evacuated. Terrified people ran once outside the building and abandoned water bottles and umbrellas littered the sidewalk. Curious pedestrians took cover in doorways. Flashing red lights assailed everyone from all directions. Reporters washed in bright lights captured it all live from behind yellow tape.

Police officers quickly dragged Hartley away from the crime scene. His wobbly legs struggled to keep up. With his hands shackled behind him, he was slammed onto the dirty floor of a waiting police van. The door banged shut with a grating sound of metal latching on metal. Hartley wrestled himself to a more comfortable position by pushing off the floor with his chin to his knees and twisting onto the bench along the wall. He bent his head forward to blot his bloody forehead on his knee.

As the van jerked into gear, Hartley peered through a small, barred window, trying to see through the dirty glass. He settled uncomfortably back onto the bench, his body rocking as the van made two short, sharp turns and then came to a stop. He heard the cab doors open and shut and the latch on the back doors rattled. Squinting in the sudden glare, Hartley stepped out of the police van on command. An officer took hold of his shoulder and spun him around toward a white-painted, cinder-block wall emblazoned with a large red cross. His head jerked around for a better look. The place was very familiar. His heart skipped a beat. The police had taken him to Northwestern Hospital. Hartley pulled back with hesitation before stepping on the mat. The motor moaned, and the doors swung wide open. His eyes were met with a sea of grave faces. He recognized many of them, even though it had been twenty years since he had been there. Only the steady, rhythmic beat of cardiac monitors punctuated the silence. Hartley kept his eyes lowered as he was eased onto a gurney and assisted gently onto his side. The vinyl covering of the mattress felt cold on his face through the thin, starched sheet. Under the gaze of countless eyes, he was wheeled into a bay. A medical student wearing a short, white coat silently locked the wheels and pressed himself against the wall, his wide eyes searching for something on which to focus. His white lab-coat pockets bulged with the *Washington Manual* and other references. Hartley curled into a semi-fetal position, trying to remember himself at that stage in his career.

A nurse entered the bay. "Are you doing okay, Doctor Hartley?" She glared at the policeman. He quickly backed away from Hartley's side and found a place to stand in the corner. Hartley glanced sideways at the nurse, remembering her face from his residency. She spaced his knees with a pillow and propped up his head. "I'd like to say it's good to see you," she whispered uneasily in his ear. "What *happened* to you?"

Sheepishly, Hartley lifted his eyes and smiled to appreciate her gestures. "Do I need stitches?" he asked.

"It's not so bad. I'll get you cleaned up. The trauma surgeon's been called. He said he was a friend of yours from your residency, and he made it clear that he would do the suturing himself."

Hartley winced slightly. "Who's that?"

"Dr. Hahn. He'll be here in a while, but in the meantime, you have a private suite with room service. Your forehead must hurt. Can I get you anything now?"

His tongue circled his mouth in search of moisture. "Some ice chips. And could you ask the guard to take off these cuffs? They're wrenching my shoulders."

"Don't worry," she answered with a warm smile as she lined the cuffs with soft gauze. "Things will get better."

Hartley laughed slightly, thinking of the contrasting anger he had observed in Anita's eyes a short while before. "They could have been worse," he said. "Can you keep me as long as you can?" he asked after a moment. "I feel comfortable here."

The policeman freed one of Hartley's hands and cuffed the other to the gurney rail. Hartley was now able to lie flat on his back, and he gazed past the officer in the doorway who partially blocked his view. ER workers were hustling in every direction, and their concerned faces made him long to help. When Hahn finally walked through the door, Hartley sat up briskly as if nothing had happened, but he kept his cuffed right hand concealed under the sheet. The tethering metal clinked on the rail. In that uncomfortable instant, Hartley saw how their lives had taken widely divergent paths. They had been colleagues once, graduating in the same year and linked together as residents. Hartley's face flushed hot with embarrassment as Hahn extended his opposite hand to shake Hartley's left. He smiled as if nothing had changed. His black hair was pulled back in a silky ponytail, and his dark eyes glowed softly. "Let's get you put back together," he said.

During the short procedure, the surgeon's soft touch was precise. "Did you ever change your mind about having children?" asked Hartley from under the drape.

Hahn peeled back the sterile, blue sheet to look at Hartley's eyes. "Why do you remember that?" he asked.

Hartley remembered the conversation they had had a long time before. Hahn had said that he chose not to bring children into a "messed up" world. It was the only negative sentiment that Hartley had ever heard from his lips, and at the time, it seemed strangely pessimistic. "I just hoped you'd changed your mind. That's all."

"No, I still feel the same," Hahn said without rancor.

The sterile drape flopped back over Hartley's face, and he felt the gentle, numb pull of the sutures in his forehead. He heard the scissors cut through the thread, reminding him of the birth of his children. Cutting the umbilical cords had made almost the same sound, but much louder. He shivered and squirmed on the gurney.

"Are you okay, Roger?"

This was the second time Hartley had thought of the kids during this disastrous morning. His tethered arm moved with anxiety, and the handcuffs clicked on the metal rail. "I'll be all right."

"Are you cold?"

"No, I'm just scared. I was thinking about my kids," he replied, relieved that his tearful eyes were hidden under the drape. "I have four."

"God has been good to you," said Hahn, cutting the final suture with a confident snip. He lifted the surgical drape from Hartley's face. Hahn's expression was twisted in a look of deep concern as he snapped off his sterile gloves and discarded them on top of the tray of used instruments. "When this is over, do you think you might come back to medicine?"

Hartley was afraid to move. With his free hand he rubbed his finger lightly over the bandage. "It's still numb, but it doesn't hurt," he said, looking away to force a pause. "At the moment, I'd have to say no."

"But you can change your mind," said Hahn with a guiding expression. "I stitched your head." He laughed. "What's in your heart is up to you. I expect you'll figure it out. Follow up with me in a week."

CHAPTER TWENTY-TWO

The doors of the police van clanked shut, and the engine roared in reverse. During the short drive, Hartley noted every turn in the road, trying to guess where he was heading. His eyes played with the darkness, opening and closing, either way seeing nothing. He heard the sounds of construction in the distance. A horn blared. The faint smell of exhaust made him nauseated. Shortly the van came to a stop. The rain had passed, and sunlight streamed down on Hartley as he stepped onto the dampened pavement. He squinted in the new light and arched his back and stretched. Looking up, he studied the puffy cumulous clouds that were streaming eastward with the wind, creating an illusion that the three-story police district building's heavy brick facade was leaning precariously toward him. Hartley had walked past this building hundreds of times before but had never envisioned going inside.

A police sergeant sitting behind a large desk confronted Hartley the moment the jailhouse doors locked behind him and asked his name in an intimidating, thunderous tone. Hartley answered, "Doctor Roger Hartley," but the title caught in his throat. His digits were rolled on a fingerprint document with painful torques to his wrists, making the nightmare-like moment more real. The sickening sight of black ink staining his fingertips made his head spin as he was photographed for the mug shots. Weakly, he held a numbered board under his chin while envisioning the haggard face he had seen in Anita's mirror, now with a white bandage slanting across his forehead. Like his wound, Hartley felt numb and the moments passed quickly. He was led into a bare room, its walls scratched full of graffiti. He sat on a small stool to take off his clothes and worked patiently at a knot in the lace of one of his bucks. Being naked in this strange, hostile place was frightening and made him acutely aware of how vulnerable his patients must feel when they changed into hospital gowns in his office. As instructed, he stepped into the orange jumpsuit and slipped on his bucks that were now stripped of their laces.

The jailer's keys rattled. Hartley was prodded down a long hall into a cell. A small wire cage on the ceiling enclosed a single, yellow bulb that cast a dim, bilious light. The cell was damp and had a faint smell of urine that made his stomach churn. With his medical mind, Hartley pictured the tiny predators that pervaded the space. Lice and bed bugs would be running amok in the bunks. *E. coli* would be infesting the floor as if it were a petri dish. Reticent to enter, he shuffled forward in the lace-less shoes.

"It's going to be a long night, buddy. Better take a bunk," issued a raspy voice from the darkest corner. As the steel-barred door clanked shut, Hartley glanced at one of the inmates who shared his confinement. The man smiled toothlessly, cheeks so hollow that it was impossible to believe he could be living. His coarse breathing was labored, and his chest heaved with an incessant cough. Hartley feared the man had TB, but he thought more likely he suffered from lung cancer instead. Hartley sat uncomfortably on the edge of the bunk, trying not to breathe deeply. He kept his legs folded close underneath out of the way of another prisoner who paced the cell from wall to wall while conversing with some invisible tormentor. *Paranoid schizophrenic*, he thought, nervously watching for signs of aggression. He recoiled with horrific visions of a long confinement. He fell back onto the bunk and contracted his knees up to his chest. Tears formed in his eyes as he feared the disappointment he would see in his family's eyes. One morning's insanity had damaged them all. But one thought gave him some comfort—his physician father was dead and wouldn't have to suffer the pain of his son's disgrace.

Heavy footsteps echoed down the hall, sinking Hartley deeper into his gloom. His name shot through the air, and a baldheaded guard smiled through the bars. "Nice weather outside for a change," he said teasingly. "Rain's gone. Sun out. Humidity down. Great day for a cold beer at a Cubs game." After scanning the cell intently, his eyes settled on Hartley. "You! What's wrong with this picture here? You a San Francisco Giants fan or something, all decked out in orange? Might make your day awful hard. Folks here don't appreciate wearing orange."

Hartley curled tighter into a ball. "What time is it?" he asked.

"If you're going to the game, you're already late," said the jailer, clearly enjoying Hartley's frustration. He opened the cell door and motioned for his prisoner to stand. Instantly, he twisted Hartley around with deft pressure from his burly thumb. Handcuffs ratcheted loudly into an unforgiving metal grip. After a nudge on the back, Hartley started forward, not knowing where he was headed. He looked down the corridor and long line of bars, his imagination filling with scenes from Dante's *Inferno* as he wondered what foul hell awaited him.

"Has the shrink been in yet?" asked the guard jovially as he led his prisoner through layers of locked doors. Hartley stared at his lace-less bucks, his mute tongue working nervously. "Real nice guy that shrink. You two doctors will get along fine. Got a lot to talk about, I'm sure." The jailer stopped at a solid steel door. Hartley peered warily at the interrogation room sign and stepped reluctantly across the threshold into the harsh fluorescent light. "No touches of home," said the guard. "Martha Stewart ain't been here yet. Not Paris Hilton, or Lindsey Lohan neither. You're the most famous person been in for a while. And sure as sure can be, you're going to be famous. Can't wait to see the papers tomorrow."

Hartley broke out in a sweat as his body writhed with torment. "Are you going to take off the cuffs?" he pleaded.

"Not this time, boss. You a felon now—impulsive and dangerous."

"Accused felon," corrected Hartley blankly.

After the door closed, Hartley dragged a mission-style wooden chair into the farthest corner, listening to every unfamiliar sound and waiting for the psychiatrist to arrive. The bleak room was nearly square, with grimy, white walls cut at waist level by a bare stripe worn through the paint where the chairs had backed up hard. Above the stripe was an ugly brown stain left by thousands of greasy heads. Hartley slumped in his chair. Without a watch, he had no sense of time's passage beyond his own growing anxiety. When a key finally turned in the lock, his head snapped to attention, and his wary eyes followed an enormous guard who almost eclipsed a slight man in a suit holding a giant, overstuffed briefcase. The man swept out from behind the guard and headed straight for the farthest point in the room from where Hartley was seated. His white Oxford shirt looked a faint yellow in the unpleasant light from the ceiling. His tie was drawn loosely up to his neck, and his worn suit had outlasted its creases. He glanced up without engagement as he indifferently leafed through a folder of legal-sized papers.

"You're case number 2012-09670," said the man in a hard tone, without inflection. "You're charged with aggravated assault and attempted murder. Were you read your rights?"

Hartley's mouth opened and closed before he spoke. The man didn't look like a psychiatrist, and Hartley thought it unusual that a doctor would treat him in such a detached manner. "I… I think so," he stammered uncertainly.

The man fixed his eyes on Hartley, looking at him for the first time. "Is that a yes?"

"Yes, I think," answered Hartley.

"Have you engaged a lawyer, or should I have one appointed?"

"May I ask who you might be? You haven't introduced yourself."

"I'm the public defender—it's my day."

"And you're going to help defend me?" asked Hartley, furrowing his forehead and blinking his eyes.

"Defend *you*? No, no, no. I hope it's not me. Besides, you're a doctor and can certainly afford to choose a lawyer of your own."

Hartley's mouth snapped closed. It was obvious that this lawyer saw him as guilty, and probably worse—a doctor who had threatened a lawyer with a gun. Maybe the man simply didn't want to defend him. "You don't sound too interested in my case," said Hartley, suddenly thinking of Moll.

When the lawyer looked up, his expression clearly showed that he had no belief in Hartley's innocence. "I don't think any lawyer will be *interested*, Doctor."

Hartley smiled sarcastically. "Or maybe you're not just interested, period. That's okay! The AMA provides lawyers—*good lawyers*—so don't lose any sleep over me."

The public defender, sneering, retorted, "Actually, *Doctor*, this is a criminal case—not a run-of-the-mill civil malpractice lawsuit. I doubt they'll be too interested in defending your actions, either." Nonchalantly he thumbed through the police report. "Let's see… Assault with a handgun. Weapon discharged. Looks like attempted murder to me." He laughed aloud. "Yes—I'm sure the AMA will be rushing to your side."

Hartley stifled a gape of disbelief, then looked away in disgust. The public defender flipped through the pages in front of him. "Look, Hartley, why don't you make it easier on yourself? Cop to the rap sheet and hope for a sweeter sentencing deal. You can be out in five years."

Hartley's brow furrowed, painfully pulling on the fresh stitches. He slumped back against the wall, irritated by the lawyer's callous suggestion. "I see why you're not a doctor," he said, disappointed. He had expected to be comforted by a psychiatrist. "Your bedside manner isn't so charming. 'You've got cancer and your chances aren't so hot. Better play the hand that you're dealt and put your affairs in order.'"

"Be careful, mister," the public defender said menacingly. "Alienate me and the best you can hope for is…"

"Don't alienate me, either," interrupted Hartley. "Sooner or later everyone ends up in the ER."

The public defender abruptly stuffed the rap sheet and folder into his distended briefcase and stood without attempting to suppress his smirk. "With a felony arrest on your record, *Doctor*, I don't think I'll have to worry about that." He marched past the guard, muttering curses under his breath.

Hartley walked ahead of the guard's nightstick and ducked into the steel bunk as if it were a refuge. Both his cellmates were gone, and the solitude was an unsettling irony. He missed seeing those men just as he might miss his colleagues when he returned to work late at night. In his daily life, he had craved moments of privacy, and now that he found himself isolated with no distractions, the quiet seemed like the last thing he needed. The springs of the bunk squeaked beneath the bare, lumpy mattress as he tossed, picturing his life without medicine. The shock of receiving the summons seemed like a distant memory, and he could barely imagine what had triggered his murderous rage. He wondered if he would ever return to the life he had failed to appreciate. He pushed himself out of the mattress's sagging depression, teetered on the edge of the bunk, and kicked off his unlaced shoes onto the dirty floor. His socks were damp, and a cold draft chilled his feet. He closed his eyes, and the hard edge of reality softened: what had seemed certain became vague. He wrenched his body off the bunk and walked to the bars of the cell. He gripped the steel with both hands in the silence. *I'm such a fool,* he thought.

After what seemed like hours, the Magic Johnson–lookalike guard returned. "Another visitor for the good doctor," he said acerbically, unlocking the door with deliberate glee. "You got a boat, or beach house, or something? You one heck of a popular fella."

Hartley looked up with a guilt-ridden, downtrodden face. "Is it the shrink?"

"Don't think so. This one's real pretty."

Hartley's heart skipped a beat, knowing who would be waiting.

"Come on now, git up," urged the guard, as if he were addressing an obstinate mule. "Don't keep a lady waiting."

Hartley could smell the pungent odor of his nervous perspiration. "Can I take a shower first?" he asked meekly.

"Sorry, no shower for you—you ain't on the list."

He touched his crusted hair. "Give me a break. Please!"

"Just enforcing the rules, Doc. There a lotta rules around here."

Hartley's heart sank as he measured his longing to see his wife against the lost freedom and happiness of his old life. He pushed himself off the bunk with a lurch, stopping in front of the guard to expose his wrists.

The guard eyed his tired face and drooping shoulders. "I'll give you a break," he said almost kindly. "You don't seem so dangerous now."

They passed through the several locked doors, stopping at an interrogation room. Hartley set his mouth squarely, but inside he was chilled with abject terror as if he were going before the board of an inquisition. He knew the act he had committed was a kind of a mutiny—a rash, impulsive reaction against an unjust system. There was no forethought. He'd had no regard for the rippling effect his reckless act would have on lives linked to his. Now it was too late. They were in this mess together.

"Good luck, my man," said the guard solemnly. "Nothing so scary as an angry wife."

CHAPTER TWENTY-THREE

Celeste sat rigidly at a table with her hands tightly clasped in her lap. Anger flashed from her eyes. Hartley wanted to run, but edged apprehensively into the room with his head bent steeply forward to hide his face. He looked down at the worn linoleum floor. He flinched as the door clanked behind him, signaling that they were now alone together. He raised his eyes to Celeste's, wanting to reach out in a gesture of supplication. Celeste stared silently straight ahead, unresponsive and unmoved. Shame knotted Hartley's stomach as he rubbed his wrists where the handcuffs had been. He slid the vacant chair a few feet away from the table and fell into it. Silence echoed from the filthy walls.

Celeste glared with dark, unforgiving eyes. "Roger, how could you?"

Hartley's head bent forward in silent embarrassment. In this moment of his darkest despair, he almost longed for self-punishment. "This isn't the trajectory for my life that I intended," he said sorrowfully.

"Does your head hurt?" she asked coldly.

The lack of compassion deepened Hartley's embarrassment. His eyes flooded with hot tears that streamed down his face. "A little."

"You have cinders ground into your chin. You hit bottom."

"On the floor of the police van," said Hartley, powerless to control his feelings a moment longer. His eyes welled with tears, and his chest heaved as he tried to speak. "How are the kids?"

She circled the table to face him to make sure he saw her simmering anger. "You might have thought of them earlier. I took them out of school and left them at Grandma's. I told her not to turn on the TV. You're all over the news, you know. Reporters are doing live broadcasts just outside the fence around our front lawn. News vans are camped all over the parkway median. It's insane! You wouldn't believe how obnoxious they are. A thousand microphones were shoved in my face when I got into the car. They hovered like hornets and kept me from closing the door. I had to almost run them over to get out of my parking spot."

Hartley glimpsed up at her face, which was etched with pain. "I'm sorry," he said with deepest sincerity. "I didn't mean for this to happen. How much do the kids know?"

"They know you had a gun and that you're in jail. But I made sure they know that no one was hurt. That made it better for them, thank God." Celeste had sat down in the chair on the opposite side of the table. "Why did you do it? How long have you been planning to do it?"

Hartley stared at the floor, shoulders sagging, his chin settled onto his chest. His jaw worked vigorously as if he were chewing something hard. His hands trembled slightly as he touched his cracked lips. His head shook back and forth in sheer futility. "Being a doctor hadn't become what I expected," he said sadly. "Someone had to do something."

"So you just decided to throw the rest of your life away?"

Under Celeste's punishing gaze, Hartley's tone became defensive. "There's no room to be human," he moaned. "We're supposed to heal the sick and never complain or even show frustration." As he slid his chair back to the wall, a paint chip fell to the floor. He covered his eyes with his cold, sweaty palms, dissecting his own expectations. "Someone had to do something."

"Oh my God, Roger! How could you think *this* was right? Why didn't you say something to me?"

"No one wants to hear the woes of a doctor." With the toe of his buck, Hartley worked a soft pink wad of gum that had been smashed onto the floor.

"Who ever told you the rules would be fair?"

"But people think it's *my* fault when I can't make them well. And sadly, I began to believe that myself. I felt that I wasn't cut out for the job anymore."

"Come on, Rosey, you're smarter than that. Next time you doubt who you are, come to *me* first. I'll remind you who you are."

At the sound of his familiar pet name, Hartley ventured a sorrowful smile. He looked up at his wife as if he were seeing her for the first time after a long absence, and his smile grew slightly wider, transforming his face entirely. "I know you've been behind me," he said, swallowing hard, "and I tried to hold everything together. For you. For the kids. But I got confused. I lost sight of you all, and I'm sorry."

Celeste checked her anger and was standing beside him in a heartbeat. Her hand reached for the base of his neck, and her caressing fingers ran down the length of his spine. He tilted his cheek into her palm as she lifted his chin. Tears dripped through her fingers onto the floor. "There's nothing wrong with crying, Rosey. Your heart was hardened—and finally you rebelled. But have you considered why you didn't pull the trigger?"

Hartley remembered seeing his haggard, unrecognizable self in the mirror. It was an image that showed the dark force inside him. "Something told me that pulling the trigger was wrong," he said.

"What something was that?"

"I don't know. The Oath of Hippocrates? My anger simply abandoned me."

"How do you feel now?"

Hartley shook his head in disbelief at what he had done. "Embarrassed and scared," he said. During a long pause his face bore a look of intense introspection as he collected his thoughts. "Celeste, have you ever asked yourself, 'If I died today, what difference did I make to the world?' For the longest time I have sensed my life had some purpose—a task I'm meant to accomplish, or a special contribution—but when I was pointing that gun, I become conscious that I was doing something totally wrong and divergent. My fear is that this will change everything. I'll be stripped of my medical license. Since I was a child, I've believed that I was put on this earth to be a doctor. But just being a physician seemed too ordinary, and for the last several years, I haven't known where else to look. I haven't found any clues. I've just been waiting."

"Destiny isn't just a grandiose dream, Rosey. We are all guided by a positive force, and we have to do our best to accept it and follow it—sometimes blindly."

"I'm sure following blindly," said Hartley, venturing a tentative, wistful grin. "For better or worse. But I can't see any way *this* will turn out with a silver lining. I hope I figure it out before they pick up the shovel to throw that first layer of dirt on my casket."

Celeste slid her hand through her husband's blood-crusted hair and kissed him softly on the lips. "So what happens now?" she asked.

"I don't know, exactly," said Hartley morosely. "I met the public defender."

"What was he like?"

"Well, if he were a doctor I wouldn't trust him to take out a splinter. I might say he was a dick-weed. I didn't tell him that I looked forward to seeing him soon."

"See how nice you can be when you want to? Nevertheless, do you have any idea how we can find a better lawyer?"

"They advertise on the wall of my cell. I haven't made my one phone call yet."

"Don't waste your dime," said Celeste, holding him tighter. "Call me instead."

Hartley stood and was just leaning in for a hug when he heard the key turn in the lock. They both straightened nervously and stepped apart with a dashed feeling of ardor. The door squeaked open, and the guard's voice bellowed politely in advance of his entrance. "Time's up, pretty lady."

Celeste mustered a smile and squeezed back the tears that she knew would make the moment harder. Hartley tried to suppress his anguish, but a split second before the barred door slammed shut, he yelled, "I love you!"

Immediately the door swung back open, and the guard's grinning face appeared. "Go on, boyfriend," he teased. "Those kinda things ain't the same as they are in the state pen. I hope you never find out."

Chapter Twenty-Four

Mates stood riveted in front of the blaring TV. He smiled excitedly when the doctors' lounge door opened, as if longing for someone to join him in a delightful moment. "Did you hear about Hartley?" he blurted the second Fogg entered.

"How could I not? It's preposterous."

"It's unbelievable! Can't take my eyes off it." He had been looking up most of the day, and he rubbed a kink out of his neck.

"Is that Hartley's house?" asked Fogg. "It looks kind of shabby."

"I must have misjudged Hartley," said Mates. "I didn't think he had it in him."

"You approve?"

"Of course I approve! It was brilliant. Nobody got hurt."

"Except Hartley," said Fogg.

"He was hurt already. His lawsuit was a life-wrecking experience. I know that for a fact. Doctors are terrified of the courtroom. They can't sleep. Newspapers quote the plaintiffs' lawyers, paint pictures of incompetence or negligence, and trash their hard-earned reputations. And the defense lawyers they have to hire eat up their time and life savings. I saw him on the day he got sued."

"I did too, and he didn't look well. This will really screw up his family and our profession."

"Our profession? What? I want to think that Hartley reacted—however mistakenly—to something that endangers our ability to practice medicine. More of us should take up the cause."

"With a gun?" The light from the refrigerator illuminated Fogg's troubled face as he grabbed a bottle of water. "I don't know how I should feel about Hartley," he said, closing the door. "This makes me so angry on so many fronts. It makes no sense. What did he hope to achieve?"

"Well, a sense of assault can inspire righteous wrath. Granted, a loaded gun shouldn't be the weapon of choice, and in his rashness, Hartley was not very righteous. But I'm not going to desert the guy. There's something here to be redeemed in the man's mistaken notion. We need to support him in his hour of need."

"Support him? Why should I stick up for Hartley? The public regard for doctors is achieved through repeated daily encounters of trust in our integrity. Patients are soothed by our knowledge and expect honest calm. But people's high regard for doctors is not a given. It can be lowered. Hartley's actions threatened this standing."

"But our profession is eroding away."

"But is that good reason to engage in hotheaded protest and civil disobedience?" cried Fogg. "He should have pursued reform by the usual channels, petitioning and lobbying avenues in his off hours, or maybe he should have left medicine behind altogether."

"Physicians have no off hours," said Mates gruffly, as if colored by his own experience. "It's the nature of the job. Besides, Hartley's too good of a doc to be out of medicine. The damage is done, and now we repair the damage by negotiating change. If we ever want to attract good young doctors into the profession in the future, we have to respond. And the government needs to work with us, too. With universal health care in 2014, thirty million newly insured patients will be looking for primary-care doctors. Let's see what the wait times in doctors' offices are then."

Fogg became nervous. "Doctors' offices? They'll come to the ER. This will be the place to go when you're sick, and you and I both will burn out. Poor Hartley. But I still don't think doctors are capable of mixing with politics."

Mates's face became red as he stood taller. "We have the right to be political activists! Doctors are citizens, too!"

Fogg was surprised by the quick reaction. "We can agree to disagree," he said calmly. "What doctors should and shouldn't do in political protest is a matter of debate. But at the bottom, public protest is most typically an ineffective, last-ditch strategy."

"But the political process has failed through the usual channels!" Mates bellowed. "Look at tort reform—passed and overturned repeatedly, like the lawyers and politicians are playing a game."

Fogg shook his head vigorously and held up his hand to suddenly stop the discord. "I won't have a part in it—I'm busy enough."

"Suit yourself," said Mates, shaking his head as well. "Keep your head in the sand. But I'm going down to the courthouse tomorrow to watch Hartley's arraignment. By the way, you have a patient to see in bay eight—lupus and renal failure. He says you're his doctor."

Fogg's mind was too scrambled to think. Eager to get out of the hospital and find freedom from the looming black cloud, he grabbed the chart for bay eight and zoomed through the opening in the curtain. As he looked at the name, Fogg's jaw fell open. "You!" he said with a surge of emotion. "You caused all this!"

Moll's face filled with glee. "Yes, I did cause all this!"

Fogg was aghast at Moll's delight. "You laugh, Moll? You're in renal failure, and you laugh? You need dialysis three times a week for the rest of your life. But that won't be very long. Make no bones about it. I won't be involved with your care. Not even this once, as I'm required to do. And I don't care if your lawyers try to skewer me on the back end. You're too much of a risk. You have a black mark. You're on your own."

Moll's eyes widened, but he could say nothing.

Mates stood in the same spot in front of the blaring TV. "What's happening now?" asked Fogg with more interest.

"There's been mixed support. But certainly many have similar feelings."

"Similar feelings to mine," said Fogg.

Mates spun and took a step back. "Similar feelings to you?"

Fogg could not return his inquisitive smile. "Remember earlier when I said that doctors should have a good reason to engage in public protest? Well, I found one—and I'm all in."

Mates slapped Fogg hard on the back. "Ah, the rational doctor has become a passionate defender. We need a handsome face to voice our opinions. You'll be our ambassador."

"This might come at great professional risk," said Fogg.

"Well, so be it. The profession is going into the dumpster, anyway."

Fogg reached out his hand. "But people will need a very clear explanation how Hartley's actions fit into the problems of health care. If we don't manage the message, the press will interpret our actions. And don't expect their version to be favorable. Our public acts might be condemned."

"Yes," said Mates sympathetically, holding Fogg's grasp. "It's worth the risk. We need to help Hartley. I don't know if you can practice medicine if you're a felon. "

"I don't know, either," said Fogg. "But why would he want to come back?"

TUESDAY

CHAPTER TWENTY-FIVE

Like a pond calming to glass, the morning ushered in stillness and quiet. Hartley eased awake to the sound of metal food trays sliding through the rectangular slot at the bottom of the bars like a short train across the gritty concrete floor. He peeked over the edge of the mattress, the foul odor of the unflushed toilet in the corner making him grimace. His unease returning, he rolled on the squeaky springs to face the wall. His eyes scanned the graffiti scrawled across the dingy surface and paused on one message etched deeply in the paint:

Have faith, brother
The grace of God is with you

He glanced over his shoulder with some suspicion, as though he felt someone were watching, but the hallway was empty and none of the other inmates paid him the slightest attention. They snapped up the food trays in silence and returned to their bunks to eat like docile, ruminant beasts. Hartley rolled onto his back and raised his hand to admire his wedding ring in the cell's filtered light. He turned his hand over to examine the long diagonal crease that crossed his palm. His lifeline.

Hartley pushed out of the bunk and slid his fingers under the edge of the last tray and hurried back to his bunk. *Grits*, he cursed silently, finding the breakfast worse than any he recalled from his residency. His stomach churned loudly. He replaced the dented metal plate cover and raised the plastic coffee cup to his lips as footsteps approached from down the hall.

"Hartley, you got more friends," the guard said joyfully. "Never seen such shiny shoes." He flipped Hartley a clean orange jumpsuit and stood back until Hartley began to stir. "Come on now—don't keep this one waiting." Hartley set the food tray on the raw cement floor and waited for a wave of nausea to pass. He unzipped the old jumpsuit, peeled it off his body, and stepped into the clean one. The smaller size constricted under his arms and the pant legs were short. "You grown overnight," said the guard. Hartley knitted his brow at his own disheveled condition. He smoothed his blood-crusted hair and frowned at the dirt under his nails, feeling every bit like a criminal. "Move," the guard ordered curtly. "And this time, it's with cuffs."

Hartley rose cautiously, working to loosen his muscles before having his arms cuffed behind his back. He made his way through the locked doors to the interrogation room and backed the familiar chair to the wall. When the door finally opened, a man stepped into the room ahead of a humorless guard. He wore a pressed suit that Hartley suspected was bought off the rack. His shoes looked American, but they shone as if today was the first day they had been worn. He was handsome, but his nose had been badly broken and had a rugged, damaged appearance. "Doctor Hartley?" he asked politely.

"Are you the psychiatrist?" asked Hartley cautiously.

"No, no, no," laughed the man. "My name is Ernest Hawkins. I'm an attorney. I was sent by your wife."

Hartley's face brightened. He rose from his chair and extended his now unshackled hand. The man took it firmly, holding his grip as he looked Hartley straight in the eyes. There were flecks of gold in Hawkins's hazel-brown irises that sparkled with light and lent a fascinating depth to his smile. "Would you be so kind as to give us some privacy?" the lawyer asked the hovering guard. He then laid his wafer-thin briefcase on the table and settled on the chair.

"Do people call you Ernest?" asked Hartley.

"My friends call me Ernie." The corners of his mouth curled up slightly. "I hate the name Ernest. It sounds meek to me."

Roger laughed and pulled his seat to the table. "My wife hates my name, too. How'd she find you? Yesterday we didn't have a clue."

Hawkins tilted his head contemplatively. "You're Catholic, right?"

"By default. I was born Protestant."

"Well, sometimes I do legal work to help the parish, and this morning I went there on a whim. I can't tell you why. But when I got to the chapel, I saw your wife struggling to open the door. When I asked to help, she stared at me with wild eyes as if she were desperate. At first I didn't know what to think. But when your wife told me her name it hit me. I knew exactly who she was, and why she was there. I specialize in malpractice law..."

"So why are you here?" interrupted Hartley.

"Let me qualify that by saying that I defend physicians."

"Bully," said Hartley.

"Please, hear me out. I first heard about you yesterday afternoon on the news. You were on every channel, all afternoon. Obviously, I was interested. This morning you were all over the papers."

"Wasn't there anything else going on in the world?" asked Hartley dolefully. His face flushed hot, and his body writhed with a physical pang of regret. "I would welcome a pedophile politician or a new pestilence right now."

"I understand why you were mad," said Hawkins with a warm, glinting smile. Unexpectedly, he slid his chair around to Hartley's side of the table, turned it backward, and sat with elbows leaning on the backrest. "Roger, what you've done here is big. Everyone has a notion as to what you were addressing, even if they don't approve of your using a gun."

"I doubt if anyone but doctors understands. But all doctors understand, and they have been silent."

"Look at me, Roger. When I saw your story, it affected me deeply. I'm part of this broken machine, and even when I'm defending physicians, I don't always feel proud of the outcome. Sometimes I lie awake at night with such a burden of guilt that I second-guess what I'm doing and wonder who I've become. The whole system has gone awry. Somebody has to do something!" he added excitedly.

"Then you'll represent me in this? This unfortunate day may take us both to unexpected places."

Hawkins's feet shuffled. "I can't. I don't practice criminal law."

"It's not much of a case," pleaded Hartley.

"It's more than you think," said Hawkins nervously. "Your story's in every newspaper in the fifty states, and a few editorials see it from your side—a doctor pushed to the breaking point—and after, all you didn't actually hurt anyone." He reached in his briefcase and placed a sheaf of newspaper clippings in a tidy pile in the center of the table. "See, you're headline news."

Hartley hurriedly eyed the first clipping on the top. "Doctor in Shining Armor?" he said suspiciously with a hint of futility.

"I put that one on top. But the rest aren't so flattering."

Hartley reached for the whole pile of clippings.

"Your medical identity is too powerful for journalists to resist," said Hawkins with a boyish grin. "Someday doctors might get tired of being blamed for all that goes wrong, and a few might step forward. They all sympathize with your frustration."

"I doubt it," said Hartley, recalling the doctor's protest Mates had complained about. "But it sounds like a good civil lawyer to try this criminal case might be a good idea. I want you to represent me."

Hawkins's head shook with uncertainty. "Roger, in medicine you call in a specialist. This is out of my league."

"Civil law messed me up in the first place. Frivolous malpractice proceedings should be in the forefront of my defense. You can get a co-counsel to help you prepare."

Hawkins looked around the room anxiously. He put both hands on the table and searched Hartley's face for signs he could trust. "If you want me to play a part in your case, I will, but I can't be blamed if it doesn't go well."

"I can't sue you," laughed Hartley painfully.

Hawkins smiled. "It *would* mean a lot to me if I had a part."

"The choice is easy," said Hartley. "It's you, or a public defender."

"I won't take that as a compliment," laughed Hawkins. He gripped Hartley's hand firmly, making it clear that he understood everything. "Sit for a minute more," he said evenly. "You have an arraignment at one o'clock today, and believe it or not, you have some choices. Your wife informed me about the events that led up to what happened on Monday," he said, pulling a copy of the arrest record out of his briefcase.

"Good. Don't make me think about *that* anymore."

"I won't—for now. But I think you know that assault with a deadly weapon isn't the appropriate response to receiving a summons in a malpractice suit."

"I hope it's clear to you that I'm not a killer."

"Quite clear," answered Hawkins. "And we're going to argue just that. The lawsuit was an emotional flashpoint, and you reacted to a frivolous attack on your professional standing. If it's okay with you, I intend to enter a plea of not guilty."

"But I pointed a gun at her face," said Hartley nervously. "There were no witnesses, but there's evidence. Even the public defender recommended a guilty plea to position myself for a more lenient sentence."

"It's clear that you committed assault, but the prosecution is also pinning you with attempted murder," said Hawkins, shaking his head. "A Class X felony is a whole different kettle of fish. Mandatory prison time for starters, and I'm guessing that you'll want to go back to practicing medicine." Hartley's shoulders sagged as he grumbled inaudibly. Hawkins smiled with amusement. "Okay—I see the answer to that. But trust me, if you didn't love practicing medicine, you wouldn't have gotten so mad. I just wish you had picked a lower-profile attorney to threaten. Lawyers are no different from any other professionals—they watch each other's backs pretty well. I'm sure Johnson's firm will pull strings to get you a maximum sentence."

"More good news. It worries me that I won't get a fair trial."

"Listen to me, Roger," Hawkins said, eyes clear and focused. "In a juried trial, the verdict doesn't depend on some judge that Johnson's law firm might have tucked in its pocket. This verdict rests with the people. Cases like yours are sometimes tried even before the defendant steps in front of the judge. We all have biases. It could go either way."

"Well, I hope doctors have been kind to the jurors," said Hartley. He studied his lawyer's sober demeanor, seeing a passionate man with noble intentions. "Doesn't defending me strike you as a professional risk?" he asked.

Hawkins face erupted into a grin. "There are all kinds of people in the legal system, Roger—just as in medicine. Some practice for the good of society, and others seek personal gain. Suffice it to say that personal-injury lawyers aren't my favorite breed. But personal preferences aside, yesterday you stopped short of pulling the trigger. Otherwise I wouldn't have taken the case."

"What do I do now?" asked Hartley.

"Just be yourself."

"If I remember who that is." Unsteadily Hartley rose to his feet and pulled down the constricting inseam of his orange jumpsuit. "Being in the slammer hasn't exactly bolstered my self-esteem."

Hawkins knocked on the interrogation-room door to summon the guard. Before the door opened, he turned back toward Hartley, shaking his head and smiling. "You never really know how your day will turn out when you wake up in the morning—do you?"

I stand for in politics. My platform on hea

"No," he said anxiously with a clear

"Your wife?" she asked, with an

"I can't—not right now. Mo

"This doesn't change any

media draws a connecti

the papers? Do you

think—this has

There w

"Everyth

it be

CHAPTER TWENTY-SIX

Anita knew who would be on the other end of the phone line when the "restricted caller" designation showed on the caller ID. She let it ring several more times as she composed herself to talk. The terrible pang of needing someone was new to her. She gripped the phone like a lifeline.

"Where have you been?" she asked in a tight voice. "Haven't you heard what happened to me? Don't you care?"

Robert stammered nervously. "I heard—I saw you on the news. I've been worried. Are you okay?"

"Worried? It's been a whole day."

"Are you okay?" Robert repeated in a low voice.

"I'm all right," she answered, relieved to know that he cared. "I'm a little sore in the neck. When can I see you? Can you come over now?"

There was a long, uncomfortable pause. "I don't know. You know that I care, but everything's changed."

Robert's bluntness caught her off guard. Her heart skipped a beat, and then at all the harder. She put a hand to her temple to subdue her dizzying fear. "ing?" she asked weakly.

s a deep huffing sound as the congressman exhaled. "I have to come on too fast. Have you watched the news? Have you read know what's going on? It would be bad for us both if the on between us. I can't risk it!"

thing," pleaded Anita. "I need to see you."

people are involved than just the two of us."

dge.

shade of annoyance. "You know what th care clearly stands on keeping the legal landscape as it is. There are people—important people—whom I made promises to that I can't break. If the details of our connection were made public, I would have to do more than just drop out of the race. My friends who are lawyers would… Anita—are you there?"

Anita had twisted off the sofa and escaped to the edge of her balcony. "That Hartley spoiled everything," she fumed into the phone. She stood frozen with a wide-eyed stare. The early morning sun had become full day. Lake Michigan was such a deep blue that it looked bottomless. Off in the distance, hundreds of lonely boats bobbed in the harbor like discarded toys. She called back the memories of her evening with Robert as the twirling red lights of an ambulance screamed along Lake Shore Drive below. Her hand tightened around the phone. "I thought that I was important to you," she said vacantly.

"Darling," he beseeched. "There's a difference between what my heart wants to do and what I am doing. Its not my choice."

"Powerful people do what they want to do. Two nights ago…"

"We were together that one time."

"And you go back to your wife, as if nothing happened?"

"I know it's hard. Right now, no one knows about us. Things will be better after the elections. But right now we have to wait."

"Wait? Wait? I can't wait four months! What should I do until then?"

"I know it's hard," he repeated with sorrow.

"You're lying through your teeth," said Anita hotly. "You're telling me what I want to hear, like a true politician, knowing full well that you can't deliver."

"Be patient, darling," he said with an edgy laugh. "True—I'm a politician. But that also means I never concede."

In the long silence, Anita thought it conceited of him to laugh at that moment. Their intimacy had been real, and his laughter cheapened it. "I can see clearly now. You've lost my vote."

"I just wanted to make sure you're okay."

"I don't deserve this," she said as her body writhed slightly with regret.

"Anita…?"

She held on to the phone in silence until the sound of the line disconnecting awakened her like the click of a hypnotist's fingers. She fled into the living room, her eyes momentarily fixing on the Degas on the wall. She gazed fleetingly at the sinewy dancers in pink tights and tiny slippers before escaping into the bathroom. She slapped at the light switch on the wall, her hands pressing to her forehead immediately to shield her eyes from the light. When her image clarified in the mirror, she felt a rising contempt and looked away. Her shaking hands fumbled through the vanity drawer, eventually clutching a bottle of Xanax. She tipped the pills out onto the counter and watched them roll to a stop. Pinching one tablet, she examined it closely. "Xanax 0.5 mg." She pictured herself taking them all in a handful, or swallowing the entire bottleful one by one. "No, I don't need that," she said. "I don't want to sleep through Hartley's arraignment."

Chapter Twenty-Seven

"Let's go, Cinderella. You got a ball to attend."

Although his deep regret was pervasive, Hartley felt a particular sense of relief when the guard arrived to escort him out to the van. He stood straight, squaring his shoulders and exposing his wrists. "My fifteen minutes of fame," he said, his sad eyes watching his hands being double-cuffed to his waist belt. The chains clanked like a specter's.

"No fame in this," responded the guard. "Good luck to you, doc."

Responding to a light touch on his back, Hartley took a faltering first step and then walked faster as he gained his balance. He stopped just through the door of the jailhouse to tip his face to the sun and savor the moment of relative freedom. The air, washed clean by the rainstorm, smelled fresh.

"Come on, get going," said the guard.

Hartley climbed into the white police van and squeezed between two other prisoners. He gazed silently through the barred windows at the familiar streets of the city. When the wind whistled invitingly through a crack in the door, he leaned over for a whiff of fresh air. But the stop-and-go traffic made time's passage conspicuous, and curious pedestrians often caught Hartley's eye. He turned away from the judgmental expressions, reminded that everyone would be a juror.

The Cook County Courthouse loomed in the distance. Hartley twisted his neck expectantly to catch a glimpse of the eight-story building. Its reflective gold-tinted windows reminded him of an enormous block of amber that had hardened to resin. The vehicle drew to a stop inside a compound. He stepped out of the van quickly, eager to be back on his feet. But there was nothing green inside the walled enclosure. He glanced around at the high walls topped with razor wire that reflected the sunlight like thousands of tiny mirrors. The

Romanesque jailhouse in front of him was faced with white marble discolored by years of urban pollution. Along its cornice was a row of proud lion heads that bore water stains down their noses like a steady flow of acidic tears. A nudge on his back started him moving.

Hartley focused on simply being himself, as Hawkins had suggested, and stepped lightly into the dim, quiet hallway of the building. People passed without smiling or offering signs of good cheer. The impersonal ten-digit number on his wristband seemed fitting.

"Hold it right there, pigeons," ordered the guard. They passed through a door and descended a flight of stairs into the bowels of the building. A harsh, unnatural light streamed through bars in what looked like a holding area. The glare reflected off the glossy cinder-block walls to make the room appear shell-like and cornerless. Hartley lowered his head, squinting until his eyes grew accustomed to the stabbing brightness. He could see eight disheveled men in identical orange jumpsuits chained together in a zigzagging line. Hartley raised his hand to wipe away the sweat that was gathering on the side of his face, but his wrist stopped halfway with a frustrating jerk. The cell door squealed open and the humorless inmates were herded into a straight line. The prisoner at the end snarled and matched the guard's aggression with a string of vulgarity. Hartley concentrated on maintaining control, but stiffened and shrank back as the guards chained him to the surly last prisoner.

I don't belong in this godless place! he screamed inside.

His chest constricted. His breathing was shallow and rapid. In a full claustrophobic panic, his eyes darted wildly to seek a way out. The edgy guard reacted quickly. With a vigorous whack from his nightstick, he sent Hartley to his knees. The room spun, and Hartley fell headfirst to the floor. He saw a bright light and felt pain penetrate deep into his skull. Then there was darkness.

Hartley awakened in stages after the blow and was delivered to his arraignment in the grip of fear. He stood alone in a modified jury box. The crowded courtroom was full of excitement that he knew was directed at him. Lawyers conversed in small, animated groups and members of the press filled the gallery, pushing toward the front rail. Hartley's eyes searched the room for the distinctive, crooked nose and bright eyes of his attorney, in need of a buoy to anchor his thoughts. But Anita Johnson was seated directly across the room, her eyes fixed on him with a caustic, defiant stare. Her black hair was drawn tight into a bun, and she wore a glistening, silver choker around her neck. A shiver of angst flashed down Hartley's spine, and his vulnerability rekindled. Just then he felt a capturing hand grasp his right shoulder. "Roger!" said Hawkins. With concern in his eyes, he used his body to eclipse his client's view of Anita. "What happened to you downstairs? I heard you had to be subdued."

Hartley focused for a moment on Hawkins's nose, imagining the strong blow that must have broken it. "I guess I had a panic attack," he said. "That's something new." His voice was beginning to strengthen. "I'm okay now. Did you find a co-counsel?"

"Nobody would do it," Hawkins admitted. "I even spoke to the public defender. What did you say to him that was so offensive? He wants no part of you either."

"Oh, now I feel better! If this doesn't go well, I don't get to go home?"

"Don't worry—you'll make it." Hawkins pulled Hartley closer. "This part is easy. Let me do all the talking. Pay attention only to the judge and to me, and don't listen to one word from the prosecution. No matter what happens, don't react. I'll have you out of here in two hours."

Hartley took a deep breath and stood straighter. "Have you seen Celeste?"

Hawkins nodded to indicate the spot where she was seated off to one side. When she saw he was looking, she kissed her hand and laid it over her breast. In Hartley's mind the possibility of being home in time for dinner began to take hold. Hartley looked back at Hawkins. "Do trials usually receive this much attention?" The bailiff shouted over the commotion before he could answer. "Case number 2012-09670. The State of Illinois versus Roger Hartley. The Honorable Judge Gadboy presiding."

Feeling stripped down and exposed, Hartley was escorted out of the modified jury box and positioned in front of the bench. He was now the center of attention, and the penetrating stares from the gallery conjured his stage fright. He took a deep breath and relaxed his shoulders. Hawkins stood staunchly beside him. The crowd hushed as everyone looked at the judge perched behind an enormous oak bench. His short, thick neck seemed to retract deep within his black robe, making his round head appear to sit squarely on his shoulders.

He studied Hartley quietly for a moment, and then his thick lips parted, and he spoke in a resounding voice. "Mr. Hartley..."

Hawkins interrupted at once. "Your Honor—with all due respect," he said, enunciating his words with disarming decorum. "My client has earned his title of address. Please address him as doctor."

Judge Gadboy's head snapped up in surprise, and he glared in scrutiny at the pair that stood before him. The crowd stirred with whispers in the silence. Hartley shifted his feet uneasily, but Hawkins stood upright and confident. After a tense moment, the judge's thick lips retracted into an amused smile. "The record should read—*Doctor* Hartley," he said, overemphasizing the title. But then his tone became stern. "You are charged with aggravated assault and attempted murder. How do you plead?"

Hawkins spoke before Hartley could open his mouth. "Your Honor, the defense moves to have the 'attempted murder' charge dismissed. The evidence is clear that my client demonstrated no specific intent to kill. He willfully dropped his weapon, and the gun accidentally discharged upon hitting the floor."

State's Attorney Griffin glared sternly at Hawkins. "The state has eyewitnesses to support the allegation," he said. The accused displayed intent to commit murder and took a number of substantial steps to kill the victim. The charge of attempted murder is supported by the evidence."

Hawkins's face showed a new intensity. "Your Honor, the trumped-up charge is politically motivated. There is no basis in fact. The door to the crime scene was closed, so there could be no eyewitnesses. Forensics will show the weapon discharged on impact with the floor. The bullet struck the wall well off to the side. The victim was never in any reasonable danger of being hit by that bullet."

"He tried to kill me!" shrieked a voice from behind the rail. Every head turned toward Anita, who sat on the front edge of her seat behind the rail. Anita's face had turned crimson. "He attacked the whole legal system! Don't make this a farce."

The judge hammered his gavel. "Quiet! Or you'll be held in contempt."

The reporters typed into their notebooks. Griffin spun away from the bench and leaned far over the rail to speak excitedly into Anita's ear. The bailiffs moved closer. Anita calmed herself rapidly as Griffin returned to the bench. "Your

Honor, as a civil lawyer, counsel fails to understand the elements of the offense. The defendant purchased a weapon illegally, made an appointment with the victim, brandished the loaded weapon in the victim's face, and threatened her life. This premeditated act is clearly sufficient to satisfy the *mens rea* of the defendant. Any lesser charge would make a mockery of this court and our legal system."

The judge toyed with the handle of his gavel, scrutinizing the two lawyers and their clients in turn. With the courtroom now hushed, he almost seemed to be enjoying the drama. "Gentlemen, I won't allow this case to be tried with premature motions and arguments. The charge of attempted murder shall stand. The defendant will enter his plea."

Anita tossed back her head in a gesture of triumph. With a look of helpless confusion, Hartley turned toward his counsel. The room was dead silent. "Not guilty!" said Hawkins, his hazel eyes dark as if the gold flecks had disappeared.

Immediately the room became loud and chaotic. "Atta boy, Hartley! Fight for our rights!" said a crisp voice that Hartley recognized. As he gawked with terrified fascination at the many white coats in the gallery, he identified Fogg and Mates among all the others. The judge pounded the gavel and yelled over the din.

Hawkins waited for the room to grow quiet without moving an inch. "The defense concedes probable cause," he said finally. "My client waives his right to a preliminary hearing. We request a trial first instance."

"Trial is set—fourteenth of August. Bond will be two hundred thousand."

The judge's fat arm swung down for one final crash of the gavel. Instantly Anita launched out of her seat, propelled by pent-up frustration and rage. Griffin reacted quickly, blocking the gate to keep her behind the rail. Hartley peered cautiously toward the fuming Anita. Bodies seemed to draw back, and a ring of clear space formed around her. Reporters scribbled furiously. But on the periphery, Celeste's blond hair and white dress drew Hartley's attention. As their eyes locked, she nodded and her mouth widened with an encouraging smile.

Griffin objected shrilly to recapture the judge's attention. "Your Honor, the prosecution requests that the defendant be held without bond. He is a danger to the victim and the community. As well, he is a flight risk. The amount named is clearly inadequate to compel his appearance at trial. His assets and income are more than enough to absorb a loss of that size."

"The defendant will pay for electronic monitoring," said Hawkins.

Hartley barely restrained himself from yelling, "Objection!" But he remained calm as he gaped at his lawyer.

Griffin's eyes grew wild as he redoubled his vehemence. "The defendant is violent and has demonstrated a complete disregard for the law. The prosecution strongly recommends that the defendant be held without bond."

"Psychiatric counsel cannot see my client for three weeks," insisted Hawkins. "He can't be held without bail for that amount of time." Despite Hartley's efforts to control his emotions, his face flushed crimson at being unable to speak out in his own defense. Subtly, Hawkins motioned for him to remain silent and still.

Judge Gadboy stared closely at Hartley amid the growing tumult. It was unusual in a case like this for the defendant to have no criminal record. As he glanced at Anita still fuming behind the rail, his lips drew back in a slightly impudent smile. "Bond is set at one million! No electronic monitoring." The gavel smacked down for emphasis and then tumbled out of the judge's hand across the top of the oak bench. He rose abruptly, disappearing into his chamber.

Noise erupted in the courtroom. Hartley's stomach churned. "Guess I won't be home for dinner," he mumbled as his eyes reached out to his wife.

But Hawkins was as bright as a child's eyes on Christmas Day. "Are you kidding? Disappointment? Didn't you watch Johnson and Griffin's behavior? They're angry and already making mistakes. That's the victory we've won!" He slapped Hartley on the back. "I said you'd be home for dinner."

"But one million dollars?"

"You need ten percent and a bond card. That's a hundred thousand."

"I don't have that in my savings," cried Hartley frantically. "And with Obamacare coming, I might as well treat gonorrhea in jail. I can't survive those horrible grits."

Hawkins laughed and shook his head. "I told you—the prosecution *wants* you to fester in jail. They're scared! Can't you feel it?"

"I see the state's attorney is kind of intense," agreed Hartley weakly.

"Exactly! People higher up must be putting on pressure. I think he needs to win this case in order to save his own skin." Hawkins beamed with a radiant smile as he checked his watch. "Now, I predicted bond would be set at a million, and I think your wife has got it together already. After posting, go home and stay there. Come to my office next Monday at ten. And *do not* talk to reporters."

"But what should I do until then?" stammered Hartley.

"There's a lot to do. Revive yourself. Let your family breathe life into you. Rediscover who you are. Find out what motivates you. Figure out why you became a physician. You might like what you discover."

"But…" said Hartley, painfully aware that he was returning home to the tattered remnants of his old life. He lifted his arms in supplication until the chain jerked against the waist-belt.

"No 'buts,'" said Hawkins. "It should be easy. Just let it unfold."

Hartley dropped his hands wearily, but Hawkins grabbed his fingers in an approximation of a handshake. "Thank you!" said Hartley with a mixture of appreciation and fear. "You're a great lawyer, and I appreciate your trying to help me."

Chapter Twenty-Eight

Hartley waited alone on the cold metal bench in the holding room, massaging the stiffness out of his wrists. It was hard to feel any sense of liberation or joy because it seemed that his life was moving in a new direction beyond his control. It would take strong faith to believe that he would pass through his troubles and come out on the other end any better. His forehead wound pulsed under the bandage. His arms and legs twitched with apprehension. He drew up his knees and locked his fingers over his shins, knowing that he would soon be home to face his family. *Some role model I've become,* he thought, pushing aside ephemeral thoughts that seemed difficult to trust. *What will I say?* He closed his eyes in a struggle to grasp what he was feeling.

While Hartley toiled to understand his changing inner landscape, a pair of footsteps echoed from far down the hallway. Celeste appeared at the worn metal bars, accompanied by a monstrous guard. "Hello, Rosey," she said cheerfully. "You ready to come home?"

It took forever for the key to turn in the lock. Forgetting his deep exhaustion, Hartley rose to his feet and rushed to the half-open door. His eyes moistened with tears as Celeste embraced him tightly. "What did you think of Mr. Hawkins?" she asked. "Was he a godsend, or what?"

"I don't understand how you found him," he said as his heart filled with joy, "but I'm glad you did."

Celeste smiled proudly and examined him closely. "Were you afraid?"

"Still am—I never want to come back to this hell."

Hartley dried his eyes with the scratchy cloth of his orange sleeve. A smile blossomed as if he believed that his wish to go home had come true. "How are the kids?" he asked.

"Anxious to see you! It's like you were away on a long trip."

"Did you come up with the bond money?" he asked, in a sudden panic.

"I did," she answered. A satisfied smile showed that she was pleased with her industry.

"How? Where? You didn't pull it out of a mattress."

"The bondsman seemed quite satisfied with the deed to our house. We've done a nice job with the mortgage."

Hartley grinned with sheer wonderment. "It's our house forever," he said. "And it's our family that makes it a home."

"Amen to that," she answered.

"Have you talked to my office?" asked Hartley.

"Mari's in denial—like everyone else. You certainly threw us all for a loop. But I think things are under control. People started calling right away to offer support. Your doctor friends at the hospital worked out a schedule to cover your patients. There're at least twenty of them on the list. They must understand what you've been through."

Hartley's deep sense of shame began to ease. "Physicians tend not to be angry," he said. "That's what surprised me about myself."

Celeste locked her hands behind his neck and pulled him back toward her. "Something good will come of this mess," she said confidently. "Have faith—and you'll find the grail."

Hartley buried his face in her shoulder. "I'm so sorry."

Celeste's words unfolded a healing calm. "It's okay. I'm taking you home now. The kids are waiting for their daddy."

Hartley reached into the bag that Celeste had dropped by their feet and drew out a neat pile of fresh clothes. The garments felt soft and light in his hands. He reached in a second time and drew out a new pair of white sneakers. "Those old shoes have to go," she said, staring down at his lace-less old bucks. "Hurry up. You need to get your head under some water and wash that gunk out of your hair."

"But how are we going to get home?"

"I got the car this morning," she said. "That police impounding lot was my own little hell. Take a cab if you decide to do this again."

Hartley almost skipped toward the jail's exit while hugging Celeste about the waist. The revolving door spun rapidly, depositing them at the top of the courthouse steps. He drew a deep breath of fresh air and glanced down at his new white sneakers. He wiggled his toes like a child. Donning his old infectious grin, Hartley reached suddenly into the bag of dirty old clothes and removed his old bucks calmly. They hung from his two forked fingers like dead fish pulled from a creel. He raised them to eye level, examining each stain as though he could remember each moment. "These shoes are retired," he said.

"Permanently?" she asked.

"I can get new ones if I choose." Hartley maneuvered them carefully through the side hole in a waste can and let go. He stuffed in the heavy bag of sullied clothes and did a quick dance in his sneakers. But his wide grin and dance were short-lived as a small horde of reporters laden with cameras and microphones mounted the steps. Each fired questions.

"What made you do it?"

"Did you plan the attack?"

"Why didn't you pull the trigger?"

Hartley flushed with embarrassment, thinking that his little dance might be seen on the news. *Don't talk to reporters*, he remembered Hawkins warning. He staggered back from the cameras and raised his arm to cover his face in a panic. He held Celeste closer and ducked his head, slashing a path through the melee. But the cameras impeded his progress, and reporters kept firing questions from all directions.

"Will you go back to practicing medicine if you're acquitted?"

"Are you the new spokesperson for health care reform?"

Hartley froze suddenly. He gawked at the constricting circle of journalists and the bouquet of microphones that bloomed in his face. His forehead wound throbbed, and he fought back a burst of nausea. "I'm in this for myself," he said with the force of his long frustration. "I'm not making a statement." He pushed through the mob with shuffling steps, becoming more aware of an increasing force at his back. As he moved faster and faster, the mob of journalists fell away.

"We've got to start taking care of our own," said a doctor close to his ear.

Hartley glanced around in astonishment at a ring of white coats. "What in God's name is happening?" he asked Fogg, who was in front of the pack.

"It's time we start fighting back," answered Fogg.

"Every one of us has been soured by a malpractice suit," said Mates, who pushed forward alongside Fogg. "We created a flash mob. How do you like it? MDs can be the activist type."

Astonished, Hartley scanned the faces of the small herd of doctors. Some he knew and others he didn't. Many had HMO logos on the breast pockets of their white coats. Hartley and Celeste reached the Suburban, and Hartley found himself sealed off from the crowd. His shoulders collapsed with relief as he ignored the mosaic of faces that danced in the windows. "That's unbelievable," he said with dismay. He shifted the car into drive and inched out into traffic, peering into the rearview mirror as he increased his speed. The crowd grew smaller and smaller until it finally disappeared altogether. "Why all the fuss? It's not like I threatened a top-ranking official."

"Decorum can't suppress frustration forever."

The political consequences of his act began to coalesce in his mind. "But I hope they're not counting on me to lead the crusade."

"It seems that they might be. They needed a catalyst to start a reaction."

"But I've had enough," Hartley said fearfully. "I'm done being angry."

Hartley traveled the same streets he had taken the previous day, but now he headed in the opposite direction. "I'm looking forward to being home for dinner," he said, picturing his children around the table.

"Rosey," said Celeste gently, nudging him out of his reverie. "Remember what you told me in that awful interrogation room? You sensed that your life had a purpose. Don't give up on that now. The election is coming—you *can* make an impact."

"Election or no election, I'm done with all that."

He touched the gas pedal harder to head north on the highway. Off to the right in the distance, the blue-black column of the John Hancock Building appeared much less imposing.

"How do you feel, Rosey?" Celeste asked.

"Tired," he answered. "But more than anything, I'm nervous about seeing the kids. I want my life to be back to normal."

As they turned onto their street, Hartley caught sight of news crews blanketing the sidewalk and median in front of his house. He slouched low, straining against the shoulder harness and seat belt, and eased the Suburban past the waiting horde. He took a fleeting look at his home, his face instantly lighting up with a smile that transformed his appearance entirely. Behind the chaotic scene, a banner suspended between the two pillars of the porch blazed the words:

Welcome Home, Daddy!

The front lawn bristled with signs in all shapes and sizes, and the fence was decorated with a chaotic montage of posters. Their bright colors formed a new landscape that sprang out in the clear afternoon sun. His curiosity piqued, Hartley hurried to squeeze into a parking spot that seemed impossibly small. He slipped out of the car and then held the passenger door for Celeste.

"Thank you, darling," she said.

It seemed like eons since Hartley had been home, and he took a firm hold of Celeste's hand. They forced their way through the chaos, closing their eyes to the camera crews beginning to hover around them, and snapped the metal gate closed behind them to seal off the yard. Despite repeated cries from the reporters three deep behind the fence, Hartley kept his back turned. The children's faces bobbed in the windows, drawing him forward, and in the next moment, they poured out of the house with unbridled joy. Hartley crouched to his knees, nearly collapsing under their weight as they all hugged him at once. He felt warm, familiar kisses on both sides of his face, and in that blissful moment, nothing else mattered. Rising gradually, he saw Evan hanging back from the gleeful reunion. He bent down in front of him to study the reservation he saw in his eyes. The irises were the same crystal blue as Celeste's, and they sparkled with deep inner clarity. "Don't go back to work, Daddy," he said, as a tear ran down his cheek.

Hartley's arm stretched around Evan's small body as he gently wiped the tear from his son's face with his thumb. "It's been tough for you, hasn't it?"

"People are saying bad things about you. I don't like hearing bad things."

His son's sorrowful expression pulled at Hartley's heartstrings. Facing his older son was harder than facing any trial judge. Explaining his actions would be difficult.

"Evan, I made a mistake. But don't believe any of the bad things that you hear about me. What are all these posters?"

Christine grabbed her father by his index finger and dragged him up the front porch stairs. "Dad, Dad, Dad, come see!" Hartley climbed the stairs and stopped on the welcome mat. Evan pointed to a large sign taped to the living-room window overlooking the porch. "Who are all those names?"

Hartley stepped closer and scanned the hundreds of scrawled greetings and short messages and signatures, his eyes welling with tears. "They're from my patients, doctors, and friends," he exclaimed, his voice catching.

"Are you famous, Dad? Look at all those camera people."

"The word would be *infamous*, son." He wiped his eyes hastily with the back of his hand and stepped slowly down the stairs into the yard, ignoring the reporters as he read in dumbfounded amazement the kind words of encouragement posted all over the fence. "What did I do to deserve this?" he asked himself, engrossed in his good fortune. He turned back to admire the large banner strung between the columns of the front porch as Celeste sidled up beside him. "How's that for a headline?" she said. "A Dr. Fogg worked on this early this morning. Job sharing, he said."

"How did I miss all this?" said Hartley, his eyes full of awe.

Celeste teased gently. "You weren't paying attention."

They pressed warmly together with their backs to the reporters. Clicking cameras sounded behind him. Grinning widely, he turned his head to face Celeste. "Here's something they can show on the news," he whispered, planting a full kiss on his wife's lips. "A happy ending."

Celeste suppressed her embarrassment. "The news hates happy endings."

Just then Sophie interrupted excitedly. "Push the magic button, Daddy."

Hartley smiled at his youngest. "The magic button? Do you have one?"

"We all do! See?" She lifted the edge of her shirt and proudly pushed a finger into her belly button. "There, see—it's all better. Now you do it."

Hartley grinned gently and glanced up at the myriad of clicking cameras. It felt good to hear everyone laughing together, so he lifted his shirt and touched a finger between the thin rolls of fat on his belly. "I did it!" he said, with a worried smile. "Everything is going to be different now—I promise. Soon these people will all go away."

"Here, Dad, I made this for you," said Hartley's younger boy. Drew reached into his pocket and solemnly handed over a sheet of notebook paper folded into a small rectangle. Hartley opened it slowly and studied the colored sketch of a doctor in a white coat with a stethoscope around his neck, flying over Chicago with small silver wings on his back. A little red cross brightened his breast pocket. There were words at the bottom: "God Loves You, Daddy."

Hartley gazed at his son's somber face. He gathered his children and held them together as tightly as he could. "God loves us all," he said.

"Pee-yew, Daddy, you stink," said Sophie, playfully pinching her nose. Celeste took his hand to tow him up the path toward the house. "Come inside, I'll make you some dinner."

"I'll have a coffee, too," he said with a smile. "I think I missed that the most."

Hartley slowed deliberately as he turned toward the porch stairs and unhurriedly took one step at a time. At the top, he glanced back at the reporters behind the yard, full of colorful posters. *We all make choices*, he thought. *Sometimes we make bad ones, but I'm learning. This isn't going to be easy.*

Chapter Twenty-Nine

Hartley insulated himself with family in his first week at home. But between sheer joy and a renewed feeling of freedom, his mind battled fear compounded by his profound personal failure. He paced the house incessantly in these moments, expecting answers to come, but finding that filling the void left by his forced sabbatical was difficult. Frustrated, he resigned himself to wait to discover where he was going and how he would respond. His second day back home, Celeste watched him from the kitchen counter. She cut thin slices of ham, folded the meat between two pieces of bread, and placed the sandwich in front of him. "Rosey, when are you going to start preparing for your trial? I know you're on an emotional roller coaster, but maybe searching blindly isn't the answer."

"Hawkins wants to see me on Monday," he answered, chewing a mouthful of the sandwich. "People forget that doctors are human," he said.

"Take that as a compliment."

Hartley said nothing. "I'm no better than that lawyer, Johnson," he said, swallowing the last bite of sandwich. He shook his head as if scolding himself for his emotion. "I actually wanted to take someone's life. Somewhere deep inside, I must really hate."

"Oh, come on, Rosey. Even Christ had His low moments. The Bible doesn't portray Him as Superman. He went from town to town teaching and healing, but there were too many sick people to heal, even for Him. But He accepted His limitations, and so should you."

Hartley recalled the Peter Principle. "Christ raised to a level of incompetence? That's supposed to be comforting?"

"No—but His reaction should be a lesson. Christ didn't quit."

"He couldn't be sued," snapped Hartley.

"But He could be crucified."

Calmly, Celeste finished composing four plates of food for the children and glanced up at her husband. "Maybe you need to get some perspective. Your friend Mark called and asked if he could help with some legal advice. He's a lawyer and one of your closest friends. How long has it been since you've seen him?"

"Years. It's been all work and kids. You know that."

Celeste put her hands on her hips. "Not anymore," she said firmly. "We're going to start having some balance in our lives."

Hartley quietly set the dish in the sink and studied the radiant joy on Celeste's face as she set the four plates on the table. Her tireless attention spoke of the pleasure she took in serving her family. He stepped to his wife and kissed her on the cheek. "Your dedication is wonderful," he whispered.

"So is yours," she answered. "You used to ride through the day on that white horse, like being a doctor was your calling."

Hartley grinned. "My calling? You mean like a priest?"

Celeste sidled closer, a spontaneous smile lighting her face. "Yes—like a priest, but with privileges." Their hips leaned in to meet.

"Now, there's a positive," he answered.

Hartley glanced through the front window of the restaurant before he entered, hoping to catch a glimpse of Mark's face. Having grown up together, Hartley and Mark had a the kind of friendship that took years to develop. He hadn't seen Mark in years, and he was curious how years of practicing law had worn him. "Mark, you look great," he said the second his friend came through the door.

"You look better than when I saw you on the news," joked Mark. "I'm glad you're still in one piece."

Hartley laughed without taking offense. After catching up, they moved to a small table near the corner. "Two beers?" asked the waitress.

"Coffee for me," said Hartley.

Mark nodded that he'd have a beer and settled onto the seat. His eyes fixed on Hartley as if in disbelief. "I might say this is a little uncomfortable," he admitted. "It's great to see you. But what in hell's nation got into you, Roger? I heard you were touched off by a malpractice lawsuit."

Hartley fidgeted awkwardly. As he slid back from the table, the chair legs caught in a crack, and he wobbled but caught himself without tipping over. Forlornly he nodded his head, not trusting himself to speak.

"Oh my God, Roger! Just because one patient sued you—you throw your whole career under the bus?" Mark leaned forward and looked up to see into his friend's downcast eyes. "Really?"

"Things haven't been going right at all. It's a Gordian knot."

"So you tried to shoot it instead of untie it?" Mark took a small sip of beer. "You assaulted a lawyer. I should take this personally."

"You shouldn't. We know each other better than that."

"You attacked my profession. I should be upset."

"But you aren't. You must know the emotional toll that a lawsuit takes on people. Win, lose, or settle—you die a little with every malpractice case. I'm sure I'm not the first to get angry."

"Indeed," answered Mark. "But you're the first to point a gun instead of your finger. You've caused quite a stir in the papers, and that's making the legal community nervous. We don't want the landscape to change."

"Why should it change? I've committed a crime—and I'll be punished. It's my problem and nobody else's."

Mark laughed with admiration. "You poker-faced imp," he said. "Nonetheless, you'd like things to change! Correct?"

Hartley's head snapped up. His face was a mix of interest and consternation. "If universal health care is a must for our country, then everyone should be forced to make concessions. We all need to contribute to the stewardship of this profession."

"We all?" asked Mark.

"Yes, all of us. Doctors need to order fewer tests. Patients need to abandon the 'I want the test so I should get it' mentality. And lawyers will have to learn to get by on less. Health care reform is doomed without an attitude shift from the lawyers."

"Sorry, but that's not going to happen. Our side of the street feels the impact of malpractice on the cost of health care is wildly exaggerated. We calculate only one to two percent at best."

"Mark!" said Hartley. "It takes only a back-of-the-napkin calculation to figure one percent of nearly three-trillion-dollar health care expenditures. And more significant are the costs of defensive medicine. In this legal environment, all doctors fear missing anything and strive to achieve one-hundred-percent accuracy by ordering a multitude of tests. We estimate that number could approach twenty-five percent of the tests that we order."

Mark rocked arrogantly back in his chair. "No one has a good handle on defensive medicine costs. We feel the burgeoning health care expenditure results from a variety of things. Our population is aging. Advances in technology are expensive. New drugs are costly. And administrative costs have skyrocketed. Almost five million people are employed in health care management and administrative support to manage less than a million physicians. That's a five-to-one ratio."

"It's a good thing managed care is reducing *that* problem."

"At least they're trying to manage the unnecessary care. We feel doctors order excessive testing to compensate for not spending enough time with patients. My doctor now clicks on his computer screen instead of looking at me. He orders tests as though my insurance insulates me from the cost. Sometimes I think he borders on irresponsible."

"Doctors don't like electronic health records any more than our patients. But those administrators you spoke about have mandated them so that Medicare and insurance payers can have instant access to our records." Hartley laughed as best he could. "At least they document every detail. My buffed charts are more lawyer-proof. But discounting the added costs of 'cover-your-ass medicine' is what's irresponsible. As it stands now, the financial and psychological costs of being sued are so severe, as you can see, that there's no amount of health care that's too much when I'm trying to prevent financial ruin. And contrary to common belief, doctors don't order tests to increase their income. We don't own CT scanners. We aren't allowed to have interests in labs and radiology centers. Reading and signing off on all those reports. Calling each patient with results. I would just as soon side with my clinical judgment and get home in time for a family dinner."

"Speaking of dinner," said Mark, "do you think we should order?"

"I'll eat if you promise not to talk about health care anymore. The subject is killing my appetite."

"I'm truly sorry—especially knowing the reason that you got into this mess. And I agree that some type of legal reform will need to occur. But the US Constitution gives citizens the right to seek retribution for damages they've suffered, and if tort reform passes, suing for smaller amounts won't be worth it for lawyers. Victims wouldn't be able to find representation."

Hartley snorted with disgust. "Protecting the 'victims' is a smoke screen. If attorneys really cared, they would accept less money to do the 'right thing.'"

"Roger! Entire law firms will go out of business with tort reform."

"Dewey, Cheatam, and Howe would go out of business? Oh darn." As Mark ordered another beer, Hartley reflected on the conversation he had had with Mates about doctors leaving their practices or relocating to states where tort reform had been adopted because their malpractice premiums were unaffordable. "Mark, let me ask you a question. Why don't more lawyers get sued when they lose a case?"

Mark smiled with detachment. "Clients usually refuse to pay us if they're unhappy, and it's incredibly difficult to win a case against your client for that sort of thing. Even if you do a good job, and your client deserved the bad outcome, you usually just let it slide."

"But in any given dispute, one side always ends up with a bad result. I can think of a lot of things that could be second-guessed. The lawyer could have been better prepared. A cross-examination could have been more aggressive. The arguments weren't presented clearly. The settlement was low. The lawyer alienated the judge. Any of those! Why don't you guys get sued?"

Mark took a satisfying sip of his beer. "Lawyers almost never get second-guessed. Where would you find a lawyer to take the case, or a sympathetic judge?"

"So lawyers have immunity?" protested Hartley.

"Not completely," said Mark. "We get sued too."

"But you have never been sued?"

"Fortunately—no. But I do carry malpractice insurance."

"Is it more than five thousand a year?" Mark shook his head. "So if the lawyer's argument against tort reform is that lawsuits are the watchdogs of our profession, how do you police your profession?"

"Attorneys take an oath to the court when we're licensed. We're not creating evidence. We merely elicit testimony from the person on the witness stand, and our rules of professional responsibility keep us from eliciting testimony we know to be false."

"I took an oath. Doctors have the same professional standards and licensing."

Mark laughed uncomfortably. "Really—this isn't a vast conspiracy."

"Then why?"

"Roger, it's just harder to win a legal malpractice suit than a medical one."

"Why is that?" asked Hartley pointedly. "Is it because there's more flexibility in how to try a legal case than in how to treat lupus?"

"Roger, simmer down. A legal malpractice case requires malice or intent be shown instead of just negligence."

"I object, Mark," said Hartley. "Shouldn't doctors be immune in cases of negligence then, too? Medical malpractice should be limited to malice! If that were the case we wouldn't need tort reform!"

Mark shook his head uncomfortably. "I seriously doubt many docs practice with malice. Fatigue, carelessness, lack of training perhaps—but not plain nastiness."

"Exactly my point," said Hartley.

"At least you have the causation element. You need to prove that you would have been healthier if the doctor hadn't fucked up. Sometimes that's difficult to do. And when it's obvious, you settle."

"Patients seemingly have very little to lose under that system."

"Do you mean contingency fees?"

"Yes."

"Roger, I know that makes you mad—it makes all doctors mad. But eliminating them is unconstitutional. People have a right to representation."

"That is misleading, and you know it. The Sixth Amendment provides the right to a speedy trial by an impartial jury and to have the assistance of counsel for defense. There is no right to counsel in a civil trial. I looked it up."

Mark checked the quick snort of an arrogant laugh. "So let's agree to disagree before we get started on that. Tell me, what it was like being in jail?"

"Like living in an unflushed toilet," answered Hartley. "It worries me that I'll have to go back."

"It worries me that I hear a civil attorney is trying your case."

"Not even the public defender was too enthusiastic in taking up my defense. It's a little disheartening."

"I don't believe it," said Mark. "Somebody will defend you."

"Yes, Ernest Hawkins. He's a med malpractice lawyer who defends physicians."

"But preparing for this trial is different!"

"With the issues, maybe his expertise will be what I need."

Mark wrapped his hands around the cold beer bottle and peeled the label off with his thumbnail. He rolled the small pieces into a tight little ball and threw them onto the floor. "How are things going so far?"

Hartley's face took on a vacant expression. "We haven't done anything yet. I'm picturing a career treating lice and gonorrhea in prison."

Mark almost choked. "You haven't done anything? Honestly, Roger. I don't know the laws after a felony arrest, but it can't be good to have a conviction if you ever decide to go back to practicing medicine."

"It's hard to think about that now. This is too new."

"But Roger, shouldn't it be obvious? Why did you go into medicine in the first place?"

Immediately Hartley's face contorted as if he recalled something horrific. "The same reason as every other doctor does," he said automatically. "I wanted to help people."

Mark's eyes didn't miss Hartley's reaction. "There's a stronger reason than that. Most kids want to help animals, but they never put forth the effort to be veterinarians. It's a long road to get where you are. What kept you going?"

"The answer buys me a stiff drink." Hartley hunched over the small table and captured Mark with unexpectedly smiling eyes. "Mark, you've known me for a long time. Do you remember when my father died of a heart attack?"

"Of course I do—we all do. Weren't you about seven at the time?"

Hartley nodded solemnly. "I was eight. And for many months before he passed, I had made a habit of going to the hospital with him on Saturday rounds. I saw how the people greeted him as he walked the halls. Patients revered him because he made them feel better. He was a healer. And because everyone could see how much I adored him, people in the neighborhood gave me a nickname.

Do you remember?"

Mark nodded. "Sure—Little Doc."

Hartley took a slow sip of coffee and replaced the cup exactly on the ring it had left on the tabletop. "At the time, hearing the nickname gave me a wonderful feeling. I imagined myself earning respect—just like my dad."

"Sadly, we've never talked about this before," said Mark.

"Nor this," added Hartley gravely, but his eyes remained dry. "I remember this like it was yesterday. I had just come home from playing baseball in the park at the end of our street. It had been raining, and I think I was cold. When I got home, I ran straight into the kitchen without removing my soaking shoes. My dad was standing there with a frantic look on his face. I looked down at the puddle around my feet, afraid he was displeased. But when I looked up..." Hartley paused. "When he dropped to the floor, he was clutching his chest. I saw the fear in his eyes as he died right in front of me."

"That's awful. I never knew."

"It was... But what I remember so vividly—and still feel today—is the sickening feeling of not knowing what to do. I felt so helpless, and I vowed at his funeral to never let that happen again—to anybody."

Mark blinked the moisture out of his eyes but never turned away from his friend. "You set the bar pretty high, Roger. It must be a hollow feeling when you try to save a life that can't be saved. You embody something different from most doctors today. Your dad would still be very proud."

Hartley recalled his father's favorite story about a man walking down a long, deserted beach, throwing stranded starfish back into the ocean. The man couldn't save them all, but was satisfied to save all that he could. He looked back at Mark. "It does feel wonderful to revive a person who is technically dead. You know, I don't think I'd be happy doing anything else."

"See, Roger?" answered Mark. "You haven't changed."

"But Mark, that's what I'm afraid of. Maybe I have to."

Chapter Thirty

Anita's office seemed half its usual size now that the thick-framed mirror was gone, leaving a discolored bare rectangle. Almost directly in the center of the darkened spot was a small hole with pry marks around its edges where the slug had been pulled out for evidence. Behind her big desk, Anita sank into her rose-colored, high-backed leather chair, half listening to Griffin, who was in the chair usually occupied by clients.

"You're a seasoned, top-notch lawyer? Really? And you behaved like that? Oblivious to rules! Your behavior during the arraignment was a disgrace!"

Anita was momentarily happy that the mirror hadn't yet been replaced so she didn't have to suffer both a front view and reflected view of the prosecutor. "Thank you for the compliments," she said. "But I'd shut up with the snotty stuff. You have no idea what I've been through. I was traumatized, and emotional and political pressures aren't mixing well."

"I know exactly what you've been through," protested Griffin. "I've memorized the arrest record and scrutinized every other document that this case has generated. You of all people should know about the political pressures attached to the underbelly of tort law. But in this case, you're the defendant. All you have to do is listen to me and tell the truth the best you can. I'm working you just as hard, or harder, in the preparation for this case as I have for all the others. And you're going to obey and do what I say."

"Obey? You mean like a dog?"

"Jesus, Anita, you frustrate me! I'm in charge here, and I don't appreciate the I-wrote-the-book attitude. Obviously that's the wrong book in this case."

"If you were in charge, Mr. Griffin, we'd be having this meeting in your office."

Griffin laughed to himself about her smug behavior. "Does this look like any other felony case you've ever seen? Have you read the news or watched the

TV? Every day the coverage has doubled. This is my trial! And you're not going to fuck it up for me."

"You can do that on your own," returned Anita. "It's my life he screwed up."

"And it may be mine, too. I've never seen such under-the-table political backlash. Hartley and I are the only names our political action groups are throwing about, and it isn't pretty stuff. Some of it one could even take as threats."

Anita's body became suddenly clammy. She was happy the news wasn't talking about Robert, but even more so, she was happy the news didn't include them both. "Griffin, Hartley accosted *me* with the gun! He left the house with money, bought the gun illegally, drove to my office with an appointment, and pointed it right at my face. Look at that bullet hole! This should be a slam dunk for a man of your talents."

Griffin's arms rose suddenly. "But the arraignment?"

"Sorry! I was outraged. My fuse burned short."

"During the trial you're going to have to tone it way down for the jury. No heels! I want you in flats. And your clothes..." Griffin exaggerated his glance at Anita's bare knee. "Something plain. I want you defenseless and weak."

"I don't know how to dress for a trial? As unwilling as I am to be portrayed in this light—or take orders from you for that matter—I'm motivated to bring Hartley down. Twice I've seen him and twice he's gotten under my skin." Anita growled loudly with disgust. Visions of the many doctors she had stripped of their medical glory paraded through her mind. It was pleasing to see them come to the witness stand, full of arrogance and outraged at being sued, and then go away embarrassed and downtrodden. She always watched carefully when the jury declared the verdict. The stunned, vacant look in the doctor's eyes was a measure of how well she had performed in the courtroom. "He thinks what I do is all for the money," she hissed. "But it won't be for the money in the future. So don't worry, Griffin, I'll wear flat shoes and put on something plain, and I'll help you break down Hartley's castle to rubble."

Griffin laughed as if he felt more at ease. "I just don't get it. Hartley has a civil lawyer for his defense. We should have a field day in court. All we have to do is not blow it."

"I've litigated against Hawkins," said Anita, sitting straight in her chair.

"Honestly, I never like to see his name as the defending attorney. Even when I win it somehow feels like I haven't. The jury's monetary award always ends up less than my settlement offer before the trial. And he never settles! I know all his cases will end up in court."

Griffin almost snickered with pleasure. "Those contingency fees will come harder then," he said in a backhanded tone.

Anita launched to her feet as if she would attack Griffin physically. "If you question my work, Griffin, you'll make me even more angry than I am now. Then we *will* have a problem. This was just an insight into Hawkins's behavior and psyche. A good lawyer should like to know his competition." Anita sat and collected herself, shaking her head from side to side. "That crooked nose!" she said, her dominant left hand closing into a fist. "I've wanted to straighten that nose. It must have been a right hook in the first place that gave it such contour."

"You can do that in your next med-mal case against him. But for now you have to behave. I should be more worried about the jurors. We need twelve good ones, and we have to get them into the courthouse without their seeing a lot of white coats."

"If you want to suffer your doubts, go ahead." Anita spun in her chair, standing to gaze out the window at the cold blue of Lake Michigan. Her eyes were immediately drawn to Monroe Harbor. "There aren't enough doctors out there to make a difference. Now I have to break off this meeting."

"Okay," resigned Griffin. "But we do need to meet twice a week." He stood and turned to the door, but his eyes caught on a decorative tabletop lectern where Anita's textbook, *The Bible of Malpractice Law*, lay open. "How ironic," he said. "You wrote the textbook on malpractice law, and you could become intimate with the downfall of its golden years. Would that be karma?"

Anita seethed as if Griffin had zeroed in on her weak spot. "Don't use the term *intimate*! This attack was thrust on me! I had nothing to do with it. And taking orders from you as a prosecutor is becoming just as painful. I know you're a seasoned prosecutor, Mr. Griffin, but keep your unease and frustration from showing during the trial."

Chapter Thirty-One

As the flashlight slipped out of his hand, Hartley held his breath in the darkness, clinging to the edge of the cavern wall. He listened fearfully until the metal casing exploded on the rocks far below. The sound of the impact seemed real, and it awakened him with a start. He bunched his pillow around his head and curled onto his side, wondering why he was dreaming about caving. Part of him wanted to quickly return to sleep and see if he would find a way out of the cave without the light, but he knew his first meeting with Hawkins was less than four hours away. He didn't know what to expect or how they would prepare a plan for his defense. Fighting apprehension, he peeled back the bedcovers and set about an abbreviated morning routine, eating his breakfast without tasting his food and hurrying out the door to leave plenty of time to stop at Northwestern Hospital. The stitches of his healing wound were ready to be removed.

The reception window was open, and Hartley checked in without special treatment or fanfare. He realized he was thinking like a patient, not knowing where he was going or how long he would have to wait. He quelled his apprehensions by leafing through the dozens of magazines to find something that captured his interest. Ultimately his eyes arrested on a copy of *Newsweek* devoted to health care reform, and his stomach began to rumble.

"Roger," called a nurse in a soft, compassionate tone.

Hartley's eyes darted to the open door as he discarded the magazine on top of the others. The examination room was generically stark, appointed with a short examination table and a small shelf that served as a workstation for a laptop. A stainless steel tray was topped with gleaming scissors and tweezers that seemed to float neatly on top of a white sterile drape. He sat gingerly on a contemporary metal chair against the wall and fixed his eyes on the doctor's empty seat. Now that it had been one week since his rage had exploded, he felt more willing to share his thoughts openly with his old friend Dr. Hahn. There was a soft knock at the door and when a physician's assistant stepped in, Hartley mustered a smile and then dipped his head. Struggling to hide his disappointment, he answered a few basic questions and then lay on the exam table as he was instructed. The conversation was cheerful, and the stitches came out with little tugs. "This wound must have been a little dog-eared, but it came together quite nicely. It must have been quite a blow. Take a look."

Hartley slid onto his feet and examined the scar in the mirror. The skin over his right eye had pulled together in the shape of a tiny cross, and he traced the smooth lines lightly with his finger, finding it soothing to touch it. He turned to the physician's assistant with an odd smile on his face. "My dyslexia tells me that my wound was 'God-eared,'" he quipped. "You did a nice job as well."

"My pleasure," the physician's assistant said warmly, covering the spot with a Band-Aid. "I have to sit down and put a few notes into the computer. Take care now, doc. Call if it gets infected."

Hartley drove across the Michigan Avenue Bridge and turned west toward the Loop, navigating the congested streets as if he knew the way. He found an old three-story building at the address Hawkins had given him and walked up the paint-speckled marble stairs hesitantly. At the end of a dimly lit hallway, a tiny brass placard was screwed into the wall next to a door. It was polished and shiny and etched with a single name. "Law Office of Ernest Hawkins, Esq." The office seemed more modest than Hartley had imagined, and he balked before knocking. But as Hartley hesitated, Hawkins opened the door. "Right on time, Roger," he said, extending a welcoming hand. Hartley glanced around nervously. The outer office was cramped with a small but neatly kept desk. On top was an old phone with only one line and a bulky computer monitor with white plastic sides that had discolored to yellow. An empty coat stand stood in the corner, hung with thin wire hangers that chimed as Hawkins stepped past them. "Sorry about the mess," said Hawkins. "My wife is my paralegal, but today our son's not feeling well."

"I'm sorry," said Hartley. "Is there any way I can help?"

"I think he's just tired. Kids are so overprogrammed these days."

Hartley smiled in agreement. There was a disarming quality in the lawyer's manner, making Hartley feel at home. "Do you have any other children?"

"No, just the one," said Hawkins with an air of contentment. "Come, follow me."

The front and back rooms of the small law office were like two different worlds. Hartley stopped at the door and stared in amazement. The terrain was chaotic, with volumes of bound law journals stacked into towers of like colors. Along the walls were dusty file boxes rising to the ceiling. The bookcase shelves bowed under the weight of the books. Except for two diverging narrow paths that led from the doorway to two chairs, there were few spots of clear floor space. "You're a hoarder," laughed Hartley, "with a wafer-thin briefcase?"

"I started collecting old law books a few years ago," Hawkins answered, hastily widening the path to his client's chair with his feet. "It's gotten a little out of hand, but believe it or not, everything in this room is right where I can find it." He repositioned a picture of his wife and son from on top of his desk to a shelf. "Please sit," he said, flicking his hand in an informal gesture. "And don't be alarmed. My practice is small because I keep it that way. And malpractice defense lawyers can't afford glitzy Michigan Avenue offices like your friend Ms. Johnson." Hawkins smiled slightly. "I've been in there just once."

"Me, too," returned Hartley sadly. He took a few mincing steps toward one of the chairs and pivoted into the seat. Confined by the volumes of books, he squirmed internally with concern. "Are those mine?" he asked, pointing a finger at a stack of file boxes marked "Roger Hartley" in black magic marker.

"Yes. I've been through them."

"I have a set just like them at home. I nearly broke my toe on them."

"Your toe?" Hawkins sat behind his desk and leaned back with folded fingers behind his head, as if relaxing just before tackling an enjoyable problem. "Tell me about your patient Moll."

"Moll spreads his misery among as many people as possible," snapped Hartley. "He has severe lupus and has been unhappy most of his life. He took his greedy revenge out on me."

Hartley's body twitched with restlessness. Clearly he was trying to sit still but couldn't. Hawkins leaned forward, eyeing his client closely. "So that's how we start," he said with dramatic emphasis. "Our first undertaking is to rid you of anger. Moll will likely be called to the stand, and the jury will be watching you closely. You'll need to keep a cool head if you want any chance of being set free."

Hartley squeezed his knees together and gripped the arms of the chair, wedging himself further into the seat. "I'm better," he said defensively. "It's amazing how much walking away from job stress improves your perspective. I feel human again."

"No," said Hawkins matter-of-factly. "You hide it well, Roger. But resentment's still in there."

"Why wouldn't there be? Patients risk nothing when they sue a doctor." Hartley's neck shortened an inch or two into his shirt. His mouth set in a tight line. "This is certainly therapeutic," he said with peevish sarcasm.

Hawkins waited patiently for his client to regain his composure. "Face it," he said finally. "If you don't deal with your anger now, it will be there next time you're served. And there *will* be a next time. Until you accept that fact, I'm not going anywhere with your defense."

"You make managing anger sound like you're treating a disease."

"Unless I fix the problem, relieving the symptoms won't have a lasting effect. Take a honest look at yourself and don't expect miracles. Preparing for this is going to be difficult. There'll be traps and false steps. Are you ready for that?"

"I'm ready to dig out of a hole with a spoon."

A smile played around Hawkins's lips. "Don't take it personally, Roger. Think of malpractice law as a grand tradition that dates back hundreds of years. What happened to you is nothing new. Alleging malpractice and seeking compensation for injuries isn't just a get-rich-quick scheme invented in this millennium." Hartley glanced up more intently to see if he could detect any anger, but Hawkins quickly began reviewing the origins of malpractice law. "Before the nineteenth century it was accepted that sickness and death was a divine punishment. The expectations for doctors and their treatments were low. People suffered, declined, and then died. It was expected. It was nobody's fault unless it was his or her own. But as the practice of medicine evolved from the dispensing of herbs to prescribing treatments that actually worked, expectations changed, and physicians became the unintended victims of their own success. Quacks and charlatans had no standards of adequate care, and there was no accountability."

"Or money to wrench from them."

"Educated and qualified physicians had texts and manuals that defined standards of practice, and these were used against them in court. Complicated therapies involved greater risks, and higher expectations couldn't always be met. *Mala praxis* became the term lawyers used to describe physician failures."

"Bad practice," said Hartley. "I hate Latin."

"The original intent of malpractice law was to guarantee a standard of quality and act as a watchdog to protect the public from quackery. But the charlatans and medical hacks had no money," said Hawkins, "so lawyers lost material incentive to prosecute them rigorously. Unexpectedly, the targets of malpractice lawsuits became the best doctors at universities and in large cities."

"The ones who took the most difficult cases," said Hartley, recalling Celeste pointing this out.

"Exactly," replied Hawkins. "The new system left tarnished reputations and bankruptcies in its wake, and physicians grew bitter. They stopped treating difficult cases and avoided new treatments. Eventually, nobody outside a hard-to-get-into university hospital provided cutting-edge medicine that people needed."

Hartley's foot flexed forward and tipped over a pile of law books. "Sorry," he said. "Not much has changed. The doctor-lawyer antipathy dates back two hundred years. That blows me away."

"See, nothing is personal. Even back then medical malpractice was a rich vein of law. Personal injury lawyers advertised aggressively in the daily papers and anywhere else they thought would bring them some business."

Hartley bent over, attempting to right the stack of dusty old books. "When will we learn?" he cried. "Soon with Medicare cuts we won't have any money either, like the charlatans. Maybe then the lawyers will leave us alone."

"There will always be bottom feeders," said Hawkins. "And that brings me to the happy part of the lesson."

"Contingency fees!" said Hartley, almost spitting as he pronounced the words. Scratching the scar on his forehead, he picked off a small scab and examined the blood on his finger. "By 'bottom feeders' you mean the shameless ambulance chasers, who fish for economically insolvent clients and entice them to sue their doctors with no money down? The ads are repulsive! A good parasite doesn't kill its host."

"Easy there, doc! I don't like that branch of law any more than you do, but even I can get offended if you slander my profession. I'm on your side. Please, remember that."

"Sorry," said Hartley, casting his eyes down and locking his clasped hands between his knees. "I know that. And I appreciate all you're doing for me. But sometimes I feel so targeted that I want to spit. Doctors are vulnerable on so many fronts."

"It's okay to spit," said Hawkins, "but not to kill."

Hartley flushed in embarrassment but said nothing.

"Let's face it," said Hawkins, his mouth lifting into a characteristic disarming dry smile. "In a medical system that's as complex as ours, mistakes happen every year by the hundreds of thousands. Many result in death or severe disability."

"You can't pin all those on bad doctors," protested Hartley. "That number must include unpreventable errors caused by unforeseeable consequences."

"No, but it does include dosing errors from illegible handwriting. Sometimes doctors *should* be held accountable for their mistakes."

With a shrug, Hartley slouched in his chair. His handwriting was better than most doctors' chaotic chicken-scratching developed through years of hurried note-taking. "Nobody's perfect," he grumbled.

"It's more serious than that."

Hartley closed his mouth, slumping still lower but finding both feet confined by a circle of law books. There was no room to move or even to fidget. "Cheer me up with your lecture about contingency fees, why don't you?"

"I know how you feel. Personal injury lawyers appeal to the greed in human nature and encourage frivolous lawsuits. All doctors feel the same way. Right?"

"We believe contingency fees foster windfall awards for personal gains that help line lawyers' pockets. It's extortion. It's unethical."

"Defending you after you pointed a gun in a lawyer's face—that I might find unethical."

Hartley's voice became a repentant whisper. "Sorry—I don't mean to offend."

"You won't," said Hawkins. "The courts have upheld the legal rights of an individual to bargain for representation. If that bargain is a contingency fee..."

"The legal rights of a patient? Or do you mean the legal rights of the lawyers?"

"Please try to listen," said Hawkins patiently. "A poor man might be denied representation without a fee system that gives him a means of establishing and asserting his claim. And contrary to what you might think, there's no data to suggest that contingency-fee contracts encourage frivolous litigation. Think about it. When fees are contingent upon a successful outcome, then pursuing groundless, speculative complaints would be a poor investment of any lawyer's time. In fact, a contingency-fee structure shifts the risk from the client to the attorney."

"But patients risk nothing—*that's* the point. I'm familiar with the statistics. Ninety percent of malpractice lawsuits settle out of court. Ten percent go to trial, and the plaintiffs win half of those. That means ninety-five percent of all malpractice suits generate income. And what do the lawyers get?"

"Forty percent is customary," answered Hawkins.

"I call forty percent incentive to seek larger awards. Don't lawyers call them home runs?" After kicking over the law books again with his restless legs, Hartley made no move to restack them.

Hawkins rocked back in his chair. "We'll agree to disagree," Hawkins said politely.

"I've heard that conclusion before," said Hartley with disgust.

"Then let's move on."

"You sure are helping to defuse my anger."

"Yes—let's talk about you. What happened to you?"

Hartley leaned in to the scrutinizing stare of his counselor. "I treated a man for lupus using the best methods available, and an altruistic lawyer tried to profit from the patient's bad luck."

"That's correct," said Hawkins. "But it's not what you did but what you failed to do that got you in trouble. There are side effects of prednisone, are there not?"

"We discussed it," said Hartley indignantly.

"If it wasn't written down, it didn't happen."

"Should I read patients the PDR and list all the possible complications in their charts, no matter how rare? Maybe I need an informed consent to treat a common cold. Tylenol can cause liver failure." Hartley scoffed. "Tell me this case isn't about money."

"Patients have rights. When something goes wrong and a patient's expectations aren't met, tort proceedings attempt to compensate the victim by bringing him as close as possible to the expected better health that would result from the treatment."

"With money?" asked Hartley.

"What else?"

"But why the multimillion-dollar awards? I can accept restitution for the patient when I make a mistake. That's what malpractice insurance is for. Patients incur medical costs, loss of income, and even giving them a little extra to make life more pleasant would be fine with me. But whose suffering is worth five million dollars?"

"I don't blame you for being angry, Roger. It's a means of deterring bad medicine, that's all. Pain and suffering are just the teeth in the watchdog. I'm simply trying to help you understand that medical malpractice is nothing more than a broken contract between a doctor and patient, where the agreement was the provision of good health."

"I can't *guarantee* good health!" said Hartley heatedly.

"Patients feel that contract's been broken. And when doctors believe they've practiced within the standards of care, they let the jury decide. I'm telling you this so you'll be prepared to get through it the next time—without buying a gun." Hawkins smiled with renewed cheer. "Now what I want you to do next may come as quite a surprise. I insist that you and your family go away for a week."

"You've got to be kidding?"

"I couldn't be more serious."

"Where?"

"The ocean. Away from the press. Clear your head. That's my prescription, and if you want this crisis to come out right, you'll take my suggestion."

"But why?"

"The jury will be studying you carefully, and I don't want them to detect anger."

"Pick up and leave—just like that?"

"Not quite. I spent an hour before the judge, arguing to get you a special parole. And I think you'll find Celeste has your trip all arranged."

Hartley's face went slack with surprise. "She hasn't said a word about it."

"I told her not to discuss it. You have a very good wife."

Hartley studied his lawyer quizzically. "Don't you think that's a week we need to prepare? Do we have a plan?"

Hawkins let Hartley explore his face for an answer. "I need the week," he said calmly. "And you'll need to be yourself—that's why you're going."

"But…"

Unable to put words to the vague fear that haunted him, Hartley's mouth opened and closed. He raised an arm in a protesting gesture, but it flapped helplessly down at his side. He had no other choice but to obey. "Be patient," ordered Hawkins pleasantly. "Everything will come together while you're away."

CHAPTER THIRTY-TWO

Mates lived in a nondescript Chicago-style bungalow in a row of similar structures. He eagerly greeted Fogg at the door. "Let's meet in my basement," he said. "I want you to see this." Together they passed through the living room and descended a dark stairway. The shorter man moved freely in the low-ceilinged room, but Fogg ducked his head as he stepped to the center. He gaped at the brightly lit computer workstation that dominated the small space. He counted six large screens forming an arc around a central black desk chair that coasted on rollers.

"This looks like a radiologist's basement," said Fogg.

"It's a media center! Six screens locked into different blogging sites." Mates proudly swept his arm about to show off his man cave. "These three screens follow medical sites, these two are on law sites, and that one stays on Twitter. I read blogs in real time, as soon as they're posted."

"How long have you been doing this?" asked Fogg with admiration.

"I've always been doing this in some form or another. It's in my blood."

"Where do the kids play?"

"No kids. Realized early there wouldn't be time." After he sat and wheeled to the workstation, his eyes focused intensely as he scrolled through a web page. "I've been waiting for this a long time," he said, slamming in a quick comment.

"Waiting for what?"

"For someone like Hartley! These things don't arise *ex nihilo*. Somebody or something has to become a catalyst. I'm just glad no one got hurt. That makes it kind of okay."

Fogg's face still showed signs of wonder. Since the incident, Hartley hadn't talked to the press, and he wondered about his intent. "I don't think he'll talk to the press."

"No?" replied Mates. "Hartley's a part of this. I spoke to him once late at night in the ER. Clearly he was fed up and agreed that somebody had to do something. Knowingly or unknowingly, he got involved. I think it's his lawyer that's putting a gag over his mouth. That makes me suspicious about whose side his attorney is on. But regardless of Hartley, this movement has taken a life of its own. Look at this thread on tort reform. It's gotten three hundred posts in two days."

Fogg stepped closer to the center computer screen, reading as Mates scrolled down the page. "Who are all these people?" he asked.

"Anyone! Doctors tired of paying exorbitant malpractice premiums. Politically minded people who believe expensive, cover-your-ass defensive medicine contributes big numbers to spiraling health care expenditures. Anyone subjected to the hostile, sometimes irrational scrutiny of greedy lawyers that results in frivolous claims. And of course half the posts are from honorable and compassionate lawyers who profess civil rights and place the blame elsewhere. I like this one: 'I tend to believe the doctors who have replied instead of the lawyers.' You can tell that one is unbiased." Madly, he pecked out another entry to a short blog and hit the Send key.

Fogg read over his shoulder. "Fear has become the new face of medicine?"

There was a hint of panic in Mates's eyes when he looked up. "I've been trying to harness our fear, and I think it's starting to happen. Look at this tweet I wrote last week supporting Hartley. It's gotten twelve thousand retweets."

"And how many negative comments? I'm sure you must read them."

"A few thousand," he said. "And I respond. There are seven hundred thousand physicians in the United States, and double that if you include physician assistants, nurse practitioners, podiatrists, dentists, chiropractors, and therapists. If only I could reach more of them!" Hastily he wheeled across the plastic floor mat to another screen and pulled up his e-mail account. "You know those chain e-mails that people hate to forward? Look at this e-mail."

"I got that," said Fogg excitedly. "I didn't know that was from you."

"It wasn't. I literally sent it to ten people. Ten of these people." His finger pointed to a blogging screen. "The people with their finger on the thready pulse of health care. And it made its way to you. That means it's working." He laughed with glee and shook his head in amazement. "I think my e-mail went viral! Ten e-mails! What a powerful tool at our disposal."

"You had to do more than that."

"A few blogs here and there, but disseminating the information was easy. Those blogs link into other blogs and the outreach becomes exponential. Talk about hotly contested issues! These posts are anonymous, sometimes from people with cute little nicknames. But it's easy to guess who's a doctor or lawyer. Their comments are polar opposites."

"You certainly can say what you feel," laughed Fogg. "Look at that one. 'Asking a lawyer what he thinks about tort reform is like asking your barber if you need a haircut.'"

"Funny, but serious as a heart attack at the same time. The bottom line is that denying that tort reform would save money is irresponsible. Let doctors use their skills and clinical judgment to decide what tests are necessary. Develop a system focused on improving safety and reducing error, not one that assigns blame and metes out punishment."

"Unfortunately, few benefit," said Fogg. "The real losers are patients and doctors. Even Obama has commented by saying, 'Anyone who denies there's a crisis with medical malpractice is probably a trial lawyer.'"

Mates laughed. "That statement lost him some funding. The incredible thing is—doctors would just as soon march in favor of health care reform as against it. But it depends on what buttons you push. It would be easy! Combine universal coverage with tort reform. Balance the weight on the other side and make it a package deal. That would have to gain bipartisan support, wouldn't it?"

"I agree, or I wouldn't be here," said Fogg. "Tort reform has to be a part of any health care package if meaningful reform is to occur. But the counterweights are heavy. This country is run by lawyers, not the gras   ̄σ shook his head in dismay. "Maybe a rash act like Hartley's was '

"It certainly has gotten people's attention. The fixed as much as the doctors. They just need to f a path to express them at the ballot box. All of ʋ away from disaster at any time. And with the ɛ perfect time for a surge of support. We need a ' how they should vote."

"But shouldn't we keep the protests to ⸱

"Ha! The way this is snowballing that might not be possible. Subjugated on one side. Exploited on the other. The incremental changes that we have endured have been tolerated for too long in the name of practicing health care. There's going to be a big pushback. I see it right here on these screens." Mates clapped his hands together and rubbed them quickly, feeling the heat of the friction. "I just hope I get a chance to do what I really like when it happens."

"Do what?" said Fogg. "I can't believe there's more passion inside you."

"My delight is speaking," Mates answered. "I've dreamt so long about having an audience that my wife bought me *that* box on eBay. See it there against the wall."

"That?" asked Fogg. "What is it?"

"An antique soap box. Of course it was a clever dig. But sometimes I do climb atop. It makes me laugh in a tickled sort of way."

Fogg felt a surge of camaraderie. "Whether Hartley turns up with us or not, I'm putting his face on some posters to distribute when we get the doctors to rally. I hope he won't mind."

"He can't mind. He started this thing!"

"And now he'll have to finish it!" said Fogg.

CHAPTER THIRTY-THREE

After walking five hurried blocks through the upscale Gold Coast neighborhood, Anita Johnson felt her toes throbbing in her sharply pointed Italian shoes. Sunday morning at six thirty was an absurd time for a meeting, and her resentment toward Griffin pinched even more fiercely than the tight leather around her feet. She unfolded the hastily scribbled note delivered via her doorman and made sure that she hadn't misread it.

> Washington visitors.
> Ambassador East.
> Back of the restaurant.
> Sunday 6:30 a.m.

Anita crumpled the note into a tight little ball and discarded it on top of the hotel's outdoor ashtray. She knifed into the revolving doors, resisting the urge to turn a full circle and flee as she imagined the identities of the "Washington visitors." Her heels clicked across the marble lobby toward a lone maitre d' standing in front of the restaurant. He was dressed in an unusual costume more suitable for a genie, with billowing silk sleeves and gold slippers that curled crazily at the tips. But more impressive was his gold turban topped by an exotic feather that nearly doubled his stature. The pluming tip bobbed gaily when he smiled as if he expected her. He motioned for her to follow.

At that hour of the morning, the main dining room was vacant, and the linen-clad tables set gaudily with crystal glasses and gold-handled utensils for brunch appeared unappetizing to Anita. She passed a long row of booths backed by a montage of ancient black-and-white photos boasting the high life the restaurant had seen over the years. She glanced at the parade of politicians and celebrities dressed in narrow-lapelled tuxedos and dining with glamorous women wearing scarlet lipstick and smoking unfiltered cigarettes. The men's carefree attitudes reminded her of the old boys' network she had infiltrated and broken up at her law firm.

A high-backed circular booth was nestled in the farthest corner in the back of the restaurant. A fine trail of cigar smoke rose into the dim chandelier and foretold that the meeting had started. The maitre d' spun and bowed so low that his feather tip nearly dusted the floor. A murmur of deep voices halted abruptly. Anita's steps slowed cautiously. Four men in dark suits sat spaced evenly around the booth. Their oversized bodies made the table seem crowded. She looked at their faces. Her heart skipped a beat. A pang of remorse ran the length of her body. Griffin rose from one end to offer his seat, but Anita had no intention of sliding in next to Robert. For a split second, she glared at the state's attorney and then glanced indifferently at the congressman. Pulling her skirt tightly around her legs, she slid into the opposite side of the booth. She pictured herself captured by a hotel photographer in one of their black-and-white photos.

The table rocked severely as Griffin slid heavily back into the booth. Robert quickly steadied the sway by spreading his hands flat on the linen cloth. His wedding ring gleamed in the overhead light from the chandelier. Anita looked at the gold band and was careful not to look up into his face. The gruff old man seated next to Anita smashed his cigar in a plate and fixed Griffin with his impatient glare. The middle-aged man in the center of the booth nodded to Anita informally. Although they had never met, she knew the lawyer from pictures and videos. On camera his high forehead and large Adam's apple gave him an intellectual air. In person Anita thought they looked somewhat cartoonish. It had often irritated Anita the way her rival sang his own praises in his legal interviews as if he represented the pinnacle of personal injury law. Her goal was to someday surpass his prestige.

"I commend you on your successes," he complimented mildly.

"And which successes would that be?" she answered sourly.

The lawyer tipped his head to hide a flush of embarrassment. "I simply hear your name a lot—that's all."

Anita folded her hands demurely on her lap and stared at the crystal glasses and gold silverware in front of her. Although she hadn't seen Robert in weeks, she couldn't bring herself to look at him now. Nearly every day the congressman had been in the headlines, stirring anew her love and hate. Nervously she glanced at his manicured hands. *That ring*, she thought, recalling every word said on the yacht. She wanted terribly to look into the depths of his eyes and discover what was hidden there. But suddenly she thought of Hartley, and her anger boiled back to the surface. Things would have been different without Hartley. This was his fault.

"Drink?" the old man asked in the guttural tone of an overused voice.

Anita shook her head, hoping she wouldn't have to stay long. "It's six thirty in the morning," she said tersely.

"Get her a drink," he ordered to his stern bodyguard, who had his back to the wall. "Something for breakfast—like a mimosa." He turned in his seat to face her directly. "Ms. Johnson, do you know who I am?"

"Of course," answered Anita.

She knew full well that he was the prominent criminal trial lawyer who headed the Trial Lawyers Action Committee. Every gift and transaction made under the aegis of the TLAC passed through his office, and it was his job to maintain the cash reserves. Every political candidate or special-interest lobby the organization backed spun off from his master plan. He waved his hand around the table to gather in the other men without moving his eyes from her face. "And these gentlemen?"

The old man's arrogant manner made Anita think twice before responding. She knew the old codger would choke on his tongue if he knew about her affair with his political ace in the hole. Maintaining her composure, she smiled mockingly at Robert, almost giving a voice to her thoughts. "Maybe I don't know everybody here," she announced. "I'm sure I know you from somewhere. Do you remember where?"

Robert forced a tight smile. "I remember exactly—like it was yesterday."

The old man coughed violently on a drop of inhaled phlegm. He groped for a crystal glass and cleared his throat with a slow sip of water. The backs of his hands were spotted and wrinkled, and his nails were a shade of yellow. Anita saw one of his eyes briefly magnified through the side of the glass. *The bloated old goldfish can't possibly know*, she thought, but she was unsure.

As the old man wiped his mouth with his napkin, his sonorous breathing was hard to discern from a moist, throaty laugh. "For obvious reasons, I'll spare the introductions. We're all bedfellows, you know."

Griffin crouched sullenly as if he knew her secret. Anita felt flush with embarrassment at the old man's lecherous choice of words and wondered how they could know. *It was only one night*, her conscience screamed, as the mild nausea she had been experiencing for the past several days returned in a sudden wave. Her hands flew to her stomach, and she could barely keep from bolting out of the booth.

The old man eyed her sharply. "We're all family, if you prefer."

When he laughed again, Anita pushed her cocktail away and rested her hands on the edge of the table. It angered her to see the cartoonish lawyer with the high forehead mutely twiddling his thumbs. She glanced quickly at Griffin's nerve-racked face. "What do you want from me?" she asked brusquely, challenging the old man.

"Have you been reading the papers?"

"Yes," she answered simply.

"And what do you see?"

Only Anita noticed Robert swallowing hard, but she felt no sympathy. "I see that our Democrats are losing ground in the polls. Especially some."

"Anyone who takes a stand against tort reform is down in the polls," the old man sputtered, no longer able to contain his ire. "People are calling candidates' offices wanting to know where their sympathies lie on the issue. And, I might add, some very private arrangements are becoming uncomfortably public! Justifying every dollar could get sticky."

Outwardly Robert remained placid, but Anita knew he feared being caught on the wrong side of an important issue. The unpopular health care bill was being branded as the Democrats' responsibility. Because of Hartley, the public was growing more sympathetic to the plight of the doctor. Their backs were up against the wall. Lawyers were getting rich at their expense. The health care insurance conglomerates were squeezing for profits.

"Hartley is hurting us all," said Robert bitterly.

"I share your passion for winning elections," Anita said coldly. "I'm a Democrat, but I'm also a lawyer. Obviously, Hartley has hurt me on many fronts, including some you can't see." Her jade-green eyes sharpened. "Some fronts should count for more—shouldn't they, Congressman?"

Robert pulled lightly at his collar. "I'm not giving up."

The cartoonish lawyer made no effort to soften the arrogant edge in his voice. "Without Hartley, this tort-reform movement will run out of steam. Doctors have no organization. They have no backing. They'll do as they've done in the past, harmlessly cancelling non-urgent checkups or withholding prescriptions. But eventually they'll go back to work. Few voters will remember the effects in the long run."

The old man's sausage-shaped fingers drummed on the table. His face was deep red. "Don't be a fool," he said, rebuking the lawyer for his unconcerned optimism. "This election might crush us!"

Griffin sat up abruptly. "Tell me how an assailant wielding a handgun can be cast in the public eye as a victim?"

"You tell me!" said the old man.

"Yes, he's touched off an avalanche of support. Health-care workers are starting to picket on the courthouse and capitol lawns. Doctors are programming their answering machines to tell their patients how to vote. We've got to do something about it!"

"You've got to do something about it! You're the state prosecutor! This man Hartley is a serious threat, and he needs to be locked away!"

"People are getting angry, and they're getting angry with us," added Robert.

Anita smiled slightly. Hartley was getting under someone else's skin as well as her own. "Don't look at me," she said with an innocent air. "I'm merely the victim of a crime. I'm a witness. He's the one trying the case."

The state's attorney glared with open hostility. The cartoonish personal-injury lawyer fidgeted nervously. Robert suppressed his apprehension that his interests no longer dovetailed so neatly with the ACTL and his voters. A lost election at age fifty-two would mean the end to his congressional career. But fear couldn't stop him from sneaking a glance at Anita.

The old man clapped his hands together with a crack. "We need solidarity!" He turned toward the congressman and smiled reassuringly. "We have this good man to support. He'll hold strong if we do."

Given Robert's narrow margin in the polls, Anita knew that she could end his career in a minute. She shot him a fleeting smirk as the old man turned and pointed a fat finger at Griffin. "I've spent great sums of money to keep this tort system in place. If those caps pass..." he fumed, letting his implied menace unfold. "You better silence this Hartley!"

Griffin's sullen composure disintegrated. "I've got it covered," he said. "He's charged with attempted murder, and he's not even represented by a proper criminal lawyer. He'll do his time."

"He better do time! I'll take him down myself if you don't," said Anita fiercely.

"Maybe you should have lunch with the judge," suggested the cartoonish lawyer to the old man.

The abrupt show of anger pleased the old man. "We will have lunch," he said, grinning. He knew the situation had become a game. Detached from his worries, he studied the black-and-white photos over the booth. "I just love Chicago politics," he admitted. "Look at those pictures. The mayor. The chief of police. The favorite alderman. Everyone's happy. It's democracy in action. Even people with bad teeth are smiling as if they don't have a care in the world. Everyone understands what's at stake."

Anita nodded absently as she pressed a hand low on her abdomen to calm a throbbing discomfort. Robert rocked forward with concern at the signs of strain he saw in her face. "Are you okay?" he asked, momentarily forgetting his self-interests.

"She'll be all right," said Griffin, narrowly.

"Yes," said the old man in a conciliatory tone. "In a few weeks, the poster boy will be locked up where he belongs, and things will get back to normal. We'll have three months before the elections to straighten this out."

Robert worked at the gold band around his ring finger. The old man breathed deeply and swiveled his body to get a better look at Anita. An apologetic smirk flitted across his face. "It's a shame such a beautiful woman got mixed up in all this. Doctors are book-smart—but they're otherwise stupid. Limitations on physician liability won't bring down their malpractice premiums or save patients money. The only impact of tort reform would be increasing insurance company profits. That's why every time there's a bear market, tort reform becomes such an issue. They're recouping their losses by squeezing it out of the doctors. The government would have to step in with fixed prices to stop that. And mind you, Ms. Johnson. This system's been working for two hundred years, and I'll suffer no reform on my watch. Mark my words—I'll do whatever it takes." He laughed coarsely as he wiped his mouth with a white linen napkin. "Now please excuse the congressman and me, because we can't stay and chat. This early in the day, we would look terrible together in a black-and-white photo."

Chapter Thirty-Four

Fall was coming sooner than usual. The earth was bone-dry and leathery tree leaves hung stiffly from the branches. Hartley was glad to be home but nervous that there were only three weeks left to prepare for the trial. Evan lay prone on the bedroom floor with his chin cradled in his palms, watching his father shave. "So, Dad," he asked, "when you start working, are you going to work on the weekends?"

"I don't know yet. Things are up in the air."

"Wouldn't you rather stay home?"

When Hartley wiped away the residual lather from his face, he was pleased with what he saw in the mirror. The circles under his eyes had lightened. The deep crease over his nose had softened. The tiny crossing lines of his fresh scar enhanced his face rather than marred it. "I can do both," he said.

Celeste entered the bathroom and set the clothesbasket on the vanity. "How'd you sleep, Roger?"

Hartley grinned widely. "I didn't have any nightmares."

"Dad's going back to work," said Evan, standing to peer through the window at the scene in front of the house. "Don't those people ever go home?"

Hartley placed his head next to Evan's. From his vantage point, he observed tall antennas rising above television trucks and reporters broadcasting outside the front gate. "They must know we're home. But why are they still taking such interest? They seem more preoccupied with my fate than I am."

"Back to doctoring?" asked Celeste joyfully, as she pulled a cluster of white socks from the clothesbasket. "Let's hope so. I want our life back."

"Me, too!" He pulled a pristine pair of suede bucks out of a shoebox and eagerly slid the laces through the eyes.

"It does me good to see you do that," said Celeste.

"Hand me one of those white pairs of socks."

"You can't wear those with white."

"I think I can," he answered. "Today I'm going to see Hawkins. I hope he has a plan that fits in with mine." He slipped his feet into the shoes and pulled the ends of the laces, tying them into small loops. Standing straight, he looked in the mirror and then took a confident step toward his wife. He kissed her lightly on the cheek.

"Thanks for the new shoes," he said, beaming down at his feet with a joyful, infectious grin.

"Don't thank me. I found them at the front door."

"Really? I wonder who left them there."

"Him!" said Evan.

Hartley immediately returned to the window, but no one was there.

Hawkins's office door was propped open by a thick law textbook. Hartley peered timorously around the jamb to see his attorney bent over a mountain of paperwork, deeply intent on what he was reading. When he knocked gently, it aroused Hawkins with a start.

"Hartley!" he said, rising and extending a hand. "How was your trip to the Outer Banks? What was the highlight?"

"We went to Kill Devil Hills and saw the Wright brothers' plane."

"Ahh," exclaimed Hawkins. "Their friends said they couldn't do it, but they did it anyway. That must've taken some guts."

"They certainly were pioneers." Hartley stepped comfortably through the clutter of law books and took his place in the chair. "Bless you for that suggestion, Ernie. I feel like the Gulf Stream dissolved away a part of me that I won't miss."

"What part is that?" Hawkins probed approvingly.

"I discovered a person could lose sight of the forest among the trees. And oddly enough, it feels like that's the whole point. Maybe it's not the same for you, but too much time studying and practicing your profession to the exclusion of normal life knocks you down a peg. It may be in my profession that socially interesting doctors become less interesting, regular doctors become nerds, and those who start as nerds become duds."

"Dedication never makes you a dud, Roger. Don't give up your ideals—just your search for perfection."

"I'm finding a balance and maybe cultivating a healthy detachment. I know I can't fix everybody." Hartley's face relaxed into a genuine smile. "I think I'm going to enjoy being a doctor again—if that's even possible after a felony. Can I practice medicine if I'm convicted?"

Hawkins studied his client's face carefully. "It's reviewed on a case-by-case basis. I would assume it will be difficult."

"But regardless, we're going to win, right? Then I won't have to worry about it."

"Right now I'm not sure I'm the right attorney for this criminal trial. You've seen what's been happening!"

"I see that the Cubs have regained first place. That's it."

"You haven't been reading the papers or watching the news?"

"We were castaways. That was your prescription, and it was a good one."

Hawkins's brow furrowed. He picked up a copy of the *Washington Post* and threw it across his desk onto Hartley's lap. "Your trial's escalated into national news! Doctors are starting to demonstrate all over the country. The editorial pages are choked with opinions. Politicians! Lawyers! Insurance companies! Everyone's blaming one another to divert public rage. Civil rights advocates are placing full-page advertisements in the *Times*. This thing has exploded and you've been the center! You don't know any of this?"

"How could I know? No television. No radio. No newspapers. And I haven't talked to the press—just as you ordered."

Hawkins leaned on his elbows and stared at Hartley with disbelief. "The doctors are rallying around you, and it's putting people in the legal community on edge," he said pointedly. "The bar association called and pressured me to defer your case to the public defender. They don't think I'm qualified to try the case."

"Are you abandoning me?"

"I simply have to be honest," he said. "This is a bigger groundswell than I imagined, and I must say this gives me butterflies. I don't have the trial and jury specialists to help you get ready for this big of a trial. It would be all our own preparation."

"What am I, the poster boy for tort reform?" said Hartley with some ire. Struggling with choosing indifference, he gazed through the dirty office window into a narrow alley. A pigeon stood on the sill and pecked at the window. "No one can make me personally responsible for fixing the system," he said. "I've learned my lesson. They can pick somebody else."

"It's too late, Roger. The doctors are rallying around you. Whether you like it or not, you're the lightning rod—the match to the powder keg. We're looking at the broadest walkout of doctors in the history of medicine."

Hartley gripped the arms of the chair. His breathing grew shallow, and sweat beaded on his forehead. "I think you can do it," he said. "I won't expect miracles, but I will enjoy them if they come."

"I don't know if you'll get a fair trial," admitted Hawkins.

"I'll take my chances. The case is decided by a jury of laypeople—right? Isn't it public opinion?" When Hartley looked out the window, there were three pigeons on the sill. He looked at Hawkins in earnest. "Remember the Wright Brothers," he said. "That must have taken some guts."

Thinking of how hard it was for a jury of laypeople to decide a malpractice case based on facts, Hawkins grumbled. It was frightening to think that the outcome of a jury trial reflected the litigation skills of the lawyers more than the facts of the case and the guilt or innocence of the defendant. "And I might say the same about you," he answered. "This trial will take guts."

The clarity of the moment made Hawkins shiver. He stood up behind the desk, grinning widely. He couldn't have explained the feeling that was coming over him, but he was beginning to appreciate what it meant to be trying a case like Hartley's. The professional and political implications might not be good, but if he stayed in medical malpractice law, what doctor wouldn't want him on his side? "This is a journey," he said.

"Then you'll do it?" asked Hartley.

"With pleasure," answered Hawkins. "Will you?"

"I'll finish what I've started," answered Hartley. "But I'm not ready to protest. Civil disobedience is a media event that I'm unprepared for. For starters, I suffer from stage fright. But mostly, I've put my anger behind me. I'm quite simply a committed doctor who intends to remain in the profession. But who are we up against in this?"

"Look at this list of campaign contributors, and you'll see." Hawkins shuffled through a pile of papers at the back of his desk and handed a long list to Hartley. He sat back contemplatively, awaiting his client's reaction.

"Who's the TLAC you highlighted at the top of the list?"

"The Trial Lawyers Action Committee. It's a political action committee representing trial lawyers. They lobby Congress and contribute big money to candidates who take their position in political races."

"Tort reform, I suppose?" said Hartley.

"The TLAC is the main reason tort reform stalls."

Hartley scanned the rest of the page, bewildered by the size of the figures. Lawyers and law firms had contributed more than two hundred million dollars to presidential and congressional candidates, with Democrats benefitting from the vast majority of those dollars. He shook his head with disgust. "It's all about money."

"Money buys votes and votes buy favors. The topic is near and dear to trial lawyers' hearts, as you can see. Who knows how much they'll cough up for Obama and the Democrats in 2012? They're hell-bent on regaining majority."

"Where's the AMA on this list of campaign contributions?" asked Hartley.

A sympathetic look from Hawkins confirmed Hartley's suspicion. "They're on there—but farther down. You doctors are completely outgunned!"

"Please," said Hartley. "Don't call us 'outgunned.'"

Hawkins laughed. "The AMA has been losing members in droves. Less than twenty percent of doctors belong. That's the difference. Trial lawyers support political activist groups that defend their status quo. Incomes are at stake! Tort cases bring nice paydays. Every one of you should belong to the AMA. They would have money to mount advertising campaigns. Do radio spots. Bombard lawmakers with letter-writing campaigns."

"We're busy caring for patients," complained Hartley.

"Too busy to contribute money?"

"We don't have any money," said Hartley with disgust. "This country has too many lawyers."

"One point three million last count, but there are a lot of doctors, too," reassured Hawkins. "This whole doctors' revolt is being organized through social networking sources like Facebook and Twitter. They just needed a voice, and you're it. Why do you think the state's attorney is sticking you with attempted murder when the charge should be simple aggravated assault? You're a galvanizing force for a league of protestors. They hope to squelch your influence for a long time."

Hartley sat back and grinned. "But I'm no longer that angry," he said.

"Well—if that's not the darnedest thing," said Hawkins. "Two weeks ago I wanted to curb your anger, and now I'm trying to fire it back up. Don't let the pilot light go out in your brain. Doctors need someone to rally around."

"I'm not leading a revolution," said Hartley. "True—the system needs fixing, but that's not my job! My job is fixing people, not politics. And quite simply, when has any one man ever made a real difference?"

Hawkins lips parted with a smile. "Don't get me wrong, Roger. You did something truly egregious, and you may be punished. But a lot of people are following your case, and their numbers are growing. Just open your eyes and take a look. You wouldn't be the only man in history to rise up against injustice."

Hartley fidgeted uncomfortably and gazed out the window at the feather-worn pigeons. "But how can we defend what I did? Do you think a jury will sympathize?"

"Will they believe that doctors save lives, not threaten them? With that in mind, I hope you don't mind if I fall back on a psychological syndrome. I found something similar to post-traumatic stress disorder called intermittent explosive disorder. It is documented that you had a witnessed panic attack at the arraignment."

"You mean temporary insanity? I'm crazy? That's a charming defense."

"Face it, the diagnosis fits the climate. Your integrity and professionalism were under attack. Your livelihood was jeopardized. You reacted with justifiable rage."

"Please, don't fall back on mental illness! Those kinds of diagnoses don't go away when we're done using them."

"Then we play our cards the best way we can," said Hawkins with dashed optimism. "Obviously there's more here than pointing a gun at a lawyer. While in some ways I'd like to show your actions are justifiable, I don't think Judge Gadboy will allow a criminal case to become a referendum for malpractice law."

Hartley sank gloomily in his chair. "I'll do whatever I have to. But aren't you worried that you'll piss off your TLAC friends? I'm sure you're on the Christmas card lists of a few lawyer buddies."

"My friends are my friends," laughed Hawkins. "But at the end of the day the plaintiff's lawyers and I aren't so chummy."

"But politically you could get into trouble. There's politics involved here."

"What are they going to do—audit my taxes? Don't feel for me, Roger. I'll sleep great for a change."

Hartley gazed at his sturdy lawyer in awe. There was so much about Hawkins that he didn't know. "Do you mind if I ask you a personal question?" he said.

"Please do," he answered.

"How did you break your nose?"

Hawkins smiled so widely that it accentuated the twist in his nose. "Everyone wonders. It was broken by an opening door—but I usually keep that to myself. People should call out a warning when they enter a room so violently." He stood behind his desk. "Roger, why don't we meet here in my office every day at ten to prepare. We only have a couple of weeks."

Hartley nodded and collected himself.

"But Roger, please be careful. I've got a funny feeling that the seas won't stay as tranquil as they were off the Outer Banks."

"Don't worry yourself," answered Hartley with a satisfied grin. "These days I take those funny feelings to heart."

CHAPTER THIRTY-FIVE

The meetings with Hawkins never turned out quite the way Hartley expected. Squinting into the sunlight just outside the lawyer's office, he glanced nervously down State Street, trying to recall where he'd parked the Suburban.

"Be careful?" he repeated.

Wondering why the warning made him uneasy, he took a few cautious steps toward the parking lot a few blocks away. The elevated train tracks cast a dark shadow, and a rare summer breeze blowing off Lake Michigan made the day colder than he remembered. He hunched his shoulders defensively as a screeching train passed over his head. The high-pitched grinding of metal on metal echoed between the buildings, and he dodged a shower of sparks that fell from the electrified rail. Dust swirled around his feet. He hesitated at the edge of the curb, fighting off a vague unnamable fear that was created by Hawkins's warning. Hartley had never considered himself paranoid, but nonetheless he was alerted by a sixth sense that someone was coming up quickly behind him. He glanced back over his shoulder, cringing as another train screeched by overhead, and then he emerged into the sunlight. He glanced back once more into the dim urban cavern as he clutched Celeste's keychain more tightly. The small Virgin Mary fit snugly in the palm of his hand.

"Hartley," called a voice.

The tone was low and hollow amid the city noises, hardly distinguishable from a daydream. He loped across State Street bent on ignoring the call, but the voice called again—this time more strongly.

"Dr. Hartley!"

Hobbling across the street was one of his favorite patients. A broad smile beamed on his face.

"I thought that was you," said the man breathlessly.

Hartley heaved a sigh of relief. "Nate, what are you doing here?"

"I'm making my rounds at the wholesalers. You're on Jewelry Row. This is my turf," he said proudly, spreading his arms wide as if to indicate that this street was his kingdom. "How in God's name are you?"

They shook hands heartily. "Funny, I was just wondering that myself."

"Of course we all heard what happened," said Nate. "And I just want you to know that I support you a thousand percent. I'm loving all the editorials." He chuckled. "It's about time someone decided to do something. I'm glad it was you."

"I'm not," said Hartley.

"This health care system is crazy these days. It's not what I'm used to. I tell people, 'That's my doctor!' when I see your articles."

"Nate, you shouldn't be running like that. Your heart..."

"And it ain't gettin' no better, neither. That new doctor I'm seeing don't care. He asks questions and types in his 'electronic records.' But we never talk like you and me used to. You're the only doc I felt ever gave a damn about me." Nate's face brightened with embarrassment, and he wiped his mouth to scrub away the swear word. "Pardon my French. But I'm excited to see you. You're looking well—all things considered."

"Thank you, Nate. To hear you say that means a lot."

"No, thank you! You were more like a friend than a doctor."

Hartley smiled so warmly his eyes burned. He wanted to look away to hide a faint tear, but Nate held his gaze like a magnet. "When are you coming back to work?" he asked. "Soon, I hope."

"With a little luck, and a prayer, I'll be back when this is over."

His optimism straightened Nate's posture. His mouth curled into a wide smile. He stepped closer and gently touched Hartley with a finger on his chest. "Do me a favor, Doc," he said quietly. "Come to my jewelry store in the next couple of days. Pick out a little something for your wife. It will be on me. I'll bet she could use cheering up."

"Nate, I..."

Nate held up his hand to stop Hartley from objecting. "No, no, no! Helping you would do my heart good. Please! You'd be doing me a favor."

"You're right," Hartley confessed. He took Nate's hand and searched his face for clues to what made him so different from his newer patients. "My wife has been through a lot, Nate. And so far she's still standing strong. If it will do your heart good, I'll be happy to accept."

"Thanks, Doc. I'll see you then in the next couple of days. Don't let me down."

Hartley watched his long-standing patient disappear up the stairs to the train platform. He fought a palpable sense of emptiness when Nate was gone.

Chapter Thirty-Six

Anita glanced nervously up the wide stairs that led into the Empire Room of the Palmer House Hotel. From the cocktail area of the main lobby, she guessed from the deafening applause that the room was filled to capacity. Once a year the TLAC, the Trial Lawyers Action Committee, hosted a regional fund-raiser to entice the area's most prominent attorneys into joining the political arena. The gala rolled out the red carpet for politicians who were sympathetic to the legal agenda of the TLAC and featured national speakers on topics germane to their cause. The contenders were out in full force. Health care was taking center stage in this presidential election year, and defending their various positions had depleted all candidates' coffers.

A group of tuxedoed men pushed through the cocktail area and led their elegant wives up the stairs. Anita stood at the bottom of the stairs off to the side, hoping that no one would notice her clandestinely watching a glad-handing candidate. This evening Robert was selling his bill on health care reform, and his platform was the topic of every discussion within earshot. Listening intently, Anita struggled to control her emotions, often clenching her fists and resisting the urge to abandon her plan. If he had seen her, Robert was deft at hiding it. He broke with a small group of men and moved toward the stairs. Anita fretted momentarily. Not knowing what she would say, she worried that she had made a mistake in seeking such a public encounter. The uncomfortable Sunday-morning meeting with the old man from the TLAC was the last time they had spoken, and Robert's cues had been mixed. She could no longer wait to find clarity concerning what direction their relationship was going. There was no turning back. Feigning casual confidence, she spoke in a bright voice as he passed up the stairs.

"So you're the keynote speaker, Congressman."

"Anita Johnson," Robert said with surprise.

If there was guilt in Robert's heart, his face didn't show it. He reached out his hand as though he hadn't seen her in ages. Anita offered her own hand limply, holding her arm close to her body and making him stretch farther to grasp it. As best she could, she pretended to be a passing acquaintance.

"Yes," he said brightly, casting an edgy glance at the two men who waited for him a few steps above. "I'm honored to speak to this august gathering. The TLAC offers huge support."

"Then you must be doing well in the polls," she said with a hint of sarcasm.

Robert beamed a confident smile. "No Democrat is doing well in the polls. You would know about that. You faced the murderous doctor yourself."

"You're right, I faced him all by myself," she said pointedly. "I should get a Purple Heart—not a black-and-blue one."

The congressman recoiled, struggling to guess what she had on her mind. Money was one thing, but Anita's version of revenge might be different. "I share your pain," he said awkwardly. "Hartley is getting more press than any of us these days. I hope that doesn't last much longer." Nervously he glanced at the two men who had impatiently advanced another step toward the top. "I'll meet you in there in a minute," he said to them.

Anita laughed after the two men had gone. "I see this campaigning has been rough," she said. "At least the discussion has been on the issues and not focused on digging in others' closets for skeletons. If that were the case, you might not fare well."

Robert wiped his mouth as if to hide his uncertainty. "If these doctors' rallies don't blow up any bigger, I'll make it. I bet it's been rough for you, too."

"It doesn't feel good to go through it without support."

"I'm sorry," he said. "But thank you for coming. I don't blame you for being angry with me, but it's nice that you came to support the cause."

Anita smiled stiffly. "I didn't have much of a choice," she said coldly. "Your messages haven't been clear. In fact, they've been so indiscernible and mixed that I feel like rooting against you. It might bring me more joy to root for the underdog."

"You may get your wish," he said sorrowfully. "I'm running behind the Republican now. My people are good at fund-raising, but the doctors are doing well at getting their message out. Seventy percent of the grassroots population is now in favor of tort reform."

"I must say their passion is admirable," replied Anita. "It's certainly more passion than you have been showing to win my vote."

Robert stifled an uncomfortable laugh. "Stay on board. This election will be easier for me to bear if I know you're behind me."

"Stay on board? I'm behind you? Those are odd choices of words." As applause spilled out from the Empire Room and flowed down the steps, Anita added a brittle laugh. "Win or lose—I won't take you back."

Robert tucked his chin and reached out his arm, but his hand fell short of touching her. Instead he grabbed the banister as if he were off balance. "It's not as you think, and I'm sorry," he said with sincerity. Their eyes locked briefly. He turned abruptly and climbed the stairs two at a time.

CHAPTER THIRTY-SEVEN

The house felt like a fortress, with hungry reporters descending upon Hartley every time he stepped out the door. Much of the day he was occupied with devising ways to outsmart and avoid them. All he could hope for was that his infamy would die down after the trial.

"You told the kids not to talk to reporters, didn't you?" he asked Celeste.

"They're sick of them, too. They haven't been able to play in the yard since this whole thing began. Can you imagine them pumping a child for information?"

"I'm frightened to face them, too," he admitted. "I'm afraid they take things out of context and spin stories to show me in the worst possible light."

"How many of them are there right now?" she asked.

Hartley took up his lookout position by the edge of the drawn dining-room curtain. "I see only two right now. They look like they're hoping for bad news to report."

"Bad news sells papers."

"Then I hope they're selling a lot to the lawyers." He withdrew his finger, and the curtain fell back in place. "The pushy little guy with the big lips is out there, and the older guy with the tie. Why does he always look so fresh? It's a hundred degrees out there, for Christ's sake."

"The polite guy? The one with the tie? I wonder if he left your new shoes?"

Hartley gave a mystified chuckle. "They'll do anything for a story. I've got to push past them one more time. Today is my last meeting with Hawkins."

Hartley kept his head down as he neared the front gate, struggling momentarily with hands full to swing the gate open with his foot.

"Can I give you a hand?" asked an affable voice in the morning quiet.

Hartley's head jerked up in surprise. The reporter wearing a tie stood politely just outside the fence, freshly shaven and neatly dressed. Up close he didn't look anywhere near the age that Hartley had guessed. His wrinkle-free face was good-natured, and he wore an agreeable smile.

Trying not to give him further reason to speak, Hartley answered hesitantly, "I think I can get it, thank you." But as he continued to struggle, he looked up with a timid grin. "I guess I do need some help."

The reporter obliged silently and remained at his post just outside the fence. "I see you are wearing your new bucks," he said, nodding pleasantly. "They look good on you."

Hartley stopped at the gate, face-to-face with the reporter. He felt oddly comfortable in his presence. "How did you know I needed new shoes?" he asked.

The man laughed. "I'm a good observer," he said.

Hartley eyed the man with uncertainty, but his kind expression changed his suspicion to gratitude. "Thank you," he said. "They fit comfortably, just like my old ones. What newspaper or TV station do you work for?"

"Oh, I don't work for anyone in particular," he answered, expressing more amusement. "One could say I'm a freelancer. I'm glad I could be of some help." The reporter's softly spoken words rang true, and it was Hartley's turn to nod graciously.

"Will you be around when we get back?" Hartley asked.

"I'm always around," he said. "I have been wondering why you bought the gun. It really hasn't been answered in anyone's story."

Hartley closed the gate with a clank. "Thinking back I don't know," he answered. "I had no reason. I wasn't myself."

"That was my guess," said the man as he stepped aside.

To Hartley's amazement, the other reporters and camera crews hadn't seemed to notice him leaving, and he relaxed. "Nice tie," he said.

"Why, thank you. It's a Countess Mara. It is the closest thing I can find to my age," he smirked.

During the long hours of preparation with Hawkins, Hartley wished that he were grooming for a malpractice trial. He would be better equipped. Often, he thought of Moll and how he had been driven forward by his spite and obstinacy. He understood Moll, but his understanding was lost in his anger.

"This isn't a tort case, Roger. Those two boxes of Moll's hospital records next to my desk are garbage. There are no gray areas here, except maybe what you were planning on doing with that gun," Hawkins said now.

"That seems to be everybody's concern today," answered Hartley. "A reporter asked me the same question when I left the house."

Hawkins's eyes opened with a start. "You didn't discuss it, did you?"

Hartley sensed that why he had bought the gun was important in both the criminal and spiritual worlds. "No, I didn't have an answer," he said. "But I think he knew by my reaction. I truly didn't have a plan."

"Good. But the real question in this trial is, 'What did you intend to do with that gun?' You might have to admit that you were buying a gun because you were considering suicide."

Suddenly Hartley's whole aspect became gloomy. "But I don't think I considered that," he pleaded, picturing all the happy times he had had in his life.

"Otherwise, we'll have to admit you were buying a gun because you were mad, and see if the jury buys into panic attacks and the intermittent explosive disorder." Hawkins shook his head. "It's your choice."

"That's a fancy name for crazy," said Hartley.

"Another Morton's Fork dilemma," answered Hawkins.

"My life is full of them. What if I'd killed her?"

"Then I wouldn't have taken the case. But knowing you now, I'm sure that you couldn't. We must get the jury to see that. Even if you feel guilty, a trial is not the time to mention that fact. Keep that information to yourself until you're backed into a corner and you have no choice but to reveal it. You don't want to help the prosecution's case at all. But I do have some good news. I've gotten a list of their witnesses. Who is this Dr. Fogg?"

"He's a colleague," he said with a wide smile. "Why would he be on the list?"

"Character reference of a sort. Even though character evidence isn't admissible to show a propensity to commit a crime, Fogg might testify to your state of mind in the hours before the crime. I hope you're friends."

"We've become friends," answered Hartley. "He knows the *mens rea* of all doctors."

Now Hawkins smiled. "Then I will include him in my list of witnesses.

Moll's on there, too, so I guess that means health care is on the agenda. So Roger, the jury will be watching you closely. Don't give them anything with which they can find fault. You want to look clean, neat, and professional. Nothing flashy. You'd be surprised how many physicians disregard this basic rule. And lastly, there is a common misconception among physicians that if they explain things well with intelligent responses, they can prove to the jury that the whole thing was a mistake. The general rule is 'the less you say the better.' There is the potential to do significant damage to your case if you take the stand. So if you do—and I'll let you decide after the prosecution rests its case—it's critical that you perform well. Somehow you'll find the strength to get through it."

CHAPTER THIRTY-EIGHT

Hartley lay on his bed, enjoying what might be his last day of freedom. He imagined living his old life exactly as it had been, but more balanced. "I think I'll take a drive to the hospital," he said to Celeste. "I just want to see it again, in case a miracle doesn't occur."

The car moved forward as if pulled by the force of a great magnet. He eased his foot off the gas pedal and rounded the last corner. The familiar buildings came into view. Hartley's grip quickly tightened on the wheel when he saw a great crowd of people gathered in front of the hospital entrance. Their picket signs stood out boldly. Some had an enlarged image of his face with bold capital letters underneath:

TORT REFORM NOW

With rapidly growing trepidation, he eased the Suburban into the parking lot and edged through the crowd. As the sea of bodies parted reluctantly, angry faces appeared at the windows. "Hey, it's Dr. Hartley!" he heard someone say. The Suburban lurched to a stop, and the circling crowd peered through the windows. Hartley recognized the physicians who had been in practice with him for years, but there were younger doctors with them as well, dressed in white coats still crisp and unstained, their faces fresh and determined. Hartley's eyes landed on Fogg.

The car door was pulled open, and many arms reached in at once to assist Hartley out of the vehicle. "Did you come to join the rally?" he heard among the questions fired at him from every direction. "What are you doing out here, Fogg?" he asked meekly.

"We're supporting you!" many voices answered at once.

"Welcome back, Hartley," others chimed in. "Join the rally!" A burst of cheers erupted.

For Hartley, embarrassment felt the same as a mortal wound. "Where did you get my photograph?" he asked.

"The hospital doctors' directory," answered Fogg proudly.

"It's pretty old," commented the speechless Hartley.

"It's your younger self. It blew up pretty nicely, don't you think?"

Thunderstruck by the development, Hartley gazed with sad eyes at the broad hospital building. A line of patients had formed at the ER entrance, waiting for their turn to be seen. Even from a distance their faces showed pain and distress. "Why aren't you working?" asked Hartley, in a tone that mingled confusion with disappointment.

"We're providing emergency care only," Fogg said with a smile. "We're in this together!"

"What about those people?" asked Hartley incredulously, pointing to the line of unhappy patients.

"Those people aren't sick—there's a skeleton crew triaging those folks."

"They look sick," said Hartley, gazing around. "Where's everyone else?"

"They're at the rallies! We split into shifts. There are some at the courthouse, some at the State of Illinois Building, and those who could went downstate to the Capitol. The hospital's staying on bypass until the end of your trial. Hospitals everywhere are. Mates is at the courthouse right now, addressing the crowd. What do you think of that?"

Hartley broke into a cold sweat. His vision blurred into a kaleidoscopic collage of the angry-faced protesters and the many images of his own face stapled to the ends of long sticks. "These protests have ballooned out of control," he said, almost in a panic. "And I'm responsible. How can I undo what I've done?" Hastily he split the circle of protesting doctors and swung into his car. The hot leather burned. The engine roared. "Don't use my face on those posters," he shouted. "Leave me out of these protests. Go back to work. This isn't my way."

Four blocks from the Cook County Courthouse, traffic suddenly came to a standstill. Hartley was awestruck by the sight of so many doctors dressed in white coats streaming past his car toward the courthouse. Buses were stranded in traffic and unloaded large groups of people at the curb. Police dressed in riot gear were spaced at short intervals like fence posts, their serious faces showing above clear plastic shields. Behind them was a barricade, blocking traffic to the congested courthouse front commons. He turned down an alley and abandoned the Suburban in a small lot off to the side. His eyes darted wildly in all directions. His picture was everywhere, and the sight caused mixed emotions of elation and terror.

Hartley stripped off his tie and reached around to the back seat for a hat. He opened the glove compartment and pulled the contents onto the floor, grabbing Celeste's sunglasses from the top of the heap. In this disguise, he made his way along the crowded sidewalk with comfort in his anonymity. At times he walked on his tiptoes, gaping at the thousands of doctors crowding the courthouse lawn and spilling into the streets. Some shouted and chanted and waved their fists in response to Mates, who was speaking from a podium at the top of the building's front steps. His clear, booming voice, amplified by loudspeakers, carried into the streets and alleys. Hartley craned his neck to see, but his view was blocked by the myriad of posters mounted on wooden stakes. Most of the messages hit close to home. *Will work for food!* said one. Hartley's heart hammered with the clash between fear and desire. He withdrew into the dappled light of a grand elm tree to watch the protest unfold. From this vantage point, Mates looked like he was realizing his dream. He was standing tall over the podium, and his message rang out through the speakers.

"We're in a medical depression. National health care expenditures have spiraled out of control. Our population is aging. Medicare is broke. Fifty million Americans live without health insurance. Pro bono work is increasing. The high cost of malpractice insurance is driving doctors out of their practices. Many doctors retire early to avoid lawsuits that would bankrupt their personal assets. More and more money is spent on administrative tasks each year. The balancing rewards of remaining in medicine are diminishing. By the year 2025, America will need one hundred and sixty thousand more primary-care and geriatric physicians. President Obama and the Democrats need to realize that health care reform must come as a package. To attract brilliant young minds into medicine and keep us practicing to the age of retirement, we need to make the system endurable. Tort reform with caps on pain and suffering would make the system endurable. Today doctors have voiced their opinion. Seventy percent of Americans now believe caps should be a part of health care reform. The answer is evident. It's time to make our voice heard. Vote for candidates who support tort reform. Unseat those who oppose it. The battle before us will take every soldier."

The burst of heated applause and waving posters made Hartley feel sick to his stomach. Deeply ashamed of his personal role in the unfolding drama, he stepped dizzily into the full sunlight and fled toward his car. He careened off a stocky cameraman, spun, and fell to the ground. "Sorry—I didn't see you," he said, scrambling to pick up Celeste's ill-fitting sunglasses. Almost instantly the cameraman's expression transformed into sheer disbelief. "H-Hartley?" he stammered. His mouth swayed open. "Hartley!" the cameraman repeated, scrambling to take aim with his camera.

Hartley didn't attempt to put Celeste's sunglasses back on. He removed his hat and lightly brushed himself off. Arms thrust forward from every direction to shake his hand. Others clapped heavily on his back. It was too late to run. "Speech!" cried a voice from the crowd. As more and more protestors took up the call, the plea rose to a swift crescendo and became a pulsing demand. The sea of white coats parted, and a path opened all the way to the top of the courthouse steps. Hartley paused fretfully, shying away from the pictures that waved atop the many long sticks. The microphones seemed to bristle from the podium. He cast off his stage fright, took a deep breath, and slowly walked forward. Mates met him halfway up the stairs and congratulated him effusively. "Look at these doctors! Listen to their applause! You did something!" He reached out and grabbed Hartley's arm. "This day has given us hope."

As he reached the top of the stairs, Hartley's chest constricted, and his breathing grew shallow with stage fright. The scene was unlike anything that he could ever have imagined, and having no idea what he was going to say tripled his terror. He steadied himself by grasping both sides of the podium and peered over the sea of white coats as far as he could see. To him the crowd of many thousands seemed like many hundreds of thousands, because all eyes were riveted on his face. They were thinking and acting as one giant body. When a few started chanting, others joined until the air was filled with a deafening roar.

"Hartley… Hartley… Hartley!"

Around the fringe of the crowd were large groups of dark-suited men. Hartley noticed their posters, the kind Hawkins had mentioned, emblazoned with pictures of sorrowful malpractice victims. Their placards and banners shook fiercely, blaming the medical profession for a multitude of injustices and innumerable misdeeds. Hartley centered his eyes and mustered the courage to speak.

"O foolish Galatians! Who hath bewitched you?"

The crackling loudspeakers distorted Hartley's opening words from Paul's epistle in the Bible, which came into his mind as if written there by some nurturing hand. The amplifiers were lowered, and his voice became stronger. In the brief silence, a lone helicopter flew in tight circles overhead, accentuating the gravity of the moment.

"I see my face on your posters, but let's be truthful. You have yielded to the influence of a false teacher. Committing a violent crime doesn't qualify me to become a symbolic leader, and I am no hero. I acted wrongly. If the innocent lawyer who I attacked was with us here today—I would tell her I'm sorry and ask for forgiveness with you as my witnesses. Anger is not my way. I would never willingly do something that damages the reputation of our profession."

Hartley stood tall over the sea of white coats, wondering how many doctors around him had been sued without cause or were financially ruined by a jury's unpredictable outcome. His stage fright was gone, and he continued with more conviction.

"One hundred percent accuracy for doctors is an impossible dream. To err is human, as I have witnessed. Medical mistakes are inevitable. Doctors need a medical malpractice system that accepts these realities without assigning blame and promoting fear. At present, they are trapped in a witch-hunt environment." Hartley paused with the crowds show of agreement. "If the system were fair, doctors would have little quarrel when reasonable settlements rectified our mistakes and all bad outcomes. Malpractice insurance would serve as intended. Compensate patients quickly, no matter who was at fault. Make a fair system that fosters openness and honesty. Address medical errors with admission. Let patients and families hear clearly why a problem occurred and how the process will be corrected to prevent future injury. An honest, heartfelt apology may alleviate resentment more than a long-delayed settlement. But within the current system, both admissions and apologies might imply guilt."

As the resounding applause confirmed that many others had walked down his path, Hartley was suddenly proud to be a part of a peaceful movement toward a universal goal of health care reform. He leaned into the podium. "Like the House Speaker from Maryland has said: 'Tort reform shouldn't be about doctors. It shouldn't be about lawyers. Tort reform should be about patients.' We need a medical-legal system that preserves the honesty and integrity of both law and medicine. Trust in our systems will promote trust amongst us all. Take the unpredictability and wackiness out of the system. Establish special medical panels to process patient claims. Make juried medical malpractice trials a thing of the past. Let decisions be made by judges chosen on merit and medical-legal knowledge. Settlements should be rapid, with generous compensation for economic losses and medical bills. But for meaningful change to occur, our current legal adversaries must accept us in partnership."

The subsiding agitation among the groups of lawyers and counter-protesters around the periphery was obvious, but Hartley did not feel satisfied. The doctors had stopped waving their posters. An aura of hope suffused the crowd. But Hartley remained bothered by the long line of patients he had seen extending from the ER door of his hospital.

"Hope is as essential as oxygen. We must move forward through other channels than this. Please... Return to your practices and go back to work. We are the guardians of our nation's health. Let lawyers be the guardians of fairness. Without both groups working together, America cannot be strong."

As a resounding ovation filled the air from all directions, Hartley stepped from behind the podium, glad-handing his way down the stairs. Doctors filled in behind him, their energy pushing him forward.

"Dr. Hartley..."

Hartley recognized the voice and searched the crowd vigorously, grinning as if charmed when his eyes fell on the reporter in the tie.

"I guessed you were wearing your new shoes," said the reporter. "Did they feel comfortable during the speech?"

Hartley gazed down to admire his feet. "They fit well. You heard the speech?"

"My views exactly. I even saw a few lawyers clapping. How's your head?"

"Fine. The wound came together nicely."

"Does it hurt to touch it?

"No! It feels soothing to touch it—instantly."

"Fine! Fine indeed! Then I will report in my columns that you're doing just fine. Splendidly indeed."

"Yes—please," said Hartley. "Report the good news."

CHAPTER THIRTY-NINE

From an amber upper window of the great Cook County Courthouse building, Anita Johnson watched over the courtyard. Judge Gadboy's dark chamber was appointed with vintage law items. The judge sank into the worn chair behind his desk. "What's going on out there?" he asked.

"Three or four policemen have encircled Hartley, and they're escorting him through the rest of the crowd. Look at him down there—stirring up those pitiful fools by attacking me from the podium," she said bitterly. She turned away from the window and stepped back into the dimly lit room. Her face was pinched with hatred. Judge Gadboy's hands were folded across his lap, and he rocked back until his chair squeaked. Anita's ire amused him as she moved nervously around the room like a gamecock.

"This seems hard to believe," he said. "A criminal trial is shutting down the whole medical system?"

"How can those doctors support him?" she agreed hotly. "He's a criminal, for God's sake. He attempted murder! And those doctors are packing into that courtyard to hear him like he's some kind of prophet. He should have been held until the trial. He's dangerous."

"Easy, counselor," cautioned the judge. "It would be highly unethical for me to discuss details of a case over which I preside. But pardon if I do make light of your unfortunate personal stake in the matter. This trial has taken on a life of its own. Those doctors out there are trying to save their profession."

"Just like we are," snapped Anita.

"It is a political powder keg, my dear."

Anita plopped into a chair across from the judge's enormous desk. "That Hartley!" Anita seethed ruefully. "Who does he think he is? We're the ones who should be out there protesting with vigor—not that Hartley bastard. It's not right that the whole system's on trial." Anita rubbed her belly, and she grimaced in pain.

"Tort reform," said the judge. "Did you hear the president speak during his last health care address? When the Republicans gave a standing ovation in unison at the mere mention of tort reform, he sat them back down with a smiling deflection—'nah, nah, nah, no, no, no.' He obviously likes his bread buttered."

"But what if this happens? What if we get shackled with caps?" pleaded Anita. "What self-respecting lawyer would represent anyone for the measly payouts they'll get after caps, especially on contingency?"

"What if the claim had some merit? Wouldn't a good lawyer take the case?"

"It wouldn't be worth my time and effort," answered Anita through tight lips.

Judge Gadboy's mouth formed a pout. "Come, come, Counselor Johnson. Money isn't everything."

"Well," she said peevishly. "I for one won't put in the effort."

"Counselor Johnson," cautioned the judge, "the rules of professional conduct require a lawyer to act zealously in the representation of *all* clients. I do hope ethics and professionalism mean something to you."

A thin blue vein in Anita's forehead bulged. "Damn it," she said vehemently. "If he's not found guilty, it's my turn. I'll drain him of every penny in civil court." Anita rose to her feet, canting forward and steadying herself on the judge's desk. Her suddenly perspiring face was drawn with pain.

"You don't look well, my dear. You're pale. Please, sit down a minute. I know this case has caused you undo stress."

Anita forced herself to appear composed, but her stomach churned loudly and again she pressed her hand to her abdomen. "I'll be all right once the trial is over. It's just all those reporters asking me questions day in and day out about the polls. It's as if this was all my fault, and I caused our politicians to fall in the polls."

"The polls?" asked the judge. "Why would you worry about them?"

Her eyes flicked nervously, and then grew soft and pleading. "Judge, this has to turn out as it was supposed to," she said.

"I can't do much but preside," he said in a paternal tone. "You should know that. But I will assure you that I'll do my best to seek justice. Of course, I have some influence during the sentencing."

CHAPTER FORTY

Hartley awakened slowly Monday morning, yielding to the soft sheets and absorbing springs of the mattress. *I did what I did—and I'll live with the consequences*, he told himself, knowing that life was no longer in his own hands. He gazed appreciatively at the cup of hot coffee waiting on the nightstand like a soft morning kiss from Celeste. Thinking that this cup might be his last, he smelled the rich aroma and sipped a tiny taste from the brim. As the caffeine started to work, he rose from the bed and fully opened the curtains. The warm sun angled onto his face. He showered a long time, shaved twice, and dressed in a crisp, button-down shirt under a new beige suit. He sat between the vanities with his favorite red tie spread across his thighs. It appeared threadbare and stained, as if it signified the last vestige of his former self. *I'll keep this as a reminder*, he thought and rose to choose a new tie off the rack. "Are you ready?" asked Celeste, seeing him cinch the knot over the fastened collar button.

"I think I have it now," answered Hartley. "God gave me two eyes and two ears, and now I'm seeing and hearing. The clues have been there all along."

"You were rowing with one oar in the water," she laughed.

Hartley smiled in agreement. "That lawyer I attacked embodied everything that was wrong within me. I'm certain that's the reason I was so angry with her."

"Rosey, how can you say that? You were nothing like her."

"No? Let's compare. She pursued her career as intensely as I pursued mine. I bet she even started out wanting to help people—the ones who had really been injured and harmed—just as I did. I wonder if she felt the same emptiness inside her that I felt at the time."

"She's a Lilith," Celeste said lightheartedly. "Half-human, half-devil."

Envisioning a demonic Anita Johnson preying on helpless, faceless physicians, Hartley's expression remained soft. "No," he said. "She just hasn't been hearing or seeing. Eventually she'll come around."

Chapter Forty-One

Anita Johnson stabbed the elevator button with her French-manicured fingertip. She waited impatiently, her hand touching the thin, gold choker that circled her neck. The fragile interwoven strands gave her face a delicate appearance. "Dress the part of a victim," she recalled Griffin reminding her. She hated the plain, single-color dress that hung on her shoulders, but she knew her part well. There were many counting on her to deliver. To prime her mind with anger, she called back her clear visions of the night spent sipping champagne with Robert, the man she was no longer allowed to be with. She pictured his manicured hands, letting the romantic image morph into Hartley's fingers circling the butt of the handgun, pointing so maliciously at her face. She evoked the terror caused by the loud report and the sound of the shattering mirror as if they were still fresh in her mind. She relived her panic when she dived under the desk and checked her body for blood. "This will be easy," she raged.

The elevator car trembled slightly as it picked up speed down the shaft. Anita was alone with the reflections in the mirrors that surrounded her on all sides. Turning sideways, she straightened her posture. But her body was changing, and she leaned to inspect her hair for signs of gray. She studied her forehead and face, lightly touching the fine wrinkles that surrounded her eyes. As the doors opened, she flew past the doorman, the dull thuds of her frumpy shoes reminding her that she was vulnerable. *The jury*, she thought with annoyance. *They're so unpredictable.*

Chapter Forty-Two

Miles from the courthouse, traffic slowed to a crawl. "Look at this mess!" said Celeste, unsure how to react. "How can we get to the courthouse with all these people blocking the streets?"

"It's a phenomenal feeling," said Hartley playfully. His excitement was tinted with optimism, even in the face of impossible odds. Doctors dressed in white coats were streaming past the Suburban on both sides. Policemen stood by, observing peacefully. "But I still don't think this is the way."

"It looks like this way is working, Rosey. Everybody's orderly. This show of public support has got to help swing a jury. People are always affected with bias, no matter how hard you try to avoid it."

Hartley stared silently out the window for a long time. "Remember my first day in jail?" he asked finally.

"Why would I want to think about that again? We've moved beyond that."

"I mean when you visited me in that awful interrogation room, when I told you that I felt some special purpose reserved for my life. The one I haven't been able to find. Well—I still don't know exactly—but something's emerging, and I can finally trust that it's there. All those years," he reflected. "I'm finally happy to be where I am, and this whole thing could blow it. I know my destiny wasn't to assault a lawyer. I just wish that I could feel better about that. But maybe the mystery won't stay a secret until my bitter end."

"I hope not, Rosey." Celeste laughed lightheartedly. "But expect God to add in some irony. You know He can have a dry sense of humor."

Hartley pushed up through the mass of people that crowded the courthouse steps, paying little attention to the voices and cheers that rang in his ears. He kept his head down, but at the top of the stairs he couldn't resist the thrill of witnessing such a powerful display of solidarity. He turned to momentarily admire the sea of white coats, feeling amazingly gratified. He glanced at the small group of lawyers squeezed far to the left, waving their posters of a grossly deformed malpractice victim that contrasted sharply with his own picture rising above the doctors. The poignant moment struck him with sorrow. With deep regret, he thought of Moll and his horrible systemic lupus. *But this trial is for me alone*, he thought, turning to enter the building. He passed through the metal detectors with somber resignation. Hawkins was waiting, his briefcase tucked tightly under his arm. He pressed close to offer last-minute instructions, but Hartley spoke first. "Are you ready for this?" he asked.

"Everything has come together," said Hawkins excitedly. "I worked all day."

"But I thought you made it a point to never work on Sundays."

Hawkins laughed. "You know what it's like—you get caught up in your work."

"When you're working on something you care about," said Hartley. He turned to Celeste and looked closely into her crystal-blue eyes. He squeezed her hand gently. "I'm in good hands."

A lone tear showed her apprehension.

The courtroom linoleum floor was badly worn. Hawkins headed toward the heavy oak defendant's table located on the right side of the well. Hartley settled cautiously at the edge of the defendant's chair and rested his elbows in the tabletop's smooth indentations, worn by thousands of elbows over the years. He looked around apprehensively, his eyes exploring the massive, tiered magistrate's bench that positioned the judge so he could oversee the whole room. Directly across from Hawkins and Hartley was a raised platform with a broad railing that sequestered twelve empty seats. Hartley imagined the dozen pairs of eyes that would stay focused on his every expression and movement for the duration of the trial.

An atmosphere of intense expectation suffused the room. Behind the heavy wooden banister known as "the bar," sheriff's deputies were wedging people into already overcrowded pew-like benches. Supporters and detractors mixed uncomfortably shoulder to shoulder. Reporters jockeyed for seats near the front. The bailiff and two deputy sheriffs closed the tall doors in the back of the courtroom, pinching off part of the crowd into the hallway. Voices muffled quickly to a low drone.

"All rise. The State of Illinois versus Roger Hartley," proclaimed the bailiff. "The Honorable Judge Gadboy presiding."

The spectators arose from their seats on cue and focused their attention on the judge's stern face as he mounted the steps to take his place behind the high bench. His thick fingers circled the gavel handle, and he hammered in measured strokes, calling the session to order. Hartley drew a deep breath as if the heavy blows were driving nails into his coffin. "Try to relax," whispered Hawkins.

Seating a jury took most of the morning. The bailiff escorted panels of nervous jurors into the jury box, and Hawkins asked them simple questions to determine their social stability. Were they married with families? Did they have jobs? He selected jurors with a stake in their community, such as property owners and businesspeople, who might have been burdened with legal fees in the past. He seemed to make his jury selections with ease, but Griffin took more time in hunting for jurors whom he guessed would be unsympathetic to doctors. Each side rejected the other's choices, and after an hour, the judge showed mounting frustration. With tested patience he cautioned Griffin to limit his liberal use of preemptory challenges. Sternly, he instructed the bailiffs to keep order and quiet the courtroom. To Hartley, the scene seemed surreal. Selecting a jury was almost like casting a movie. Yet these twelve seemingly random people would decide his fate. He relaxed to a degree, but his unease renewed with every veneer. "A bias favoring lawyers over doctors isn't easy to find," whispered Hawkins, casting his eyes to the frustrated Griffin.

Well-practiced in putting on the right face in the courtroom, Griffin loosened his tie a fraction and began questioning the potential jurors less deliberately. He circled and pivoted in front of the jury box without evident indecision until the jury selection was complete. "Look at the jurors and smile," instructed Hawkins as Griffin strode back to his table. "Don't look away for anything. I think we got a fair panel."

Hawkins was especially interested in a well-dressed man seated in the far corner of the back row. He was a small-business owner who might have to provide expensive health care insurance to his employees. A sickly woman next to him probably had a long history of hospitalizations and might have accumulated copious prescriptions and bills, along with a deep mistrust of doctors. There was a housewife in the front row who might be sympathetic to hardship. A well-dressed businesswoman sat to her left. Griffin had worked hard to keep this woman in the jury box, and her vaguely hostile glares at Hartley suggested that she might side with a successful professional woman. There were two attentive African American women, a Hispanic man, and a schoolteacher, all of whom appeared proud to decide a momentous case. But only a thin-faced college professor in the middle of the back row seemed to look upon Hartley with definite sympathy. He wore a tattered tweed jacket that appeared too heavy for a hot August day. He peered over his reading glasses at the crisply dressed lawyers as they scurried about. Hawkins sensed that this juror might hold Hartley's key.

Sternly, the bailiff read the charges. "The charges in themselves do not prove guilt," cautioned Judge Gadboy. "You must start with a presumption of innocence. Listen to the witnesses. Consider the physical evidence. It is your duty to determine the facts from the testimony you hear and the evidence you see and then distill the truth. Make judgment based solely on guilt beyond a reasonable doubt." He carefully explained the Fifth Amendment to the jurors. "The defendant shall not be compelled in any criminal case to be a witness against himself." Hartley stared nervously into the grave faces of the jurors. Thoughts of testifying in his own defense caused heat to rise under his collar and sweat to moisten his face. His mind whirled backward in time to picture the dramatic events that had led up to this moment. Hawkins had instructed him to take the stand if he could, but at that moment, he didn't feel sure.

Rapt attention gripped the audience as Griffin began to deliver a composed opening statement. The state's attorney appeared older and thinner than at the arraignment. His tousled hair was gray at the temples, and dark circles bulged under his eyes. He roved restlessly around the room, laying out an overview of the important facts supporting his case. His hands gestured vigorously to emphasize his promise to prove Hartley guilty of a heinous crime. And each time he underscored a key point, he paced to a new spot on the floor, as if Hartley's guilt were evident from all directions. Finally, Griffin planted his feet in front of the bar. His lips curled into a smug smile as he witnessed telltale expressions on the faces of the jurors.

By closely watching Griffin's performance, Hawkins had learned a great deal. Wearing a faint, unreadable smile, he walked to the exact spot that Griffin had vacated at the bar. The doctor's anger and rage was his backdrop. "I agree that the facts might indeed demonstrate guilt in the defendant. No doubt within his profession there is a general resentment of personal injury lawyers." The gallery stirred with a rippling murmur of surprise that quickly mingled with scorn. Judge Gadboy banged the gavel to call for order. Hartley lowered his face to hide his chagrin. "The defense will admit—right from the start—that the defendant is guilty of possessing a handgun without a license. The defendant is guilty of pointing this weapon at an innocent victim and thereby committing assault. But as you will see, the defendant is innocent of the more severe charge leveled against him—attempted murder. We will establish the defendant had no malice aforethought and confirm beyond a reasonable doubt that the defendant had no specific intent to kill. I will ask the twelve members of this jury to consider the facts very carefully and look beyond what is immediately apparent to see that the defendant was not responsible for his actions at the time the assault was committed. We will argue that Dr. Hartley has selflessly dedicated himself to the welfare of others throughout a long and distinguished career as a healer, and as a faithful servant to society, he paid a personal price. The price of his sanity."

The jury remained staid and gave no outward sign of disapproval or disagreement, but Griffin rose suddenly to his feet, interrupting. "Objection!" he yelled in disbelief, exasperation, and disgust. "Argumentative. The defendant is on trial here! The defense is attempting to switch the focus of the trial away from the accused with an improper opening statement."

Judge Gadboy's fingers drummed on the bench. "Objection sustained. Mr. Hawkins, I caution you to restrict your comments to the matters of the defendant's guilt or innocence. You will not make a travesty of this case by attempting to unravel health care policies."

Hawkins approached the bench and stood at the base of the massive oak tier looking up. Judge Gadboy's eyes were calm and more tolerant than his stern warnings had implied. Hawkins stifled a smile of delight and nodded before he returned to the bar in front of the gallery. His eyes focused as he quickly organized his last thoughts. "Ladies and gentlemen of the jury—I ask you to imagine yourselves in the shoes of the accused. Try to appreciate the pressures and stress..."

"Objection! Mr. Hawkins is making a closing argument and an improper one at that," yelled Griffin. "The defense can't ask the jury to 'imagine themselves in the shoes of the defendant.' The jury has been instructed to consider *only* the facts of the case."

Judge Gadboy glared down from high on the bench. "Objection sustained. Mr. Hawkins, you will abide by the rules of the court."

Affecting humility, Hawkins gazed down at the floor. "Your Honor, I'll rephrase my request. Ladies and gentlemen of the jury, I simply ask you to carefully listen and consider the evidence that will explain the broader context of the defendant's history and his actions that bring us here today. He has been a healer most of his life." Calmly, Hawkins turned and walked past the bench toward the defense's table, appearing to ignore the murmur of the crowd and the sound of the falling gavel. But the emotions were not lost in the jury. "Your Honor," he proclaimed casually, "I have nothing further."

In his opening statement, Hawkins had flouted convention by arguing the case at first chance. Emotions on both sides erupted in the courtroom. Murmuring in the gallery grew heated. But the men in dark suits were the most upset of all. The judge pounded hard with his gavel. "Bailiffs!" he hollered. "If this courtroom won't come to order, I'll close the proceedings. Prosecution, call your first witness!"

Griffin cleared his throat and began calling a parade of minor witnesses. The receptionist in Anita's law firm described Hartley as edgy and tense, as if captivated by a murderous plot. The lawyer who had tackled Hartley into the desk stated the accused was in the process of reaching for the gun on the floor, giving the impression that he planned to use the weapon again. The security guards portrayed the confusion, chaos, and terror created by a man on a shooting spree within a workplace. They described Hartley's behavior as typical of a man bent on revenge. A cohort of arresting officers confirmed that Hartley's apparent anguish stemmed from profound disappointment in failing to accomplish his homicidal plan.

Hawkins followed Griffin's questioning of each witness with strenuous cross-examination of his own to show that Hartley had dropped his weapon voluntarily and that the gun had discharged accidentally upon hitting the floor. But what remained clear was that the whole incident had taken place behind closed doors, before any witness had entered the room.

"The state calls Maxwell Moll."

The people in the gallery craned their necks to observe how Moll looked and acted. He shuffled into the witness stand, with only glints in his eyes showing that he enjoyed his grand stage. Clearly, he was pleased to have a front seat across from Hartley, as if it were his day of retribution. It was hard for Hartley to picture his anger the night of their argument in the ER. The weight of the summons had mostly lifted. He remained stoic during Moll's testimony, even proud that he could look back on his decisions with confidence.

"Did Dr. Hartley change as a physician during the years?" asked Griffin.

"He became short and always seemed rushed. On the last day I saw him, he abandoned me, like he no longer cared."

"Did he say something that showed intent to do harm?"

"When I tried to get him back as a doctor—then he threatened me."

"How did he threaten you?"

Moll felt, rather than pictured, the moments with Hartley. His dialysis shunt bulged like a giant purple vein. "He threatened that he would 'shove a thousand prednisone down my throat.'"

Griffin strutted to the front of the jury box, smiling as if he had emphasized a key point. "Mr. Moll," he said, "Hartley's motive in buying a gun is in question. Did he ever mention to you, in regard to the emotional toll of your lawsuit against him, that he might be thinking of suicide?"

"It wasn't suicide!" sneered Moll. "He wanted revenge."

"Objection!" yelled Hawkins. "Please instruct the witness to answer the question with a 'yes' or 'no' response."

Judge Gadboy sustained the objection, striking the answer from the record and instructing the jury to disregard the opinion of Mr. Moll. Having made his point, Griffin had no further questions. Hawkins approached Moll quickly, asking him to explain how many doctors he had burned through before his relationship with Hartley, how long his other doctors had lasted, and why his relationship with Hartley had endured for nearly ten years. "You wanted to take him back as a doctor?" confirmed Hawkins.

Moll squirmed at the door of an obvious trap. "I did at the time—but never after he threatened me."

"To clarify—you wanted to keep him as your doctor, even after you filed a lawsuit. Wouldn't that imply that Dr. Hartley's behavior wasn't egregious enough to warrant a five-million-dollar lawsuit?"

Griffin objected. "The validity of a civil lawsuit is not in question here and has no relevance."

"But the impact of the lawsuit on the defendant's state of mind is critical in understanding the intent and actions of my client," returned Hawkins. "In that regard, validity is highly relevant and should be addressed."

Moll's eyes darted rapidly around the room. Judge Gadboy's fingers drummed on the bench. He glanced at Hartley and then the gallery. "Sustained," he answered in a subdued tone that carried a hint of dissatisfaction.

Hawkins turned away from Moll and unceremoniously dismissed him from the witness stand. "Then I guess I have no further questions."

The afternoon court session was called to order at one o'clock to the second. Spectators scurried in from the hallway and pushed into any available space. The doors snapped closed and the excited galley quieted down in a hurry. "The state calls Anita Johnson," said Griffin loudly.

Nothing about Anita's appearance was as Hartley remembered. She emerged from a side door in a plain, gunmetal-gray frock unadorned with accessories. Her black hair was pulled into a bun. A fine necklace made her entire aspect seem introverted and meek. She trailed the deputy to the base of the witness stand and swore in, maintaining a stiff, expressionless face. She stepped primly into the witness stand, avoiding all eye contact with Hartley.

"Please state your name," said Griffin.

The shadows under her eyes made it appear as if she had been crying. "Anita Johnson," she answered in a self-conscious timbre.

At a few sarcastic words from the back of the gallery, a small group of spectators started pushing and shoving. The audience turned quickly. Judge Gadboy scowled and pointed his gavel. "Quiet back there," he shouted menacingly. "I'll hold any of you in contempt on an impulse." The commotion ceased immediately. Griffin positioned a floor plan of Anita's law office on an easel between the witness stand and the jury and began to establish the details of the crime scene. He marked where the assailant had stood and highlighted the proximity to the victim. Two plastic bags were selected from the evidence table and held up to the gallery. "This is the evidence," he said, "as identified earlier by a law enforcement agent. A silver-plated revolver bought in an illegal transaction, and the bullet fired from the gun, pried from the wall near where you stood." Anita's hands writhed in the crease of her dress as Griffin asked the judge's permission to unpack the gun. The bailiff inspected the weapon and threaded a leather strap through the barrel to secure it. Griffin captivated the jury with descriptions of the crime steeped in menacing language. He brandished the weapon within a few feet of Anita's face, his lip stiffening in a believable expression of cruelty. Light gleamed off the silver-plated barrel. Anita shrank back in the witness stand, her face re-creating her fear. But at no time did she look directly at Hartley. The jury reacted with unbridled disgust. The businesswoman surveyed Hartley with dismissive scorn. The male juror's faces reflected disapproval. Even the face of the stoic Judge Gadboy betrayed condemnation. Feeling rekindled dishonor at watching Griffin's re-creation of the crime, Hartley glanced nervously at Hawkins. His eyes were fixed on the witness stand. From the side, his crooked nose lent him an aspect of weathered determination that Hartley appreciated and embraced.

"Have you ever seen this weapon before?"

"Yes, that is the weapon of my attacker."

"Ms. Johnson, for the benefit of the jury, would you identify the attacker who brandished this gun in your face and fired this bullet?" said Griffin, holding the evidence at arm's length before her.

As Anita stared at Hartley for the first time since the arraignment, a combination of factors began to tear down her composure. Unable to trust her voice, she glared with cold, caustic hatred. Griffin pushed the gun closer, forcing her to look down the barrel. Hawkins raised his hand to object, but seeing her reaction, decided to let her emotions play out. Though the riveted gallery was silent, muffled comments could be heard in the background. Anita glared at the gallery and then at Hartley. "That's him," she spat, pointing her stiletto-like finger. "That doctor tried to kill me!" She leapt to her feet and leaned over the witness-stand railing as if ready to launch out and attack Hartley physically. "He's to blame for this nonsense," she howled. "That man has the heart of a killer."

Instantly a wave of anger spread through the gallery, with muttered insults disseminating along the lines between the doctors white coats and lawyers dark suits. In the corner, a pocket of erupting hostility escalated into a pushing match, which attracted the bailiffs from all sides. Judge Gadboy's eyes were wide with astonishment, and his face flushed with anger. He began pounding his gavel as if he were staking the heart of a vampire. "Bailiff! Bailiff! This court will recess for thirty minutes. Clear the courtroom!" he yelled. "We will reconvene at two—closed session! For the record—the decision to exclude the public will give the witnesses a chance to speak truthfully and not be intimidated."

In the defense counsel's chamber, Hawkins plunked heavily into a chair. His eyebrows were knitted, and his expression was vexed. But his mood had no effect on Hartley's enthusiasm. "Holy cow! Did you see that?" exclaimed Hartley.

"What I saw was trouble," answered Hawkins in a somber tone.

"Trouble? What do you mean?"

The traces of worry cleared from Hawkins face. "You did great, Roger. You had no trace of hostility."

"And she attacked me! Isn't that great?"

"What was great was you didn't smile or gloat when she lost her cool. You seemed remorseful when Moll was on the stand—not heartless or vengeful. The jury notices things like that—and they remember. You blew the top off the prosecution's game plan by being yourself, just as I said."

"So why the concern?" asked Hartley, not grasping the meaning of what had transpired.

Hawkins's face creased with concern. "This may be grounds for a mistrial," he said flatly. "They would have to try the case at a later date."

Hartley froze, staring blankly. "A mistrial?"

"But I think we'll be okay," added Hawkins quickly. "This judge is journeyed and knows how to run a trial. Obviously, there's pressure on him, too. I'm sure he wants to dispose of this case in a hurry." Hawkins glanced at his watch. "We have thirty minutes. When this court reconvenes in closed session, we must try to keep the jury from rekindling any sympathy for Johnson. So far, both of you have made my job easy."

Chapter Forty-Three

The proceedings in closed session were more calm and orderly. The dialogue unfolded at a normal volume, and the court reporter pecked undisturbed at her keys. Anita delivered her responses to the remainder of Griffin's questions with a veneer of equanimity, making it clear that she had returned to their game plan. Hawkins began the cross-examination by clarifying a few contested facts and then drove into the pivotal points of her testimony.

"Would you call the case you filed against Hartley a frivolous lawsuit?" asked Hawkins.

Anita's countenance hardened. Ethically, she couldn't answer. "Objection," shouted Griffin, before Anita could comment. "Relevance! The merits of a malpractice lawsuit call for a legal conclusion."

"Sustained," said Judge Gadboy. "Mr. Hawkins, rephrase your question."

Hawkins nodded in compliance, and asked Anita to describe Hartley's appearance the day he came to her office. "Possessed with revenge," she answered, touching her necklace with a delicate hand. "Murderous."

Hawkins objected to the witness stating opinions rather than measureable observations. "Strike the response from the record," ruled the judge.

"What was the tone of Hartley's voice?" asked Hawkins. "Was he sweating? Were his eyes fixed on you, or was he looking wildly around the room?"

"His voice was harsh," answered Anita calmly. "Panicked. He was sweating profusely, and his hands were unsteady. His eyes moved rapidly around the room."

"Like he was having a panic attack?" said Hawkins.

"Objection," said Griffin. "That would require a medical opinion."

"I will provide that opinion tomorrow," said Hawkins. "Did the accused say anything about intent while you two were alone in the room—behind closed doors?"

"He said, 'Convince me that I should let you live.'"

Anita's face churned with scorn, and her ire was not lost on Hawkins. "And how did you answer?" he asked, trying to bait her into losing her cool once more.

She answered evenly but with a curt sentence. "I said he wouldn't be able to do it."

"Well—obviously you were right," quipped Hawkins. "Describe what you saw immediately before the gun fired."

"The gun was pointed at my face. I saw blackness down the length of the barrel. I heard several clicks as he cocked the weapon."

"Immediately before the gun discharged, was the defendant looking directly at you?"

"I think he looked at the mirror to the side of my desk."

"And his arm—had it lowered?"

"Only to point the gun at my heart."

Hawkins approached the bench and requested that the judge admit into evidence a forensic expert's analysis that re-created the moment the gun had discharged. Without objection from the prosecution, Hawkins described the poor quality of the Saturday night special and the path of the bullet to confirm that the gun had discharged upon hitting the floor. "The bullet passed far wide of the victim, shattering the mirror," he said. He returned to address the seething Anita. They had opposed each other in civil court for malpractice cases several times, but this was far from those circumstances. "Let it be evident to the jury that the victim was never in imminent danger."

"I was in danger," she said. "He tried to kill me."

"That's for the jury to decide," he said, as if settling past scores. "Ms. Johnson," he said in a falsely patronizing tone, "where Hartley was standing after dropping the weapon for whatever reason—was he close enough to attack you with his hands? He could have killed you with his hands after the gun fired, could he not?"

Anita glared at Hawkins as if he were a turncoat. "Objection," yelled Griffin. "Opinion."

"Rephrase the question," requested the judge.

"If Hartley had wanted to kill you, would he have had the opportunity in that moment?"

"He might have if he hadn't been tackled."

"But he didn't?"

"No."

"Then what was he doing?"

"He stared at the shattered mirror frame."

"Without moving?"

"Yes."

"And after that?

"I don't remember," answered Anita, hiding her face with her hands. "The door flew open, and he was tackled. I dove under the desk to protect myself. My life was in danger."

"But you saw Hartley tackled. He fell from a standing position and then hit his head on the desk?"

"Yes."

"Then he wasn't crouching, as if scrambling to get a hold of the gun."

"I don't remember," said Anita with disgust. She had fallen into a trap.

Smiling approval, Hawkins turned to the jury. "I surmise that the accused saw something so surprising in the mirror that he lost awareness and muscle control. The weapon fell out of his hand. After the discharge, he was staring at the broken mirror. It must have been irrelevant to him at the time that the gun had slipped out of his hand. At that moment, he had no intent to kill."

"Objection!" screamed Griffin. "Drawing conclusions from facts. Move to strike the testimony. If Mr. Hawkins is sworn as a witness and would like to testify, I'd be delighted to examine him."

"Mr. Hawkins," scolded the judge, "in criminal law you ask the questions, and allow the witness to testify. I instruct the jury to disregard the last testimony and draw their own conclusions from the facts."

Anita was excused from the witness stand without a last word. The bailiff opened the small half door and waited to escort her from the courtroom. Suddenly realizing that she was being led out of the room, Anita turned to Judge Gadboy. "Do I have to leave?" she asked, desperate to watch Hartley's downfall.

"You know the rules, Ms. Johnson. You're subject to recall, and the defense has motioned for you to be excluded from the courtroom and admonished to not talk to anyone regarding your testimony. Please leave the courtroom." His eyes hardened when Anita hesitated by taking another stern glance at Hartley. "Immediately," he commanded. "Bailiff!"

The late-afternoon sun began to stream through the western windows. Hartley felt relieved when court was adjourned. He longed for the trial to be over—almost no matter the outcome. He'd been humiliated most of the afternoon by vaguely familiar witnesses who recounted the fine details of his misconduct. Only he smiled gratefully at the last policeman, who testified that the defendant had been peaceful and cooperative during the arrest. The officer had smiled at Hartley unexpectedly, as if he appreciated a great contribution a doctor once made in his life.

"Court is adjourned for the day," said Judge Gadboy. "Both attorneys meet in my chamber."

"You have a right to be present," whispered Hawkins.

Hartley's face fell immediately. "Do I have to stay?" He had paced himself to that moment and was quite eager to rejoin Celeste. "Would you suggest it?"

"You're eager to get home, aren't you? Go home." Hawkins paused with a rare smile and asked, "Did you notice Griffin at the end of his day? He's under pressure. His case has been presented, and for the rest of the trial, he can only cross-examine witnesses I bring to the box. Frankly, it worries me to have you take the stand. He is a seasoned lawyer, and I'm sure he can be vicious."

"I know who I am. I'll be myself. I have to speak up."

"Griffin has many close friends who care a great deal how he performs. He's tight." Hawkins's eyes meandered around the nearly empty courtroom. "Okay," he said, gathering his thin briefcase and clutching it in both hands.

Hartley wondered if it contained a single paper. "You did a great job today, Ernie," he said. "Thank you."

Hawkins smiled shyly. "A 'thank you' may come at the end of the trial, but not now. And I have to ask you—if the prosecution offers a plea bargain, are you interested in pleading guilty? I need to know in case Griffin asks during this meeting with the judge."

"Maybe that's why I should be there?"

Hawkins shrugged his shoulders in noncommittal confirmation. "I'll just see you tomorrow. A plea bargain would be a big disappointment."

Hartley grinned widely. "That's what I wanted to hear."

"Gather your strength. Tomorrow you'll take the stand." The gold flecks in his eyes twinkled brightly. "Remember, the prosecution bears the burden of proof."

"It's my word against Johnson's," Hartley said proudly. "Right now we've heard only her side of the story."

Judge Gadboy motioned for Hawkins and Griffin to sit across from his desk. "Where's the defendant?" he asked, glaring at Hawkins.

"My client chose not to be present."

"For the best," said Griffin humorlessly. "You won't hear a reason from me that requires him to be present."

Both angled their chairs farther apart before sitting. As if in prayer, the judge pressed his hands together and meditatively touched his thick bottom lip. He shook his head slowly back and forth. "Sometimes it's hard to find common sense in the world. Take this case for example—a simple assault becoming a national media event?"

"Attempted murder," corrected Griffin.

The judge eyed him sternly. "I'm trying to remain objective, Mr. Griffin. But in this case that is becoming increasingly difficult."

Encouraged by the judge's voiced pessimism, Hawkins blurted out a solution like a cannon shot over Griffin's bow. "The defense moves for a dismissal of the attempted murder charge. There is no evidence of specific intent. A reasonable resolution is simple assault. We'll change our plea to guilty of the lesser charge if the defendant is given probation. Griffin—you'll get your guilty plea. On middle ground everyone will be happy. This can all go away."

"Not a chance," Griffin replied curtly. "This won't all go away with simple assault!"

"Exactly!" said Hawkins with a winning smile. "I'm glad you agree. But I thought I would give you a chance."

Griffin's face flushed with suppressed rage. "Just why did you take this case anyway, Hawkins?" he fumed. "You're a civil lawyer, for God's sake—you shouldn't pretend."

"You have a habit of being partially right, Griffin. I usually do litigate civil trials, but I'm not pretending. All trials rectify wrongs, and I step in when I see man's inhumanity to man. This issue I view from the doctor's perspective."

"Then you'll certainly see a different perspective tomorrow."

Quickly the judge rose from his chair to put an end to the banter. "For all I care, Barack Obama can litigate," he said sternly. "Obviously there seems to be a great deal at stake here, though I'll be damned if I care. But let us not forget, gentlemen, this is a criminal trial, which requires a verdict. Mr. Hawkins, your motion is denied. The charge stands: attempted murder. I want a clean trial. It should be over with quickly. The tort reform controversy won't become our matter."

At that moment the phone rang so loudly that it startled the judge from his commanding pose. His face appeared troubled, and his arm rose as if to smash the phone with an invisible gavel. "Who's next?" he asked sternly. "Another person I've never met wanting to meet me for lunch?"

"At least it's a jury trial," said Hawkins calmly.

The judge pointed a stiff finger at both Hawkins and Griffin. "But I control the sentencing," he threatened. "I want a verdict tomorrow."

CHAPTER FORTY-FOUR

Gripped by frustration, Anita stormed out of the courtroom. She barged into the prosecution's office, grabbed a sheet of paper, and began to scribble a hasty note to Judge Gadboy. Her pen moved furiously until suddenly she paused and shredded the note in her hands. A deputy sheriff and a court secretary sharing the room were wordless as torn bits of paper floated to the floor like confetti. They eyed Anita askance, half-expecting her wrath to be redirected against them. "It's a travesty," she fumed. "I have rights! If that judge doesn't do the right thing, I'll finish him off myself."

The deputy sheriff paid closer attention, fixing his eyes warily on the spluttering lawyer, his police sense inspiring him to be ready. Anita's hands were clenched as if to strike out, so he chose his words carefully. "You need to get out of here. Go home and cool off. Trial's done for the day."

"Mind your own business or I'll…" Anita's head swung ferociously toward the court secretary, whom she caught staring openly. "What are you looking at?" The secretary froze with alarm. The deputy sheriff had risen to his feet and taken a subtle step toward Anita. "You need some help, Ms. Johnson. You don't look well. Let me see you out to your car. We don't want any trouble."

Anita had inhabited the fragile, vulnerable victim role long enough. She freed her hair from its bun and violently fluffed the strands with her fingers. "I don't need your help," she said with an icy finality.

The secretary and deputy glanced at each other incredulously, but before they could say another word Anita stormed out of the room and headed for the lobby. The deputy sheriff scratched his head. "Should I follow her?" he asked the court secretary. "The lobby is full of reporters."

"Somebody's going to get hurt," she answered. "She's gone plumb crazy."

The deputy slipped out the door and followed Anita at a safe distance. He could hear the din of reporters and spectators down the hall, and the noise escalated abruptly as Anita entered the front lobby. The deputy quickened his pace and pushed into the chaos, but before he could catch her, a ring of newspeople had tightened around her like a noose. White lights of the cameras pulsed. Suddenly a searing pain shot through Anita's abdomen, and she felt like her chest was constricting. She flailed her arms, spinning and pushing in every direction to escape. "No comment! No comment!" she screamed.

Knifing into the entangling horde, the deputy sheriff latched on to her arm. "You don't want to hurt these reporters, Ms. Johnson." He pinned her close to his side and cleared a path to the stairwell using his body. Their passage was slow and difficult, and when they reached the safety of the stairwell the deputy released his grasp. "Ouch—that hurt!" he howled, writhing in sudden pain and lifting the foot Anita had smashed with her heel. Helplessly, he watched her flee toward the parking garage, a few harried reporters trying to follow.

Anita Johnson's red Lamborghini screeched through the parking garage toward the exit ramp. "Slow down," yelled a security guard, waving his arms wildly as he jumped out of the way. By instinct he glanced at her license plate. "ILLSUEU," it read. Still in first gear, the engine braked loudly. The guard's face pressed close to the driver's side window. "You gotta slow down, Lady—there's doctors all over out there."

"Do I look like someone who cares about doctors?" she hissed.

The stupefied guard jumped back from the surging Lamborghini and fretfully watched as its screeching tires entered the ramp. Daylight streamed into the car at the bottom of the ramp, and Anita was forced to slow down. She inched forward into the swarm of bodies, forcing a narrow path to part the sea of white coats. Her belly was hurting. Her breathing was shallow. Doctors outside the car pressed close to the window, making her feel claustrophobic. She saw none of the faces in detail, but collectively they made a profound impression. Their expressions weren't scared or deflated, as she was used to seeing when she confronted them in the witness stand. They were stern. Determined. A poster at the end of a long stick flattened against the windshield and an oversized image stared her full in the face. "Hartley!" she fumed aloud, compressing the horn and mashing the clutch and the brake simultaneously. When she released the clutch, her body sprang forward and the seat belt cut into her waist. A still worse pain shot through her abdomen. The poster was thrown off, and the red Lamborghini swung onto California Avenue. Anita clutched her belly and moved rapidly through the traffic toward home.

The condominium's underground parking garage was deserted and dark. Anita coasted into her parking spot and shut down the car. The engine fluids boiled in the silence. Closing her eyes, she laid her head back on the headrest. The gripping spasms of searing pain below her navel were unrelenting. She crawled out of the car and limped into the elevator that accessed the lobby. The bellman peered up casually from his small television set hidden under the marble-topped console. Today he didn't stand to open the door and spout his usual effusions. He studied her face silently over the top of his glasses and leaned back in his chair. "I just seen you on television, Ms. Johnson, and here you is now. That's some fifteen minutes of fame you had today," he exclaimed, removing his worn cap and rotating the brim slowly in his hands. Anita heard stern judgment in his voice, but she was too much in pain to react. The doorman stared, shaking his head, unaware that she was in pain. "I'm too old to tell lies, Ms. Johnson," he said. "You got to leave those doctors alone. Already I can't get no primary doctor, and someday I might need their help."

Without reacting, Anita pressed her hand on her abdomen and stumbled into the elevator. She weakly turned the key that accessed the top floor. The car rose quickly, the tug of gravity intensifying the throbbing sensation in her gut. She fell back against the wall, feeling faint, and steadied herself with a hand on the railing. When the elevator doors opened, Anita stepped precariously across the dark, narrow strip that opened into the deep abyss of the elevator shaft below. The plush white carpet of her living room felt soft under her feet, and she hastily kicked off her shoes. All the trouble in her life seemed to have surfaced with the vague sense of a brewing illness, which had begun as a hollow feeling in her abdomen several weeks before and now amplified into a brutal torment. She dragged herself to the bedroom, falling onto the bed. But lying flat, her head spun with vertigo and nausea deepened her breathing. She wanted to cry out in pain, but pride and self-reliance made it hard to call someone to help. Suddenly, as if something deep inside let go, her body doubled over in agony. She groped for the phone on the nightstand and dialed the three emergency digits with a shaking finger. And for the first time in her life when she was in need, she found someone was there. A kind voice calmed her fears and told her an emergency team would arrive soon.

Somewhat relieved with hope, Anita sat on the toilet hoping to pass the pain out of her body. Her body rocked and her hands wrung together, attempting to comfort her fear. Something warm slid out between her legs. Gingerly, she turned to look into the bowl, and her eyes widened in terror. Rising to her feet quickly and spinning, she slammed the flush lever and studied the crimson, apple-sized blood clot that circled and passed down the drain. Then she blacked out.

Chapter Forty-Five

Hartley and Celeste exited the back of the courthouse soon after the judge's gavel signaled adjournment for the day. They took a circuitous route to their car, hoping to move briskly away from the spotlight. Hartley kept his head down, nodding self-consciously to a few excited protesters who called him by name. His pace quickened as the crowd thinned, and his tension began to dissipate with every step. "Where are we going?" he asked, feeling the splintered afternoon sunlight on his face.

"I got a room downtown at the Allerton. With the lights and noise from the camera crews outside last night, it was hard to sleep."

"What about the kids?"

"They're with your mom," she answered. Seeing his face tense up with disappointment, she added, "Don't worry. They'll be fine. And so will we."

Hartley stepped out of the car cautiously at the front curb of the hotel. "No TV trucks," he said as he glanced around. It felt wonderfully liberating to be able to drop his guard. He signed his name neatly on the registration slip and loosened his tie. An ancient metal key rested in the palm of his hand.

"Any baggage?" asked the bellman.

"Just a little," Hartley replied. "I'm traveling light."

"Can I show you to your room?"

Hartley held out a five-dollar bill. "I'll find my way. But thank you for asking."

Once in the room, Hartley flopped onto the plush hotel bed and propped up his head with a pillow. Celeste lay by his side and nestled her head on his shoulder. "Are you beginning to feel better about this?" she asked.

"Anything can happen. Right now, I'm missing the kids. I hate to think that I might miss several years of them growing up."

"One way or another, all things will work out," she said.

Hartley's arm curled around his wife's shoulders. "Did you notice the warm sunlight when we were leaving the courthouse?" he asked in the moment of serenity. "The sun was just at that certain afternoon angle that makes all the colors so vibrant and clear."

Celeste lifted her head off his arm and regarded him closely. He wore an expression of resolve and acceptance that was new. "Maybe the world looked more beautiful because you've let go?" she said.

Hartley laughed at the uncertainty of his future. "Tomorrow's a big day."

"But no matter what happens, you should feel good about yourself, Rosey. You've almost made it through this. And you'll make it through whatever happens tomorrow."

Hartley stared at the blank, white ceiling, searching his mind and estimating his desires. "It's almost as if I don't want this journey to end. I've finally pulled my head out of the sand, and I'm convinced that this is what I've been waiting for. You saw the doctors out there. I'm part of a movement that could improve the whole system. And I trust that things will end up the way they're supposed to. It makes me feel safe."

"It sounds to me like you're discovering your soul, Rosey."

Hartley laughed incredulously. "Where—exactly—is your soul located?"

"You must have slept through that anatomy class," she said teasingly. "Your soul is the part of you that's not your brains or your groin." Celeste remained comfortably motionless next to her husband, feeling his warmth. "What do you feel inside of you right now?" she asked.

"Something rock solid," he said. "I can't explain it. Can you explain it?"

"This isn't medicine—not everything needs to be explained. Some things are taken on faith."

Feeling secure, Hartley rearranged his leg over Celeste's and snuggled closer. A terrible burden had slowly been lifting from his shoulders all afternoon. No longer did he feel the need to resolve every problem—even this one. He closed his eyes and took a slow breath. It seemed that this was a process that every person went through, and he didn't understand it completely, but he felt blessed. "Something good will come of this," he whispered.

Celeste nestled closer. "The first fruit is love."

Hand-in-hand they left the hotel room in search of some food. Hartley felt an unexplained excitement in Celeste's fingertips and perceived a spring in her step as she pulled him along to the elevator, pushing the button to the hotel's top floor as if she knew where she was going. As the doors opened, Celeste's hand fell away, and she gave him an encouraging push forward.

Hartley froze. "Celeste…?"

In an intimate, octagonal meeting room lit by candlelight sconces that lent a Renaissance air, Hartley beheld a small company of people he loved—his mother, brother, and many old friends. His four children emerged from behind the crowd of adults and ran to take hold of his waist. His joyful eyes swept over their smiling faces, and then he peered back at Celeste, his expression transforming into a bashful grin. "A little early to celebrate—don't you think?"

"It might be our last chance," she said in jest.

Hartley appeared even more stunned as his mind questioned fleetingly whether the past six weeks could have been nothing more than a practical joke.

"We wanted to come," said Christine sweetly.

"Don't feel alone anymore, Daddy," said Evan.

A mist clouded Hartley's eyes as the last vestiges of reserve crumbled. He gathered his children tightly, and their squirming bodies felt warm. He had never felt more alive. "I'm glad that you're here," he said. "Going through this without your support is the only thing that could make me afraid."

"You'll never be without us," exclaimed Drew.

"Never, ever," added Sophie. Hartley was enjoying their small pats on his back as he met the eyes of his mother. Her forgiveness and unconditional love were evident in her expression, and his heart filled with new strength.

After a beautiful dinner, an exhausted but happy Hartley stood with a warmer and wiser version of his old infectious grin brightening his face. He lingered for a moment, holding his glass. The candles flickered, setting his silhouette in motion on the wall. As the room quieted, he spoke in a tone gauged to quell pity. "I'm sorry I let you all down," he said with sincerity. "Practicing medicine has been a privilege for me, and regrettably I came close to throwing it all away. But because of your love and support, I've found that I can make a mistake and still trust that I can come home. I am so grateful. No one knows what will happen tomorrow—but I'm prepared. I'll accept whatever verdict the jury delivers. And no matter the penance—I will abide. I realize I won't be alone. When this is over a new life will be waiting. I recognize this wonderful blessing. In every end, there is a new beginning," he said, raising his glass. "To love and lasting friendship."

Hartley tried to comprehend the loneliness and hopelessness that had carried him down the path he had chosen, and marveled at the changes that had taken place inside him since then. Disorder and chaos were sometimes painful, but they were integral to the process of change. He had journeyed down a path that tested his faith. And now he was ready to go back and take the other fork. Tomorrow he would take the witness stand to speak out in his own defense. *I'm getting closer*, he thought, giving himself permission to go wherever tomorrow would lead him.

CHAPTER FORTY-SIX

Anita's taut abdomen was filling with blood. The surgeon worked quickly with nimble fingers, guiding a cauterizing electric knife to cut the outer layers of the skin and divide the thin fat planes. As he entered the peritoneal cavity, blood flowed out of the wound. The surgical team hurriedly cleared the field with suction and sponges and retracted the bowels to look for the source of the hemorrhage deep in the pelvis. Illuminated by the bright lights, the cause of Anita's misfortune came into view. The central section of her left fallopian tube was swollen into a bulge and burned red with inflammation. Blood streamed from the rupture.

"Did she even know she was pregnant?" the surgeon asked.

Conceived six weeks earlier, the fertilized ovum was supposed to have followed nature's intended course to implant into the nurturing uterus. But this conception had become trapped short of its intended destination, and pressure had built in the confining space until it exploded.

"An ectopic pregnancy," said the surgeon. "Even God isn't perfect."

Using procedures that he had performed hundreds of times, he removed the left fallopian tube and ovary. Examining the excised tissue confirmed what he suspected. As small as a tiny seed, a fetus lay curled at the center. The inflamed area in Anita's pelvis was now sterile and void.

The surgical wound was sore when Anita awoke the next morning. The stabbing pains in her abdomen had vanished, but a new pain gripped her when she moved. She didn't want to recall the night with Robert on the boat and the fruitful love that she had relinquished. Her eyes circled the room self-consciously. The surroundings were basic and barren, without signs of life. There were no comforting flowers or cards wishing her well. She sank deeply into the hospital bed and clutched the sheet to her neck to hold in her warmth. There was nothing familiar about this situation. Her strong self-reliance was useless. There was no feeling of professional superiority to buoy her esteem. She looked away when a young nurse entered the room to check the unit of blood that dripped slowly into her arm.

"I need to check your bandage," she said with soft compassion, her mouth lifting into a comforting smile. She wore a clean, white uniform as if she were just out of nursing school. "How do you feel?"

Anita strained to regain composure while the nurse checked the bandage. "I'm okay—I think." These first words she had spoken since her emergency surgery came out weakly. She cleared her throat to strengthen her speech.

"Do you feel any discomfort? Can I get you something for pain?"

Anita touched her belly to assess her distress. "I think I'm okay. It's hard to tell."

The nurse placed the call button on the bed within reach. She seemed to enjoy performing small tasks that would comfort her patient, and attended to every detail to keep her safe. "Are you warm enough?" she asked as she lifted Anita's head to fluff the pillow.

"I'm okay," answered Anita. "Thank you."

The nurse beamed with the words of appreciation. "You're so very welcome," she said. "I'll be back in a little while. The call button is by your right hand. You rest and get better."

"Will my doctor be in?" asked Anita.

"Dr. Fogg is your hospitalist. He usually comes a little later."

"Is he good?"

"He's a good doctor."

Anita felt a vague anxiety. "Who's better? I want that doctor."

"That would be Dr. Hartley. But we won't talk about that."

Shocked by the reality that she needed to be under the care of someone who knew her reputation, Anita's anxiety tripled. She followed the young nurse with her eyes, wondering how much she knew and how much she cared. Fear battled her gratitude. She thought of Hartley with waning hatred, a dreadful feeling of solitude sweeping in to replace her anger. She raised her forearm and studied the IV that dripped life-giving blood into her vein. Her fingers fanned out, and her French-manicured nails looked out of place. Squirming uncomfortably, she grabbed the TV remote and clicked through the channels before halting abruptly to go back to a familiar sound that made her cringe. *"Have you been harmed by a doctor?"* The voice she heard was her own, soliciting malpractice clients. She smashed the button with her thumb, and the TV turned off. But she couldn't tune out what she had heard. *The nurse must know who I am,* she thought, shrinking lower in the narrow hospital bed with a sense of embarrassment. The cold plastic mattress felt uncomfortable through the thin sheet as her conscience began an assault. *The surgeon must know what I do for a living. If he had refused me as a patient, I might have died.* Her legs shifted restlessly and sudden nausea deepened her breathing. Her body flushed hotly while a cold sweat chilled her skin. There seemed to be something unfair in her callously ruining the lives of physicians. Her motivation in malpractice lawsuits had never been righting wrongs. She imagined the newspapers squaring her reputation with the news of her illness. *Everyone must be against me.*

Anita sat up in bed holding her belly and anxiously searched the room for a clock. It was just before eight on what would likely be the final day of Hartley's trial. Her hands groped for the phone, and she dialed the courthouse, her pain replaced with urgency as the number connected. "State's Attorney Griffin," she asked breathlessly. Somehow she had to make good. "Griffin, this is Anita," she said.

"Where are you?" he asked, with a clear edge in his voice. "Court's about to start."

"I'm in the hospital. I had emergency surgery last night."

"What are you talking about? There's nothing wrong with you."

"Something was wrong—and they fixed it. I'm not going to explain."

"Damn it, Anita! You need to get down here. We have no time for this. You are under a court order and subject to recall as a witness. The defense may call you as a witness. Hartley's ass is on the witness stand. I can't worry about you."

"I've changed my mind. I'm dropping the charges. Hartley can't go to jail."

A sharp clattering indicated that Griffin had dropped the phone. She pulled the speaker away from her ear, enjoying how Griffin's voice became squeaky and faint. "What makes you think you have a choice in the matter?" he demanded. "Both our careers are on the line."

Anita eased deeper into her hospital bed. The hospital made her feel safe and secure. "I'm not testifying," she said quietly.

"What did you say? Not testifying? Have you lost your mind?"

"No—I think I found it. And I'm asking myself where it's been."

"Hartley pointed a gun in your face, for God's sake! Make him pay for what he did! Where's your self-respect?"

"Self-respect? No—I think he's already paid enough."

"Anita, please, just one more day. Keep the wheels on—for my sake."

Anita sat up in bed, summoning strength. "I won't," she said. "There's been enough blaming, and Hartley has had more than his share. If crucifying him is the only way to save the tort system, then the system needs to be changed."

"Rubbish," yelled Griffin. "What's gotten into you? Your career…"

"If my career suffers, so be it," interrupted Anita. "My life will be worth something more."

Griffin's mind raced to understand. "Listen," he pleaded. "Every trial lawyer I know is expecting me to slam-dunk this son of a bitch. The whole case hangs on your testimony. It's his word against yours. Get your ass down here, or I'll be toast."

"I'm dropping the charges."

"The hell you are," screamed Griffin. "It's my case, and you're only the victim. Only I can drop the charges, and I'm not going to do it!"

"Griffin—I'm in the hospital, just out of emergency surgery."

"It's professional suicide! Your neck's on the line, too."

"The prosecution is done with me," she said calmly. "For my absence to matter, the defense would have to call me back to the stand."

"I'll ask for a bench warrant and have you arrested! You're in contempt."

"Nobody can order me back into the courtroom. I'm in the hospital."

"You'll pay for this, you… you… God damn you. There'll be no continuance. There will be no mistrial because of you!" Griffin slammed down the phone with an earsplitting crash.

Anita smiled as she hung up the phone and pushed it away. *I'm minus a tube and ovary. And now I'm minus an asshole.*

Chapter Forty-Seven

Hartley lay flat on his back with his hands crossed over his chest. Celeste could tell by his peaceful breathing that he was at ease. She rolled onto her side and gently stroked the side of his cheek. "Hotel beds are so comfortable. How did you sleep?" she asked.

He had been focusing on a distant point beyond time, and his attention crystallized gradually. "I felt like I was sleeping in a room lit by a nightlight."

"What do you mean?" she asked.

His energy suggested that he had been up thinking for a while. He rolled to face her, fully awake, and balled the pillow under his head. "My dream was more like a vision. But I don't even think I've been asleep. It was bizarre. I was flying high over Chicago in my white lab coat with little transparent wings on my back. They beat like a hummingbird's, and I hovered and darted around at whim."

"That picture that Drew gave you when you first came home from jail," she said. "Don't you remember?"

Hartley thought back through the confusion. "Yes—I think I kept it somewhere. That's it exactly," exclaimed Hartley. "It felt so real."

"It must have been one of your nightmares," she answered calmly. "You've never liked heights and you hate flying—I don't blame you with all this stress."

"But I wasn't afraid—isn't that strange? I flew around healing and comforting people, and there was a real sense of pleasure and joy."

"You sound like Jimmy Stewart," joked Celeste.

"But the dream wasn't flat like a movie. Everything was so real."

All of a sudden, Hartley's face saddened with less enthusiasm. "I remember seeing you and the kids. I felt like I could reach out and touch you, but when I tried—I couldn't. That was the only sad part."

He rose from the bed and walked to the window, drawing back the curtains as if to see where he was. "When I woke up I was right over there, suspended over Northwestern Hospital. I was looking down at scenes from my residency, reliving moments that actually happened. I had been to Ravenswood Hospital. The Hancock. I had flown over the courthouse rallies. I could see into the trial, and I saw myself on the stand. Isn't that interesting—it hasn't even happened yet." Hartley stopped and strained to remember the outcome. He regarded Celeste with amazement. "Do you think my story has been written?" he asked.

Celeste crawled to the edge of the bed, reached out, and pulled him back gently. His face looked thin, and the tint of his hair had subtly grayed. "How do you feel?" she asked with concern. "You have a big day."

Hartley paused to think, feeling like he was trying to determine the flavor of ice cream with just a taste. "My life has unfolded and run together—all at the same time. I sort of feel proud."

"Are you worried?" she asked.

"I feel like I start a new life after today," he answered evenly. His sparkling blue eyes were deep and clear. "From now on, things will be different."

As if a chill breeze had brushed her skin, Celeste shuddered. She stood and walked broodingly into the sunlight that streamed through the window. "Sundays," she murmured. "Sundays will be our day."

Hartley moved to hold her. "We'll get back to spending the whole day as a family—just as we used to."

Celeste's face fell into the nape of his neck. "I don't want you to go," she whispered. "This day will be tough."

Hartley's voice was peaceful and strong. "You've been a great comfort, Celeste. And I love you more than anything else in the world. It's out of our hands. We should get ready. I don't want to be late for my judgment."

Hawkins was bent over a newspaper in the defense counsel's chamber when Hartley entered the room. "You're late," said Hawkins. "I was starting to think you'd jumped bond."

"How can I be late for my destiny?" answered Hartley.

Hawkins's brown eyes beamed as he extended his warm hand. "Look here—you made the front page."

Glancing at the picture of him leaving the courthouse, surrounded by a sea of white coats, Hartley sensed somewhere inside his body that his judgment had already been handed down. "My life has taken on a direction of its own.

This is my fifteen minutes of fame."

"Then you must be eager to find out where this is going?"

"I'm certainly ready."

"Well," said Hawkins. "There's a twist."

Hartley rocked back on his heels. "You plea-bargained?"

"No. Anita Johnson had emergency surgery."

Instantly, Hartley's expression became grave. "When? What for?"

"I don't know. But she'll miss the rest of the trial. You should see Griffin this morning. He's panicked over the possibility of a continuance or a mistrial."

Hartley's eyes widened with fear.

"Let's move for a mistrial," said Celeste, hastily. "That's got to be good."

Hawkins grinned like a child after telling an off-color joke. The prosecution had rested its case, and it would be up to him to decide whether Anita would be called again as a witness. "Your testimony is all we need. But of course I haven't let Griffin in on the secret. The poor guy's so frightened—I hate to say I'm enjoying it. We'll strike Johnson from our case in chief. The judge will be pleased, and hopefully he'll recall it later. He wants this finished up, too. I'll bet he's hoping you win. Besides—do you really want to see her again?"

Hartley's smile was unreadable. "Only to say that I'm sorry."

"And what about Moll?"

"He'd have to be pretty sick."

Hawkins chuckled in appreciation of his client's humility. "Well, we won't see either of them today. They've done enough damage already. But are you ready, Celeste?"

Hartley gawked from one to the other as if there were a conspiracy. "I won't allow it," he said instantly. "This is my problem, and I don't want her involved."

Celeste reached out to steady his arm. "It's okay," she answered in a hush. "I knew about this, and I'm prepared. I have a lot of nice things to say about you. I want them heard." Hartley looked quizzically at his wife. "I didn't want you to worry," she added with a shrug of her shoulders.

"But Griffin? You heard—he's panicked."

She patted his arm patronizingly. "I know what to expect. You'll get your turn after mine."

Chapter Forty-Eight

A polite knock broke through Anita's narcotic-induced fog. Her head rose from the pillow, and she peered sleepily at the door. "Who's there?" she murmured. As the door creaked open a touch, a man's elbow appeared at the edge of the frame. Shyly, the visitor stood just out of sight, as if he were awaiting permission to enter. A gigantic bouquet of red roses concealed his face. The blossoms were fully open and their scent quickly permeated the air. Anita couldn't see the face of her unexpected visitor behind the flowers. "Come in," she said hesitantly. The flower heads on the ends of the long stems waved gently, as if the visitor's hands shook. Anita pointed to the windowsill. "Put them there."

Suddenly she gasped, and her eyes opened wide. Her heart beat faster as her hands reached to cover her body with the blanket and smooth out its creases. Robert's soft, manicured hands were gripping the vase. "Will you forgive me?" he said from behind the bouquet.

It was the one voice that Anita had been longing to hear. The vase lowered, and Robert's face finally came into view. His mouth was drawn into a tentative smile. "Robert?" Anita tried to say more, but the medication had muddled her thinking. Was this love or sympathy? In the ensuing silence, the distance narrowed between them, and she felt his gaze caressing her face. "It's been seven weeks," he said in a voice deep with longing.

Anita's eyes lowered, and her hands folded protectively over her fresh wound. A dull ache was all that was left in the emptiness. "How did you know?" she asked.

"The news," he mumbled with embarrassment. "Was it ours?"

Anita gazed blankly at the bouquet of roses, her heart drained of all feeling. Awkwardly, Robert hugged the vase to his chest and cleared a space on the windowsill. He set down the bouquet, carefully spacing the flowers. The arrangement splashed color into the drab room. He stepped to the edge of the bed and pressed Anita's hand between his own. She wanted to say, "I forgive you," but instead her hand pulled back. "Does anyone know that you're here?"

"I don't think so—but I don't care if they do." His face was trapped in a smile. "It was ours—wasn't it?"

A wave of pain passed quickly, and comforting warmth spread through Anita's body. Years in the courtroom had made her a close observer, and she was hesitant to believe. She studied his eyes, waiting carefully for a sideward glance or any other hint of insincerity.

"I told my wife," he said simply.

Abruptly, so many different emotions emerged at once. Anita found it hard to choose one to trust. Her mouth curled shyly at the corners. "But the election..."

"It's okay."

A rush of tears made Robert appear blurry. Anita wiped away the tear streaks on her cheeks with her free hand. Robert took the hand encumbered by the IV and kissed her fingers lightly. "Seven weeks," he said, showing agony. "I've been devouring the papers every day to read everything about you I could. It's been horrible guessing your feelings. I've watched you interviewed on TV, wishing we were together. And then this." He squeezed her hand lightly and pressed it to his lips. "I let you go once—and I won't let it happen again."

"Robert, what are you saying?"

"It's okay," he said again, seeing her notice the band of pale skin on his ring finger. "Good sometimes emerges from the unpleasant. It was time for a change." He gazed serenely at the bouquet of roses. "Things will be as they should."

Anita's mind raced as she pictured the old TLAC lawyer's gargantuan eye magnified by the crystal water glass. "But what will you do?" she asked.

"If I lose the election, maybe we'll travel for a while. Somewhere nice. Out of the way. Maybe somewhere you'd like to go?"

Anita found the strength to sit up in bed. But she wasn't willing to give herself away so suddenly. "I tried dropping the charges against Hartley," she admitted, showing genuine conviction.

"You did what?" asked Robert, recalled out of a passionate daze.

"Anyone can make a mistake. We're all human. Me. You." She lay back on the hospital bed, picturing her father and the Degas that hung in her living room. The delicate but powerful frames of the dancers. Their tiny white slippers painted clear as glass. Even the dancers were human. A tear re-formed in her eye as she clutched Robert's hand and pressed it to her abdomen. "I want to feel something," she pleaded. "Something different."

Robert laughed kindly. "Well, I'll be damned. Are you trying to put me in the hospital with a heart attack? What are you going to do now?"

"Maybe I'll switch to his side," she mused.

"Stop—you're scaring me," said Robert. "I'd have to become a Republican."

"Now you're scaring me," she answered.

Robert pulled a rose from the vase and nestled it onto her chest, the blossom under her nose. The fragrance was alluring and deliciously sweet. "If you're going to give up the cause, then I can, too. We all *should* work together and compromise. So however this trial turns out—the doctors have already won."

Anita took the rose off her chest and handed it back. "And so have you."

Chapter Forty-Nine

Head up and shoulders squared, Hartley led the way into the noisy courtroom. Doctors sparred with reporters for positions in the gallery, and lawyers squeezed into the spaces in between. With barely contained hostility, Griffin glared at Hartley. Dark circles shadowed his bloodshot eyes. Hartley diverted his eyes to the empty chairs of the jury box. The sheriff's deputy stood at attention as the bailiff called the court in session. Everyone rose. Judge Gadboy climbed the stairs and sat behind the bench. The jurors filed in and took their seats, only the sound of shuffling feet breaking the silence. Each one looked at Hartley, carefully studying his face. "Good morning," said Hartley, smiling politely as he greeted the panel.

Hawkins leaned toward his client. "Don't address the jurors," he whispered.

Hartley studied Judge Gadboy, who was sorting some papers in silence. The judge seemed calmer than he had the day before. His white hair was carefully brushed, and his shiny, black silk robe was pressed into pleats. As if sensing someone's eyes upon him, he raised his head and focused directly on Hartley. He flashed a brief smile as if they were the only two in the courtroom. "Good morning," he said. Hartley nodded unassumingly, glancing sideways to take pleasure from his lawyer's obviously astonished reaction. Judge Gadboy brought down the gavel more civilly than he had the day before. "Court is in session."

Confidently, Hawkins called Hartley's mother as his first witness. She moved quietly from her front-row seat, mounting the witness stand still full of vitality. She had graceful waves of gray hair, and her clothing was tidy and plain. For Hartley, things had not changed—forty-five years after his birth she was still on duty. After adjusting her position, she focused her smiling eyes on her son, deliberately blinking once as a signal that they both were going to be fine. Proudly, she painted a picture of her son's good character to the stretch of the judge's tolerance and answered every query with as much objectivity that a parent realistically could provide. Hawkins's gentle questioning completed quickly, and Griffin began his cross-examination. His calculating, probing manner was designed to reveal well-hidden secrets.

"Was there anything 'unusual' about your son?" he asked, as if knowing there was something irregular.

"He was born with a caul, if that's what you mean."

Griffin stopped pacing, and eyed her with surprise and disdain. "What is a 'caul'?" he asked in a scornful tone, as if the answer wasn't the one he expected.

"It's quite rare, actually," she answered excitedly, steadfast and loyal. "When Roger was born, he came out with a fetal membrane stretched over his head. It's a curious phenomenon. The thick, extra skin dries up and falls off over time. I still have the thing. It looks just like a scrap of white leather."

Griffin was stunned into silence. He had no idea where this path was leading and he had no intention of following the trail to the end. But the interested silence in the courtroom forced him to continue one question further. "And this being unusual, is there some special significance?"

"A caul is thought to bring good fortune. It's a sign that no evil will befall the child. In the olden days, sailors bought cauls and kept them to protect themselves from drowning. It's also called a 'lucky hood.' I just knew I should have brought it," she added with pleasure.

When the gallery laughed, Hartley's face reddened. He was embarrassed as well. Where she had learned all this, he didn't know, but she was clearly playing games with the state's attorney, and he enjoyed watching the courtroom stir with sympathetic emotion. Griffin was clearly peeved that she had sidestepped his trap. When his questions became increasingly prying and needling, Judge Gadboy's gaze sharpened and followed the attorney as he wandered around the room. Annoyance simmered in his eyes. Even the gallery betrayed their dissatisfaction with the way Griffin's badgering cross-examination unfolded. Alone in a sea of judging faces, he abruptly dismissed the witness and retreated to his table while trying to hide his resentment.

Following Griffin's retreat, Hawkins called his next witness with respectful decorum. Fogg entered the room through the side door, wearing a suit that looked suspiciously new. He glanced stoically at Hartley as he took the stand, his glimmering eyes revealing his sentiment. After dispensing with introductions and background, Hawkins plowed into developing a picture of Hartley's true character for the jury. "You report spending a few moments with the defendant in the days preceding his arrest. Describe his behavior the day he received his summons."

"Hartley cares deeply," said Fogg. "His generation of doctors expects to work brutal hours and maintain close relationships with patients. They're used to total control over their domain. I think he was struggling."

"Struggling how?"

"Younger doctors are better equipped for the demands of today's medicine. Fresh out of medical school, they are pre-programmed to understand that they can never expect to enter private practice, instead accepting a salary. Their proficiency as insurance-company advocates is now as critical as physical exams. They accept measured performance with decision-making and frugality scrutinized against internal and national standards. In the eyes of their employers, the 'best' docs see the most patients each day. In Hartley's eyes, seeing lots of patients didn't equal good care."

"Did Hartley ever mention that he might be considering suicide?"

"Many physicians have suicidal thoughts just after being sued. Even when the case is baseless, as he felt his was."

"Objection," yelled Griffin.

"I'll rephrase the question," said Hawkins, without taking his eyes off Fogg. "Would you say that the medication 'prednisone' is appropriate therapy for lupus?"

"In certain situations, such as if someone has no insurance or money to pay for newer, more costly drugs. But prednisone treatment usually works better," he said, grinning with an understanding smile. "Hartley knew what he was doing. He's thought to be one of the best doctors we have at our hospital."

"And do you feel that way too?"

"Without a doubt. I will welcome him back."

When Fogg was his witness, Griffin seemed eager to downgrade Hartley's character. Having memorized Fogg's prior statement to the police, he cut into his case. "You have known the defendant for five years. Have you ever seen him act surly around patients, other doctors, or anyone else?"

Remembering his resentful behavior that Saturday morning in the doctors' lounge, Hartley felt a twinge of anxiety. Fogg also remembered the conversation. "Yes," he said smartly, bringing a visible smile to Griffin's face. "But that surliness is new."

"Regardless," said Griffin. "I understand that the defendant had an outburst with his patient, Moll, and threatened him in the days just before he purchased the weapon."

"I was not present if he did," said Fogg with gravity. "But I also had a similar outburst with Moll. He is a difficult patient."

Griffin's eyes became focused. "Did you ever witness anything resembling a panic attack with Hartley in any moment in the five years you have known him?"

"No," said Fogg, unsure how to answer.

"Not even during a code blue—when things can become very tense?" pressed Griffin. When Fogg confirmed his answer, Griffin returned to his table. Hawkins redirected Fogg's testimony and established again that Hartley's ill behavior was new, and that unwitnessed panic attacks might have occurred outside the hospital without his knowing.

"The defense calls Celeste Hartley," he announced next in a moderate tone. Despite the fact that Hartley now expected his wife to be called, his head jerked up sharply, and his fingers clutched the table. Celeste strode through the well toward the witness stand. Her slight smile was neither pretentious nor overbearing. Eyes followed her as if she were a captivating celebrity. "I do," she said, with no overemphasis in response to the oath. Hartley choked back his emotion. The last time he had heard her utter those words had been on their wedding day, and he saw her crystal-blue eyes shining with the same benevolent spirit.

In a measured voice that fortified confidence, Hawkins began his examination by standing at the side of the witness stand, so that every juror had a full view of his witness. Carefully he avoided any past tense in his speech. "Mrs. Hartley, please tell the jury how many hours your husband typically works in a normal workweek."

"I've never thought about it before. It varies. He just takes care of whoever needs help at the time."

"But can you guess how many hours per week?"

"Well—from seven to seven during the week. All day Saturday. Parts of Sunday. Nights for emergency calls. Should I count phone calls, too? Sometimes he consults over the phone. That can seem like half the night."

"Would you say seventy to eighty hours a week?"

"Maybe. But I don't really know. It wouldn't be something you calculate on your fingers."

"But almost twice a normal forty-hour workweek?"

Celeste shrugged, but agreed verbally when the judge asked for a response.

"Does he *always* work weekends?"

"Unless someone covers. But he prefers to go in himself."

"Can you tell me why your husband works so hard?"

"He has always known that medicine is not a nine-to-five job. Why he does it—" She smiled with genuine respect at her husband. "You'd better ask him."

"Understood. Do you have family dinners together?"

"Objection," interrupted Griffin. "What relevance do family dinners have in a case of attempted murder?"

"Overruled," cut in Judge Gadboy abruptly. "Mrs. Hartley, please answer the question."

"Sometimes we do—and sometimes we don't."

"Do the children miss their father when he's away so frequently?"

Griffin stood up to object again. "The defense is simply trying to paint the defendant as a sympathetic character. Family life should have absolutely no bearing on the outcome of this case."

"With all due respect, Your Honor," responded Hawkins without missing a beat, "this line of questioning is relevant to the defendant's state of mind at the time of the incident. I'm trying to demonstrate that the man portrayed by the prosecution is essentially not the same Dr. Roger Hartley who worked hard to both serve his patients and provide for his family."

"Overruled," said the judge, intrigued by the skill of a civil lawyer who had chosen to take on a criminal trial. "But I warn you, Mr. Hawkins. Keep your questions relevant. Mrs. Hartley—you will answer the question."

"We're used to his absences," she said, with moving sincerity. "He does special things with us whenever he can."

"Would you say his life is well balanced?"

"Physicians work long hours. Roger is no different from any other doctor."

"But in your opinion, is he able to maintain proper balance?"

Celeste looked down at the floor, avoiding all the eyes that were watching her so intently. "His practice has gotten busier during the past few years," she answered, in a wary tone. "It seems there's a lot of sick people lately."

"Does he ever take sick days?"

"I don't remember one," she answered, looking up proudly.

"Would he work on days when it might be medically indicated for him to stay home?"

"Every physician works…"

"Nonresponsive," Griffin objected. "The question calls for a yes-or-no answer. 'Every physician' is not on trial here. Just this one—Mr. Hartley. Move to strike."

There was obvious intent in Griffin's misuse of Hartley's title. Having been corrected himself, Judge Gadboy scowled down from the bench. "Overruled. I will allow it—Mr. Griffin."

"I'll answer yes, Your Honor," said Celeste convivially.

"So your husband practices medicine even when his own health is suffering? Is that correct?"

"Objection—leading the witness."

"Sustained."

"Let me rephrase the question," Hawkins resumed pleasantly. "Mrs. Hartley, when your husband is ill, does he ordinarily choose to go in to the hospital, or does he stay home?"

Celeste stared down at her feet. Her ankles were tightly crossed, and she uncrossed them. She didn't want to look at her questioner or at anyone else in the courtroom except her husband. Hartley flushed warm as Celeste beamed at him with loving pride. "He feels obligated, and he would go in."

"So for Roger Hartley to not go in on the day he entered the law firm of Hendricks, Kennedy, and Johnson, he must have been ill."

"He was ill."

The courtroom gallery stirred. Hawkins was focused. "I'll get back to that. But first let me finish here. With your husband working such long hours every week, do you or your children ever feel neglected?"

"No," she replied, without delay. "My husband is a loving person and a wonderful father. Quality counts."

"Has there been any loss of intimacy?"

Celeste smiled indulgently. "Everyone gets tired from time to time, Mr. Hawkins."

"Has there ever been talk of divorce?"

"Hearsay," Griffin objected.

Judge Gadboy looked sharply at the state's attorney. "Counselor Griffin, you're missing an interesting trial. If you pay attention, perhaps you'll learn something that may help you later in your career. Overruled."

"No," Celeste answered, acknowledging the judge with a wry smile. "The subject of divorce has never been raised between us."

Hawkins allowed Celeste to catch her breath while he walked back to the defense table to survey the jury box. The housewife wore an expression of admiration and empathy. The businessman appeared introspective. The academic gazed at Celeste attentively as if solving a problem in his mind. After taking a slow sip of water and asking his client how he was faring, Hawkins walked with a measured pace back to Celeste's side. "Overall, Mrs. Hartley— would you say your husband is satisfied with life as a physician?"

Celeste gazed sadly at her husband. "He loves being a doctor. Until lately."

"Until lately—can you elaborate?"

Absently, Celeste smoothed the hem of her dress on top of her knees. "He's worried. He gets discouraged."

"About what?"

"Finances, for one thing. Payments from insurance companies have been dropping year after year. They value his time less and less. Malpractice premiums are spiraling through the roof. Employee salaries keep going up. The conversion to electronic records cost him more than one hundred thousand. He worries about losing his practice to an HMO. He has to provide for a family of six. The children are getting older, and more costly." Fighting back tears of hopelessness, she tried not to look at her husband. She rubbed her eyes and dried her fingers on her dress.

Hawkins spoke sharply to make her look up. "Mrs. Hartley."

Celeste glanced at her husband, who was sitting upright and proud, as if his soul had been repaired. Seeing his courage, she too straightened her shoulders and prepared to finish her testimony. Hawkins walked to the side of the jury box, forcing her to look at all twelve jurors at once. His aspect was grave. "Mrs. Hartley, how did your husband react when he found out that he was being named in a malpractice lawsuit?"

Celeste looked to her husband before answering. "He was very hurt," she said, remembering only the facts of the day. A nod from Hawkins rewarded her honesty, encouraging her to continue. "He gave all he had. His patients loved him. He was dedicated to making them well. He felt betrayed. He didn't do anything wrong to that Moll patient." She wiped another slight tear that escaped her control. "But mostly—I think he was scared."

"You said he didn't do anything wrong. Why was he scared?"

"He realized that any patient could sue him at any time—just to have someone to blame for their illness. The deputy sheriff delivered the summons at our home early Saturday morning… He was treated as if he'd committed a crime. The children watched. The neighbors were there to see. It was an awful morning for everyone."

"I can understand why it changed his whole outlook, but…"

"Objection," cried Griffin.

But sympathy and understanding had already warmed the faces of the twelve people sitting in the jury box. "At any time during the next two days did your husband ever mention Moll or his lawyer with malicious intent?"

"Objection," said Griffin. "Calls for self-serving hearsay."

"I will allow it," answered the judge.

"Definitely no, he didn't make any statements. I don't think he knew who the lawyer was."

"So your husband never mentioned the name Anita Johnson before the incident?"

"No."

"Did he ever threaten to harm anyone, including Maxwell Moll?"

"No."

"Mrs. Hartley, were you ever aware that your husband owned a gun?"

"No. I don't even think he knew how to use one."

Hawkins crossed the well and drew close to her side. "Mrs. Hartley," he said solemnly, "has your husband ever seemed suicidal?"

Hawkins quickly stepped aside to give the jury a full view. Celeste gasped slightly and gazed at her husband. He sat stoically, his eyes instructing her to go on. "If he did—I can understand why. He needed help."

Hawkins walked back to his table. "I have no further questions, Your Honor."

The suspense-filled silence in the courtroom snapped like a twig. The doors burst open and a stream of doctors spilled through the packed gallery until even small spaces in the gallery were filled. The bailiffs resealed the doors. And in the next instant, Griffin sprang to his feet. "Mrs. Hartley, you implied in your testimony that your husband suffered 'undue' stress on the weekend before the alleged crime of attempted murder. How would your husband usually react to stress?"

With a look of pure honesty in her eyes, Celeste sat forward. "I said he was under stress, if you please. Not 'undue' stress."

"Please answer the question," snarled Griffin.

"I don't understand," said Celeste patiently.

Griffin's mouth curled into an ingratiating smile. "Then let me help you. Has your husband ever been prone to outbursts of rage? Explosive rage?"

Celeste regarded him coldly. "Which do you mean? There's a big difference."

"Explosive rage," Griffin clarified.

"Only once," responded Celeste, with fervent intensity matched to the prosecutor's. "And that was the incident that brought us here."

"Has he ever been subject to just plain old outbursts of 'unexplosive' rage?"

Celeste smiled quietly. "A normal amount."

"And what is a normal amount?"

With Griffin only a few feet away, Celeste inspected the prosecutor closely and glared back with clear contempt. "My husband's not an angry person, Mr. Griffin. We all need to vent frustration on occasion. Nobody's perfect."

Griffin's eyes narrowed, and his words were almost accusing. "What about phone calls in the middle of the night? Did he ever lose his temper with a patient, or perhaps a nurse?"

"Calls can be inappropriate at times," Celeste replied coldly. "In such cases, he may be short with the caller."

"What about with the children? Can he be short with them?"

Celeste looked hard at the prosecutor, glancing down at his empty ring finger. "Do you have children? If you do, you know the answer."

Griffin took a step back. "Please, just answer the question," he said defensively.

"He can be irritable. But he never threatens or becomes abusive."

Hunting for any weakness in Hawkins's defense, Griffin probed for signs of depression, insomnia, anxiety, and self-medication. Finding no easy foothold, he pressed all the harder. "Mrs. Hartley, did your husband suffer from panic attacks?"

"Twice," she answered flatly. "One the day of the crime, and one downstairs before the arraignment. Both were reactions to what I would call 'undue' stress." Celeste smiled furtively.

Griffin leaned on the edge of the jury box and rested an elbow casually on the railing. "Do you think that your husband was capable of taking his own life?"

"No," Celeste stated firmly. "I trust that he wouldn't."

"Then I suppose that we can conclude he had some other intention when he illegally purchased the handgun that has been entered into evidence." Hawkins sat up, but didn't object. Griffin faced the jury with an arrogant swagger and raised his hand to make a point. "If suicide was unlikely, then murder is the only other reason I can think of to purchase a gun intentionally," he said, smiling conceitedly. "There are no further questions."

Taken aback by the abruptness of Griffin's dismissal, Celeste's mind raced backward to review what she might have said that would allow the prosecutor behave as if she had confessed her husband's guilt. She gripped the rail, wanting to expand on her testimony and clear up any misrepresentations. The bailiff opened the gate. Celeste's thunderstruck face pleaded with the jury. Reluctant to leave the witness stand, she smoothed her dress and peeked at her husband. As their eyes met, it was as if their bodies had touched. He would be next to take the stand.

CHAPTER FIFTY

"Just be yourself," whispered Hawkins. "The defense calls Dr. Roger Hartley," he said at full volume. As Hartley's name resonated around the gallery, the courtroom doors burst open and more doctors penetrated from the hallway. The sudden intrusion alarmed Judge Gadboy, and he banged his gavel. "Bailiffs!" he yelled severely, eyes bulging at seeing the overcrowded gallery. "These proceedings will become a copy of yesterday morning if this courtroom doesn't quiet. The public has a right to be present, but I have the right to exclude them, as you have seen." The room hushed immediately. The deputy sheriffs pressed the doors closed, and the flow of spectators stopped. But many had managed to squeeze in and hurried to blend in with the others. It comforted Hartley to be backed by his peers.

As Hartley mounted the witness stand, the small wooden box seemed to take on a new prominence. Griffin's eyes brightened, and he wet his cracked lips with his tongue. "Do you promise to tell the truth, the whole truth, and nothing but the truth, so help you God?" asked the bailiff. The room was too noisy to hear Hartley's response.

Judge Gadboy banged the gavel repeatedly until the gallery quieted enough for him to speak. The judge began his instructions to the defendant. "Dr. Hartley, by taking the stand in your own defense, you are waiving your right to protection under the Fifth Amendment. You must understand that you will be subject to cross-examination by the prosecution. You must answer all questions truthfully. False representation of any kind will be considered perjury. Do you understand your right?"

"I do," said Hartley, confidently sitting in the chair and nodding to the collection of jurors. His stage fright was gone. *Inch by inch*, he thought,

The jurors inspected Hartley closely, hungry to hear him tell his story. They studied his voice. His facial expressions. Even his posture in the chair. Hawkins addressed his key witness with low intensity from the start to keep him from becoming nervous. "Did you receive any distinctions or awards in medical school?"

Hartley responded proudly. "One—at graduation."

"Could you tell us what it was for?"

"Compassion and competence in my last year of clinical training."

"Dr. Hartley, where do you practice medicine now?"

"Now?" Hartley asked blankly, glancing solemnly around the room. "It worries me greatly that that is in jeopardy. I practice at Ravenswood Hospital on the north side of Chicago. And that's where I hope to return—if I'm able."

"Have you ever been reprimanded or been the subject of a written complaint?"

"Only the lawsuit," Hartley said gravely. "That was my first black mark."

Hawkins flinched slightly. "I mean at the hospital. We may get to the lawsuit later."

"Then—no. I haven't been disciplined. And never during training, either."

"Are your examinations and licensure up-to-date?"

"I'm board certified. I pass the exam every ten years and complete a hundred and fifty hours of continuing education every year—as I'm required."

"Do you like your job as a physician?"

Griffin objected. "Relevance—the defendant's job satisfaction has no bearing."

"Overruled. Please answer the question."

"Yes!" he said with a quiet smile. "I do like being a doctor."

"Do you find that being a doctor is difficult?" probed Hawkins.

"I've been fortunate," Hartley answered with genuine modesty. He had never completely understood why the concepts of medicine had come to him so easily. He could assimilate a twenty-pound textbook in six weeks, without having to read anything twice. It simply came to him as a gift that he had taken for granted. He easily kept up with new treatments, and he mastered innovative procedures, as if he had performed them hundreds of times.

"Do you find being a doctor is psychologically taxing?"

"Only when I can't make someone better. The fear of losing the battle is never far below the surface. You can miss something that might make a difference."

"Would you call that 'undue' stress?"

Hartley took a short sip of water. "I would—unless we get tort reform."

There was a loud reaction in the gallery. "Objection! There is nothing political in the Oath of Hippocrates," screamed Griffin.

"Overruled," hollered Judge Gadboy. "Hawkins…" he said, pointing the gavel head. Hartley shifted uncomfortably to relieve a cramped muscle.

"Do you worry about malpractice?" asked Hawkins.

"I did after the summons. But now I'm trying to hold on to good," said Hartley.

"And what is good?"

Hartley gazed at Celeste. "God," he said, smiling widely.

"Objection!" said Griffin. "What the defendant believes has no bearing."

The judge's belly laugh transformed into a cough. He looked at Griffin with amusement. "Sustained. Strike the word *God* from the records."

Hawkins smiled and continued. "What about physical stress?"

"Long hours? I manage. People are sick—they need care."

"Have you ever thought about quitting?" asked Hawkins.

"What would I do? I've spent hundreds of thousands of dollars on specialized training. I have four children." Hartley glanced at his new bucks, wondering how one of his difficult patients was doing without him. He recalled the story about the man throwing starfish back into the ocean. "No, there is no other career for me."

Hawkins took a long look at his client's face, which radiated a basic unshakeable goodness. In his heart, he felt Hartley's trial was already won. Lowering his eyes to hide any sense of personal triumph, he gathered his thoughts to complete his examination of the doctor.

"Dr. Hartley, do you believe the case filed against you was a frivolous lawsuit?"

"Objection! Relevance! Your Honor—we've been through this," scolded Griffin disgustedly.

The judge laid the gavel at arm's reach and drummed his fingers introspectively. "Mr. Hawkins. You have been warned. I must keep these proceedings in order. There is a fine line here that may not be crossed."

"Pardon," said Hawkins, reframing his question. "Dr. Hartley—do you feel that your treatment of Mr. Moll with prednisone was justified?"

"Objection!"

"Overruled!" said the judge sternly.

"I did my best," answered Hartley sadly.

"Then what were you feeling after being served with the summons?"

"It was like a death, and I began to experience the five stages of grief."

Hawkins stepped close to the jury box. "For the jury's benefit—the five stages of grief, as introduced by Dr. Elisabeth Kubler-Ross in her book *On Death and Dying*, are denial, anger, bargaining, depression, and acceptance. A clue to the defendant's motive can be found in which stage the defendant was in at the time of the crime. If he were in the stage of anger, it would be likely that Hartley harbored intent to do harm. If he were in the stage of depression, it would be more likely a suicide. Dr. Hartley—which stage do you think you were you in when you went to Anita Johnson's office the morning in question?"

As Hartley searched for words to express how he had felt on that awful morning, his expression turned reflective. The jurors leaned forward to hear his response. The silence was broken by a loud cough in the audience. The cough came again—this time louder and more artificial. When Hartley glanced toward the gallery, his eyes fixed immediately on the reporter sitting behind the bar. He wore a fresh tie and beamed with a familiar warm smile that had greeted Hartley each time before. Hartley sat upright in the witness stand and in some inexplicable way felt the courage to speak. "I reacted impulsively," he admitted, lifting his head regretfully toward the jury. "That morning I couldn't believe that things would ever get better. I had passed through anger, and I was in the bargaining phase. I asked Ms. Johnson to plead for her life—as I bargained for mine."

"Did you ever think of Ms. Johnson before buying the gun?"

"No. The first I thought of her was when I saw her billboard and then heard her ad on the radio."

"How did that make you feel?"

The question set Hartley reeling back for the moment to recall the wayward desires of his fevered mind. "Honestly, I don't know," he stammered. "I wasn't thinking clearly."

"Were you planning to kill her?" Hawkins asked softly.

Hartley's body curled forward as he reflected. "I was gripped by panic. I am so deeply sorry for what I did."

"Please answer the question," the judge demanded.

"Were you planning to kill her?" asked Hawkins softly.

Hartley bowed his head to stare at his hands folded in his lap. "I wanted to take a stand against the abuses and injustices of the system," he said in a voice that trailed off to almost nothing. He twisted his head as if to plead with Judge Gadboy. "Killing was not my intent. I could never intentionally injure anyone. Not Mr. Moll. Not Ms. Johnson. Not myself. I had no plan."

"Then tell me what happened in the instant before the gun fired."

The reporter smiled sympathetically. His head was inclined forward as if he too waited for an answer. "I simply let go," said Hartley. "I saw the image of a hopeless, desperate man in the mirror by the side of Anita Johnson's desk. I didn't recognize myself. Instead of anyone dying—I woke up. My hand went limp, and the gun dropped to the floor."

"Objection!" yelled Griffin desperately. "What the defendant saw in a mirror has no merit or relevance."

"Overruled!" responded the judge. "Dr. Hartley—continue."

"In the next instant, I was shocked to hear the gun fire. It was so loud. The mirror shattered, and my hideous image was gone. And when I looked back at Ms. Johnson, she was gone, too."

Hawkins paused, letting the gallery stirrings subside. "How do you feel now?" he asked in a voice full of compassion.

Hartley glanced to the place where the reporter was sitting, but the seat was now empty. He gazed around almost startled, his finger touching the scar over his right eye. He sat up in the witness stand with an expression of profound humility. "I'm accepting," he answered. "I'll go wherever I have to. For however long. But after that, I hope I get a second chance. I'm going back where I'm needed."

The corners of Hawkins's mouth turned up in a satisfied smile as the rapt jury relaxed with barely a sound. "I have no further questions, Your Honor."

Abruptly Griffin stood up and approached the witness stand. He glared at Hartley. The circles under his eyes had darkened. His jaw was set, giving his face the fearsome aspect of a man bent on revenge. "Doctor Hartley," he said harshly, trying to provoke a reaction. "Is it true you suffer from dyslexia?"

The unexpected beginning stunned Hartley. This was a private pain, and a topic that he rarely discussed. He gawked at Hawkins for reassurance, but caught in surprise, his face reflected ignorance. "Objection," he said. "Outside the scope of the direct examination. No foundation. No relevance. A background of dyslexia has no bearing on criminal intent. The prosecution is beginning a blatant attack on the defendant's professional character."

"Your Honor," said Griffin in a sickly-sweet voice. "The defense has suggested that the defendant's professional character has an important bearing on the case. Please keep the playing field level."

A murmur swept through the crowd as the judge pursed his lips to consider. "By taking the stand, the defendant has opened the door to this line of questioning," he said finally. "I direct the witness to answer the question."

"Dyslexia isn't a flaw in my character," answered Hartley complacently. "It doesn't indicate incompetence. It isn't a mark of a criminal."

"But hasn't dyslexia made it harder to be a physician?"

"Being a doctor can be a struggle for everyone," said Hartley. "But to answer your question—no, my dyslexia hasn't presented a particular difficulty."

Griffin's tone implied that he had caught Hartley in a lie. "You mean to say that learning long medical terms didn't pose a frustrating problem?"

Hartley resented Griffin's parading in front of the jury box, but he answered by carefully controlling his voice. "I learn by association," he said smartly. "My dyslexia allows me to create mental pictures, that I associate with difficult terms. Right now I'm associating *microcephalic, gonadal agenesis,* and *proctalgia fugax.* I have a clear picture."

As the doctors in the audience laughed, Griffin knew he was being attacked without knowing how. He wheeled on the defendant. "Dr. Hartley, did you graduate near the top of your medical class?"

"Mr. Griffin," said Hartley coolly, "do you know what they call the medical student who graduates last in his class?" Griffin glowered angrily without answering. "Doctor," said Hartley, releasing a satisfied breath. "But if you must know—I didn't graduate at the top of my class. And those students don't always make the best doctors. Great physicians need common sense. Unfortunately, sometimes we learn by making mistakes."

The judge extinguished the extraneous dialogue with a loud rap of his gavel. "Dr. Hartley, please answer the questions without editorial comments. Mr. Griffin, please attempt a new line of questioning."

Pricked to indignation, Griffin turned angrily. "Dr. Hartley, tell the court how you acquired the gun with which you threatened Counselor Johnson."

"I bought it that morning."

"Did you buy it from a legitimate firearms dealer?"

"No, I bought it from a person outside a gun shop."

"Did you solicit this person to purchase the weapon?"

"No, he followed me out of the store."

"Let me make sure I get this correct. You purchased a gun from a man on the street? I assume this dealer didn't accept credit cards." Smiling broadly at what seemed a rich vein of questioning, Griffin walked to the side of the jury box and set one hand on the wooden rail. "Did you have cash on hand?"

"The money was in my pocket."

"How much did you pay for the gun?"

"Three hundred dollars," Hartley confessed. Saddened by the waste, he looked down at his feet, calculating the hours he would have worked to earn that sum of money.

"Do you normally carry that much cash?"

"No."

"Did you leave the house with that much cash? Or did you stop at an ATM?"

"I had it when I left the house."

"So you left the house with the money, intending to purchase a gun?"

Hartley's shame showed plainly on his face. "Yes."

"And what did you intend to do with the gun?"

Griffin had no tolerance for silence. When Hartley didn't answer immediately, he seized control of the proceedings and imposed his will. "Dr. Hartley," he said loudly. "When you left the house, were you planning to purchase a gun?"

Hartley nodded, but the judge commanded him to speak. "Yes."

"You left the house planning to purchase a gun, with the sole intent of killing the lawyer who had recently filed suit against you—isn't that so?"

"Objection," called out Hawkins, if only to allow his client time to breathe. "Argumentative. Assumes facts not in evidence."

"Overruled," bellowed Judge Gadboy at once.

The jurors watched intently, foreseeing arrival at the crux of the matter. For a brief instant, Hartley regretted forfeiting his Fifth Amendment rights and taking the stand. Sweat beaded up on his forehead, but his hands were still, and his eyes fixed on the twelve people who decided his fate. "When I left the house, I didn't know who the lawyer was," said Hartley.

Dramatically, Griffin threw up his arms. "You left your house with a large sum of money in your pocket, intending to purchase a gun that you had no intention of using? Then how is it that you phoned Counselor Johnson's office to ask for an appointment?"

"I heard her ad on the radio, and it enraged me," answered Hartley simply. "It was a spontaneous, impulsive reaction."

"A spontaneous reaction? Impulsive?" Griffin glanced at the jury and pressed through another uncomfortable, judgmental silence. "So, after hearing the victim's advertisement on the radio, you called to make an appointment to meet her?"

"Yes."

Griffin glared at the defendant as if he had caught him red-handed committing a heinous crime. "The law firm's secretary states in her testimony that you insisted on making an appointment for urgent business. You made that appointment under an alias. Is that correct?"

Recalling how irrational he had been, Hartley grinned slightly. "Yes, I posed as Jack Turner," he answered simply.

"You posed as Jack Turner and claim that you had no intention of using the gun to kill Counselor Johnson? Yet what other motivation could lead you to aim a gun just three feet from her face?" Griffin approached the witness stand with sinister features. Forming his hand into the shape of a gun, he waved it close to Hartley's face. "Just three feet away!" Hartley could feel the prosecutor's hot breath and see the red veins in his eyes. "In fact—you planned a murder," snapped Griffin. "A premeditated murder. Didn't you, Dr. Hartley?"

"Objection," Hawkins said calmly. "Argumentative."

"Sustained. Remember, Dr. Hartley, you're under oath."

With mounting frustration, Griffin twisted his head still closer to Hartley. "I'll rephrase the question," he hissed. "At any point did you intend to kill the victim?"

"No! I told you—I've never wanted to kill anyone."

"Then what were you doing in Counselor Johnson's office, pointing a loaded gun at her face?"

"I don't know what I was planning. Or why I went there. Buying the gun was impulsive. I wasn't myself. My heart was filled with despair. Certainly I'm different now, and it's hard to re-create what I was thinking."

"Answer the question. You said you were bargaining. How were you bargaining by using that weapon?"

Hartley recalled his sentiment on that sad Monday morning and wanted to scream. "At first I wanted to escape from the pain. The system had killed me. I no longer cared. And I couldn't live with that feeling. There was no hope. But then..." Hartley's chin came to rest on his chest.

"But then, what?" asked Griffin.

Hartley's voice bore no trace of anger. "Then—I wanted revenge. I imagined that I should do something."

Content that he'd extracted a full confession, Griffin strutted back to the prosecution's table with a self-congratulatory air. But just before sitting down, he turned abruptly to address Hartley again. "I have one question more, Dr. Hartley. Your wife testified that you might not know how to fire a gun. Would that be the case?"

"Yes, that's true. I've never held a gun before in my life."

"Then might it be true that you didn't release the gun from your hand? More likely you accidentally dropped it due to your own inexperience. You dropped it by accident before you could carry out your murderous intent."

"Objection!" yelled Hawkins. He stood suddenly. "Calls for legal conclusion."

"Sustained," said the judge. His face hinted at anger. "Dr. Hartley, you are instructed not to answer the question. Disregard the comment of counsel."

Griffin smiled slyly as if the conclusion were obvious to all in the room. "Your Honor, I have no further questions."

CHAPTER FIFTY-ONE

"How'd I do?"

Taking the chair next to his attorney, Hartley released a deep breath.

"We knew it was a risk," said Hawkins. "But you held up. It's hard getting around your pointing a gun in someone's face. I don't know how real trial lawyers would work around that, but I'm not finished. It wasn't what you said up there just now, it was the way you said it. You weren't yourself that morning, and I think the jurors understood that. Now let's show them why."

Hawkins rose to call his last witness. "The defense calls Dr. Murray Feinstein."

An erudite-looking man with gray hair and half glasses entered the courtroom through the back doors and worked his way through the gallery. He waited at the rail until a bailiff opened the gate, then strode through the well carrying a cane in his hand. He smiled constantly and continued to do so even as the bailiff read the oath. "I do!" he said loudly.

Hawkins formally thanked him for coming, which put the jury and witness at ease. "Please—tell the court your name and occupation."

Dr. Feinstein beamed proudly at the jury as he described himself as a professor of psychology, specializing in the area of physician burnout. "I've testified dozens of times," he said.

"Objections from the prosecution?" queried the judge. Griffin had no choice but to agree. "The court recognizes Dr. Feinstein, expert witness on physician burnout," he proclaimed.

Hartley studied the august old man with keen interest. "Physician burnout is more than simple fatigue," the psychologist explained, glimpsing frequently at Hartley and smiling. "All physicians endure heavy workloads and most are chronically tired. But burnout is a state of physical, mental, and emotional exhaustion that occurs from long-term exposure to overly stressful conditions. It's a process of gradual depersonalization. Physicians are particularly susceptible," said Feinstein, this time gazing suspiciously over the top of his half glasses at Griffin, who was scribbling furiously on a legal pad with a scowl stamped on his face. He cleared his voice loudly until the prosecutor looked up. "Burnout can happen to anyone, Mr. Griffin."

Hartley recognized the changes in attitude that marked his downward slide. Negative feelings about work. A loss of empathy toward patients. Decreased self-esteem. Self-blame. A sense of personal failure. A general loss of interest in life. He remembered clearly his callousness toward patients when he began practicing defensive medicine. There was the negative spiral of cynicism through anguish, depression, and finally explosive rage. These were precisely the symptoms that Feinstein was laying out before the court.

"But most painfully," said Feinstein, "there's a profound loss of the ability to love. Your family, your friends, and even yourself. You feel alone. And when coping mechanisms fail—the results can be catastrophic."

Gravely, Hawkins paused to circle the well. The gallery of interested doctors served as a backdrop. "Dr. Feinstein, could you enlighten us on the extent of the problem in the medical community?"

Feinstein chuckled sympathetically and the rubber end of his cane tapped lightly on the floor. "Let's face it," he said. "Being a doctor isn't a healthy lifestyle. Doctors are workaholics. They accept too much stress. They're trained to be super-achievers. They're obsessive. Driven. They deny weakness. They're compulsive perfectionists. These are all characteristics that make great doctors, but they also oblige behaviors that drive doctors to exhaustion."

Hawkins flicked a glance at the jury. They seemed to be processing the information as if it were hard to believe that doctors could suffer hardships. "Has the incidence of burnout increased for any particular reason?" he asked.

"That's why we're all here today, is it not?" asked Feinstein.

Hartley's lip protruded defiantly. Doctors were losing their traditional position of respect in society. It was the last of the balancing rewards.

"So," said Feinstein. "With the erosion of financial compensation and social prestige, the stress of this lifestyle becomes hard to endure. The public generally has no idea of how desperate the situation has become. Just look outside! That's a whole nation of disillusioned, discontented physicians."

"The public wasn't aware until now," Hawkins commented lightly.

"Objection!" said Griffin tersely. "This rambling diatribe about health care is irrelevant to the case."

"Mr. Hawkins—" cautioned Judge Gadboy. "This discussion must lead somewhere quickly."

"Oh—I hope so, too, Your Honor—or I wouldn't be here."

Judge Gadboy settled back, his head retracting slightly into his robe.

"So, what are the final results of all this undue stress?" asked Hawkins.

"Increased divorce rates. Alcoholism. Substance abuse. And regrettably, suicide."

Hartley stirred nervously as the word *suicide* resonated in the courtroom.

"Dr. Feinstein," said Hawkins. "Let me clarify one point. Are you implying that the increased pressure on physicians from all stress factors can engender suicidal tendencies?"

"I have encountered many cases. There is a demonstrable connection."

"Can a suicidal urge be confused with an aggressive impulse?"

"A suicidal urge is an aggressive impulse that one focuses inward. In other words, when we are enraged by circumstances beyond our control, we may seek to enact vengeance upon ourselves."

"Why do some people choose suicide in such cases, while others commit assault—or even murder? How do some people manage to control their destructive impulses? Are there specific determining factors?"

"The stability of a subject's family life. The strength of his character. The depth of his affliction. It's impossible to speak in general terms, but when any person is on the point of acting out either aggressive or self-destructive impulses, some may see or hear something that gives them a reason to stop."

"That sounds familiar," said Hawkins. "Like seeing himself in a mirror?"

Hawkins turned to the judge without needing an answer. "Thank you, Dr. Feinstein. I have no further questions."

Feinstein nodded and smiled modestly. His hands rested on top of his cane.

Scowling deeply, Griffin approached the witness stand, eager to twist the expert's testimony to his advantage. "Dr. Feinstein," he said sternly, "you've testified that doctors experience job-related stress, which can lead them to desperate acts. Would physician burnout constitute a mental illness per se?"

"No, not a mental illness per se. But it is as serious as a chronic illness."

"So—if not a mental illness, then mental competence shouldn't be an issue in these cases. Correct?"

"The subject is usually mentally competent and usually very intelligent. That may be one reason why the syndrome is so insidious. Coping mechanisms hold out for many years."

"Following this line of reasoning, if the defendant was suffering from 'physician burnout' at the time of his attack on Ms. Johnson, then he was mentally competent, and can be held legally responsible for his actions. Isn't that so?" Feinstein glanced sympathetically at Hartley. "Since I have not examined the defendant, I cannot speak to his mental state at the time of the alleged crime, or at any other time in his life. I have been speaking in generalities about a syndrome that is common among people in his profession."

Griffin's face twitched as if he had been stung. "We're not speaking in terms of generalizations, Dr. Feinstein! If the defendant were in fact suffering from the syndrome you call 'physician burnout,' he would still be considered mentally competent. Therefore he would be legally responsible for his actions—yes or no?"

"Assuming that there was no other underlying condition," answered Feinstein. "Yes, he would be legally responsible."

Vindicated in the face of scorn from the gallery, Griffin drew himself up as he excused the psychologist from the stand. He strode back to his table, taking satisfaction in the expressions of accord he had generated in the twelve jurors. But at the same time, Griffin was warily watching a cluster of lawyers tucked to the side of the gallery. The outcome of the trial was uncertain and so much was at stake. As the state's prosecutor, he had become the guardian of the tort system, and the high-profile situation made him feel that *he* was on trial. Hartley needed to be out of the public eye, away from public discourse on tort reform. As the judge slammed down his gavel, Griffin shuddered as if the blow had been dealt to the back of his skull.

"This court will recess until two thirty."

Hawkins flipped a chair backward and sat down with his arms over the backrest. Hartley strode into the defense counsel chamber behind him, taking a chair against the wall. "You've got to feel good about this," said Hawkins effusively.

It was heartening to see Hawkins elated, but Hartley's own delight was more tempered. Griffin's display of anxiety and rage deeply affected him—he had been in that dark place himself, and it was exactly as Feinstein described. "I can't feel too good about myself. We don't have a verdict."

Hawkins beamed with undaunted enthusiasm. "But even if the jury finds you guilty, your case will still be a watershed. Doctors all over the country view you as a hero. You've done something unprecedented. You stood up against a system rife with injustice and gave a voice to people who have suffered from its abuses."

"Let them take Hippocrates as their hero. A doctor should set an example by saving lives, not by threatening to take them." Hartley stood and paced the room, barely listening to his attorney. There were no windows looking out on the street. A sense of isolation seemed to increase his notion that political influences were at work, veiled from the judge's full view. "The system is badly in need of reform—I know that," he said at last, trying to control a potent mix of agitation and excitement. "But seeing the effects of tying tort reform to my trial makes me wonder if I can get a fair verdict. Did you see Griffin?"

Hawkins smiled slightly to himself. He knew that the politicians who had responded to the pressures from legal special-interest groups to support tort reform would be taking a beating in the election. He hoped that with bipartisan cooperation there might be some hope that a solution to the health care conundrum could someday be found by some sort of compromise. But right now the battle was too overheated, and it was obvious that Griffin was feeling the pressure. During the morning session, he had watched him struggle to control a facial twitch. He had observed his unsteady hands and wandering feet, and it was becoming painfully evident that Griffin was losing mastery over his emotions. Hawkins now recognized the signs. "That's undue stress," he said. "Burnout can happen to anyone."

Hawkins abruptly stopped pacing to inspect his lawyer's demeanor. "Ernie," he said pensively. "Do you think the professional relationships between doctors and lawyers will ever improve? For the good of our patients?"

Hawkins laughed cheerfully. "Doctors and lawyers working together? I'm sorry, but I have to be honest. Lawyers will never pull doctors up on their pedestal. Medicine provides too much opportunity. You'll always be vulnerable.

There are too many variables and too much room for error. At least I will never be out of a job."

His laughter made Hartley relax. "Good civil attorneys give me comfort."

"You mean competent civil attorneys—there's a difference."

"I know. And you are both."

Hawkins acknowledged the compliment. "There will always be greed in my profession," he said apologetically. "But you've helped to show us that malpractice law has strayed too far from our ideals. Maybe we'll begin to understand that your profession should be regarded with more esteem."

The clock showed a few minutes till noon. When Hartley lifted his head, deep lines showed on his forehead. "We've done all that is earthly possible," he said somberly. "But I don't think this is enough. There has to be more of a catalyst before any real change can occur."

CHAPTER FIFTY-TWO

Griffin launched into his closing arguments, waving his arms to punctuate frequent bursts of indignation. "Beyond a reasonable doubt," he declared, shaking his tattered legal pad as if the pages bore some authority. "Dr. Hartley had a premeditated plan of revenge, with a definite intent to commit murder!" Once again he illustrated the brutality of the attack. Airily he dismissed that Hartley's defense should rest on a state of emotional imbalance. "He should be held accountable for his actions!" said Griffin, stating the crime challenged a malpractice victim's right to seek counsel. "If the defendant remains at large without punishment, he will continue to pose a threat to any lawyer or patient who makes his life difficult. Clearly he is prone to violent behavior and is not ready to be released back into society. Find the defendant guilty as charged for attempted murder. Recommend the maximum sentence. Incarceration is the design of our democracy to deter others from committing similar destructive acts."

Although the prosecutor had redoubled his efforts to cast a negative light, Hartley endured the closing arguments without feeling appalled or frustrated. There was no fear as Griffin pressed for the maximum sentence. "Good luck," he whispered as Hawkins rose in his defense. "Whatever sentence I receive—I will accept it."

"Remember," Hawkins whispered back, "you're not a murderer."

To overwrite any memory of the prosecution's arguments, Hawkins by habit began his closing by standing in exactly the same spot that Griffin had vacated. He spoke in a calm and confident manner, indicating that a clear conscience and full force of reasoning were backing his words. "Roger Hartley did not plan to buy a gun. He did not plan to commit murder. What he had planned was to become a great doctor, earning a great reputation by attending to the many needs of his patients. He planned to support his wife and four children and eventually to retire in a reasonable amount of comfort that would be well-deserved after a life devoted to the service of others. But when one resentful patient sued him for malpractice—those plans seemed to unravel and vanish."

Hawkins circled the well, stopping just inside the bar frame with the solemn, attentive doctors. As his arms fell heavily to his sides, he became a man who had given up hope. He spoke deliberately softly so those in the audience had to sit forward and tune in their ears to his closing remarks. "A person can form the specific intent to murder in the time it takes to move from one thought to the next. By way of argument, you could say that you can lose or dismiss the specific intent to murder in the same short period of time. Let us consider for a moment the kind of reasoning that would be required for Hartley to plan a murder. The motive for his buying a gun would require a plan for revenge. On the contrary, the prosecution has presented no evidence of malice aforethought. In the days and hours before the crime was committed, there was no plan. Not until the moment the defendant saw Counselor Johnson's billboard and heard her voice on the radio soliciting malpractice victims was there any perceived intent to do harm. The only reasonable conclusion would be the crime was a consequence of an emotional meltdown. Our expert has clearly illustrated the grave consequences of physician burnout—including suicide. Dr. Hartley was a desperate man at the end of his rope. And in the moment before he acted, regardless of his intent, he realized something and dropped the gun. What did he see in the mirror by the side of Ms. Johnson's desk? The face of desperation was not recognizable. As Dr. Feinstein has said for the record, undue stress crafts depersonalization, but Hartley had come to his senses. Voluntarily, he dropped the weapon. And while his actions are not justifiable, there is an explanation—a heartfelt response to the flagrant injustice that had undermined his esteem: a frivolous lawsuit. Hartley expressed in the purest sense the moral outrage that is shared by a group of individuals represented behind me. Plagued with similar abuse. Disemboweled by the legal system. There has been no other public forum to voice their complaints."

The crowd stirred fitfully. Hawkins stepped in front of the jury box to confront the confused stares of the twelve jurors. "Ingrained in our legal system is the presumption of innocence," he said in a loud, resonant voice.

"The prosecution has not proven the defendant's intent to commit murder. The testimony presented is not sufficient beyond a reasonable doubt to fulfill the burden of proof. For the charge of attempted murder, we ask you return with a verdict of not guilty. But beyond that, we only ask for the court's mercy in sentencing. If rehabilitation therapy and monitoring are imposed, we will accept it. Dr. Hartley would like to return to his practice and live the life of his destiny." Hawkins calmly returned to his seat at the defense table.

Griffin leaned away from the jury in a disconcerted manner. His cheeks and ears were reddened, and his teeth were clenched. His lips moved silently as if he cursed under his breath. Hartley recalled the reflection he had seen in the mirror, and from a place in his soul that he now clearly recognized, there arose such a deeply pervasive feeling of forgiveness that he turned and whispered to Hawkins, "I'm guilty of at least assault. I don't want to be let off scot-free."

"Careful what you wish for," whispered Hawkins. "There are people in this room who are quite ready to put you away. They could make an example of you and show the doctors out there what happens when you try to tamper with their system."

When the gavel fell, Hartley jumped as if it were a pistol shot. Quickly, Judge Gadboy gave the jury their final instructions, pointing his fat finger sternly to caution them. "You must remember that the nation's health care and legal systems are not on trial here. The defendant stands accused of aggravated assault and attempted murder, and in your deliberation you must consider only the facts of the case as they have been presented. Nothing more... nothing—" Suddenly, a paroxysm of coughing seized the judge. His round face flushed red, his muddy eyes bulged, and his thick tongue protruded. Hartley stood up immediately in a reflex born of long habits and rigorous training. The judge groped for water and motioned him back.

"I thought he was going to code on the bench," whispered Hartley, picturing the morning's headlines—"Accused Doctor Resuscitates Judge."

"He puts work before health, too. We're all nuts," said Hawkins.

Still winded and gasping, the judge continued his jury instructions. "You must bear in mind that the burden of proof rests with the prosecution. Based on the testimony presented, the prosecution must establish the guilt of the defendant beyond a reasonable doubt. If you deem that they have failed to do so, you should find the defendant not guilty. Take your time. Carefully consider before you arrive at a verdict. You are entrusted to act as objective representatives of our society."

The judge's paroxysm of coughing had sent a surge of adrenaline through Hartley's blood. He stood observing the closed door to the judge's chamber after the jury had filed out of the room. His body had felt the old call to action as in the early years of his training. He yearned to return to the practice of medicine. He walked to the window during the moment of calm and stood alone gazing west over Chicago. Below in the courthouse square, the sun was shining brightly on the sea of white coats, and the peaceful scene contrasted sharply with the turmoil he had witnessed in the preceding days. His colleagues were united. There was hope that tort reform might someday be possible. *I found my sun spot*, thought Hartley, relishing the sense of fulfillment that welled up in his breast.

Celeste slipped through the gate into the well and crept up beside him. Her husband's arms hung loosely at his side, and the slanting sunlight lit his face. She lifted one of his hands and cradled it softly, kissing the backs of his fingers. "I'm so proud of you, Roger," she said, as she peered into his sky-blue eyes.

"Roger?"

"Yes, Roger. I think it's okay for you to say 'yes.' and take care of patients the way your heart tells you. Something bigger has found you, and it's okay to accept it. Tomorrow things will change for the better because of you. You're their hero and also mine."

"It's too bad discontent is the first step toward progress, but I'm thankful to learn from my mistakes."

Celeste gazed at him joyfully. "What have you learned?"

Hartley grinned. "I'm a starfish thrower."

As their fingers entwined, a mist formed in Hartley's eyes. Celeste's golden hair shone in the light. Her face was luminous. "I'm truly blessed," he said, drinking in his wife's radiant beauty. He wiggled his fingers out of her grasp and reached deep into his pocket, pulling out a small, red, velvet box tied with a bow.

"What's this?" she asked, cupping the box in her hands.

"Red is for love," he whispered. "It's a token of my appreciation."

When she opened the lid to see a pair of diamond earrings, Celeste inhaled with a delicate gasp. They caught the slanting sunlight perfectly, sparkling like twin stars. "Oh, Roger! Appreciation for what?"

"For all those years that you brought me coffee. Sometimes the smallest gestures are the most meaningful. You may have wanted to rescue me—but you never did. You let me work it out on my own."

"I just waited," she said proudly.

"And prayed," said Hartley. Lovingly, he kissed her on the forehead. "I prayed, too," he said. "And I hope that my prayers are answered."

Chapter Fifty-Three

Hawkins peeked nervously at his watch. It was sometimes a bad sign when the jury deliberated for less than an hour. They filed in slowly, some glancing furtively at Hartley as they took their seats. The judge ascended the bench. "Have you reached a verdict?" he asked, turning his head for a quick study of the defendant.

"We have, Your Honor."

The jury foreman held out a folded piece of paper that contained the verdict. The bailiff took the paper without emotion and walked it to the judge. Hartley's eyes nervously followed the document, knowing that it would help reveal the secret plan of his life. But whatever the verdict, he was convinced that he would row with both oars in the water. Griffin seemed buoyed by the short deliberation, but despite his eager smile, his legs jiggled restlessly under the table. Maintaining a practiced, stoic expression, Judge Gadboy opened the paper and silently studied its content. After a moment, he passed the paper back to the clerk.

"Dr. Hartley, please rise."

Hartley rose to his feet with Hawkins by his side, their faces fixed in neutrality. The courtroom was tomblike. The clerk read the verdict in a monotone. "In the case of the State of Illinois versus Roger Hartley, we the people of the jury find the defendant not guilty of count number one: attempted murder."

In a single motion, the doctors jumped out of their seats in the gallery, cheering and slapping high-fives to show their approval. Griffin pushed the heavy prosecution table forward several inches. Celeste blushed beautifully amid the chaos. Hartley exhaled with relief. Unable to look away from his wife, his eyes shone with new rays of hope. He felt like a lucky man. But seeing the trial through to the finish, his expression remained neutral. Judge Gadboy banged his gavel to make the court come to order and let the clerk continue. "We the people of the jury find the defendant guilty of count number two: aggravated assault."

The emotions in the courtroom turned quickly, as anger burgeoned from joy, and satisfaction blossomed amid frustration. Hartley was just bowing his head when Hawkins's loud voice cut through the erupting chaos. "The defense requests the jury be polled on count number two."

After explaining the proceedings, Judge Gadboy began to poll each juror by number. The well-dressed small-business owner hesitated as if weighing personal bias against civic duty. He glanced at Hartley with a look of apology. "Guilty." The sickly woman reacted self-righteously, letting the defense table know that she resented their attempt to buck her authority. She let her voice be heard. "Guilty." The housewife glimpsed shyly at Celeste before casting her verdict in a barely audible tone. "Guilty." The businesswoman appeared bothered by the inconvenience of the extended duty. "Guilty," she roared. The two African Americans, the Hispanic, the schoolteacher, and three others followed suit. "Guilty." But the thin-faced college professor in the middle of the back row appeared hesitant. Nervously he pushed his reading glasses into the breast pocket of his tweed coat. "That's not my verdict," he said when his number was called. "I was pressured. I didn't understand. Not guilty!"

Knowing a unanimous vote was required, Griffin slammed his legal pad on the table. Judge Gadboy stepped in quickly, rapping his gavel only once to quiet the confused courtroom. "We have a hung jury. Both attorneys come to the side bar."

"This should be interesting," whispered Hawkins to his stunned client.

He strode to the far side of the well, keeping his distance from Griffin but sidling as close as he could to the judge. The small group looked more like it was fighting than huddling. "Motions by either party to resolve this issue?" asked the judge.

"I motion for the court to set this matter for further hearing in a new trial," said Griffin.

"Your Honor," pressed Hawkins, knowing Griffin was down. "Griffin— really? You want this whole mess to repeat itself? That might be okay for the doctors' cause, but the politicians? Don't tell me they haven't pressured you for this thing to be over."

"Hawkins, keep it above the bar," cautioned Judge Gadboy.

Caught in a Morton's Fork of his own, Griffin was silent.

"Your Honor," pleaded Hawkins. "You have heard the witnesses, seen the evidence, and have surely felt the strong undercurrents. You understand better than anyone the facts and circumstances. Clearly, the jurors are divided over some justification of the defendant's actions. We motion for dismissal of the second count."

"I will appeal," ranted Griffin.

"If I decide to dismiss the case, you will do no such thing," the judge warned sternly. "Back to your tables."

The judge took his time mounting the stairs and sat heavily in the chair. His eyes circled the room. "We have a hung jury," he said, his hand stroking his chin in a single motion. "This case is dismissed!"

The gavel's bang sounded more like a click amid the celebration. "This court is adjourned," he yelled by formality. But this time the judge didn't race away after closing the trial. Instead he paused to observe. Griffin was slumped in his chair, the verdict clearly representing a professional failure. When his eyes met with Judge Gadboy's, he clenched his jaw tightly, scooped up his legal pads, and stuffed them with sharp jabs into his briefcase. He flung a dark glare at Hawkins before he stormed past the bench, letting the side door slam behind him. Spectators had already surrounded Hartley and Hawkins. A great weight had been lifted, and both were absorbing the full impact of the ruling. Hartley's mother remained behind the bar, choking back tears. She reached out with a trembling hand, cupping the air as if to cradle his chin from afar. Judge Gadboy finally rose to his feet, his eyes twinkling brightly as if satisfied with the result.

"We did it—not guilty," said Hawkins. "I knew that professor in the tweed coat would hold the key. He's educated enough to have a valuable opinion."

"No jail time," said Hartley, still stunned by the finality of the verdict. He clapped Hawkins on the back. "Ernie—you were a godsend."

"Not me," corrected Hawkins. With a humble shake of his head, he gestured toward the crowd of rejoicing physicians who were pouring into the courtroom. "I think you were the godsend."

Hartley touched the scar on his forehead as if to see if he was experiencing a dream. He wiggled his toes in his spotless new bucks. "God sure went to a lot of trouble to teach me a simple lesson," he said, his joy equaling what he felt the day he graduated from medical school. "The finality of this moment makes me wonder if I still need to do more to help change the system. There's still a piece missing."

Celeste and his mom were now close by his side and both held him tightly. A faint chant was filtering in from outside and drew Hartley's gaze to the window. The sun was sinking toward the horizon. "Are you going out to speak to your supporters?" asked Celeste, seeing his gaze fixed toward the window. "Listen—they want to hear you. You don't have much time."

Hawkins agreed instantly. "Take up the cause. Encourage them on. Without you, this flame might fizzle out."

The memory of his own image bobbing on the ends of picket sticks made Hartley shiver. He recalled the thousands of hopeful faces looking up when he'd spoken from the top of the courthouse steps. "I am still not an agitator," he said, feeling untrained for politics. "I simply want us all to work together."

"Then tell them," prodded Hawkins.

Hartley's frightened eyes were comforted as they locked with Celeste's. She gripped his hand tightly and pulled him close. "Drew and Evan both say they want to be doctors," she whispered. "Just like their dad."

The corners of Hartley's mouth turned up in a smile as he welcomed the love that rushed into his heart. He held his wife closer and kissed her on the temple. "I love you," he said, feeling a shiver of ecstasy.

Letting go with all the resolve he could muster, Hartley stepped carefully through the maze of well-wishers, appreciating their gratitude and relishing the happiness along the way. The doctors were still gathered outside, and he gazed through the glass front doors of the courthouse with a satisfied smile.

"You can do it," urged Hawkins.

Hartley's face grew smooth and serene. "Thanks for all you have done," he said, shaking hands warmly. "You've helped me more than you'll ever know."

"And you have helped me," returned Hawkins. "Whether you like it or not, change is coming because of you."

Hartley pushed the revolving doors, circling without looking back. The five-o'clock sun streamed over his body at his favorite angle. The sea of white coats brightened as the doctors pushed forward and came together. Their cheers transformed into a chant. "*Hartley, Hartley, Hartley!*"

Hartley's body tingled with sudden delight. He stepped to the podium and leaned into the microphone. As he cleared his throat, the crowd rapidly quieted until there was almost no sound. "Put down your posters—your voice has been heard." The cheering had to die down before Hartley continued. "Although I made a terrible mistake, the court has delivered forgiveness. God has given me a second chance. And now I have to make amends with myself. Over the past several weeks, I have been through enormous personal changes. I've admitted to myself that I'm human—fallible and full of flaws. I now accept myself with all my failings. I return to the practice of medicine with renewed humility. I understand the limits of pride. We should admit when we fail and make amends no matter the personal cost. Training programs should prepare us for failures and align us with honesty. The legal side of the malpractice crisis may not give us help. We can't expect others to change. But we can change ourselves. We are bound to commit human errors."

As Hartley turned from the podium, the reporter with the tie was there by his side, holding out his arms as if to embrace him. His enveloping smile was even warmer in the light of the departing sun than Hartley remembered. And for a moment it seemed as if they were the only two souls at the top of the stairs. "This news is worth reporting," he said.

Chapter Fifty-Four

The windows had been open all night, and cool morning air suffused the kitchen. Hartley sat at the kitchen table listening to a gentle rain falling outside. He distinguished the depth and layers of sound as birds sang in the tree canopies and took flight in a fluttering of wings. The verdant foliage outside the window appeared hydrated and fresh.

"Would you like another cup of coffee?" asked Celeste as she placed a hot breakfast on the table in front of him.

Hartley shook his head. "I'm only having one cup a day. If I get tired, I'm going to rest."

"You were at the gym early—maybe that helps."

"Put the big rocks in first," he answered, chewing slowly to enjoy the salty taste of a long strip of bacon. One by one the children filtered into the kitchen to join him at the table. "I'm really happy," he said, watching them get settled and do things on their own. "I'm not worrying about what I should be doing or how I could be doing things differently. I'm doing what I like to do best."

"You live in the moment."

Hartley released a lighthearted chuckle. "It's funny, but I don't think that I'll need to hear patients say 'thank you' anymore," he said. "In fact—I should thank them. Their grateful smiles are as good a reward as a million-dollar bill."

Hartley's mood became infectious, like in the old days. Evan peered over his cereal bowl, smiling. Drew spoke with a jovial snort. "Going to work has got to be better than going to jail."

"That's positive," laughed Celeste.

An infectious grin spread over Hartley's face. "Everyone should get a second chance. And that reminds me—I'm visiting Anita Johnson in the hospital today."

This drew Celeste to him as if he were magnetic. "Do you think she wants to see you? After the judge let you off?"

"I checked it out with her internist. Dr. Fogg agreed—and so did she. I can't get over the irony. My victim's misfortune somehow led to my victory. It's one of those serendipities that I was missing before I started to listen." Hartley laughed with delight. "I'll be home after that."

Hartley's conscience had taken the driver's seat. Since hearing of Anita's misfortune and her desire to drop the charges against him, he wanted to provide an apology that he felt was long overdue. A pleasant sensation bathed his body as he approached the hospital. There were no picket signs or lines extending from the ER door. Maybe his destiny *was* to help change the system.

Fogg was waiting when Hartley entered the hospital lobby. "Great to see you back," he said, warmly extending his hand.

"Thank you for the kind words on the witness stand."

"Was I bad?"

"You lied like a politician," laughed Hartley. But then his face became serious. "Is she ready to see me?"

"I saw her this morning, and she wasn't smiling. Remember, she still has a lawsuit against you."

"I don't need a smile—just an acknowledgment."

"An acknowledgment of what?"

"My apology. I can't pretend that I'm innocent just because the judge and jury let me off. I've got to live with myself."

"Jeez, Hartley! If you have to salve your conscience—good luck."

They stepped into the elevator and rode up together. Fogg fidgeted and appeared as if he had something to say. "I hope you understand that I didn't choose to take care of Johnson," he said at last. "She was assigned through the ER."

Hartley grinned. "We can't pick and choose our cases, can we?"

"But knowing what she does for a living..."

"Obviously, you do a great job," said Hartley.

They stopped hesitantly outside of Anita's closed door. Hartley looked Fogg straight in the eyes and spoke without a pause. "There are many traits in you, Fogg, that I have come to admire. Before this happened, I was under the impression that you weren't so involved in your work. You represented everything that was wrong with the system—a Generation X doctor—but I know now that was wrong."

Fogg raised his eyebrows with surprise, but a disarming Hartley grin caused him to adjust his reaction. "A what?" he asked cautiously.

"You seem to accept being a widget. I thought you viewed your position as nothing more than a salaried job. I wondered if you were one of those medical students who sidestepped pledging the Oath of Hippocrates at graduation, as if not realizing what a privilege it was to become a physician. But now that I see and hear clearly, I agree with that small protest at the podium. Those young, idealistic doctors are unwilling to make promises that economic forces will keep them from upholding. Generation X doctors simply understand how to cope with the changes. They compensate for their loss of autonomy with improvements in lifestyle. And after what I've been through, I see a contented physician being more effective than a miserable one."

Fogg's eyes sparkled brightly, appreciative of what he was hearing. "But sometimes you've got to draw a line in the sand. This time we have you to thank for that." They shook hands as colleagues. "Shall I announce you?" he asked.

"I'll be okay." But Hartley's heartbeat quickened as he knocked.

"Come in," said a voice that he didn't recognize.

Hartley stepped hesitantly into the room, stopping just inside the door. Anita was sitting in a large chair next to her hospital bed, dressed in her street clothes. She was not the imposing figure that he remembered, as she winced when a nurse removed an IV from her arm. "Dr. Hartley," she said, summoning all her dignity.

Immediately the nurse straightened as if she were coming to attention. Her mouth fell open when their eyes met, and she smiled. Without saying the words that seemed ready to explode from her mouth, she finished her task and scurried out of the room.

"It looks like you're going home," said Hartley.

Anita's eyes were cast down. "They've just released me," she answered, looking up with intensity. "Why are you here?"

"To express sympathy for your illness. But mostly, I'd like to apologize for my behavior and ask your forgiveness." In the prolonged silence, Hartley thought his heart would beat out of his chest.

"I've never handled a case where the physician asks for forgiveness," Anita said.

"Then—could I be your first?"

She peered up with her jade-green eyes, exploring Hartley's face as she chose her answer. "I need some time before I can discuss it."

"I understand," said Hartley. "But I hope you know how sincere I am in my request." After a polite nod accompanied by a slight smile, he turned to walk out of the room.

"Wait—Dr. Hartley," said Anita abruptly, her face flushing red. "Even if I begrudge saying these words—you won the trial, and I suppose congratulations are in order. But there's something else that I need to say. I'm truly sorry, as well. It was Moll's lawsuit that touched off this whole mess. Being a good lawyer, I'd like to put things back as close as I can to the way they should be. I've dropped Moll as a client. That's the best I can do."

"Things can't be the same," agreed Hartley, grinning boyishly with the delightful surprise. "They can be better."

Anita wasn't hesitant to take up Hartley's hand. Her delicate fingers squeezed harder than he expected in a handshake that was more like a man's. "I look forward to seeing you again," she said. As if floating on air, he turned lightly and left the room in a few even strides.

After lingering at the nurses' station, Hartley strode happily across the parking lot toward the red Suburban centered in the middle row of the doctors' parking lot. His arms swung loosely, unhinged with the comforting sense that he could finally forgive himself for letting his imprisoned passion explode. He was amused that Anita had had the last word, expressing renewed fairness rather than gratitude. But even if she hadn't said it, her actions showed she was thankful for the care she received. Feeling blessed with a second chance and renewed hope, Hartley gazed up at the familiar hospital buildings. There were no patients standing in a line extending from the ER door. There were no protestors with his face perched on the ends of long sticks. *This is my destiny*, he thought.

Feeling a light touch on his shoulder, Hartley glimpsed a hand withdrawing behind him. He pivoted as if the hand pulled a string, instantly recognizing Moll. He was dressed in a worn flannel shirt buttoned up to his neck. His shabby overcoat was too warm for the season.

"Moll, you've lost weight," observed Hartley in a neutral tone.

"I haven't been eating," Moll spat back, his face a mask of resentment and anger.

"How come? Where have you been?"

"Where have I been? You saw me testify against you in court. And I was in the audience yesterday in front of the courthouse—along with your other adoring fans." His hands moved nervously over his coat as if searching. "Do you think saying you're sorry really does any good? I'm all messed up because of you—and did you ever say you were sorry? But apologies won't change anything now."

"I am sorry," Hartley said simply.

Moll's dull eyes were nonetheless piercing. "Not sorry enough!" he responded defiantly. "I trusted you with my health, and all you gave me was pills. Pills. Pills. Pills. My body is ruined because of your pills. And now I'm alone, without a pot to piss in."

"Moll, have you been drinking?" asked Hartley.

Moll's plethoric, swollen face split with a fiendish grin, exposing a mouth of rotten teeth. "What good is a trial? What good is this system?" he seethed. "Everyone feels sorry for you! Curses! And now I'm the criminal. I'm the fiend! My name is infamous as the patient who wrongly accused his doctor. Even Johnson won't represent me. Winning that money was my only hope. You spoiled everything! Curses on you!"

"Moll," pleaded Hartley. "Have faith. Curses can turn out to be blessings. Why don't you—"

Threateningly, Moll raised his bony hand. "Quiet!"

In the short silence that followed, Hartley searched his patient's face to determine if he had any malicious intentions. He knew him well from dozens of visits over the years, and quickly he searched his memory for Moll's list of medications. He remembered an antipsychotic. "Are you taking your risperidone?" asked Hartley, recognizing paranoid delusions. "You're not yourself."

"I told you—I stopped all my pills! Your pills ruined my life! Now it's my turn to spoil things for you."

Suddenly Moll pulled a small black revolver from his overcoat pocket and pointed the barrel at Hartley's chest. He was now in control. "I've been thinking about this for a long time," he said with sinister calm. "A hung jury isn't the way things were supposed to turn out."

Hartley raised his arms instantly. "Moll, I am truly sorry," he said, a sharp pang of guilt gripping his heart. "I wish there was more I could do."

Moll fumed with rage. "There is more you can do—you can die!"

Hartley eyed the gun wearily as his new pager vibrated on his belt. He lowered his arms to grasp the device. He pressed the button and read a message about a patient: *Trouble breathing.*

"Moll—please excuse me," said Hartley. "I have to go."

Turning and attempting a first stride, Hartley felt the hard barrel press into the upper part of his back and heard a searing shot ring out. The deafening noise echoed crisply off the facade of the hospital, resounding through the surrounding streets in all directions. Hartley slumped forward with a groan and crashed to the ground in a heap. He curled into a fetal position in pain and then rolled onto his back, working hard to breathe. Blood poured from the sucking wound in his chest and formed a crimson shroud on the concrete. A red mucous bubble rose from his mouth, glistening and popping as he tried to speak. His hand gripped his pager as he lay motionless, arms splayed out to his sides. Moll's dark silhouette clouded the blue sky above, his face close, his mouth twisted with blind, implacable hatred.

Even though no words came from Hartley's mouth, a smile began to blossom on his face. At last his eyes bore a look of infinite peace.

ACKNOWLEDGMENTS

*I wish to thank the following people
for helping this book find its voice:*

Dale Griffiths, Brad Hawkins, John Warton, Lucy Boling,
Robin Ross-Henning, Sue Padula, Bob Bradley, Robert Waltz,
Greg Warren, Tom Weidenkopf, PH Book Club, John Martin,
Michael Code, Dana Crowley, Kevin Gadbois, Rayanne Coy,
Dr. Brent Johns, Richard Hawley, Dwight Clarke,
Chris Nelson, and Susan Olmstead

Thank You!